ZERO
REPEAT
FOREVER

ZERO
REPEAT
FOREVER

G. S. PRENDERGAST

SIMON & SCHUSTER

Author's Note
The sign language used in this book is fictional and not based on
American Sign Language (ASL) or any other existing sign language.
Any resemblances are purely coincidental. If you are interested in
sign languages used by the deaf, you can find out more at
www.nidcd.nih.gov/health/american-sign-language.

First published in Great Britain in 2017 by Simon & Schuster UK Ltd
A CBS COMPANY

First published in the USA in 2017 by Simon & Schuster Books For Young Readers,
an imprint of Simon & Schuster Children's Publishing Division

1 3 5 7 9 10 8 6 4 2

Simon & Schuster UK Ltd
1st Floor, 222 Gray's Inn Road
London WC1X 8HB

www.simonandschuster.co.uk
www.simonandschuster.com.au
www.simonandschuster.co.in

Simon & Schuster Australia, Sydney
Simon & Schuster India, New Delhi

A CIP catalogue record for this book
is available from the British Library.

PB ISBN 978-1-4711-5805-6
eBook ISBN 978-1-4711-5806-3

Printed and bound by CPI Group (UK) Ltd, Croydon, CR0 4YY

MIX
Paper from
responsible sources
FSC® C020471

Simon & Schuster UK Ltd are committed to sourcing paper
that is made from wood grown in sustainable forests and support the Forest
Stewardship Council, the leading international forest certification organisation.
Our books displaying the FSC logo are printed on FSC certified paper.

For Lucy, a very Canadian girl

PART ONE
Summer

"I have no faith in human perfectibility."
—EDGAR ALLAN POE

There is a light floating above me. Nothing I recognize. I remember moving, so I try to move.

"Don't move," someone says, so I stop. "Do you know where you are?" I try to answer but find I can't speak because there's something in my mouth. I shake my head. I remember gestures and signs. Something about memorizing them and being tested on them. "Do you know who you are?" I search that part of my memory and find it a void. Not small, or undeveloped, but empty. Emptied. I shake my head again.

"Good," the voice says. "Close your eyes." I can't remember ever choosing for myself, so I do as I'm told. The idea of obedience fills me, flowing through me like warm, viscous fluid. Obedience and anger, as though that's all I'm made of.

"Eighth," someone says. There's another noise, like a hiss. "You'll manage," the first voice says. "He'll learn from you."

Behind my eyelids thoughts squirm around, jumbled and messy, out of order. I try to catch them, but they skitter into cracks and holes, like frightened animals.

"Try to relax," the voice says. "It's just residual neural impulses. It will go away."

But what if I don't want—

There's a bright flash. And a noise like thunder. And everything shakes.

Her hands blur in front of my eyes.

What are your directives?

I only nod. I can't answer. I'm holding my rifle with both hands.

The heel of her hand connects hard with my forehead, slamming me back against the metal wall behind me.

Look! Listen!

I nod. Nod. Nod.

Yes. Yes. Yes.

Dart each one. Leave them where they fall. Understand?

Yes. Yes.

I know this anyway. The directives are humming in my mind like a swollen river churning over rocks.

You must obey.

Yes.

I am obedience. I am malice. I grip my rifle tightly, fingers and hands absorbing the weight of it, the feel of the trigger, the faint vibrations.

Then I am running behind her, my hand on her shoulder, clanging over steel and stone as we're consumed by heat and fire and noise. At first all I hear are weapons. Our precise ones and their brutal, noisy ones. But under that is another sound.

Screaming. They are screaming. I put my hands over my ears.

What are you doing?

I nod. *Yes.*

Stupid defective low rank mud for brains.

Yes.

She drags me, pulling my hands away from my ears. Ahead of us on the road, emerging from the flames and smoke, a human vehicle appears. I fumble for my rifle, but she has already fired; the dart punctures the glass and the face of the driver. There's a screech as the car swerves toward us, and I'm leaping for it, pushing it away into a high wall as she stands there, undaunted, her rifle still raised.

Break it, she signs with one hand, marching toward me.

I turn and drive my fists through the window of the door. Inside, small humans scream.

Dart them, she says.

They scream and scream. I can't move.

MOVE!

I step back as she raises her rifle. *Thunk. Thunk. Thunk.*

The screaming stops. She drags me away before I can take a breath.

Follow me! Her hands slash through the air. *Obey me!*

We run between two high buildings, emerging into chaos. Hundreds of humans with guns and shields fire at our lines.

Bullets bounce off my back as she leads me into the fray. Behind the humans with shields others are pushing and running, trying to get into a building. Our line breaks, and we follow a group that plows right through the shields and guns. The armed humans fall around us. One of them gets its fingers around her arm, pulling her rifle down. I grab the human by the neck and fling it away, watching it tumble into a heap with others.

Good, she says.

Her praise enlivens me. As the humans pour in through the door of the building, I leap up and tear open a window. She clambers ahead of me, and I dive after her, landing among the screaming humans as they scatter, desperately scrambling for exits. Her rifle whines as she darts them, one by one. When she stops, there are a dozen humans motionless on the floor.

Good, I say, though I feel dizzy and hot. I'm burning. I sway on my feet, reaching for her.

Think cold, she says.

Yes. I do what she says and feel my body cool down and my head clear. Malice is cold. Obedience is cold. I am cold.

There's a huge noise outside, one of their crude weapons. The force of the explosion blows the remaining windows inward. Instinctively, I pull her under me, curling my back over her as the glass tinkles down around us. She shoves me away, stepping over bodies, and turns back to the door the humans came in.

Outside is smoke and flames. Those of our soldiers who don't lie in pieces among the darted humans stagger to their feet. A transport swoops down, hovering over the carnage. She pulls me away from the transport, back along the ruined road. Over our heads a human aircraft explodes, raining debris. She worms away from me before I can shield her and stands with her arms out, defiant, her face turned to the explosion in the sky as burning embers drift down around us like . . .

Over the roar of our transport and the screams of fleeing humans I hear something else, a kind of whistle. A flash of light shoots past us and cracks into the side of a human car, shattering the windows. She takes one step toward the car before I can stop her.

Then I'm falling. Shards of metal careen at me before I land. My arm twists up to block one, another smacks into my face. I hit the ground hard and sink.

Obedience. Anger. I'm swimming in it. My insides twist and churn and thoughts scurry out of the holes in my mind.

Snow . . .

A sunset . . . the smell of . . .

It's just residual neural impulses. Pain stomps on them, killing them.

Breathe.

I blink away the blood in my eyes. She's hanging over me, kneeling by my head.

Breathe. Obey.

I try. The air is too thick. I'm choking. My head is open and everything is escaping. And I'm on fire.

Cold. Think cold. Obey.

Are you damaged? I sign with one hand. The other hand is not working.

No. Breathe again.

I obey. Each breath is like a flaming knife. I turn my head to the side and let my thoughts drip out. I'm forgetting everything. I've forgotten how to hold on to thoughts. I put my good hand over the hole in my head to try . . .

Stop. Be still.

She touches my face. Her hand is warm and firm. *You will live*, she signs. *Keep breathing.*

The agony of the next breath erases everything.

My eyes snap open in the dark. The battle is over. We are alone now in the building with the darted humans. Silver moonlight through the broken window outlines her as she moves.

You scared me, Eighth, she says. *I thought you would die.*

That makes me feel so happy that the pain becomes meaningless.

Our own stars betray us.

First, when they fall, we make wishes, then more wishes, until we realize it's not a meteor storm. We watch fighter jets shoot across the sky, and missiles streak upward.

Pip and David, the camp directors, gather us into the main building and tell us what they learned before the phone line and Internet went down.

"Is this real?" Emily says, her voice high pitched and child-like. The lights flicker. Flicker and die. David goes out to crank up the generator. We all flinch as it roars to life and the lights burst brightly on the ceiling. David comes back saying something about rationing fuel. Topher wants to know how much there is, how long it will last, as though there is some answer that will make this more bearable.

His twin, Tucker, curls around me, breathing in my ear as we watch the few horrifying news reports cached on Pip's laptop. Cities on fire all over the world: Bogotá, Denver, Addis Ababa, Mexico City. Armies of death-wielding shadows pouring out of multitudes of monstrous ships. Videos make it real.

We hold each other as Pip and David outline a plan. Those with weapons experience are armed with hunting rifles and put on sentry duty for the night. The rest of us will barricade ourselves in the girls' cabin until dawn. The remainder of the plan can wait for daylight. We tiptoe in the dark, listening to the low rumbles in the distance.

Boom. Boom. Boom.

As long as I have Tucker, I tell myself, everything will be all right. The world has fallen apart around us before. We were suspended from school. Once we were handcuffed and driven off in separate police cars. We both faced my parents, and his parents. We survived that. We can survive anything. I thread my fingers into his, firm in my belief that we are an immutable force. No army of shadows will change that.

"Who are they?" someone says as we trail across the sports field, the stars still flashing and falling in the sky. "Terrorists?"

No one wants to say "aliens" that first night.

The next thing I see is white, then gray, then green. And as things take shape, my mind awakens in a field, walking behind her, my hand on her armored shoulder. Slowly, thoughts click into place, memories, like parts of a rifle recently cleaned and oiled. We have been out in the world for some time, away from the battle in the city. It's as though I've only just noticed. I turn and look behind us. Some way back, three humans lie facedown, the long grass crushed under their bodies.

When she hisses at me, my feet move and I turn from the humans in the grass, turn from the brief sense of loss their lifeless shapes stir in me. I take a step with her, hand on her shoulder, and another step until we regain our rhythm, walking steadily away, as any feelings I had about the fallen humans peel away from me like dead skin over a healing scar. She shot them. I haven't touched my rifle all day. She prefers it that way.

As we walk, I remember more and more. About myself. And about her. Sixth, I call her. She is above me in the ranks, and it shows.

Her aim is flawless, and her disappointment with mine is

palpable. *Let me shoot; you can manage any close contacts*, she signed once, back when she could be bothered to give me instructions. "Close contacts" means fighting. I can fight. I know this. I'm strong; my strength surprises even me. I can tear heavy locks open with one hand, and once pushed a moving vehicle right off the road. I think I would be lethal in a hand-to-hand fight, but no one comes close enough. Even if they did, they seem so weak, these humans, so small and vulnerable; it scarcely seems fair. Even the ones with guns hardly wear any armor. I turn my eyes away now when she shoots them.

I suppose I could break one, if I had to. I did it once. She counts on me for that. I would kill to protect her, but I can't see that sort of danger ever coming up again. She shoots; I follow or precede her, break down doors and smash fences, hunting out the last dregs of humanity. We are preparing. I don't know what for, and I'm scared to ask.

I'm not supposed to ask. I'm not supposed to be scared.

Eighth is defective, she signs frequently, using both hands to show me how broken I am. I would tell her that her disdain hurts my feelings if I thought that was permitted. Instead, I swallow the disdain, as much as I can, and let it sink into the pool of oily obedience inside me. There it turns into an urge to break things.

Breaking things is permitted, even encouraged. I will break whatever is in her way. I want her to be happy with me.

PART TWO
Autumn

"It is by no means an irrational fancy that, in a future existence, we shall look upon what we think our present existence, as a dream."
—EDGAR ALLAN POE

Tucker died this morning.

My soul was split in two this morning. The war that we have evaded, hidden from, and occasionally pretended was all a bad dream crashed into us this morning, when Topher, after searching for hours, found his twin dead under a pine tree, a dart in his spine, dark metallic tears in his open eyes.

After ten weeks of hiding and hoping for rescue, we have been touched by the invaders at last.

The *aliens.* We have no trouble saying it now.

I scream myself hoarse when they bring his body back. Topher lays him on the sunporch off the mess hall and collapses down beside him. The other camp staff leave us, too stunned to process it. They disappear into the cabins and close the doors.

Who knows how long we sit there, ruined by grief, paralyzed and helpless. The sun is high in the sky when I use the corner of my T-shirt to wipe the gray fluid from Tucker's brown eyes.

"Close them," Topher says.

But I want to look at him a little longer.

"Close them. The sun is too bright."

I have never liked Topher, and the feeling is mutual. He and Tucker have . . . had that bond that twins have, and look so alike that even their parents mixed them up until Topher cut his dark hair military short. They look alike. They are not alike.

Tucker was carefree. Topher is contained to the point of repression—a rule follower, a future judge or prison warden. Tucker is wild and wicked . . . was . . . was wild and wicked. Tucker is dead. Topher is stern and steady and grave. Tucker was dark and deep and complicated and infuriating.

Topher is straight and dull. Tucker was a risk taker. He jumped off cliffs and bridges, swallowed unknown pills that kept him awake for days, rode his longboard down impossibly steep hills. He set out hunting alone at night, disobeying our strict buddy system—an insane thing to do, even for him. Topher said his twin had a death wish. He got his wish. Tucker is dead. And Topher is alive. I wish it were the other way around.

"Close his eyes, please, Raven, or I will."

He uses my full name, not "Rave" as everyone else does. Raven doesn't suit me. When I think of ravens I imagine something serious, clever, and sleek. My puffy golden Afro and smattering of freckles make me look frivolous and festive, like a firework, which doesn't suit me either. "The raven is inside you," Mom used to say, and I always thought that meant it would hatch out one day, that I would morph into someone less . . . chaotic.

I still look in the mirror sometimes and am not sure who I see. Black mom, long-gone white dad. Does that make me mixed? And does part of that mix have to be the white family I don't even know? A halo of tawny hair, full lips, rich mossy eyes, golden skin. Adding all that to my mom's posh English, my stepfather Jack's Michif, and the French they taught me at school makes me feel like about ten people at once. Rave suits me, like a party, but only some of the time. Not right now. Rage would be a better name right now. My karate instructors used to joke that Rage could be my fighter name, in between telling me that anger needs to be controlled, especially in martial arts. But of course, they couldn't have known what was going to happen, how we would lose control of everything.

I feel a small twinge of guilt for wishing Topher had died in his twin's place. A small twinge of guilt, until I remember that if Topher could have chosen any of our little band of survivors to sacrifice, it would likely have been me, the girl who was never good enough for his brother, the troublemaker who got us all arrested in the park. He would choose me because he has convinced himself that Tucker's misbehavior was my fault. Or maybe he would choose me because I took him down in about eight seconds whenever we sparred at the dojo. Tucker says . . . said . . . Tucker said. Tucker will never say anything ever again.

He said Topher claims he lets me win. I never believed that.

Topher would choose me because of a raft of things that can't matter anymore, now that the world is gone. He clings to the lost world, like an infant to the corpse of its mother, or a dog lingering by its dead master. Maybe now he'll finally let go. It's been ten weeks; that's more than enough time for rot to set in.

The world is gone. It was taken from us, the way a massive heart attack takes a life. Swiftly, ruthlessly, almost as though there is nothing personal about it. It just has to be done.

We survived because we wanted to spend the summer volunteering with kids in a remote wilderness camp. Well, some of us wanted to. For me and Tucker and Topher, the judge, and our parents, gave us no choice but to accept a last-minute negotiation to keep us out of juvie—two months' free labor and we would "talk about further restitution in the fall." I guess Tucker's panic-stricken threats to run away or do something worse if they separated us moved them too. We got to stay together and quickly adapted to the idea of a summer as junior camp counselors. Ten weeks at a wilderness camp? For Tucker anyway, what could be better? Why should the label "community service" change that? He had no shame. Topher felt enough shame for both of them.

As for me, I bore my shame. A small part of me felt guilty for dragging these two nice white boys into my messy life. A bigger part of me felt guilty about dragging my hardworking, long-suffering *parents* into it. The rest of me focused on the goal—a good summer, a debt paid, a lesson learned—and gave thanks that I didn't lose Tucker as part of the deal.

But then . . .

Had it been two weeks earlier, I might be dead too. I would still have been in high school in Calgary, which, from the glow in the sky, from the days of low rumbling booms, we assume was bombed to nothing but ashes and ghosts. A week later there would have been a hundred campers here, with enough food and fuel for a week. Instead, there were only nine of us, junior counselors and trainers, for two weeks of training with Pip and David. Food for a hundred divided by eleven equals eight or nine weeks of supplies, ten if we ration carefully. Simple math. The end of the world doesn't change that. We even have weapons; basic hunting and archery were planned camp activities, and remote camps like this always have rifles, in case of bears. So we train with them, carefully, responsibly, conserving ammo as much as possible, since there's every chance we will need it. We have no way of knowing if the rifles or crossbows will be of any use. We have few ways of knowing anything. Communications were cut somehow, along with the main power that first night. We wait in the dark, armed and

19

fatalistic. If they notice us, our chances are slim. They haven't noticed us yet.

Pip and David set out in the van to find answers but never came back.

After two weeks of knowing nothing Felix rigged something up with the satellite phone and the old radio tower on the hill. We tried to send distress calls, but all we got in return was a low-frequency humming that Felix finally figured out was a video signal. He theorized that someone had hacked into one of the emergency broadcast system servers. Some of it *was* emergency broadcast stuff. There were repeated generic instructions to "shelter in place," but eventually those stopped and were replaced with amateur videos.

The bandwidth was prehistorically slow. A one-minute video took hours to download to Felix's laptop. The videos were like something from a shooting game or a horror movie. The creatures were named "Nahx" by some Russian gamer on the day of the invasion, and the name stuck. They are like walking night, moving shadows, blindingly fast and utterly ruthless. They shoot with whining dart guns. The darts do little physical damage, like tranquilizer darts, but they kill in seconds, filling their victims' eyes with weird metallic tears. The Nahx kill indiscriminately—women, children, soldiers or not.

There are videos of humans vainly fighting back. It is often young men—they hoot and swear with feigned courage as they waste their bullets on armored enemies who won't fall. The Nahx are unstoppable, is what the videos tell us, even the ones where we fight back. Felix spent hours a day downloading the videos, his laptop charging from the radio tower solar panel. Who is making and sending the videos is mysterious, but the message inherent in them is clear, to me anyway. They remind me of the futile bleating of a mortally injured animal.

I called the videos "revenge snuff" and stopped watching them, but Tucker watched them over and over, his eyes growing glassy with something almost like desire.

Tucker's eyes. They stare up at the clear sky, but see nothing. I close them, then bend down to kiss his cold lips. Topher, sitting across from me, hangs over him and sobs, his tears falling onto Tucker's sunburned arm. He takes one dead hand and presses it to his mouth.

I wonder which one of us hurts more, and if Topher will use sorrow as a final contest for his brother's love. I can't quite imagine his grief; I've never had a sibling, much less an identical twin. And though I may never know if my parents survived, or my cousins, my aunts and uncles, my massive stepfamily up north, at least I haven't had to confront any of them dead in front of me. Except in frequent nightmares.

War, love, loss, grief, and me and Topher, each holding a hand of someone we will never get back, not even to share.

The sun is too bright, he said, as though Tucker could still see and still be bothered by the sun in his eyes. As though he could see through Tucker's eyes. A fraction of the bitterness I feel for him crumbles, then a chunk, then pretty much all of it. He's been sitting here with me for hours, crying. How can I continue to hate him? We have nothing to fight over anymore.

In the end, it is just a war, but we seem to have lost.

We lost the world. I lost the chance to make it up to my parents for all my stupid mistakes.

And I lost Tucker. Without him those things I thought I could survive threaten to overwhelm me.

When Topher sets Tucker's hand back down on his chest, I do the same with the other hand. Wordlessly, we lace his fingers together. He could be napping in the sun but for the blackened veins in his neck and face.

"Earth or fire, do you think?" Topher says, and without hesitation I answer, "Earth."

He nods, agreeing with me for once.

Xander and Lochie offer to dig the grave, but Topher wants to do it. While he sweats down by the lake, digging deep under a birch tree, Emily, Mandy, and I wash Tucker's body. I can't imagine undressing him though, not in front of them, so we wash his face and neck, his arms, hands, and feet. We bury him in his clothes, cargo shorts and a grubby camp T-shirt, but Topher keeps his hiking boots. I take his gold earring and hook it into the hole at the top of my ear. I slip my beaded bracelet around his wrist.

Sawyer and Felix, senior counselors who have taken charge since the camp directors disappeared, stand hand in hand, leading the service even though they are only a few years older than us. They are a couple. It was a big secret for the first few weeks, even after the invasion, but gradually they stopped hiding it. And none of us care, anyway. The end of the world is not the time to get hung up on labels.

Sawyer speaks calmly, but Felix grips his shoulder as he finishes. I don't really process the speech beyond the general gist. Something about bravery and survival and living to honor Tucker's memory. I'm glad he didn't make out that Tucker was some kind of angel, because that was definitely not the case. Except maybe to me.

We take turns shoveling dirt into the grave. I scoop it in with my bare hands, because I am trembling too much to hold the shovel.

Emily and Mandy have made a wreath of pine and birch boughs. Xander plays a mournful tune on his harmonica that has us all shuddering with sobs. But Topher stands as still as an ancient tree, tears streaming down his cheeks. I don't even bother to stay standing. I fall to my knees and try to suppress the urge to scream and scream until I'm shivering uncontrollably. Someone—Xander, I think—puts a sweater over my shoulders. Someone else reads a poem, or a Bible passage. Someone sings. My blood rushes in my ears.

By the time we finish it is dusk.

This time two days ago Tucker and I snuck down to the lake and swam naked in the icy water, then forgot the end of the world for a blissful private moment under a blanket on the beach. He told me he loved me and that he was sorry for . . .

Well, nothing like that matters anymore.

War and grief—this is my life now.

"Raven."

At first I think it is Tucker's voice in a dream. Have I been sleeping? Time seems to have passed. I am kneeling at the graveside, my knees and ankles stiff. Topher kneels across from me. We are surrounded by half-burned-down candles.

"They shot him in the back," Topher says.

I nod, unable to form words.

"He was running away. They could have let him get away."

Everything we know about the Nahx, which isn't very much, suggests that this is unlikely, but now is not the time to disagree.

"I'm going to find the one that did this and kill it." He sounds so much like Tuck at this moment that I have to look up to check. But no, it's Topher with his neat hair and clean camp T-shirt, as if we're still on duty. His face reflects Tucker though. His fierce and sure expression says Tucker. Tucker never approached anything without a gallon of certainty. Tucker was so sure he would come back with fresh meat last night. But he never came back at all. Two arrows were missing from his quiver. The rifle hadn't been fired. His smartphone was on the ground next to him when Topher found him, smashed beyond repair, as though he'd been trying to call for help on networks that no longer functioned.

"Toph, how will you find it, this particular Nahx?"

He shakes his head, wiping tears with the back of his hand. I notice the broken blisters on his palms from digging the grave.

"Swear to me that you're with me on this," he says, as if he's angry at me.

"I swear. I'll kill it too, if I find it." I'm too tired to argue. Topher needs this. He needs to think he can fix this somehow. And he's all I have left to fix.

"Swear on his grave." He must know it's an impossible promise. But I suppose many things that once seemed impossible happened anyway.

We place our hands on the loose dirt, leaving handprints into which we drip candle wax and tears. A long time passes before either of us speaks again.

"Do you want to sleep here tonight?" I ask. Topher simply nods. We walk back to the cabins to get sleeping bags. Halfway up the hill he puts his hand on my shoulder, and we walk like that until the trees clear and we're on the open field.

"We have to do this together, you know," he whispers, as though those treacherous stars might be listening. "We can't fight anymore."

"I know," I say, and wonder whether Topher can hear the echo of his brother's laugh, as I can.

Muddy death, someone help me.

Help me.

What do I do now?

RAVEN

I watch the sky with Topher, neither of us able to sleep. Sometime after midnight, when we hear footsteps crunching down the hill, Topher wriggles out of his sleeping bag and slips an arrow into Tucker's crossbow. But a burst of giggling and a whiff of sweet smoke let him relax. He unloads the crossbow and sets it aside.

Xander appears on the path with Lochie and Emily, the two Australians. Wisps of smoke trail behind them. I sit up as Xander passes the joint to Topher.

"Where did you get this?" Topher asks, taking a deep drag. He passes it to me and I puff on it silently. When it becomes clear I'm not giving it up, Xander produces another one and lights it on the embers of our fire.

"Broke into the office," Xander says. "Sawyer and Felix are hoarding medicine in there. And this."

"They confiscated it from me when I arrived," Lochie says, in a halo of smoke. Lochie *looks* like a stoner, a typical sunburned and bleached-hair surfer dude, but he's also a hard-core survivalist who can make a fire by rubbing sticks together and eats insects and slugs for our amusement.

Soon we're all as high as the silver moon. Emily sits behind me, arranging my tangled curls into a dozen little braids and twirling and tying them with ribbons of dry grass. She's a pale and dreamy hippie chick, who paradoxically is also something of a weapons expert, from her outback farm upbringing with three gun-crazy brothers. She taught Tucker to use the crossbow. They practiced until his aim was lethal.

Not lethal enough though, apparently.

I never liked having my hair fussed over for longer than a few minutes. When I twist away from Emily, she turns her attention to Xander, making him a crown of pine fronds. He wears it with surprising dignity, like Chinese royalty, a beautiful Ming dynasty prince.

As he starts another tune on his harmonica, I lie back and gaze up at the stars again. By now we are used to the large bright ones that move in unexpected patterns, and the occasional flashes. Sawyer thinks the Nahx are destroying satellites, one by one, and space junk that interferes with their ships. This is why our satellite phone stopped working. Our cell phones turn on, if we charge them with the solar generator, but apart from reading old e-mails or looking at photos of people we'll probably never see again, they're useless.

Ten weeks. It's been ten weeks. There are eight of us left. Right now five of us are so wasted, a band of invading Smurfs could paint us blue and eat us. But who cares? I have nothing left to lose.

The stars move, and move back. One pops in a flash. And one shoots out of sight.

Yes. Like that last beautiful night on Earth.

The first group of campers were due to arrive in two days. We had been training, building on skills we already had. Pip and David had to make the most of us, since half their crew had been denied work permits due to some kind of immigration screwup. Self-defense and martial arts was my class. Topher would do canoeing and fishing, Tucker, what else? High ropes, climbing, and zip line—the dangerous stuff. Mandy would teach first aid, Emily weapons and hunting, and Lochie botany, maybe what mushrooms to eat, depending on how you want to feel. Xander, a friend of Tucker's whom we roped in at the last minute after another permit was denied, was down for orienteering. He threw himself into it with typical zeal. We all did. To avoid a sentence of vandalism and destruction of city property, it was a pretty good deal for Topher, Tucker, and me. And the rest were getting a nice wage. Oh, what fun we were going to have helping kids learn "How to Survive the Zombie Apocalypse."

Shit. The irony.

That night Tucker and I disappeared down to the lake right after dinner, stripped down to our bathing suits, and sparred, old-school karate style, on the dock until I was able to knock him into the lake. At the last second he grabbed my wrist and pulled me down after him.

"Illegal hold," I said, spitting water.

"Hold this," he said, pressing my hand to his crotch under the water. But Xander and Topher appeared on the shore.

"Have you seen the meteors?" Topher said. But of course they weren't meteors.

On the second night of the invasion we hiked up to the ridge and watched the repeated blinding flashes from the horizon, waiting each time for the sound wave to reach us like a thumping blow to the chest. We had no word from anyone in Calgary. By this time the phone, TV, Internet, and radio were all dead. Without ever discussing it, we all came to a silent consensus that Calgary was gone. And with it Tucker and Topher's parents, Xander's family, and all our other friends. In the early days, we spoke of these losses as though they were real and confirmed, but eventually we stopped discussing it. Tucker confessed to me that he still thought of his parents as alive.

"It's easier," he said, which was odd. He was never one to choose the easy path, even when it came to emotions. Maybe he meant it was easier for Topher.

As for my parents, they were planning to make their annual drive out to the coast, leaving on the day of the invasion. Maybe if they weren't in an urban area, or were able to get off the main roads, they could be hiding somewhere too. Jack was an experienced wilderness camper, and though Mom wasn't a big fan of camping, she knew what to do. But it all depends on what time of day they left. And how far they got. I try not to think about it, because there's also a chance that they're dead with everyone else. And everything I wanted to prove to them, everything I wanted to apologize for, everything I promised to fix is gone. Forty-eight hours was all it took. Our world is gone too. We grieve. And survive.

But for what?

I blink away the afterimage of exploding stars as Topher lies down beside me.

"We have to get out of here," I say.

"I know."

"The food is almost finished, and anyway there won't be enough daylight to properly run the solar for much longer. And we have hardly any fuel. We should have rationed better."

"I guess we thought we'd be rescued. Or something. We were supposed to shelter in place, remember?"

More irony. Of all the government advice and instructions I have ignored in my life, that "shelter in place" is the one I ended up following. I'm pretty sure it was the wrong choice.

"The fuel will run out before the snow comes," I say. "Then we're completely fucked."

"Hunting is obviously dangerous," Xander offers. I look up

to see that everyone is facing us, listening.

"Where can we go?" Lochie says. "I don't know much about this area, but I think Xander and I can keep us alive in the wild for a little while. As long as we keep clear of the baddies."

"We're about a day's hike from the nearest town," Topher says. "But Tuck was heading that way."

"It might be safer to go in the other direction," Xander suggests. "Toward Calgary, stay off the highway though, go along the river. There's a kind of tourist resort at Whatsitcalled, in the foothills. Right? Maybe people are hiding out there. That's what I would have done, if I'd been in town. Headed to high ground."

"How long?" Emily says.

"Two days maybe. There's a lot of uphill. It depends what we take with us."

"Don't you guys think we should go away from Calgary?" I ask. "Head west, toward the coast?"

Topher gives me a meaningful look. He knows what I'm getting at. We've talked about my parents and where they might be a hundred times. "We'd never make it across the mountains. Not now."

"And we don't have the supplies for such a long hike," Xander says.

"Hike?" Emily snorts. "Isn't it like six hundred miles?"

"It's smarter to see what's happening nearby," Lochie says.

"We might find supplies, food. We could always come back here."

"Or head west," I say stubbornly. The four of them stare at me, and I start to feel like we're going to have a vote, and I'm going to end up looking like a dickhead. "Fine. You're right. We should look for other survivors around here first. So we should take food and weapons. Maybe warm clothes. We'll need them soon." We could have blankets of snow by late September, if we live that long.

"Right. Lots of weapons. Everything we have." Topher curls his fingers around Tuck's crossbow.

"Do you think Sawyer and the rest will go for it?" Xander says.

"I don't care," I say. Nothing left to lose, I remind myself. "I'm going. I'm not staying here to starve or freeze without even trying." A few cells of my weed-addled brain cling to a faint hope that my parents are safe somewhere. And something in me wants to at least try to get back to them. Even if I die on the way, I have to try, because maybe trying will make all that other stuff go away. The suspensions, getting arrested, probation, the judge and his disapproving glare. My utter failure to make something of everything they did for me. And all the things we said to one another that none of us meant. I wanted to make it all better. Tucker would have understood. He knew how important it was. The others see only my surface: tough, reckless, and snarky. I hate to dissuade them of that, even now when a little attitude adjustment might be sensible. But since when am I sensible? "I'd rather throw myself into a Nahx cooking pot," I add, for effect.

"It may well come to that," Lochie says.

EIGHTH

Wait.

Wait here.

Stay here for a while. Try to think.

Disconnect and find something to eat, and a drink of water. The hole in my chest is shrinking, and the armor plates have knitted closed. It aches, but I can breathe again, without wanting to scream anyway.

Pain filled up my mind for a while. I couldn't think at all. Pain is not supposed to do that to me. They even tested me, I think. I don't remember that very well. Except for the pain part. I might have pretended it didn't hurt because that's what they wanted. That was stupid, I now realize.

That was before Sixth joined me. Before the battle. Before I figured out the only thing I'm good at is doing really stupid things. And breaking stuff.

I need to find some others. I'll tell them she didn't get up. I'll tell them I waited with her while the sun rose and set and rose and set again. She didn't get up. I left her there. I'm scared that was a mistake. Maybe I should have waited for a transport.

I'm not supposed to get scared.

Eighth is defective.

I'll tell them. Maybe it'll be okay. Maybe they can take me back to a hub and fix me. Fix my mind. Restore my directives. Or give me new ones. I barely remember what the old ones mean. They buzz in my brain like bees behind glass.

Dart the humans. Leave them where they fall.

I hope no humans find me.

I don't think I can do that again.

Sweet painless muddy death, my chest really hurts.

RAVEN

This is not a democracy!" Sawyer shouts in my general direction.

"I'm sorry. I don't remember joining the marines, either."

We've been arguing about leaving the camp for over an hour. Topher and Emily are outside training the others with rifles and crossbows, so our conversation is punctuated with gunshots and the *snap-twang* of the bows.

"You are a minor, Raven. So are Topher and Xander."

"So we don't get a vote?"

We've already ascertained that if those of age vote, Mandy, Sawyer, and Felix vote to stay, and Emily and Lochie vote to leave. Three to two. Sawyer knows the vote would go the other way if us "minors" had a say.

"Leaving is suicide," Sawyer says. *Snap-twang* goes a crossbow outside. "We've seen their ships over the foothills. They'll pick us off like ducks on a pond."

"Staying is slow suicide. Those ships will find us eventually."

"They might not. They haven't yet. We're well hidden. And

we can survive here. We have excellent shelters and plenty of land to grow things come spring. We've kept all the seeds from the fresh fruit and vegetables. We can hunt. We have guns."

Jesus. He's hard core. Even Lochie with all his bug eating, is not as dedicated to this post-everything way of thinking. Sawyer and Felix are the real deal. I suppose they'll expect us girls to breed, too.

As though he's reading my mind, Felix adds this: "We could be the only humans left on Earth. We have a duty to keep our species going."

Though this makes me groan, his fatalism is not without cause. Weeks have passed since we've managed to capture a video signal. Felix's theory is that a point-to-point base station up on the mountain has been destroyed. But Sawyer is all *I Am Legend* about it, without the flesh-eating zombies. Actually, for all we know, the Nahx might be zombies. Though, so far, we haven't seen any flesh eating.

"So, what?" I snap. "We pair up and start popping out babies?" There's a *bang! ding!* from outside as someone shoots down a can. I twitch.

I don't think Sawyer knows how ridiculous he sounds, or how delusional. Because to me, and maybe to Topher, too, Tucker's loss cemented this reality: Death is already inevitable. Not inevitable in the sense that everyone dies one day, but the sense that we are all going to die *soon*. The only remaining question is how. Do we die fighting, or crying in our beds? No one who knows me would be surprised that I choose to go down fighting. I've always been a fighter.

Illegal hold, I think, of Tucker pulling me off the dock with him. All of us who would vote to leave loved him in some way, I realize. Me and Topher, obviously. Xander had been friends with both of them for years. He and Lochie bonded instantly when they discovered their mutual love of Belgian beer and hanging upside down from tree branches. And Emily . . . well, girls always loved Tucker.

Tucker is our vanguard, our pioneer into death, even though he was running away from it when it caught up with him. I want to be running too, when it comes for me. At least running, if not fighting. Tucker's memory deserves that.

"Look, Your Majesty," I say. Felix rolls his eyes. "There is no age of majority after an apocalypse. Can we agree on that? And even if there was, how could you stop us from leaving? Five of us are going. I'm not going to lobby Mandy, though I'm pretty sure she will be joining us when it comes down to it. We'll take a fair share of what's left of the food and weapons and see you later. How does that sound?"

I don't wait around to hear their response.

"Someone give me a gun," I say when I reach the others. Topher hands me a rifle obligingly.

"Just the targets, right?" he says with a nervous smile.

I shoot three rounds with the rubber bullets we have for practice, none of which come close to the cans propped on the fence at the other side of the field. The recoil of the rifle pounds into my shoulder painfully on the next round, but the bullet hits a fence post with a satisfying *crack*.

"Nahx armor is bulletproof," Topher says quietly as he reloads the rifle. There was a surprising amount of both live and rubber ammo in the gun locker. Maybe they were expecting a plague of bears.

"Bulletproof? How do we know that?"

"It was in one of the last videos we caught. Those emergency broadcast network ones. Facts-about-our-enemy sort of thing. You didn't watch that one?"

I shake my head. I watched a few of the early videos—battle scenes mostly, if it can be called battle when civilians are mowed down as they run away. Some were long-range shots of cities on fire, or explosions. There was one, which streamed every day for two weeks, of what looked like a Nahx ship blowing up, but that might have been faked. Anyway, I stopped watching. I decided to pretend it wasn't happening, that Tucker and I were on vacation together. All that seems like a very long time ago already, like a half-forgotten story from childhood I didn't know I was quite done with.

I press my eyes closed. Topher has seen me at my worst,

and I him, but this doesn't seem like the moment to show weakness, or emotion, or that I'm a human being. I feel him give my arm a squeeze and a pat. When I open my eyes, he's walking back to the cabin, the rifle propped on his shoulder.

"Wanna try the crossbow?" Emily says.

I ignore her and follow Topher to the cabin.

"So what do we do?" I ask him. He's sitting on the edge of one of the beds, looking out the window at the lake. "If we can't shoot them, what do we do?"

He has the rifle resting on his knees, one hand gripping the barrel. "One guy thinks there's a weakness in the neck. Another thinks knives or arrows might work. You know, since they go through Kevlar and stuff. Maybe it's the same kind of armor."

I take a moment to run my own little video in my head. "Arrows, okay, maybe I can see it. But knives? How do you think a knife fight with a Nahx would go down?"

"Best-case scenario is you'd both end up dead."

Down on the lake a group of Canadian geese takes off, heading south, as if nothing has changed in the world. I wonder if they even notice, or care. The sky is clear, the air is still. It could be any other autumn day.

Snap-twang!

Except for that.

"We're all dead anyway, though," I say. "Right?"

Topher nods, watching the geese.

The relief of being able to think more clearly is worth the effort it takes to breathe without my mask. What a choice, breathe or think. I check my elevation. Just over 5,000 feet. I could breathe better if I went higher up, but I'm scared now. Sixth said the Rogues, the noncompliant lower-ranked Elevenths and Twelfths, are up there. I prefer to avoid them, as she instructed. They are dangerous, as inclined toward violence against their own kind as humans. Each other, too, Sixth said.

I need to focus on remembering the things she said, on what she taught me. If I stay at this elevation, I have a few hours before I need to reconnect. I can think. I can try to organize my thoughts. I wasted an hour sleeping, but I needed the sleep. When I woke up a lot of the fear and confusion had drained away, and I could assess my situation a little more rationally.

I've really screwed up. I should not have left her. I'm sure the transport came eventually. Or maybe it will still come. When I reconnect, I'll walk back down there. Maybe she's still there. Maybe she got up at last. She might be wondering where I am.

I wonder whether she'll look for me. I think I would look for her if it were the other way around. But . . .

I've never heard of one of us getting up after so long.

The color and the smell of the trees up here help me concentrate. This is the kind of thing I could never tell her. I know enough to understand I'm not supposed to care about the color and smell of pine trees. I knew enough not to tell her how sometimes I would lose thoughts right after thinking them. She would tell me something, and a moment later it would be gone, leaving a blank space in its place.

Eighth is defective.

I'm more defective than even Sixth knew. But at least I can think now, better than when I'm connected anyway. I still have a giant empty wasteland for half my mind, but the other half works okay. It's hard not to worry about the emptiness though, about the missing thoughts. Have I forgotten important things? Even not knowing what they are, they feel important, if missing things can be important.

I miss Sixth. She is important.

Important. Defective.

I need to get back to a hub somehow. Find a transport, get back to a hub. If she's still alive, then I'll rejoin her and we'll continue the preparations. If not . . . I don't want to think about that. I'm sure I'm not supposed to care.

Maybe another one will like me more than she does, won't get angry when I make new signs.

You have all the signs you need, defective low rank. She would hiss as she said it.

Another one won't call me defective and shove my hand off her shoulder. We're supposed to walk like that, so I can push her down if there's any threat.

I think she's dead. I hope that thought will slip away too, but it doesn't.

If I close my eyes and reach out, it's almost like my fingers could find her shoulder. It's easier to walk, easier to forget the pain in my ribs if I think like that. That's wrong too, but I don't care.

RAVEN

We leave two days later, at dawn. Sawyer, Felix, and Mandy agree to come with us finally, because Mandy could see that being left in a remote wilderness camp with a gay couple might not be all that she dreamed of from life. And Sawyer and Felix couldn't let us all go on our own. They are the senior camp leaders, after all.

Before I leave I want to visit Tucker's grave. Alone, I plan, but of course, when I reach it, as the sun is peeking up over the valley ridge, Topher is there, sitting cross-legged, his fingers trailing in the loose earth.

"What a surprise to see you here," I say. A pathetic attempt at levity.

Topher sighs. "My parents will want to know where he is."

If they're alive, I think.

"If they're alive," Topher says, looking up at me. I've dressed for the journey and armed myself. "Knives?" he says, eyeing the two hunting knives, one in each thigh holster, strapped over gray cargo trousers. A third is tucked into the top of my hiking boots.

"I never could get the arrows to go where I wanted them to," I confess. "And the rifles make my ears ring."

"You're quite the soldier." He gets up and brushes the dirt off his jeans. He has a rifle and a crossbow slung over his back, a quiver of arrows, rounds for the rifle, *and* a hunting knife strapped to his thigh. Quite the soldier. "I'll leave you alone, if you want."

"No, it's okay. I wanted to say good-bye. You can stay. I want you to stay."

He clasps his hands in front and looks down.

I stare at the grave. The pine and birch wreath still looks fresh and green. Our waxy handprints are undisturbed. I wonder how long the grave will look like this. With no permanent headstone, soon it will be lost among the fall leaves, the snow. Eventually, no one but us will know he's here. I try to memorize the more enduring landmarks, the birch tree, the angle of the lake behind it. Will I be able to find this place again in years to come?

Am I going to have years to come?

Once I imagined a future with Tucker. I knew it wouldn't be easy, the two of us being who we were. I knew there would be dark moods and mistakes made. I knew it would be hard. But nothing could be harder than leaving him here in his grave. I never imagined that.

"Good-bye, Tuck," I whisper, glad that Topher is here to

witness it. "I love you, always." I've said this to Tucker a million times, but it feels important for Topher to hear it. He never understood our love. He was like all the adults around us who called it "a rebellious infatuation." Maybe now he sees it differently.

"That's it, then," Topher says, nodding. As we walk away, he squeezes my hand. Just for a second, but it means the world to me. I'm not even sure why.

We don't know what we'll find outside the security of our little hidden valley. Tucker was nearly five miles away, over the ridge and deep into the foothills, when Topher found him. So there are some Nahx that way. We're going the other way, around the lake and following the river that feeds it, to the mountain at the other end. There are so many nooks and crannies in the Rocky Mountains; people could be hiding anywhere. If we find them, we'll join them, or they'll join us. There is strength in numbers, or so they say.

We make a motley group. We're all dressed in dark clothes, with generous amounts of camouflage and army green making up our attire. We're also armed to the eyebrows—rifles, crossbows, knives. Only Emily has a traditional bow and arrow—she's the only one who is fast enough to make it practical. We all have bear spray too. Wouldn't it be ironic if in this post-invasion world, at the mercy of a hostile superhuman foe, we were set upon by bears? Or wolves? I wonder whether bear spray deters the Nahx. Do they even breathe?

We each have a heavy pack. The boys are carrying the last of the food, which is heavier. The girls have clothes and blankets. We have sleeping bags tied to our packs, wet-weather gear, and a few cooking supplies. None of this is new to us. We spent the summer with nothing to do but train for the end of the world. And we all already had some game. Tucker and I could fight. Lochie and Xander are practically mountain trolls. Topher just knows everything. Emily grew up in a yurt or something, and Mandy spent last summer living up in the far north working with Inuit nurses. Sawyer and Felix were in the British armed forces. They both joined up at seventeen and served eight years.

We are well prepared to survive anything, excluding an invasion by a hostile alien race. Even nuclear holocaust would be easier to survive than this. We have *iodine* pills, for God's sake, for the radiation. Sawyer has a Geiger counter. He was going to teach a workshop on how to use it. It's all so funny I could cry.

We hike for three hours, stopping for a break where the lake narrows into the riverbed. Some of the trees are just starting to turn, which is not a good sign. It's been getting colder. Perhaps we haven't noticed, what with the end of the world and all, but the nights are going to be cold. And no more are we all cozied up together in an insulated cabin. Xander better be right about the resort being a two-day hike. Our sleeping bags are not all-season. We weren't exactly planning on spending the winter, or even the fall, out here.

Add freeze to the list of possible deaths. Starve, get shot with a toxic dart, blown up, or die of melancholy. I understand freezing is peaceful, at least. The pain stops and you fall asleep in the snow, maybe not even knowing you're going to die. That might be quite nice.

We barely speak while we rest, drinking a little water and nibbling on dry noodles and chocolate. We had an obscene amount of chocolate in the camp pantry. Apparently, they had planned for s'mores every night. That's a lot of chocolate and marshmallows. Diabetes might be another way to die.

I need to break out of this morbid state of mind. Obsessing about the manner of my death is going to suck all of the fun out of actually dying.

Late that afternoon, we come across a narrow swath of burnt forest. Charred black trunks spike upward like medieval torture devices. The forest floor is scorched and featureless.

"This looks recent," Sawyer says. "This summer recent. There's no regrowth."

It's bleak, but to me it looks pure, and clean. Cleansed. This is a natural part of forest life. I remember this from bio classes. The forest will regrow. Fireweed first, then other things. If it had been last season, the forest floor would be bursting with purple and white and green. As it is, it's black and dead. I find it sort of beautiful though. Like turned earth, or a . . .

Well, I was going to say a fresh grave, but what's beautiful about that?

Walking through the harsh landscape, I drag my hands on the blackened tree trunks until my palms and fingernails are stained with soot. The fine particles make my hands satiny and soft, as though dusted with expensive powder. But the smell is earthy and ancient, the smell of fire and wood and time, like a campfire from long ago. It makes my heart ache.

"The Nahx did this," I say. My voice surprises me. I didn't mean to speak, but words came out anyway, unbidden.

"It was probably lightning," Felix says, his appraising eyes drifting over the black charred spindles.

"Has there been a thunderstorm since that day?" I ask. One of the many ironies of this whole nightmare has been the perfection of the summer weather. We've had sunny days, with enough drizzles of rain to keep the dust down and the trees green. It's been warm and moist, but not humid. Like the climate is teasing us, reminding us of this perfect world we've lost.

We walk on, coating our boots with soot. Sawyer, at the lead, stops us with a raised fist.

"Fee?" he says, staring at something on the ground. Felix moves forward to the front of the group.

Sawyer points to the forest floor with the barrel of his rifle. "Seen treads like this before?"

Topher, Xander, and the rest freeze. We are lined up in the scorched trees, like pins in a pincushion. I push forward.

"What is it?"

Sawyer and Felix are looking at footprints in the soot— large footprints with a tread made up of triangular patterns in a kind of segmented formation. There are several. Whoever was wearing these boots, there were a few of them.

"Nahx?" I say. Somewhere around my bladder, something clenches.

"We have no way of knowing. Their tread pattern was never in the videos we saw. But I've never seen boots like this. They look . . . mechanical."

"Mechanical" is the mystery word no one talks about. It's easier to think of the Nahx as organic, humanoids. Obviously, they are armored, but if we imagine them with biological innards, it's more realistic to conceive of defeating them somehow. If these are nothing but robots, we're completely fucked. Because whoever is controlling them has no compunction whatsoever about annihilating us.

Topher steps up behind Sawyer. "That's one more thing we know about them," he says pragmatically. "We can track them. That helps."

"Track them?" Sawyer says. "Aren't we trying to avoid them?"

Topher steps backward, his eyes fixing on mine. "Yeah. Whatever."

I can almost feel his rush of energy. Of vengeance. Topher could follow these tracks to the ends of the earth. He believes he will.

I see Tuck so much in him right now it hurts like fire. And I don't know whether to run away or follow.

We camp not far from the burnt forest, in a dense grove of shaggy willows and scrub. Sawyer doesn't think a campfire is wise, but we have a few cans of Sterno fuel, so we're able to heat water and cook some noodles, eaten with cubed Spam and canned peas. Then we spend several hours trying to perfect a way to melt marshmallows with matches and lighters.

Darkness falls, and the mood changes. The Nahx are known to be much more active at night, when they can barely be seen. We shrink together, wrapping open sleeping bags around us, rather than crawling inside. This way we can get up and run faster, if the need arises. Sawyer has decreed that if we are attacked, we should all run in different directions and rendezvous, those of us who survive, at a designated point farther down the river. The idea doesn't exactly fill us with confidence. Only the exhaustion of the day-long hike offers us any hope of sleep at all.

Topher volunteers to take the first watch, and I volunteer to join him. With our friends curled up, backed into the mangled remains of a fallen tree, we sit back to back on a smooth rock. Topher has both rifle and crossbow on his lap. I settle for one of the rifles, even though I'm loath to fire it.

"How long is the drive from Calgary to Vancouver?" I ask when I'm fairly certain the others are safely asleep.

Topher sighs heavily. "We've had this conversation," he says. "About twelve hours."

"If they left early that day, they would have been nearly on the coast."

He shifts his weight forward, away from me, and the cold night air makes goose bumps rise on my back where his warmth has left me.

"Maybe, but . . ."

"But what?"

"That doesn't mean they're safe," he says. There is no empathy in his tone. He's back to being irritated with me. I guess the brief reprieve of our shared grief is over. "If they were in Vancouver . . . well, Vancouver probably got bombed too."

"But if they were on the road when it started, there's no way Jack would have . . ." I shake my head. My stepfather was a survivor, a fighter even more than me. "He would have turned onto some little back road, headed into the wilderness. Or hooked up with one of the First Nations out there and gone deep into their land. Someplace white people never go."

"The Nahx aren't white people."

I hear him moving behind me and turn to look at him, barely visible in the light of the sliver of moon.

"If I really wanted to go west, would you come with me?" I ask.

He looks back at me and shrugs. And then shakes his head.

Somewhere an owl or a bat flutters in the treetops. We both clutch our weapons and tense, watching the sky. After a moment Topher sets his weapons down.

"This vendetta. This is for Tucker, not for you," he says. "What's best for you is to go with the others, find shelter, find other people. I get that I'll probably never find the one that killed him. I'm not stupid. But maybe I can kill enough of those bastards to make up for it. I could find a base or one of the ships and blow it up. It's a suicide mission. I don't care. It's for Tucker."

"Didn't we make a pact to do it together?"

"Yeah." Topher sniffs. "That was a dumb idea."

We sit silently, in the dark, waiting for an owl to hoot or a coyote to howl, or crickets to start chirping. Something to create a little atmosphere, to fill up the void around us.

"I don't know why you hate me so much," I say, though I had no intention to until the words were already floating away. I've said such things to Topher before, and his standard answer has always been that he doesn't hate me; we're just too different, or some other platitude. But this time he surprises me.

"You mean *before* you got us all arrested? I thought you would get Tucker killed. He never took drugs before you came along, never snuck into clubs or broke curfew. It was like he was trying to be exciting enough for you. The long hair, the earring. He stole a car, for God's sake. Punched that douche bag math sub who got you suspended. He could have done time for that. And setting fire to the bandstand. Jesus, that was an ode to you. So yeah, I hated you. And you pretty much did get him killed, because he did all those stupid things to impress you."

This is the first time I've heard Topher correctly assign the blame to Tucker for the fire that got us all arrested. His change of heart makes me dizzy. Up until this moment he accepted his part in it and took his punishment, but I was sure he blamed me. He's still blaming me indirectly, but for Topher even that is progress.

"I didn't need any of that, or ask for it," I say.

"Whatever. I could see after a week that your relationship was a time bomb. I could never get him to see it."

"So you tried to break us up?"

"Yeah. Sue me."

I'm not going to sue him, but I am going to punch his lights out when the time is right. I squeeze both my hands into fists under my sleeping bag. Topher leans back on his elbows and looks at the clouds drifting across the moon. His face goes in and out of focus as the moonlight ebbs and flows. In low light I can almost see Tucker in him. As the light gets brighter, there is no mistaking Topher's tense, pinched expression for Tuck's easiness.

Topher frowns at me. "Look, sorry," he says.

"For what?" I say, feigning calm. I should feel nothing for him. If not for his connection to Tucker, he would be irrelevant. As it is, I'm developing a pathological obsession with keeping him alive, while also wanting to murder him.

"I don't blame you," he says, oblivious to the epic battle inside me. "I don't hate you. Not anymore."

Through the thick trees I can see the moonlight glinting on the blackened strip of forest we left behind. The Nahx footprints are there, a trail that will take us to them. I imagine following them mindlessly, driven, like Topher, by anger and a desire for revenge for days, weeks, months, never finding them, walking and walking through the soot, then the snow, until everything about me is gone and I forget who I am. Because Topher has just reminded me of something.

I blame myself. For everything. And it doesn't matter to me how he feels.

E I G H T H

The transport must have come after all. She's gone.

I suppose it's possible she got up and walked away, but I think she would wait for me. Or look for me.

The grass where she fell still holds the imprint of her shape, each blade pressed sideways, broken. She lay on her back like . . . something, something, from before that is behind a door in my mangled mind.

The shape in the grass is too much to look at. The wings of blood where her life seeped out from a torn-open throat, they make my own throat ache like there is something hard inside it. I want to use my knife to let it out.

There's a weakness there, in the armor. They told us that.

Keep your chin down, Eighth, she would tell me. She was looking up to the sky, looking for the transport. It was late.

I try to think. The thick syrup flowing through me dulls things, slows my thoughts down. I think of running or fighting easily enough, but there is nowhere to run and no one to fight. My other thoughts are sluggish. Like a slug. Slug. Slugs can be eaten, if necessary. Humans don't normally eat them. My brain is not quite working, like every time I reconnect. I feel powerful but stupid. I could run across the mountains or break down a thousand doors, but I can barely string two thoughts together.

She lay here for days. The earth beneath where she lay has not forgotten. The broken grass, the stain of blood. My fingers find the mark on my chest where my own blood spurted out. My wound wasn't bad enough to make me fall, and I dove for her, to knock her down, but I was too far away. Or she was already falling. I don't remember.

She had pushed me away minutes before.

Defective.

If I had reached her and saved her, she might have stopped calling me that. Terrible aim, and stupid. Only good for breaking things. If I could have saved her life . . .

Is it possible she got up? Did the transport take her? Could they fix her?

I want to disconnect again. I can't think with all this armor closing me in and filling me with slug syrup. I'm too far from a hub to receive directives if they change. I don't know how to send a signal. I don't know what to do without her.

Sixth. I miss you.

Sweet painless death, I know that's wrong. She hated me. Called me stupid and useless and made me find my own food and let me drink some sweet thing she found in a car that made me throw up and throw up until blood came out of my nose. Then she laughed at me.

You scared me, Eighth. I thought you would die.

I think of the way my head snapped back when the missile fragment hit me. So sudden and disorienting. Sixth was like that sometimes.

If I close my eyes and reach out to the left, I might find her steady shoulder there. She might let me walk like that.

I close my eyes. I reach out to the left.

Sixth?

Someone, please help me. I don't know what to do.

I walk away. Walk away from her shape in the grass and the wings of blood. Walk away from her. The sun is rising. I walk during the daylight, even though it's not safe.

I will shoot the first human I see. And the second one. And the one after that. I will do it for her. I know I can hit them now. I hate them.

I hate them, as much as she hated me.

I walk away from her, reaching out with my left hand. It is easier to keep my balance this way.

W hen I wake I can hear the others stirring around me. We are quiet, cautious, but more at ease now that the sun is up.

Moments later, all hell breaks loose when Sawyer does a half-serious head count and comes up one short. Topher is gone.

"Did he say anything to you? Anything?" he says as Felix, Xander, and I prepare to go looking for him.

"He wants to find the Nahx that killed Tuck. I didn't think he would go." This is something of a lie. I didn't think he would go without *me*. "Maybe he went to follow those tracks."

Sawyer is furious. He agrees to wait at the campsite for six hours while we backtrack to the burnt forest. If we don't return with Toph by then, he and the others will continue on to the resort. There is no way of knowing when Topher left. If he left just before dawn like a sensible person would, we may have a chance to catch up with him. If he left in the dark—by anyone's measure a reckless thing to do—he's hours away by now. So was he thinking like Topher or Tucker when he left?

Back at the burnt forest, it is easy enough to find his tracks.

He's not trying to conceal himself. Perhaps he wants to be found. I hope he's not making himself conspicuous in the hopes that the Nahx will find him. That would be stupid as well as reckless.

Sweating in the rising heat, we follow his tracks up the side of the valley. The sun beats down on the ashes at our feet, warming them, causing waves of the rich earthy scent to rise up around us. It is silent and still with barely a breeze. All the sound is in the crunch of our boots on the burnt debris and the twittering of morning birds. We listen for anything, any footsteps, any engines. None of us has ever seen a Nahx or one of their ships up close, so we don't know what we're listening for. All we know is that their dart guns make a whining noise before they fire. Felix learned this from the videos before they stopped. You hear a high-pitched whine and then you die.

It's an hour before we come across the landing site, just on the other side of the ridge. A large patch of blackened forest is flattened, the triangular, segmented shape mimicking the footprints we and Topher have been following.

"It's kind of small," Felix says. "Must be some kind of transport."

Xander examines the scorch patterns around the landing site. "This is how the fire started," he says. "But it was weeks ago. See these?" He points out some small green shoots, straining out of the ground where the ship flattened everything.

"But the Nahx footprints are more recent," I say. I'm not the greatest tracker, but even I know that prints won't last in loose ash and soot much beyond a couple of days. The weird segmented tracks don't look much less defined than the ones Topher left a few hours ago. "Earlier yesterday? We might have only missed them by a couple of hours."

"I could kill that boy," Felix says, looking around nervously. "Next time you get wind that someone is on a suicide mission, you tell me, got it?"

"Yes, sir." I hope my insincerity comes across as strongly as I feel it.

Felix tramps off, away from the landing site. Xander and I follow.

"You know what, Rave?" Xander says to me. "Tell me. I know Toph thinks this is his own private *True Grit*, but Tuck was my best friend. And this is ridiculous. What does he think he's going to achieve?"

I stare at Felix's back and try to formulate an answer. But my ability to speak is overwhelmed by anger as I properly process the danger Topher has put us all in. And more than that, I'm furious at him for leaving without me. How can I keep him alive if he walks away from me? And why do I even want to, if he's so determined?

"There he is," Felix says suddenly. He's gazing across the ridge through a pair of high-powered field binoculars. Pointing to the edge of the burned-out swath, he hands them to me.

I scan the spindly black landscape. At first I see nothing. Then, taking another scan, I spot Topher, sitting, his back to a tree stump, his head hanging. I have to press my lips together to keep from calling out to him. He doesn't move. My ears strain to hear anything.

"It doesn't make sense for us all to go down there. It's too dangerous and exposed," Felix says, shaking his head. "What was he thinking?"

"Let's go back up. We'll have a better angle," Xander says. "We can provide cover if anything comes up."

We move farther up the slope. Every few minutes I check through the binoculars. Topher still hasn't moved. "Wait here," Felix says. He eyes the rifle I borrowed from Lochie. "Can you shoot straight?"

"Not really," I admit.

"Wonderful. Shoot high, then. I'd rather not get hit with friendly fire today. Let Xander go for the kill shot."

What is Topher doing? I wonder as Felix leaves us. He still hasn't moved. Felix jogs down, sticking close to the trees and ducking out of sight wherever he can find cover. I follow his descent through the binoculars.

"Shit," I hear Xander whisper beside me.

"What?"

"The birds have stopped."

Suddenly, a guttural, animal screech pierces the air, and two black shadows descend from the sky. They seem to have come from nowhere.

"Topher!" I yell. Down the ridge Felix is running. I flatten myself on the ground and yank the binoculars back up to my eyes. Topher is gone. Felix bolts past the tree where he was sitting and disappears, leaving a puff of ash and dust in his wake.

Where the hell did they go? The two transports touch down on the hillside between us.

Xander crashes to the ground next to me, his rifle fixed on the ships. "Did you see where they went?" I shake my head. "Right," he says, gritting his teeth. "Shoot or run?"

The door of the first transport opens. Two shadowy figures appear in the doorway. Human shaped, but too large, armored in dull, deep gray. Everything about them is like a living weapon, hard, metallic, and lethal. My insides turn to Spam, which threatens to come back up. We can't cover Topher and Felix if we can't see where they went.

"Run," I squeak. "Run!"

Xander leaps to his feet, yanking me up after him.

I hear the hiss of the other transport door open and the clatter of armored feet on the gangplank.

I'm lost. Despite our weeks of survivalist games, neither Xander nor I have any proper combat training. I have no idea about strategy in a situation like this. If they go after Felix and Topher, we might as well say good-bye right now. But we can get over the top of the ridge and head back down into the valley. We would have the advantage of being out of sight for a minute or two. That might save our lives. But what about Topher? What about Felix?

Xander lets go of my hand as I stumble to a stop. I spin around and point my weapon in the general direction of the squadron of Nahx gathered at their landing site.

"Are you crazy?"

Well, yes, I think. Yes, I am.

"Get behind me!" I scream at him.

I fire into the center of the group of Nahx. Unbelievably, I think I hit one. It spins around and seems to shove one of its colleagues to the ground. I'm pretty sure the bullet just bounced off the armor, but now the whole group of them turns as one and starts barreling back up to the ridge.

"Oh Jesus, we're going to die," Xander says. I pull him, diving over the ridge and running full speed back down to the river, which glistens in the sun like an emerald necklace. It feels like only a few seconds have passed when I hear a high-pitched whining noise.

"Paintball!" I yell to Xander. He gets my meaning right away. All the kids from the dojo played paintball at least three times a year. We both know the best way to avoid getting hit is to run like a convulsing lunatic. He veers away from me.

A dart zings past my head as I begin to weave in and out of the burnt tree trunks. Xander ducks and leaps like his shoes have springs. A tree splinters next to me as another dart misses its mark. The Nahx behind us aren't even running. I have heard they can move at inhuman speeds, but they are calmly marching, their weapons whining and firing. Bizarrely, one is walking with a hand on another one's shoulder.

Another dart whizzes past. Ahead of me Xander tumbles and rolls.

"Xander!" I shout, but he leaps back up to his feet on the other side of a cluster of burnt logs. When he reaches the riverbank, he turns and raises his rifle.

"Get down!" he screams.

Clearly, he's even crazier than me. I dive to the ground and roll toward him as he fires off rounds. A glimpse of the Nahx tells me his tactic is not slowing them down even a little bit. Two darts zing past his head, and he ducks. I use the momentum of my fall to keep rolling, clutching my rifle to my chest as Xander keeps firing. I stop rolling, leap up, and tackle him. We both fall off the riverbank, crashing to a small muddy outcrop below. Xander lands in a heap on top of me.

The river's edge is a tangle of mud and roots from the trees on the riverbank above. I know we have seconds before the Nahx reach us, seconds to do about the stupidest thing I've ever done. "Take a deep breath and hold on," I say, grabbing Xander by the shirt and rolling into the river.

The water is frigid and instantly knocks about forty points off my IQ, but I manage to stick to my plan and pull us both under, reaching out to the roots under the surface for something to hold on to. Worse case is I will let go, and the river current will pull us back into the lake we left a day ago. That would epically suck, so I wrap my arm around a large root, pop to the surface to take another breath, and slither deep into the water.

My brain freezes to the point that I barely take in the fact that Xander is still with me, also clinging to roots, his cheeks puffed out and eyes wide. We are a good five feet under the surface, with a healthy current of murky water flowing over us, dressed in dark clothes and making a point to look like a couple of rotting trees.

Above the water, however, the bright sunlight allows me to see three Nahx appear on the riverbank over the outcrop. Damn it, that was stupid. I should have let us drift downstream a bit. We are hiding in the river directly under the spot where we rolled off the bank.

Beside me, Xander twitches. My lungs feel like they're going to pop like two balloons. The Nahx up on the bank show no sign of leaving. We could let go and drift away, but the Nahx might notice the movement despite the murkiness of the water. I need to breathe. I need to breathe. My vision starts to turn black at the edges.

Above us, the Nahx move back and disappear from view. Xander and I shoot to the surface and gasp in gulps of air, still clinging to the roots and pressed into the river edge. Stars twinkle in my eyes, and my teeth start to chatter. Shaking my wet hair from my face, I see something, a smudge of shadow on the opposite shore. Xander sees it too. We both spin our heads around.

"Oh fuck," Xander says wetly.

Instinctively, I pull him behind me, pressing him into the weeds.

A single Nahx stands on the bank, looking at us, its dart rifle hanging at its side. It tilts its head for a second, then reaches down for its rifle. I don't waste time.

"Let go!" I yell. Xander obeys, and together we are sucked out into the river, sailing downstream with the rushing current. I struggle to keep my head above water, expecting the Nahx on the far shore to start running, chasing us down the river, but it just watches, rifle still raised, as we tumble away.

EIGHTH

I never considered that the next human I saw would be a girl. I don't know why that made me hesitate.

When I stepped out from the trees, I had a clear shot to where she clung to the river's edge. I could have darted her, I think. But it seemed a shame. She was so brave, the way she pulled that other human down, and she succeeded where I failed. She protected her Offside.

I think I admired her too much to fire my rifle.

Admiration. I don't even have a sign for that. I would make one up but . . .

The soldier on the other shore sees me and signals for me to wait. *Lost*, I sign, and one of them nods and signs.

Wait there.

They are higher ranked than me, or even Sixth, I think. The one who nodded to me might even be a First. They are so regimented and controlled. Nothing fazes or distracts them. Sixth would have stomped in frustration about losing the humans in the river, but these ones just turn and march back over the ridge. Sixth would have blamed me and called me stupid, shoved me away and refused to talk to me for days.

I wait, the fingers on my left hand seeking something to hold on to. I wonder whether I shouldn't slip back into the trees, go up higher, and disconnect again. I don't trust these high ranks. I know what they think of me. What happens if they find out I'm defective?

But how would they know? We are not decorated in any way. We all look the same, especially in our armor. It is behavior that indicates rank. The higher ranks think *all* the Eighths are defective, and the Ninths and Tenths even worse. Even I'm scared of the Elevenths and Twelfths. Mostly, they disappear and are never seen again. But if I can manage to act like a higher rank, then what's to stop me going with these ones? I can watch them and do exactly as they do. I can be regimented and controlled like them, not become entranced with green things, or distracted by the smell of baby wolves or spiderwebs.

I can't be a First, because I'm a boy and the male Firsts are all still on the ships. I can't expect to be as perfect as a Second—a Second would never get lost, for starters—but maybe I could make a convincing Fourth. Then I would be higher ranked than she was. Sixth would like me as a Fourth. If she's not dead.

My fingers reach, reach, and find nothing there.

One of the transports takes to the sky and skims over the water to collect me. I would tremble if I could. My apprehension makes me forget the girl in the river for the moment. I think of Sixth instead, and reach for her.

RAVEN

When Xander pulls me out of the river, I am so cold my limbs feel like seal flippers. We are both battered from rocks and other debris crashing over us as the river twisted and turned. Xander finally managed to haul us toward the shore and drag himself up into the tangled rocks and roots. I clung to his legs as he gathered his strength to tug me up after him.

He lets me fall in a heap on the shore and collapses down beside me. We lie like two dying fish, gulping and gasping for breath. Soon we are both shivering. With the lateness of the day and the season there is little hope of warming ourselves up without a fire.

"I don't s-s-s-suppose you have m-m-m-matches," I stutter.

Xander snorts, and coughs up river water.

So no hope at all, then.

"We have to get back to the others."

Xander looks at his divers' watch. "We have about two hours. We should run." He clambers to his feet and, offering me a hand, tugs me upright. "Shall we race?" he asks with a cheeky grin. "I'll even give you a head start."

I show him my middle finger.

If there's a feeling as desperate as running in wet clothes and sloshing boots along a muddy riverbank with the threat of being killed by a hostile alien around every corner, I don't know what it is. Running, with no food in your belly, a half-frozen brain, clumps of river-drenched corkscrew curls slapping you in the face, and a lukewarm commitment to actually not lying down and letting a bear find you and eat you. With no hope of ever reaching anywhere good. It's hard to muster up enthusiasm for a run like that.

After twenty minutes of straining to keep up with Xander's long-legged, loping pace, tears are streaming down my face. Barely slowing down, I turn to the side and vomit about eight cups of river water onto the roots of a sick-looking sapling. Xander stops and looks back at me as I stagger on.

"Break?"

I shake my head, wiping my mouth on my damp sleeve. I've done longer runs than this, though I've never enjoyed any of them. I'm not one of those girls who run for hours every day in the hopes of being skinny enough to fit into some sexy dress. I hate dresses anyway, and I never wanted to be as skinny as I am right now. Ten weeks of rationing food has moved all of us down in the weight categories.

I have no concept of how long we've been moving, when I begin to feel almost warm again. When sweat drips into my eyes, it is a reprieve. We reach the burnt forest just as the sun dips below the valley ridge. We pause there, making sure the way is clear.

"We can walk from here," Xander says. "It's only about another half hour."

The light is fading though, and our last encounter with the Nahx was in this exact spot in broad daylight, so I can't say that I think slowing down is a good idea. My legs disagree. I heave them, like lead pipes filled with concrete, dragging one after the other. When I realize that my clothes are nearly dry but still freezing cold, I begin to giggle.

"You're losing it," Xander says with a smile.

"Oh, you noticed?"

Past the burnt forest we finally veer away from the river, up toward the dense scrub where we left our camp. I turn back and take a last look at the rushing current, now dark and brooding in the dusk rather than emerald and sparkling. My eyes drift to the other shore, and my mind to the solitary Nahx that stood there, watching us but not shooting. There is something more to think of that, but I can't quite connect with it.

As we lose the light, every tree and branch becomes a shadow. By the time we reach the campsite, my nerves have unraveled like an old sweater, expecting a Nahx or some other horror with every footstep. Somehow, I end up walking ahead of Xander, so I'm the one who hears the distinctive creak of a bow being drawn back and finds an arrow pointing in my face.

"Boo," I say halfheartedly. Emily lowers her bow, squinting in the dark.

"Bloody hell, we thought you were dead."

"Don't look so disappointed."

For my part, I'm flooded with relief, relief that they waited longer than six hours, and relief because in the darkness behind Emily, I can see Topher's shocked face. Among the others the news of our survival is greeted with restrained jubilation until we confess we lost two rifles in the process. Then Sawyer is furious again, but lucky for us, he takes it out on Topher. I have a few things I want to say too.

"You left without me," I say, plopping down beside him.

"Are you all right?"

Suppressing the urge to punch him makes me grind my teeth. "Cold, bruised, but unbroken," I say. "What the hell were you thinking?"

"There was a firebreak, a trench. I was going to lure them into it and then . . ."

A question forms in my mind. Something like *Have you taken leave of your senses?* But then I realize there is no real reason to ask it. It's clear he has.

We stare out into the dark together, a dark so deep it's hard to tell if my eyes are open or closed. I blink, and in that blink see the lone Nahx on the shore, not shooting, letting us float away. Its shape, blurred like an indistinct shadow, is like a photograph of a moving object. The memory of that instant stretches out like a slow-motion film. It tilted its head to the side before it raised its gun. It didn't shoot. It *thought* about it. The Nahx think? What was the Nahx that killed Tucker thinking in that moment? What do they think of us, the occupants of this planet that they have taken by force?

The strength of these questions derails me. It's as though I'm able for a moment to see the world through their eyes, see myself through the eyes of that lone Nahx on the shore. What did it think of me when it decided not to fire? The idea of it thinking about me at all is repellent and violating. Topher senses my unease. He has the same infuriating sixth sense that his brother had. Always able to tell when something was the matter, never able or particularly willing to do anything about it.

"If you have something to say to me, say it," he says, as though I've been sitting there thinking about him the whole time.

"This isn't about you," I say. "No one here is going to let you disappear into the night. Everyone is just stupid enough to get themselves killed going after you. So . . . wait, okay? Wait until we get everyone somewhere safe. Then you can go off on your vengeance quest."

"So you don't want to come with me?"

"God, Topher, the days of being allowed to *want* things are over. We're running on absolute nothing left to lose, we're dead-unless-something-miraculous-happens desperation here. Maybe I'll go with you to kill some Nahx. What's the alternative? Wander around, freezing, starving? Waiting for them to find us?"

At least the more I think about it, the less likely it is that I'll let Topher go off on his own.

He doesn't speak again for a long time. Behind us we hear the murmurs of our friends, the rustle of sleeping bags, the rattle of a plastic wrapper. They seem like normal noises, but nothing about this is normal.

"We all thought you were dead," Topher says. "When you fell into the river, we thought they must have shot you and you were both dead."

"So I heard," I say. "How did you feel about that?"

I don't even know why I'm asking this. I suppose to make the commitment to go on a murderous vendetta with someone, or to make their salvation your life's project, you should really know how they feel about you, or something. Or maybe I'm attempting to strengthen our bond, so that if I go off with him, eventually I might be able to convince him to abandon his vendetta and head west.

There's another long pause, during which I get slightly

nervous, like I'm about to hear something I'll never be able to unhear.

"I don't think I could explain it," Topher says cryptically. "Even if I wanted to."

That answer is not unexpected. Topher was always the one who kept his feelings in check. But those hours we spent together next to Tucker's body and lying by his grave tell me there are depths to Topher that are rarely plumbed. Depths to his capacity for grief anyway. Perhaps if I was really dead he could explain it. Perhaps one day I'll die in front of him just to get to the bottom of his emotional repertoire.

Maybe Topher got the brains and Tucker got the soul. Wouldn't that be perfect?

I crouch in the back of the transport, next to the ammunition storage. The First pilots, meticulously searching the dark landscape below, while her Offside, a Third, faces me, silently watching.

Rank? he signs at last. I was beginning to think he would never lower himself to speak to me. But I lose my nerve somewhat, tapping my left thumb with my right index finger.

Sixth.

Third nods and does the sign for "good," a palm flat on the chest, so fast that the sarcasm is painfully clear. I'm beneath him and the First, and he's not happy to be stuck with me. I sense his suspicion, too. There is no trust among my kind. Maybe he can tell I lied about my rank. He might think I'm a Rogue, searching for others like me, an Eleventh or Twelfth bent on desertion and disobedience.

In our signs "disobedient" is the same as "defective." I remember Sixth snapping it at me angrily.

What are your directives? Third asks.

I reply without hesitation. *Dart the vermin. Leave them where they fall.* Making the sign for "human," I read my own hands as "vermin." Sixth used this sign for a nest of mice we found once and for large insects I wanted to eat.

Vermin. Human. I suppose they were the same to her.

Have you received revised directives?

No.

Is your transponder malfunctioning?

Now I'm in trouble. Only the higher ranks, the First through Sixths, receive revised directives this far from a hub. When I hesitate to answer, the Third shoves me against the metal wall of the cargo bay, rattling my armor.

Rank! he signs violently, his fingers slicing inches from my face.

I press into the wall. *Eighth*, I sign. *Eighth.*

Offside? he signs, holding his left hand out at shoulder height. I close my eyes behind my visor.

Dead.

I feel him kick me hard in the shin, but by the time I open my eyes he's in the cockpit, signing to the First. She turns back to me for an instant, the briefness of her glance expressing as much disdain as any signs or words or facial expression could. I'm irrelevant, and a burden, farther down in the ranks from them than I was from Sixth, even pretending to be a Sixth myself. And worst of all, I let my Offside die somehow. They would be justified in pushing me out the hatch. Even I couldn't survive a fall that far. We're not supposed to kill each

80

other, but I know it happens. Sixth threatened it enough times.

I busy myself by reloading my rifle from the ammunition stock. Only a few darts are missing anyway. Out of habit I check the six backup darts concealed in my armor, but of course they're all still there.

The transport banks suddenly and begins to shake. First and Third reach up and grab handholds in the cockpit. I have nothing specific to grab here in the hold, so I wedge myself in between the ammo stockpile and the curved metal wall. Out of sight of the others I press my left hand onto the top of a weapons locker, curling my fingers around it, imagining . . .

I have to stop thinking of her.

A word pops into my head. It's familiar and unfamiliar. "Friend." It squeezed under the door somehow, with all the rest of the emotional stuff that is not supposed to bother me. We don't have friends; we don't have feelings, apart from anger and efficiency. I think of the way the human girl defended her friend. Humans are like this, bound not by rules and order but something else, something chaotic and unpredictable. It's familiar to me, too, and not, like so many things. But I'm defective. I tried to make Sixth my friend and she ridiculed me for it, laughed at me for being so pathetic.

Once when we were disconnected, I pointed out that laughter wasn't permitted either, even if it was mean spirited. She hit me in the face so hard my jaw ached for days.

I suck down the shame of this, swallow it into the thick slime below, hoping that it will turn into the strength of hate toward the vermin on this world. But the person I hate right now is myself. I wish the First and Third *would* push me out the hatch. We're quite high up. I could pretend I'm flying on the way down.

I sometimes dream I can fly.

The next day breaks brightly, but unexpectedly cold. The temperature drops further as we ascend to the resort on the mountain, and then, as though to mock us, just after midday, it clouds over and begins to snow. We hunch and shiver, tramping upward. The first thing we see is the trailer park outside the more affluent village. Rows of shabby trailers perch on terraces in the steep hillside. They seem pretty quiet, deserted.

"This doesn't look good," Xander says.

Instinctively, we all draw our weapons. All I have left are knives, which seem pathetically small against Topher's crossbow and the rifles, but speed is what matters with the Nahx. So the videos tell us anyway.

Sawyer takes charge. "Pair up and search. Take note of any food or weapons. We'll come back after we scope the village. Emily and I will stand watch."

Felix and I pair up. Topher and Lochie form another team, while Xander pairs with Mandy.

We work our way down to the end of one of the rows of trailers. Felix holds his rifle loosely at his side. My knives are holstered again, but I'm unnaturally aware of where they are. We check behind every trailer and in between every car. There are no signs of recent habitation. Everything is quiet, neat almost, like it was left tidy for visitors or something. There is a noise behind us. Felix spins, rifle raised, dropping to one knee before I even manage to get my knife pointing in the right direction. But it's only blobs of snow falling from a trailer roof. The day is warming up and snow is melting in the sun.

Finally, we reach the end of the row.

"We'll start with this one and work our way backward," Felix says. He tries the door of the last trailer. With a low *click*, it opens.

Inside looks as though someone might have been living here yesterday. Dishes litter the table, a magazine lies open on a bench. Behind a narrow open door near the small kitchen I can see a toilet.

The trailer appears to have two rooms. While Felix opens cupboards, finding a few cans and some dried food that look promising, I check out the door to the back room. It's closed but not locked. Perversely, I feel like knocking. But instead I turn the handle and it clicks open.

A man and a woman lie dead in the wide bed. Each of them has a black dart embedded in their forehead. Steel-colored veins spread out from the hole, covering their faces with the weblike lines. The man's dead fingers are still curled around a baseball bat.

I feel sick to my stomach. Felix comes up behind me.

"Oh," he says.

"They killed them in their sleep." I'm struck by how discreet that seems—I mean, for a species that blows up cities.

"Yes." Felix bends to look closely at the woman's gray face. "Recently? They haven't decayed."

"I don't know. That's weird, isn't it?" I swallow something sour in the back of my mouth. In the corner of the small room is a cradle. A tiny cradle. In it is a tiny desiccated baby. Definitely not recent. The baby's mouth is open, fixed in a permanent scream. I pull back the pink blanket and see that the diaper is soiled, the excrement as dried out as the rest of the body.

"These newer trailers are well sealed," Felix says. "And hotter than hell with the sun shining on them." He's calm, as though we're not talking about a baby being baked.

"There's no dart," I say. I take my gloves off and gently move the corpse, but find no sign of any wound or injury.

Felix pulls the blanket over the tiny mummified face. "The Nahx killed her parents in their sleep and left the baby to starve, I guess."

Somehow it is this injustice, this small act of disdain that finally steels me, welding me to Topher's mission. I close my eyes, a silly girl with a broken heart, and open them as a soldier who will never surrender. I know what kind of hope remains when the likelihood of getting out of this alive is gone. I hope I can take down a hundred Nahx with me, a thousand.

"Did you find much food?" I ask, turning from the dead. I feel as though I might never eat again.

"A bit," Felix says. "Next trailer?" His calmness disturbs me, but I remind myself he served in the military. He's seen all kinds of death before. Maybe a baked baby is nothing new to him.

Felix steps down from the trailer before me, collecting the pack he left by the door. He turns to look at me where I stand in the top of the doorway when I hear a loud whine and then a *thunk*. Felix's eyes bug out and he staggers forward. His rifle clunks to the ground and tumbles down the stairs and outside the trailer.

"Sawyer!" he manages to yell before falling, splayed on the floor of the trailer at my feet. There's a dart in the back of his head. He twitches painfully as I fall to my knees, pull the dart out, and throw it away. I try to turn him over, but he's wedged in the doorway, and it's too narrow for me to move him. Finally, I lie on the floor so I can see into his face. It is already filling with the dart toxin, the veins turning black, his eyes filling with dark blood.

"Hide," he chokes out, clutching at my arm. "Hide . . ." Then oily blood bubbles from his mouth, his eyes fix on me, and he stops breathing. The light leaves his eyes as I watch him die.

Outside the trailer, I hear shouting and gunfire. I edge back inside, past the kitchen. My choice is the bedroom with the corpses or the tiny toilet. I can't think. I hear Topher call Sawyer's name. And gunfire. And someone screaming "No! NO!" I climb into the toilet closet and pull the door closed after me. It's then I realize I've pissed myself.

Run. Run. Run, I think. I'm trapped, but the others can run. Above the toilet is a tiny window. In the sky outside I can see a hovering transport. Somehow this one is more menacing than the ones we faced yesterday. It looks like an awful organic machine. The sound of the engine is terrifying. Not loud so much as deep and throbbing. My teeth chatter uncontrollably. And I taste bile in the back of my throat again. The yelling outside stops for a moment. Are they all dead? Is Topher dead? I think of Felix outside on the floor and the tiny baby in the crib. They blur together. My hate is all that keeps me from fainting of fear.

Then I hear a voice. It's Sawyer.

"RETREAT! Back down the hill!" he shouts. I don't hear anyone looking for me. Someone says, "Help me carry him!" in a desperate voice, and I think they must mean Felix, but I don't hear any movement in the trailer. Someone else got hit. A him.

Not Topher. Please, not Topher. I pull my other knife from its holster and try to focus on remaining silent while my thoughts scream at me. *Not Topher. Not Topher.* He's all I have left of Tucker.

Seconds go past, minutes. Silence.

Have they left me? I look up through the small window and can still see the transport in the sky. It moves and dips out of sight. I hear its engines rumble low and the sound of metallic footsteps. Then it roars away.

I hold my breath, straining to hear anything. There are footsteps outside the trailer. No voices, just footsteps, heavy-sounding and a whining noise, then another *thunk*, very close by. The trailer vibrates a bit.

Have they shot Felix's body? That means they've spotted him in the trailer doorway. This trailer. The one I'm in. I don't dare open the bathroom door when I feel the trailer rock as someone comes up the stairs. I know it can't be one of us. They've left me. They've left me here to die with a dart in my forehead. I prepare myself. There is no way I am going to die sitting on the toilet. I clench one knife in each fist and coil up, ready to attack whatever comes through the door.

I feel the trailer rock.

Oh please, oh please. I'm not sure if I want them to leave or to open the door so at least I have a chance to kill one before I die myself. *The weakness under their chin,* I think, tightening my grip on the knives. A minute goes past, then another. I'm still trembling when I feel the trailer rock once more and hear heavy footfalls. I haven't locked the bathroom door! I look up at the latch hanging uselessly. I could reach up and attach it, but I would have to put down a knife. And move. And maybe breathe. I don't dare. My last hope now is that the Nahx won't open it.

A second later that hope fades, as I watch the door handle turn. I think of my parents, and Tucker, and Topher as I transfer that last dreg of hope to him. I hope he survives this, because I know I won't.

The door opens. A Nahx stands there with a dart gun pointed right at me.

I leap at it, both knives aiming for the throat. The armor blurs as in one movement it drops the gun and grabs both my wrists, one in each hand, stopping my knives an inch from its neck. I try not to scream as it squeezes my wrists and lifts me up. An instant before I'm sure my bones will be crushed like dainty porcelain teacups, I let go of the knives and they clatter to the floor.

I hang for a moment, suspended by my wrists. I try kicking out, landing several good shots on its torso and at least one that would leave a human man writhing on the floor. It barely flinches. I bend my elbows and pull myself up until I'm level with its black glass eyes.

This is the closest I'm ever likely to get to a Nahx. The armor is a thick dull gray that seems to absorb the light around it. It is segmented, like a beetle or a spider, and has valves and wires and reinforced panels all over it. The plates over its face seem to move slightly, revealing sharp-looking spines in thin strips. Some kind of extra defense? Or is this anger, fear? Can it feel fear, as I do? I wonder if they are just machines or if there is something inside there. There's a faint pulsating buzzing noise coming from the armor and a peculiar smell, almost like coal or burnt wood.

This Nahx is very tall, probably nearly two feet taller than me, and broad shouldered. It stands with knees slightly bent and feet apart. I hang there, biceps burning with the effort of holding myself up. Finally, with cramping muscles, I drop down. It doesn't let go of my wrists, and pain shoots through them as I realize they are burning. Its hands are burning me.

Growling with fury, I swing my knees up and wrap one leg around the dart rifle, which hangs from a strap at its side. When I almost pull it away, it lets go of one wrist, yanking the gun away from my legs, but the effort makes it lose its grip on my other wrist, and I crash to the floor, my head hitting the toilet behind me. I roll forward and gather my knives where they dropped. I crash and slash into its armored legs, setting it off balance and staggering back into the kitchen. Dishes clatter to the ground. When I manage to get onto my knees, it has the rifle trained on me again. I have one knife raised above my head and one pointed forward. I haven't got a chance. The best I can hope for is that I slice it before it kills me. I open my mouth to hurl more obscenities, but something else comes out.

"You don't have to do this," I say through chattering teeth. "You don't have to kill me. We don't have to be enemies." The words are pointless. I'm sure it doesn't understand. Maybe the tone of my voice will do something, make it feel something for me. Isn't that what you are supposed to do with attackers or if you get abducted? That's what they taught us in self-defense. "I'm no threat to you. Walk away. Just walk away."

The Nahx reacts with a barely noticeable twitch of its head. It doesn't lower its rifle though, or move.

We remain there, poised to kill each other for what seems like an hour, until I notice the Nahx's shoulders and chest rising and falling in time with the pulsating buzz from the armor. It is breathing. The second I take to register my surprise is all it needs. With blinding speed it lunges forward, gun arm knocking one knife away, hot armored fingers closing on the other. I take a breath to cry for help. The last thing I see is the butt of the rifle flying toward my head.

EIGHTH

Ah no. What have I done?

Wake up.

The girl human lies unmoving on the floor at my feet, blood blossoming from a gash in her forehead. Her cheeks are wet with tears, her mouth slightly open. That last little cry never quite escaped.

Breathe.

Her chest rises and falls once. My own breath catches somewhere near the back of my mouth.

Breathe again, please.

I press my fist into my chest. Sixth used this sign with me. It's an imperative. *You must. Right now. Obey.* It feels different when I do it. More polite.

Breathe, human. Obey. Please.

Her chest rises and falls again and begins a slow rhythm.

Stupid, stupid, stupid. That was so stupid. She's tiny compared to me, like a bird that has fallen from its nest. She couldn't hurt me with those pathetic knives. Think. Not anger. Not fear. Think.

I hate humans.

I *don't* hate humans. Not this one, anyway.

I have directives.

I know the directives. I can't . . . I can't do it . . . not this one. This one is so . . . brave, so wild, the way she snarled at me, like a wolf mother. She's so part of this chaotic world. So unlike me. My head spins. I was frightened, I think, truly frightened of her. That's ridiculous.

You don't have to do this, she said.

Her friends are gone. They ran down the hill. Will they come back for her? Humans do that. They come back for lost ones.

I look at her crumpled on the floor, her arms splayed at awkward angles, knees falling to either side. It seems, vaguely . . . improper to look at her. I look at the door instead, tempted to walk away, as she suggested.

If she woke up now, she would scream and scream. I could not make her believe I wouldn't hurt her again. No one could blame her for putting one of those knives in my throat.

But if she doesn't wake up . . .

She's still breathing. *Keep breathing. Obey.*

Her hair is so beautiful. Like a spiderweb or a dandelion halo around her face. Why do I even think about dandelions? That seems like the kind of thing that might be a waste of my diminished brain power. Dandelions, spiderwebs, setting suns. Why do I even notice such things?

Defective.

Would it be wrong to smell her hair? She would never know.

Ah. Her hair smells like the rushing river and pine needles, as though she grew from the earth like a tree. A pang of guilt quickly turns to fear, then anger. I hate these vulgar . . .

Stepping back, my rifle aims at her almost of its own accord. It would be so easy. The rush of fluid makes me dizzy. The humming directives in my head seem to pulse. *Dart the vermin. . . . Leave them . . . leave them . . .*

Pine needles. Think. I need to think.

I can't leave her here. What if her friends don't come back? It's getting cold. She could freeze if she doesn't wake up. Humans can freeze. And what if my people come back? They would dart her.

She breathes. Her eyes move behind her eyelids. Her thick black eyelashes are like a caterpillar's feet, though . . . I'm not sure that caterpillars *have* feet.

Slinging my rifle over my back, I slide my hands under her legs and shoulders and lift her up. She sags, limp in my arms, but I hold her tightly, like . . . like . . . something I can't quite remember, something behind the door. She is as light as a dandelion, or a spiderweb, or a snowflake, or a wisp of cloud. I can smell the tears on her face.

There is no sadder smell in this world than human tears.

Stupid defective Eighth, what have I done?

I dream, so I must not be dead. I dream I float through falling snowflakes. The dream changes. A bright star presses down on my forehead. It's so cold and white it hurts, the pain shooting down all the way to my ears, my jaw, my neck, down my spine, making me shiver.

Then I dream silence and darkness, but in the darkness, something moves. I dream of charcoal and waves of buzzing bees floating back and forth. The dream changes again. Suddenly, it's all flames and heat. My body stops shaking. I see a shadow move in the flames, then nothing.

I awake with my bare hand wrapped around someone's throat.

"Raven," a voice gasps. "It's me."

I let my hand fall, straining in the dark to see who's there. "Topher?"

He sits back, rubbing his neck. My vision begins to clear. I'm lying on a ridge. I can see the valley floor spreading beneath us, the remnants of a fire glowing next to me, and the stars above. Topher is gathering some snow into a ball, which he carefully presses onto my forehead. I begin to notice the throbbing pain. The cold numbs it somewhat.

"I dreamed this," I say. He doesn't reply. He pulls off his gloves and slides them onto my hands.

"I don't think you have frostbite," he says. "How did you manage to build a fire?"

"I didn't," I say. "I dreamed it."

"You're delirious," he says. "You've been out here for hours."

I try to sit up. The pain in my head is like a hot coal. Topher presses the snowball on my forehead again.

"Felix," I say.

Topher's face confirms what I already know. "He's dead. So is Lochie. We took their bodies up into the village. I came back to look for yours . . . you. . . ." His voice breaks here. I realize he thought I was dead. He takes a moment to compose himself, a marvel of restraint and dignity. So very Topher. "We're nearly a mile from the trailer park. I came when I saw the fire. How did you get here?"

"I dreamed . . ." *No, that's not right,* I think. The pain in my head is making it hard to talk, hard to make sense of what I remember. The smoke of the campfire infuses my next breath, and a memory floats to the surface. "A Nahx brought me here."

Topher frowns. "You're delirious, Raven. You must have wandered off after the Nahx left. Were you hiding?"

"Felix told me to hide," I say dumbly.

"He saved your life." Topher stares up the hill. "We need to go," he says. "Can you walk?"

I try to stand. Every inch of me hurts, stiff with cold or aching with bruises. When I sway and can't get up, Topher helps me, his arm around my back, holding me upright. I'm self-conscious about the smell of piss, but he doesn't mention it. Halfway back to the village, I'm feeling stronger, so I ask him to let me go. In the moonlight I can see there are tears on his cheeks. He doesn't try to hide them.

"I peed my pants," I say before I can stop myself.

"That's okay," Topher says.

We walk in silence. We're close to the village again now. Just before we reach it, Topher stops me.

"Where did you hide?"

"In the bathroom of the trailer."

"The one Felix died in? But I went back there. We went back for his body after the Nahx were gone. Where were you?"

"A Nahx found me," I say. It's a bit blurry though. Did I dream that?

"If a Nahx found you, you'd be dead," Topher says. "You hit your head. You wandered off."

Maybe he's right, I think. Nahx don't hold their fire. Nahx shoot first and never ask questions. I don't tell Topher about the breathing. I don't tell him about the long minutes the Nahx and I spent facing each other. I don't tell him that somehow in the time between being knocked unconscious and waking up with Topher hanging over me, I stopped thinking of that

Nahx as "it" and started thinking of it as "him." I'm not sure why that makes a difference, but it does.

Before we even reach the village, I can hear Sawyer crying. What's left of us gather in front of what looks like a little chapel, with the two bodies laid out in the snow.

"Oh my God," Xander says when he sees me. He leaps up and throws his arms around me. "You must be a cat, Rave. Seven lives left."

Sawyer lies with his head in Emily's lap, shaking with sobs.

"Why don't we go inside?" I ask. My senses are starting to return, and even I can see that it can't be safe having a fire out in the open like this.

No one answers. Mandy stirs something in a pot, poking at the fire listlessly. Xander and Topher help me to sit. Sawyer sobs as Emily strokes his hair. Her face is stained with tears.

"We should go inside," I say firmly. With Felix dead and Sawyer incapacitated, someone has to take command. "Let's go into the church, at least."

"What do we do with them?" Mandy asks, indicating Felix and Lochie lying there in the snow, dead, spiderweb veins tattooing their faces.

"What would they want us to do?"

"Get to safety," Mandy answers. "Keep going." She picks up the pot of whatever it is and heads up the steps of the chapel. Finding the door locked, she simply steps back and gives it a good kick. It flies open with a bang. Sawyer twitches in Emily's lap.

The boys lift him up and follow us inside.

The chapel is tiny and cold, but soon the soup Mandy heated is warming those of us who can still eat. I change my clothes and try not to think of Felix and Lochie out in the snow.

When we finish eating, Mandy comes over with her flashlight. Shining the light in my eyes, she ascertains that I don't have a serious concussion, but her careful fingers find a hard, painful lump on the back of my head as well as the gash on my forehead.

"How on earth did you do this?" she asks, dabbing at the forehead wound with a stinging wet cloth.

"Is it shaped like a lightning bolt, at least?" I ask.

She coughs a little half laugh and decides to leave it without a bandage, since it has stopped bleeding on its own. She checks my fingers and makes me take off my boots so she can check my toes.

"No frostbite," she declares, giving my nose an affectionate tap. She instructs me to sleep, and helpless to resist, I climb into my sleeping bag and close my eyes. "Check her every hour," she says to someone as sleep captures me. Hourly, I guess, I'm disturbed, but never enough to fully wake.

When I next open my eyes properly, daylight is streaming through the stained glass windows of the chapel, my nose is pinched with cold, and Topher is asleep beside me, one hand scrunching a handful of my sleeping bag. I look up at the ceiling rafters and sigh, wishing that the slow deconstruction of what I thought was my life might be a little less complicated. It's easier to hang on to Topher as an obstacle, an antagonist, than cling to him as a lifeline. But all that changed when Tucker died. Slowly, our obsession with each other as the last remnant of the wild boy we both loved is evolving into something else. I'm not sure, but I think in this postapocalyptic world, Topher might be turning into a friend.

I carefully uncurl his fingers, trying not to wake him. He moans a little, but rolls over, snuffling and pulling his cold hand inside his bag. I wriggle out of my own bag, unzip it, and wrap it around my shoulders like a cape. Standing, I consider my traveling companions wrapped up on the floor. Xander and Mandy lie together like spoons in a drawer, curling around each other's warmth. Emily's ring-bespangled hand rests on Sawyer's sleeping bag, but Sawyer has vacated it. He's sitting on the altar, back against the wall, right under a stylized crucifix.

"You were his last word," I say, sliding down beside him. Not strictly speaking the truth, but what does truth matter anymore?

He nods. "I heard it."

"Why did you come back up here? I heard you yelling to go back down the hill."

Sawyer's demeanor changes, from heartbroken to officious. He becomes a soldier debriefing after a disastrous mission. "The Nahx trailed us back down into the valley but gave up the chase near the river. They disappeared in their transport. We figured they'd come back to take us out where they left us, but might not think we'd be crazy enough to come back here."

I nod. It's a sound theory. It seems to have worked so far anyway. But I doubt the Nahx will stay away for long.

"Where to now, chief?" I ask. If becoming a soldier again helps him recover, I'm happy to play my part. We need him.

Sawyer pulls a small canteen from his thigh pocket and uncaps it, taking a swig. "Back to the camp? Or onward? Shall we vote again?" That's how he makes it clear I'm not off the hook for Felix's death. Felix, Lochie, Tucker. I suppose I'm the reason that the Nahx invaded in the first place. Hell, I'm the reason Adam ate the forbidden fruit. Anything else anyone wants to blame on me?

A faint thumping noise saves me from further accusations. Sawyer's face shows neither fear nor surprise, but the others begin to stir. After a second Topher shoots upright.

"What's that? Nahx?"

"It sounds like a helicopter," Sawyer says.

"What?" Mandy's face breaks into a huge smile. "It must be humans, then. Rescuers?"

We fall silent, listening as the thumping grows, becoming

more familiar, more certainly something from the human world. When there's no longer any doubt, Mandy, Emily, and Xander share a celebratory hug, Xander lifting the girls in turn and spinning them around. But Topher and I just look at each other. Do we dare hope? I'm not even sure this is what Topher wants anymore. As for Sawyer, his face is still fixed and emotionless.

"Gather your gear," he says, picking up his rifle and heading to the chapel door.

I'm not lost anymore, but I wish I were. I wish I could have stayed when she started to stir, but I didn't want to scare her. So I hid nearby, watching, until one of the other humans took her away.

I'm concerned that he took her somewhere safe. The First and Third are unlikely to come back to finish what they started; this kind of work is beneath them. I'm sure they've noticed I'm missing, but of course they don't care. If they could be relieved, they would be.

But others might come. This territory is designated for complete preparation. The darts are stockpiled by the thousand, by the million. I have what is in my rifle, about forty, and the six spares. But I doubt I'll ever use them.

I can see quite far from up here. I can see the deep green trees poking out of silvery snow, and the river, like a thin snake winding through the bottom of the valley. I can see the burnt strip of forest where I first saw her as the river sucked her away. What strange forces made me go into that trailer, open that door, and find her again? It's hard not to see some meaning there, but that's ridiculous too.

I'm disconnected, so my thoughts drift into a more orderly state. But I can think only of the girl human and her friends. Did they get away? Did the high ranks come back? I'm sure I'll stop obsessing eventually. And now that I have nowhere to go and nothing to do, I'm in no hurry. I'll keep out of sight of her people and mine. I need a new plan, because I can't go back to the mission. Not now.

You don't have to do this.

I'll pretend I don't exist. Stay away from hubs, so I don't get sucked in by new transmissions, ignore the buzzing directives and what they tell me to do. I can resist them. I know that now. I can hunt for food, melt snow for water, even make a little fire during the day. Sixth laughed at my fires, since we don't need the warmth or to cook our food. But I like the smell and the color of fire. And I like making them and keeping them bright. I wish I could make one at night, but that might draw my people here, thinking I'm a human.

I'd rather not see any of my kind again. Perhaps I might even turn away from my reflection in puddles or my shadow on the snow. My distaste for all this is much stronger when I'm disconnected from the armor. It's almost like being . . . something, something hidden, not remembered. Something that leaves a negative space behind it, where it used to be. Like the shape of Sixth on the crushed grass with the wings of blood. Like the feel of the little human in my arms and the smell of her hair.

Dandelion.

I'm a vile and terrible, monstrous creature who doesn't deserve to live. What a relief to be able to think that properly, not having it sucked into the slime inside me and turned outward again, turned into hate for the humans. I refuse this mission. I refuse. If I can stay disconnected for long enough, I'll be able to hang on to that. I won't get drawn back to the others again.

There's nothing complicated about the directives that flood my thoughts when I'm connected. *Dart the vermin. Leave them where they fall. Move on.* But as time passes, away from the hubs, without a fresh transmission, the directives have degraded to a low humming sensation. I'm starting to see them as separate from me. It could be the armor that's vile, the monstrous armor and the slime that infuses my blood when I'm connected to it. Maybe I'm . . .

Defective.

I can reconnect only when I need to, when it becomes hard to breathe. But first I can sleep. I need sleep. I'm high up enough that I should be able to sleep for several hours, maybe even a whole night.

I know I'll dream about the human girl. That's how my half-ruined brain works. But that will stop eventually too. It won't be so bad, not like the dreams about Sixth, I hope. I kind of look forward to the dream, as long as it's not too scary. I look forward to seeing the human girl again.

RAVEN

The base appears in the snow haze as the helicopter slowly descends into a deep valley between two high mountains about a two-hour flight north from where they found us. At least I think it's the base. From the air it looks like drifts of snow and piles of rocks, a railway track that leads from nowhere to nowhere and something that could be called a road if all cars were actually amphibious snow tanks.

"Why didn't the Nahx shoot us down?" Topher asks. We've all been thinking it during the flight. Expecting it, even. Maybe wanting it.

"We've analyzed their patterns. They don't spend much time in these remote areas, and when they do, they don't come back for weeks," says a skinny and pale young soldier sitting across from me. He introduced himself as Liam before we took off. "It was a risk, but we spotted your fires. We've been sending out spy drones at night. They look like owls. You might have seen them. They're the latest technology. Don't need GPS or anything. The Nahx haven't got a clue." His bluster gives me a strong next-to-die vibe, like he's that guy in the movie who has to fly one last mission, or retires the next day. I wish I weren't sitting right across from him, in range of any potential blood splatter or flying organs.

As if to increase my anxiety, Liam adds: "My mother is the base commander. We came out here after, you know, and she lets anyone who wants to, to serve. You guys look like you'd make good soldiers." He sniffs a little too haughtily for my tastes. "Even you girls. With some training."

Emily and I lock eyes. I happen to know she can take apart and clean a rifle faster than most people can blow their nose. As for her archery, she can hit targets I can't even see.

"What's your rank?" Sawyer suddenly says, with a dark expression.

Liam hesitates. "I don't really have one," he says. "Not yet."

"That makes you a recruit. I'm a lieutenant. I outrank you, and I'm telling you to shut up."

To his credit Liam mumbles, "Shutting up, sir," before falling silent. Next to him, Xander's head lolls to the side. He's asleep.

We touch down quite far from anything recognizably man-made. Three other uniforms help us out of the helicopter.

"Where are we?" I ask.

"I'm sorry, the location is classified," Liam says. "But it's an old nuclear bunker from the Cold War. I can tell you that. Finally put to good use, I guess."

As the helicopter blades wind down, he gathers us together. "May I?" he says to Sawyer, not even attempting sincerity. I've barely known Liam two hours, and already he annoys the shit out of me.

He continues. "We're not a real command unit here. We don't exactly use ranks, and mostly we go by first names. My name is Liam, like I said. My mother's in charge. Her name is Kim. You'll meet her later. I didn't get all your names."

We do some brief introductions before he goes on. "The entrance to the base is about a half mile from here. There's a climb down a pretty steep canyon. The whole thing is underground, so I hope no one is claustrophobic."

I think we're meant to laugh or something, but no one does. Liam gathers what's left of his dignity and continues. "I could radio for a jeep if you don't feel up for the walk, but we're supposed to be rationing fuel, and the jeep has to go the long way around."

"We can walk," Emily says. Liam gives her an approving look that makes me vaguely nauseous. We hoist our packs and head off into the snow.

"This snowstorm has been great," Liam says as we walk. "Even though it's cold, it's made us much less visible from the air."

"Will you go back for the bodies?" Sawyer asks, following his own personal agenda. I can't really blame him.

Liam turns and walks backward as he talks to us, like he's

conducting a museum tour. "Not likely. It's too dangerous. You know they don't decay, right?"

No one says anything, but I can tell the others must have seen some evidence of this, as I have. Liam keeps talking, because he doesn't know the horror of what he's saying to me and Sawyer and Topher in particular. "It's the toxin in the darts. It's some kind of embalming thing, or a preservative." A shadow crosses his face like a cloud, but it soon passes. "Weird, huh? Wonder what they plan to do with all these bodies."

Tucker at least is in our hidden valley, under a blanket of earth and birch leaves. It's a strange thought that I might be able to go back there in years and find him just as he was the day he died. One glance at Topher tells me he's having the same thoughts. It's a whole Dorian Gray thing for him, too. He'll age, while Tuck will be an image of him as he is now, forever young.

God, I hate this planet.

I look around at all my friends, and their stony faces. We should all be giddy with relief, but instead maybe this rescue has confirmed what we were all hoping wasn't true. We're refugees. And we've all seen enough news stories to know how that goes.

As we arrive at the edge of a canyon, Liam leads us all onto a narrow path downward, so narrow that we have to walk single file. I walk behind Mandy, and Topher walks behind me. After five minutes I'm surprised at how deep the canyon is.

After ten minutes I'm amazed. It seems to be going down and down forever.

"Is this natural?" I say to no one in particular, but Liam, who is clearly eager to show off some more, gamely answers.

"It was a quarry with a mine at the bottom of it. In the fifties, the government bought the mine and built a military bunker here. It's pretty big, accommodation for about five hundred, but we have about two fifty now."

"And who are *we* exactly?"

"About half, like me, are military families who bugged out of a base south of here during the first attack. The other half we've picked up along the way. Survivors from the towns, a couple of Native communities, and people like you we've found with the drones."

"What communities?" I say it without thinking. We're dipping into a topic I've learned to avoid, especially with people I don't know.

"Mostly around Calgary," Liam says. "The villages themselves have been pretty well iced, but some families escaped out onto the prairie, where we found them."

Topher puts his hand on my shoulder, steadying me as I stumble on a patch of gravel.

"What about up north, by Slave Lake?" I ask.

Liam shakes his head. "We never got that far north. Not sure what's happening. Why? You got people up there?" He turns, assessing me, eyes narrowed. I imagine him trying to calculate the color mix of blood in my veins. It's a look I'm used to.

"Sort of," I say dismissively. I have no desire to try to explain my stepfather's family and the Métis settlement full of aunts and uncles who aren't really aunts and uncles but claim me as a niece regardless. It's too complicated, and anyway . . .

"Some of the information we get suggests the attack zones were fairly limited," Liam says with a shrug. "There's a chance that up that way things are okay. Word is a lot of survivors were evacuated, we're not sure to where."

That changes things, a shift in outlook so radical I'm rendered speechless. It's Topher who puts it into words. "How many survivors are there?"

"In the world?" Liam says. "Hard to say. But there's no way out of here, east or west. That much we know. And communications are totally toast, so we're sort of poking around in the dark for information."

"Even after all this time?" Sawyer says. "If this is a military base, don't you have secure landlines?"

Liam looks uncomfortable for a moment. "Maybe you should talk to the commander about that."

By the time we reach the quarry floor, the snow is blowing so thick that Liam recommends we hold on to each other the rest of the way. So we stomp through the dense snow, like a kindergarten class, me with Topher's fingers crushing one hand and Mandy clinging to the other wrist.

"This feels like a bad dream," Mandy says. Then we walk in silence for about five minutes before she adds. "I guess my parents are dead."

The word "parents" makes me twitch. The constant rhythm of missing them and regretting the things I said and didn't say has become background noise to the life-and-death game I've been playing over the last few days. Nearly drowning, being knocked out by an alien. And death, of course. Tucker. Lochie. And Felix, who died right in front of me. It all makes setting fire to a park bandstand seem small by comparison. I have to believe that if we're ever reunited, my parents will just take me in their arms, and we'll never speak of it again.

I try to exhale everything, but all that comes out is a cloud of frozen air.

There are about a dozen people hanging around outside when we reach the entrance to the base. Some of them are heavily armed; the others are smoking or chatting. Two young boys are making a snowman. Watching them, I suddenly understand why Mandy said what she did. Hiding in our little camp in the valley, we could pretend it was all a mistake, that the world outside was just as we left it, with family and loved ones waiting for us to come home. But the last few days have taught us something different. The bad dream is the world. We're going to live in some kind of underground refugee camp for the rest of our lives. Maybe, if we're lucky, that won't be very long.

From the outside, the entrance looks like an abandoned mine, rough stone with heavy, weathered wooden supports. A rusty rail track leads in. There are even overturned coal carts, adding to the authenticity. But inside the entrance, the outlook changes dramatically. As we enter, automatic lights flick on, revealing a large open area, cluttered with jeeps and other supplies and equipment. Two more armed guards leap to their feet.

"Only me," Liam says. "We found them right where the drone clocked them." He thumbs back at the six of us, now shivering with the change of temperature. It's much warmer inside than it was outside, but the hike in wet snow has left us damp and disoriented.

Liam and a guard reach inside their jackets, pulling out key cards on heavy chains. When they swipe the cards there's a heavy-sounding *clang*, and they swing open a large door. The door is over a foot thick and solid metal.

"This is a nuclear bomb shelter?" Emily says. "Like NORAD?" Liam smiles at her in a way that makes me grateful I didn't eat any breakfast.

"This is the NORAD even NORAD didn't talk about. A long-lost deal between us and the Americans against the Russkies. It *was* a total command center, but full operations shut down years ago. Since then it's been a bit of a ghost town around here. The commander and a few others had codes and keys. Someone reactivated it when the whole terrorism thing started to look bad, but on a much smaller scale. I'm not sure who that was. Whoever it was, we haven't heard from him. He's probably dead."

Liam leads us into a long passageway. It's wide and high enough for a small vehicle, and lit by motion-sensitive electric lights, which flick on and off as we pass.

"We'll get you sleeping arrangements, and then you might like to wash. We have running hot water." Liam looks proud to inform us of this.

"Doesn't that waste fuel?" I can't resist saying.

"Geothermal," he says, a prim expression on his face. "The base itself is fully self-sufficient. Only the vehicles need fuel. And we use solar, wind, and hydro for luxuries like music and stuff."

Topher and I exchange a glance. I know exactly what he's thinking. This is as good as he could have hoped for, a safe, permanent refuge. Somewhere we would be fools to leave if he were to disappear in the night. My heart flickers at the thought of following him. Or stopping him. I haven't decided which.

"What do you do for food?" Mandy asks. Mandy loves to feed people. She was going to teach camp cooking and perma-culture, along with first aid. Mandy may run screaming out of here if it turns out we all have to eat some kind of Soylent Green paste for sustenance.

"We have a pretty big stockpile, and people brought stuff with them. But it won't last forever." Liam looks uncertain again. A tiny chink appears in his bravado, the son of the commander of what might be my last refuge on earth. "This place hasn't been set up for something like this for decades. So it's . . . well . . . we're not that well prepared. I guess we'll figure it out somehow."

It's a pity, I think, that I might be long gone before Liam realizes that death by starvation is coming for him too.

EIGHT

The dream of the human girl ends up being both terrifying and sensational. I wake up, heart pounding, blushing with shame, and with parts of my body doing things that are not normal, though not entirely unfamiliar.

It takes several whimpering minutes for the urgent heat of the dream to wear off and for my heart rate, and other things, to calm down. The humiliation sticks with me though. How could I think of a human that way, even in a dream?

The disgrace of it makes me want to break something. I spend an hour snapping enough branches to build a hundred fires but feel only a fraction better. Then I light a fire and fuss over it until hunger makes me think of getting up and finding something to eat. Soon I'm crunching the bones of some hapless animal I dug out of its den. I barely register even what it looks like, never mind the taste. But having food in my stomach alleviates the effects of the slug syrup somewhat, and my anger and hate dissipate back to ordinary embarrassment.

For the first time since she died, I'm grateful Sixth isn't here with me. I would never tell her willingly what I dreamed, but she would find a way to make me confess. Then she would punish me for it somehow. Whack me behind the ear with her rifle, or maybe just tell me over and over that I'm defective. Possibly she would add the words "perverted," "disgusting," "pitiful." Sixth hated humans more than I ever could. I can only imagine what she would say if she knew I dreamed of one like that. It's so wrong, I feel sick.

I reach up and pull a branch down from the pine tree above my head, crushing a handful of needles under my nose. The smell clears my head a bit, then a bit more. I press my free hand into the fresh snow around me and fix my gaze onto the green treetops and the rolling clouds behind them. It's enough to nearly bring a smile to my face. A fleeting sense of peace and happiness calms my mind sufficiently to formulate one perfectly coherent thought.

I want to see the human girl again.

Not like in the dream. Nothing like that.

Throwing the needles into the fire, I close my eyes and press both my hands over my face. One hand now smells of pine needles, like the girl's hair. I lean forward, plunge that hand into the fire and hold it there until the skin starts to burn off.

That's going to hurt for a few days, but I deserve much worse.

We all indulge in sinfully long, hot showers. Emily and Mandy giggle at the state of their unshaven legs and underarms and pay no attention to my own unremarkable nudity, even though I'm covered in some fairly impressive bruises. I take special care with the rings of bruises around my wrists. If not for them I might think that the Nahx I met in the trailer was part of a dream. I let the warm water flow over my wrists, soothing the lingering ache but not easing the disorientation the experience left behind. He could have killed me, darted me, snapped my neck, or smashed my head in. But he didn't. That changes things somehow. It's a slight shift, but it feels like an earthquake.

We dry off and dress in the clean army-issue casuals that have been laid out for us. I twist my hair into a half-assed roll, held with the one elastic band I can find in the bottom of my pack. I end up with kind of a weird puff at the back, but it will have to do.

The boys have been waiting in the common area for some time when we three girls finally join them. I scan the other unfamiliar faces lounging on drab sofas or strolling in and out, noting with relief that at least I'm not the only brown girl here. But I don't see anyone else I know. No one from the dojo, no friends from school, no one I recognize at all. Before we had our showers, they gave us a list of people here, but I didn't see any familiar names there, either. Looking at the friends I arrived with makes me ache over losing Felix and Lochie, even Pip and David, whom I barely got to know. Maybe I shouldn't make eye contact with anyone new for fear of losing them, too. I stare at my hands instead.

Liam appears through a door marked RESTRICTED AREA: PASS HOLDERS ONLY.

"Is someone in charge?" he asks, sitting on the edge of the sofa.

We turn to Sawyer. Even Liam looks at him, but he is hanging his head, eyes on the floor.

"We are," Topher says, pointing back and forth between himself and me. Sawyer glances up, but says nothing. No one else comments, though I notice Xander's little smirk.

Liam looks uncertain for a moment, but finally stands up and beckons us to the door. "Come on, then. Kim wants to meet you."

He leads us down another long, sterile hallway. Again the lights flick on and off as we pass through a few unlocked doors. It's disconcerting, like I'm being watched somehow, but Liam seems to be used to it.

"A lot of the security has been disabled for safety reasons," he says. "We're relying on trust to keep people out of restricted areas for now. But I have a pass, so I can go anywhere."

Topher glances at me, eyebrows raised.

At the end of the hallway we reach a set of stairs.

"It's nearly twenty stories up. Can you make it?" Liam says, a gloating look on his face. He's daring us to say no.

Topher just grunts and takes to the staircase two steps at a time. Liam rushes after him. I could probably keep up, despite my hunger and exhaustion, but I decide it might be more effective to make them wait for me. So, plodding upward, I make my own pace and enjoy the anticipation of their impatience when I arrive at the top. Which I do, calm and unsweaty, about five minutes later. The expression on their faces is worth the climb.

"Good things are worth waiting for," I say.

Topher sighs. Liam doesn't know what to make of me, I'm sure, which is exactly how I want him. And it feels familiar anyway, something left over from the old world. I'm pretty sure we'll have the whole what-are-you? conversation sometime soon. Or he'll want to touch my hair.

He leads us along another corridor, this one with doors along one side. The doors are all open, and I can see daylight streaming through them.

"Where are we?" I ask.

"We're halfway up the mountain," Liam says. "These are

observation chambers. Designed to be bomb and radiation proof, for watching . . ." His voice trails off.

"The end of the world?" I supply. Liam shows some of that uncertainty again. There are depths to him too, I realize. Perhaps ones I would prefer not to know about, but they're there anyway.

Halfway down the corridor he leads us into a room. A woman and two men stare out the bright window, watching the featureless sky, and the jagged, forbidding mountains rolling away to the horizon. It drives home how hard getting out of here will be. I hope Topher has noticed it's not a journey you'd want to take alone.

"Leave us," the woman says to the men. When Liam lingers, she gives him a stern look. He backs out of the door, closing it behind him.

"Topher and Raven, I hear," the woman says. "I'm the commander here. I'm a CAF officer, but you can call me Kim."

I feel privileged. I was certain she would insist on being called "Your Majesty." Listening to Kim and watching her makes me think of someone in a vise, as though something is squeezing her together, tightly, painfully, and the pressure is what prevents the pieces from falling all over the floor. She's fractured, badly. And it takes one to know one.

She asks us where we came from, and Topher gives her a quick summary. All the while she nods approvingly.

"I can't tell you what a relief it is to have some refugees with actual survival skills," she says. "Most of the people here can barely tie their shoelaces without help. You have weapons training?"

"Some," Topher says.

"Are you willing to use them?"

"Against the Nahx?" Topher says. "Are you kidding? Tell me when and where."

Kim grins. She has the same vaguely parasitic smile as her son. Like someone who might lay eggs in you that will hatch and then eat you from the inside out.

"And you, Raven? How do you feel about shooting at our enemy?" The hate in her eyes is like a living thing. I'm afraid to answer. Afraid my answer won't be sufficient. Her hate for the Nahx is in its own category. But when I think of them now, I think of the one in the trailer, and the strength of my hatred wavers. I'm not sure I have that kind of power for any emotion, not even love. Not even for Tucker.

"I'm a terrible shot," I admit after a moment. I can't think of a reason to lie at this point. "But I'll do whatever is necessary."

Kim looks at us, both smug and satisfied. "Good," she says. "I know this looks like a refugee camp, but we are amassing an attack force here. You and your friends, if you're willing, will see some action. We are not going to lie down and take this, you can count on that. And we're not going to sit around until help comes either. The fight continues all over the world. We'll take our planet back."

Topher glances at me. "How many survivors are there? In the world, I mean."

Kim frowns for a moment, and I catch a glimpse of that intractable sorrow I saw when we arrived. But her face soon hardens, like drying clay, and I can no longer read her. "Most of the coastal areas were relatively unscathed. That's the report, anyway. Communications have all been cut. We get some videos though, and that tells us . . ."

"Wait," Topher says. "You still get the videos?"

Kim nods. "Some. There's a landline direct in and out of here, deep underground, and all the way to a base station on the other side of the mountains. We think the Nahx disrupt most of the data with some kind of microwave jammer that knocks out the point-to-point system between that base station and the coast. But the Nahx jamming signal itself gets jammed at least once a day, usually around midday. We don't know how yet." She shrugs. "It's a last-resort comm system built years ago for exactly these circumstances. Disaster. War. It's working the way it's supposed to, but the quality of data is still poor because of all the interference. And it's . . . we're not sure whether to trust what we're getting. There are no security codes. It's not military. We untangle what we can. There are people still fighting all over the world, it seems. Millions, maybe billions, survived. This isn't over."

"Why did the coastal areas pull through?" I ask. "Why didn't the Nahx take them out? They firebombed the cities around here, didn't they?"

"We think Calgary and Edmonton were bombed," Kim says. "But possibly not destroyed, though we haven't been able to confirm that. We try to send data back via the landline, but we can't know if anyone gets it. They might not know we're here. And it's risky using radio or wireless, because we're pretty sure the Nahx are tracking that. And all the satellites have been taken out."

I look down and see Topher's hand gripping the back of a chair so tightly that his knuckles practically glow. And I know what he's thinking. All this time we assumed everyone we knew back home was dead. But they could all be alive. Somehow. Somewhere. And the coast . . . God. If my parents left early enough that morning, they might have made it.

Kim continues, oblivious. "We don't know why the coast was spared. Vancouver seems to be functioning as a refugee camp."

"Can't we go there?" I ask. "Surely that's safer than here."

"We've already lost two choppers trying that," Kim says. "The Nahx have a kind of web of attack drones west of here. They hit any aircraft with some kind of scrambler, like an electromagnetic pulse or something. Knocks them right out of the sky."

"What about over land?"

"The main roads are heavily watched. And we don't have enough vehicles. There are over two hundred people here. And anyway, most land vehicles lose power too. And then Nahx move in and dart you. We watched exactly that happen with one of our drones."

"Walk, then," I say, and even I can hear the desperation in my voice. "You'd be much less visible from the air. Hike along the Fraser River and then . . ."

My geography fails me as Kim gives me a withering look. "All the way to Vancouver? In this weather? We've got children. Elderly. We'd never make it."

"So we're just . . . sitting here?"

"Raven . . . ," Topher says.

Kim continues, her tone becoming impatient. "We're not sitting here. We're fighting back. We're gathering intel. We're looking for weaknesses. Anything we find out will be useful. You'll see."

"But—"

"What have you found out so far?" Topher asks her, glaring at me.

With a wave of her hand, Kim invites us to sit at a long conference table. There are maps and schematics spread out like fallen leaves, along with black and white chess pieces strategically placed in various locations. Kim grabs a white chess piece from a spot by a curve in the river and repositions it off to the side with a pile of others.

"That was you," she says with a wry smile. "Rescued."

"We're very grateful," Topher says. He said these exact words a lifetime ago when the judge explained we'd be working off our sentence instead of going to juvie. I suppose I should be grateful too. That judge might be the reason I'm alive. Also the reason Tucker is dead though, so maybe gratitude isn't quite right.

"We put together a briefing package," Kim says. "Summarizing what we know. The brief is updated weekly. I'll get you a copy and you can add to it, if you've learned anything new. In the meantime, anything specific you want to know?"

Before I have time to think, Topher speaks. "How do you kill them?"

"With difficulty. Their armor is very tough. And no one seems to have been able to capture one, or even bring one in dead to study. The ships have wicked countermeasures against missiles." She shakes her head.

"Arrows," Topher says. "One video said arrows could disable them."

"Yes, I saw that one. I heard you had a pretty close encounter yesterday. Did any of you get a good look at them?"

Topher glances at me, but I just shake my head.

As Kim opens her mouth to continue, there's a knock on the door. Liam pokes his head in. "Commander? The tech staff need to see you."

Kim nods, with a grim look. "I'd better check this out. You can go. I'll get copies of the briefing for you, and we'll talk more later."

Topher disappears with Liam soon after Kim dismisses us. After exploring for a while, and having a meal, I follow directions to the quarters I've been assigned and am almost happy to discover I don't have to share with Emily, who snores like a tiny consumptive hamster. It's Mandy who has to suffer my company, but she doesn't seem to be around to either tolerate me or complain. The room is like a prison cell, about six feet wide and ten feet long, with a set of bunks and a tiny table and chair. No bars though, just a regular door, so that's worth celebrating. I note that Mandy has claimed the top bunk, which suits me. I like to be able to put my feet straight onto the ground when the shit starts flying.

When, not if.

There's a window, a nice surprise, although I would have to have been dead for a month to fit through it. It's a wide, low rectangle, and looking out I realize the room is mostly belowground, like a basement room. The window looks out into the quarry.

By the light, I estimate it to be late afternoon, maybe close to sunset. The snow has stopped blowing and now falls softly in fat flakes like turkey feathers. It looks like the aftermath of the kind of pillow fight that we all once believed would happen naturally at sleepovers, after we stripped down to our lacy underwear and painted each other's toenails. I was never much for sleepovers. I pretended to be disdainful of them, but the real reason was . . . I shake that thought away—the thought of my mom, of how much I once needed her. It seems wrong that I have lived this long not knowing whether she's dead or alive, as though it's a discredit to her and all the things she did for me that I probably didn't deserve.

The falling snow does something medicinal to my head, and I find I can't look away. I almost feel like laughing, putting on snow pants and running outside to make angels. Or I could just lie down in the snow, maybe, and never get up. Either way, watching it makes me smile, with nostalgia bubbling inside me, painful and potent as white liquor. Snow pants, snowmen, me and Jack making snow angels in the front yard of our house. Stuff from before my life went off the rails.

I don't know how long I've been standing there when I feel someone come up behind me.

"This is where you've been hiding?"

Topher, sounding so much like Tucker again I clench the windowsill with my fingers to keep from spinning around.

He puts his hands on my shoulders, resting them there before gently massaging my neck, like we used to have to after the cooldown stretches at the dojo.

"It's hardly hiding, since this is my room," I say. "Where have you been?"

"Watching videos." He leans forward, resting his chin on my shoulder, and looks out at the falling snow, now barely visible in the dark canyon. "We should go back to Calgary. I want to look for my parents. I need to tell them about . . ." He turns his head to the side and sighs forlornly. I smell the alcohol on his breath.

"What's that, moonshine?"

"Vodka," he says. "Stolish-stoliks . . . some Russian *pish*." He moves in and presses his lips onto my neck.

Great. Drunk Topher. So drunk he doesn't even know what he's doing. Just what I need. I'm actually perfectly positioned to flick him off me like a bug, slam him down on the floor, and smack his stupid face with the heel of my palm. His lips move to my ear.

"Toph, don't do that, come on."

He moves his hands down, wrapping them around my waist, pulling me back to him. I can feel his drunken enthusiasm pressing into my hip.

"Topher, please let go."

I really don't want to hit him, not in his current state. At the dojo I took every opportunity to humiliate him. Outside the dojo I had to restrain myself from decking him several times an hour when we had the misfortune of being in the same room. But grief has softened me toward him. *His* grief and mine. Now I just feel sad. He's hurting. I'm hurting. Maybe this is all we have. And I miss Tucker so badly suddenly, it's like being strangled. If I close my eyes . . .

"What's the harm?" Topher slurs, one hand drifting up to cup my breast. "Turn around."

I turn, though the sensible part of my brain is telling me not to, that's it's stupid, that I should just punch him and be done with it. The only light on in the room is a small reading lamp in the bottom bunk. It's just enough to see his face, his eyes looking into mine. Enough to see his expression slowly downgrade from teenage lust to resignation and then something else. Maybe boredom, or heartbreak. His hands fall away from me.

"You don't really like me that way, do you?" I say.

He doesn't even pretend, or try to be polite. "Not really, no. But you don't like me that way either."

Like that's an excuse.

"Actually, I hate you, Topher," I say, outward calm concealing something inside I barely recognize. He has somehow made me feel like a thing he's scraped off the bottom of his shoe, while at the same time making himself look the victim.

"If you don't get out of my room, I'm going to drop you so hard right here that your brains will come out your nose."

He takes a step back, laughing a little. "Hard-core," he says. "Tucker always liked the badass girls. Couldn't resist them. Not even for you."

"What's that supposed to mean?"

He chuckles blearily. "Ask *Emily*."

My fist lashes out into a straight jab before I can stop it.

Drunk or not, Topher ducks and blocks like the black belt he also is. He doesn't try to hit back though, something to be grateful for. That really would get ugly. He holds my wrist for a second, making the ring of bruises throb. I yank my arm away.

"Get out, please," I say, my eyes starting to sting. "You're drunk. You're horny. Or you wanted to hurt my feelings for some fucked-up reason. Mission accomplished. You can go. Please go before I'm forced to kick the shit out of you. Tomorrow . . . tomorrow . . ." I can't finish because my mind is screaming at me.

Emily. E.M.I.L.Y.

The sudden rage is so disorienting, I feel nauseous. And it has nowhere to go. I can't fight Topher here. I can't go chasing around the base at night like a madwoman, looking to confront Emily.

And Tucker is not around to deny or admit it.

Tucker and Emily. And all that time they spent alone in the woods practicing archery. It could be true. Or it could not. It wouldn't be the first time Topher has said something nasty to get on my nerves. Maybe being drunk has made him forget we're friends now. We were friends. Now I want to kill him. Or someone.

I close my eyes and say a little prayer, to whom I don't know. *When I open my eyes, Topher will be gone.* Then I count silently backward from ten, pressing my fingernails into the palms of my hands. When I open my eyes, I'm alone.

My mind is like a horror story, told to scare children. Later, after Mandy comes back to the room, also smelling of vodka, and I lie in the dark, listening to her breathe above me, Tucker and Topher swim behind my eyelids until my head spins so vigorously I feel like I might vomit. Tucker, who loved me, is dead. Topher, who probably hates me, cried when he thought I was dead. Is that hate? Tucker, who might have cheated on me with Emily. Topher, whose hands and lips felt like needles under my skin. Tucker, whom I miss so much, I sometimes daydream about crawling into his grave. Is that love?

My parents love me. I should know what it is.

As I finally begin to surrender to sleep, my body recalls a rocking motion, and unnatural warmth wrapping around me, and snowflakes drifting down on my face. I smell charcoal and hear the buzzing of bees. I see my own face reflected in black glass. My bruised wrists still ache, as though I'm being pulled along in chains.

He built a fire and pressed cold snow on my bleeding forehead. He carried me and left me somewhere safe, somewhere warm, where Topher could find me. A heartless, soulless Nahx did this for me.

EIGHT H

The Rogues find me in the darkest part of the night, in the thick of the forest. I'm connected, at least, so my reflexes are fast and my strength sufficient to fight them. But they don't attack. They surround me in a circle, as I step back, pressing into the straight trunk of a tree. Even the way they stand is disobedient, disorderly. Lazy almost. It's as though the rigidity of our armor doesn't affect them. They are dirty, too, though so am I.

One of them raises a human bow and arrow, drawing back the bowstring and pointing the arrow at me. I fix my eyes on it. If she lets it fly, I can catch it before it hits me. I think. I think I can. It seems like something I should be able to do.

Rank? her Offside signs. The other Rogues draw weapons too—some have our rifles, some human axes or knives.

The Offside growls and takes a step toward me. *RANK?!*

Eighth, I sign. *Eighth.*

They exchange a look. The first Rogue lowers her weapon, tucking both bow and arrow behind her back.

Join us? she signs.

Fear makes the fluid pulse through me. And the directives

buzz, making the back of my neck itch. *Dart the humans. Leave them where they fall.* I want to answer, but it seems impossible to choose anything but the directives. And Sixth. I should go and look for her.

In the low light, the other Rogues surrounding me come into focus. Some of them seem injured. I notice the one to the right of the Offside is missing part of her arm. She has woven branches with sharp thorns around the stump. Another is missing half his helmet. The exposed skin is mottled and twisted, like the roots of a burnt tree.

Sixth. I should look for Sixth.

The Offside lunges toward me again, hissing. His hand slices through the air.

JOIN US!

I shake my head. *No.*

The Rogue reloads her bow and points it at me. Her Offside raises his rifle, a large and heavy human rifle. I have seen these kill us.

I dive to the side, pushing the girl with the half arm out of my way as I sprint into the trees. I hear them crashing after me. I should stop and assure them I won't tell anyone where they are. That's what they think, that I'll report them to the high ranks, but I won't. I don't think I will. I don't want to. What would I say?

I hear the *ping* of an arrow being released and twist in time to catch a glint of starlight on its metal shaft. My hand lashes out, sending the arrow spinning into the dark as I run.

The trees begin to clear, and the sky beyond them is the deep blue color of shadows on lakes. It will swallow me if I can . . .

The cliff beneath me falls away just as I hear a rifle's loud *crack*. I land hard, falling forward and rolling over another edge and down to rocks and ice. Turning onto my back, I can make out the silhouettes of the Rogues, peering over the cliff, their weapons still raised. I lie still, not even breathing. If they think I'm dead or badly damaged they will probably leave me.

After a long time they slip back behind the cliff face, one by one, until only the leader remains. She lingers there watching me until I'm taking tiny stolen breaths and trying to resist the urge to stand and move. The fluid flows through me, pulsing relief where the fall left bruises. But it also makes me jittery, longing to get up and move, to walk, to run, to keep moving.

Dart the humans. Leave them where they fall.

After the last Rogue finally retreats, I wait, letting the stars drift across a swath of sky, before sitting up. My head throbs where I hit it on the rocks, and the fluid flowing through there leaves empty spaces behind it, lost thoughts and memories. What was I doing up in the mountains? The answer to that question flickers like a dying flame as I clamber to my knees. I wait there, feeling the stiffness in my armor and limbs release.

By the time I move, the sky is lightening in the east, over the flat land back toward the city, so I walk in that direction.

I find a squadron just after dawn, boarding their transports on the shore of a frozen pond. Falling in beside two others, who I think might be low ranks, like me, I board with them. They reload their rifles. I hope they don't notice mine doesn't need reloading.

I'm not sure why I'm here. There's something I've forgotten. My head hurts, and my hand hurts, burns inside my armored glove, despite the fluid. I wrap my thoughts around the pain and cling to it, to the reason I stuck my hand in the fire in the first place.

A human girl, and something about our mission. And the Rogues and Sixth, and the reason my rifle doesn't need reloading. And the human girl. And pine needles. Spiderwebs.

And the human girl. The human girl. The thought of her gets so big I can't think of anything else.

Another video party starts right after I choke down a few bites of flavorless porridge for breakfast. Liam strolls over, whispers something in Mandy's ear, and leaves.

"You coming?" she says to me, as she gets up to follow him.

"Are you sure you want an audience?"

Mandy rolls her eyes. "Don't be gross," she says. "We're going to watch videos."

I trail after her, wondering what pointless action movie has drawn not only me and Mandy, but also Topher and Xander, to Liam's quarters. A large-screen laptop is open on his desk. Mandy and I slump into the lower bunk. Topher squashes in beside me. He turns his head half in my direction.

"Sorry," he whispers, so quietly it sounds like a snake taking a breath. "I didn't . . . I shouldn't have . . ." But before he can finish, Xander dives into the bed, threads his head between us, and rests his chin on my thigh.

"I bet you're the only one here without a ball-shrinking headache," he says.

"I don't have balls," I remind him.

"I've heard otherwise."

Mandy snorts beside me as Liam turns and gives me an appraising look. He clicks a few things on the laptop until a media player comes up.

"I hear you're not crazy about the videos," he says to me.

Nahx videos? This is what they were watching last night? And here I thought it would be James Bond or something. "I don't see the point of them. Just a whole lot of death and destruction. Who wants to watch their team lose?"

It's like some personal development teacher suddenly possesses him. "It's complicated, but the point of watching the early NKVs was to learn as much as possible about the enemy. How they operate, what their weaknesses are. Admittedly, the thing we learned first was that they were utterly ruthless. But even that was useful. That is what feeds the resistance. Understand?" He clicks a few things on the computer, pausing a video and making it full screen.

"What's an NKV?" I ask.

"Nahx kill video," Xander says. He has produced a bag of raisins from somewhere. His chewing makes his whole head wobble on my thigh. "Remember in the early days, how those dudes were always trying to get a video of someone taking one out? Wait till you see these new ones, Rave. They're wicked."

At first when the video plays, it's hard to recognize what I'm seeing. Dark figures on a blurry background go in and out of focus. As the picture quality improves I realize it is a group of four Nahx picking their way down a steep embankment. The two larger Nahx walk with one hand on the shoulders of the smaller ones. The video has no sound, so there is nothing but Xander's chewing to accompany what happens next. One of the larger Nahx jerks backward, its free hand grabbing at its throat. As it falls, it pulls the smaller Nahx down with it.

The other two Nahx fall to their knees with their rifles raised and begin firing. The camera rolls and falls and the picture goes dark. There follows a slow-motion recap that shows a spray of something black as the Nahx gets shot in the neck. Blood?

Liam pauses the video. "That was the first confirmed sniper kill ever, about two weeks after the invasion," he says. "Hunting rifle and deer killer bullet right in the neck. The cameraman paid for that one with his life. But that's how we know that they don't get up from a shot to the neck."

Emily appears in the doorway as Liam scrolls through a list on the laptop.

"Oooh, are there new ones?" she says, curling up on the floor in front of Topher's legs. I glance over at his face, noting his blush and his tense posture. He's always been a bit cool with Emily. I never thought anything of it before. But now . . . God.

It's true. He was telling the truth.

"The scan hasn't finished yet," Liam says. "I'll download any new ones from the mainframe later."

My brain does the equivalent of shoving piles of crap into the closet and under the bed and calling it a cleaned room. I can't deal with the thought of Emily right now, so I just push it aside, biting my lip, wondering if everyone knew but me. I realize I've been sitting perfectly still with one hand resting on Xander's hair and the other twisted in Liam's bedcovers. Next to me, Topher leans forward, elbows on his knees, his eyes on the laptop screen.

Liam starts a video. "Here's a more recent one. This one is a high-caliber assault rifle, military issue, armor-piercing bullets. Check it out."

This one is a better quality video, high-powered zoom, digital focus, and sound. Two Nahx cross a clearing to a transport. There's a deafening crack, and one of the Nahx falls. I'm not sure whether I blinked, but it looked like . . .

"Did you see that?" Liam says. Topher and Xander are shaking their heads in admiration.

"Its head just disintegrated. Direct head shot with high-caliber armor-piercing rounds. They don't get up from that, either. Look, I'll play it again."

I force myself to watch, so I know I saw what I saw. The Nahx's head literally *disappears* in a cloud of blood and shrapnel before its body crumples to the ground.

"Awesome," Emily says.

I feel a bit nauseous.

Xander produces a bag of chocolate chips now and passes them around. I take a handful and close my fingers around them. They start to melt on my palm as Liam lines up another video. I have to force myself to look at the screen and not at the back of Emily's head with her long blond ponytail.

"This one came yesterday," Liam says. "But it was encrypted. The tech dude just unwound it this morning. I haven't even seen it."

Chocolate melts and melts in my hand.

The video starts up with a page of text:

On September 9, armed human militia came upon a group of Nahx in the mountains north of Vancouver, Canada. Reports vary on how it was achieved, but the result was that one Nahx was taken and held prisoner for a period of approximately four hours. The militia attempted to interrogate the prisoner, but it either couldn't or wouldn't communicate. The prisoner was executed when attempts to restrain it failed. Under attack from approaching Nahx, the captors were forced to flee. Because of the danger of returning through occupied territory, the body has not been recovered.

"Jeez," Xander says, chewing, as the video starts.

A Nahx kneels, hands on head, in the center of a circle of armed and masked men. Each of them has a nasty-looking rifle pointed at the prisoner's head. All I can think is, where did they get guns like that in Vancouver and why are they wearing masks? The sound is muffled, scratchy. You can hear someone yelling things, and occasionally one of the gunmen prods it . . . her? There's something subtle about the shape of the armor. Maybe if I hadn't had such a close look at the Nahx in the trailer park, I might not have spotted it, but this one is noticeably more slender, and smaller, the shoulders narrower, the neck thinner. It . . . she still seems very tall, even though she's kneeling.

One of the gunmen approaches closer. He has an automatic handgun in one hand and something in the other. It's hard to see.

"Is that a sword?" Mandy says.

"Machete," Emily answers. "A big one." She mouths a handful of chocolate chips. "I have a feeling this doesn't end well for our Nahx mate here."

I'm dimly conscious of the small pool of melted chocolate in my clenched fist. I want to turn away from the screen. I feel like I'd rather look at almost anything than what is about to happen, but I can't look away.

The machete-wielding gunman yells something at the Nahx. The sound is too distorted to hear it clearly. But when the Nahx turns her head to him, we all clearly hear her response. She *growls*. Like a cat or a wolf. The machete man recoils. Another gunman steps up behind the Nahx and kicks her hard in the back. She tumbles forward, stopping her fall with her hands so she's on her hands and knees. She lifts her head up, turning it slightly to look at the man with the machete. It's not an aggressive position. More like . . . supplication.

"God, no . . . ," I hear myself whisper. Machete man makes a split-second decision. He throws his gun to the side, raises the machete with both hands, and brings it down on the back of the Nahx's neck.

Separating her head from her body as neatly as clipping a bud from a rosebush.

There's a collective gasp. I slap my hands over my mouth, stifling a whimper, then furiously wipe the chocolate from my face with my sleeve.

The decapitated Nahx lingers on her hands and knees as her head rolls away and black sludge pours out her neck. Machete man gives the body a swift kick, and it tumbles in a dead pile. There's a shout from one of the men, and they scatter, leaving the dead female where she lies.

The camera jolts into motion as the video ends.

Finally, I'm able to tear my eyes from the screen. Liam is grinning madly, his eyes bright. "That was *awesome!*"

"Didn't really look like they tried to restrain it," Topher says, popping a chocolate chip into his mouth. "Play it again."

I leap to my feet, feeling like I might scream. I need to get to a toilet, or a sink, or outside *fast*. Eyes streaming with effort to keep my breakfast down, I push out of the room, tripping over Mandy's chair.

"What your problem?" Liam snaps as I leave.

Faintly, I hear someone calling after me, but I barrel down the hallway, barely able to see where I'm going. If this men's quarters is anything like the women's at the opposite end of the residential wing, there should be a bathroom . . .

I throw a door open, finding myself instead in a kind of garage, with two thick blast doors open to a long passageway to the outside. The door blows shut behind me. The cold and fresh air allow me to take some control over my stomach, and I gaspingly manage to suppress the urge to vomit.

Two guards outside the blast door notice me. "Are you all right?" one of them calls out. I wave him away, resting my hands on my knees, hanging my head. I hear the door open behind me.

Expecting Topher, I'm surprised it's Xander who has come after me. Well, am I surprised? Not really. For some guys there's nothing more interesting than a girl who is about to completely lose her shit.

He puts his arm around me, leading me out into the snow-dusted passageway. "Come get some air," he says.

Just inside the door there are reflective coats hanging on hooks. Xander helps me into one before donning one himself.

The guards nod at him as we exit. They're smoking, despite not being quite outside. "Light?" Xander says as we trudge over to them. When one of them produces a lighter, Xander pulls a neat little joint from his pocket.

"This won't be a problem?" he asks lightly.

"Not if you share," the guard says, flicking his cigarette into the snow.

We pass it around, puffing furtively. The guards bluster and boast about nothing, trying to impress me, but I can barely hear them over the pounding of blood in my ears. When they finally giggle off to check something back inside, Xander gazes at me.

"It's because they're shaped like us," he says.

"What?" I'm having one of those buzzes that are more paranoia than any kind of pleasure. I'm deeply suspicious, among other things, that Xander is trying to get me into his bunk, but he seems willing to talk first. And I want to talk, for once.

"They're shaped like humans. They walk and move like humans, mostly. Even some of the things they do, the way they walk with their hands on each other's shoulders. It's unnerving. But they're not human, Rave. I felt a bit sick when I saw the exploding head one too, but, well, they're not human."

I'm having second thoughts about my desire to talk, to Xander anyway. But my mouth seems to have other ideas. "Dolphins aren't human either. Do we blow their heads off for entertainment?"

Xander looks pretty convincingly impatient for a stoned

dickhead. "Dolphins aren't predators. We shoot . . . I don't know . . . mountain lions in the head. If they've killed someone."

For some reason this is the moment where the Nahx from the trailer crashes back into my mind. I combine my dim memories of him with the decapitation video and what I have just learned about Emily into a thought so horrific I have to grab Xander's shoulder to keep from falling over.

"Jeez, Rave, are you okay?" he says. "You look a little green. Also, you have chocolate on your face." He reaches out to wipe it, but I pull away. Apart from Topher, I haven't told anyone about my encounter with the Nahx, and I'm not about to start with Xander.

"We don't shoot mountain lions for entertainment," I say instead. "I know this is a war, and people are going to die on both sides, but those videos are sick."

Xander considers me quietly. My balance back under control, I take my hand off his shoulder.

"There's only *people* on our side, Rave. The Nahx aren't people. They're like machines or something."

"We don't know what they are," I say. "They breathe, you know, and they bleed."

"That oily stuff? It's some kind of lubricant or fuel or something."

Nothing he's saying is making me feel any better. Being high as a cloud and churning with paranoia isn't helping either. I need to get back to my bunk *alone* and try to sleep it off. But once again my mouth has a few more things it wants to say.

"They took her prisoner. Even in a war, we don't just execute prisoners of war. She didn't resist or fight back. She . . . she . . ."

Xander looks at me like I've lost my mind. Oddly, he also looks surprised. "She?" he says, shaking his head. "Rave, you either need to stop smoking this stuff or start smoking a lot more." Then he leaves me alone in the long passage, shaking his head again as he walks. "She . . . Jesus, that's funny."

Each time the transports touch down in the city, I march down the gangplank with the others, rifle raised, convincingly emotionless, though I'm bristling with fear. I hate the city. There are survivors here, humans who didn't evacuate but somehow survived the ground assault and firebombs. They crawl out of holes, and our job is to dart them and leave them where they fall. But each day I slip away, down a dark alleyway, or into a stairwell, empty my rifle into a drawer or pile of garbage. Then I curl up somewhere hidden and wait for the transports to come back. I occupy my mind with capturing memories and trying to fix them in place. But the armor and the black syrup make them slippery and quick to escape, like eels in a rushing river.

The human girl floated away down the river. I remember that easily enough. And the feeling I had when I thought I might have killed her. I do more than remember that. I relive it, my heart jumping in my chest, making my notched ribs ache. I choke on the tube in my throat, but I can't take it out and disconnect, not at this low elevation. The syrup calms the gag reflex and my heart rate after a moment, but leaves me giddy and confused. This happens at least once every day.

The directives have changed slightly. *Search for humans. Dart them. Leave them where they fall.* And because it is a fresh transmission, it is loud, persistent. I have to focus to resist.

I somehow manage to not forget that I refuse this mission. Though sometimes I still see the humans as vermin, each day my rebellion repeats. If I am discovered, they will kill me, painfully probably, and leave *me* where I fall. I creep out when I hear the transports return, and blend in with a group of Ninths or Tenths, who are so dull witted they are unlikely to notice me.

When we return, they ask us about hits. The first time I wasn't prepared, so I answered forty, which is how many rounds my rifle carries. The Second who asked grabbed my throat, kicked my feet out from under me, and slammed the back of my head down on the hard floor until sparkles floated in front of my eyes. *No lies*, she signed to me. After that I reported twenty or twenty-five, and once ten, but that got me punished again for not being enough. I lose count of how many days we have been doing this. The winter settles in and coats the bodies left where they fall in drifts of thick white snow.

I don't disconnect, so I don't eat or sleep. I can feel my sense of self being saturated in slug slime, in the oily syrup that circulates through my armor, being replaced with mindlessness and malice. Only watching the snow fall or smelling the dormant trees keeps my mind from dissolving into nothing but obedience.

Disobedient. Defective.

Eighth. Will. NOT. Obey. The cloudy-haired girl in my memory gives me strength.

I crouch in dark passageways, hidden between abandoned vehicles or burrowed into the rubble of ruined buildings, my mind spinning. Some of the memories I grab on to as I wait don't make any sense. I try to hold on to them anyway, but they slither away.

RAVEN

As the weeks pass, the public screening of the videos becomes a near daily event in the cafeteria after meals. Both civilian and military watch, with more civilians volunteering to train as fighters every day. Despite this, we seem no closer to launching any kind of attack even after being at the base for two months. It is because the winter is too harsh, Kim explains to the ones she calls "enlisted," the pseudo-military ragtag renegades she has assembled—mostly kids, like us.

The winter is unyielding. It has not stopped snowing for weeks. Giant drifts seal off many of the exits, and all of us, civilians included, are assigned to working parties to keep the other exits clear. Topher and I find ourselves one morning outside the observation windows, digging away at snow that has blanketed them overnight.

"I'm tired of waiting," he confides, attacking the drifts with a shovel.

I pause, leaning on my own shovel. "For what? Going after that Nahx? How are we going to find him after all this time?"

Topher digs and digs, frowning with concentration.

Suddenly, he hurls his shovel far out into the snow. "I need to go after something. To do something." He lets himself fall backward in a snowdrift, which opens up to a sort of throne for him. He leans forward and holds his head in his hands. "Tucker wanted to go look for our parents. We talked about it before . . ."

"If he had done that, he would have gotten himself killed."

"How do you know that?"

"Because he did get himself killed, of course!" I toss my shovel away too and fall down beside him. The snow is as soft and yielding as an old sofa. If it weren't for the cold, we could be sitting in Topher and Tucker's basement lair, playing video games and eating junk food to quell the weed-induced munchies. "We're not prisoners here. We could go back to Calgary, in theory."

Topher stares at me for a second. "But you think it would be suicide?"

"Not if we were allowed to take weapons, supplies. If we had a vehicle, a Jeep or something."

I'm indulging him again. There are ways to make a mission like this more feasible, but I can't see Kim going for it. Even with a vehicle it could take days on remote snow-covered roads. We would have had a much better chance if we'd left before the real snow started. And went west instead of east.

"Why now?" I ask. "What brought this on?"

Topher exhales heavily, surrounding himself in a cloud of mist. "A video," he says, and I think *These fucking videos will get us all killed.* "An NKV yesterday. Liam doesn't know where it came from, but it shows a Nahx getting creamed by a Molotov cocktail."

"Charming." I hoist myself out of the snow throne and revel in the irony that I now have to dig my shovel out with my hands.

"It looked like it was in Crowfoot Park."

I pause, hands full of snow. "*Our* Crowfoot Park?" Crowfoot Park was a hangout for kids from the dojo and other karate clubs. We had semi-illegal martial arts scraps there some Friday nights. Not exactly *Fight Club*, but I occasionally woke up with a black eye.

"You know the weirdly shaped slide and that bug climbing thing? I could see them in the background. And the rock wall that Tuck broke his thumb on. You can just catch a glimpse of it."

I adjust my knitted hat, pulling it farther down over my ears, which I'm sure are about to freeze off like an alley cat's. "So? That means there are survivors. We knew that."

"Yeah, but we didn't know the Nahx were still there. Some kind of secondary ground assault? And there are humans there, fighting back. We could join them. Every day that goes by . . . if they're still alive . . . Fuck it, Crowfoot Park is blocks from my house. They don't even know . . ." He struggles to regain his composure. Another thing Tuck would never do. Tuck would give into it, weep and rage and rail against whatever was bothering him, usually his own weaknesses, until I couldn't stand it anymore, and I'd take him in my arms and tell him everything would be all right. But Topher lets himself get tied up in knots. And I'm probably the only person left alive who can unknot him.

"I should have gone weeks ago," he says. "I should have left as soon as . . . It's just . . ."

I stare out into the white expanse, knowing what's coming. But he is silent next to me. After a few seconds I finally work up the courage to turn and look at him. He's hunched over, one mittened hand covering his face.

"Toph . . ."

He speaks without looking at me. "I shouldn't have told you about Emily. That was a dick move."

I wasn't expecting that. He hasn't mentioned it apart from that one drunken time. "It's true though, right?"

"Yeah."

"And there were other girls, before that too, right? Before camp?"

He hesitates before answering. "Yeah."

I have to close my eyes to let that sink in, as fundamental beliefs about what Tucker and I had reorganize themselves in my head. I made excuses for the way he acted around other girls sometimes, telling myself it didn't mean anything, that he loved *me*. But clearly I wouldn't know real love if it smacked me in the forehead.

"I'm sorry I was such a dick about you and Tucker." Topher is practically whispering now. "It's was because . . . you spent so much time with him and I didn't . . . couldn't . . . kind of . . . function . . ." His voice breaks, shrinking to the pitiful cry of a little boy. "I never knew what to do . . . without him."

He suddenly sobs. "It's so hard to make a decision without him." He cries as he speaks, tears freezing on his cheeks. "I barely even know how to get out of bed or get dressed. I can't think. I can't sleep. . . ."

Kneeling down in front of him, I slide between his knees and put my arms around him.

"I sometimes wonder how I'm even still alive," he says, pressing his face into my shoulder.

"I've wondered the same thing," I say. "Don't get snot on my coat, okay?"

This makes him snort out a desperate little laugh.

"Everything will be all right."

He pulls back and looks at me as though I've gone mad. "No, it won't," he says, wiping streaks of ice from his face with the back of his mittens.

"No, you're right. I just thought I'd try it out."

This time he laughs properly and wipes what I'm almost sure *is* snot from my shoulder, letting his hand linger for a moment.

I sit back on my heels and look up at him. The morning sun makes his brown eyes seem gilded, like they are made out of gold. His cheeks are ruddy and flushed from the cold. A chin-length strand of dark hair has escaped from under his hat. And he needs a shave. I breathe, reminding myself that he is not Tucker, though each day that goes past, it gets harder to remember that, harder to resist Topher's pathos. Maybe if I closed my eyes and fell into his arms, it would feel like going home. Maybe all the bits of Tucker that we both carry around combined would be enough to reconstruct a kind of facsimile of him. It's a tempting idea. And at least Topher has never seemed very interested in Emily.

"So the plan has changed," I say, swallowing. "Vengeance goes on the back burner. We get to Calgary somehow. We look for your parents or other survivors. We kill some Nahx, to make it worthwhile. Deal?"

He closes his mittened hand around mine.

"Deal," he says.

When we tramp back into the bunker entrance, shaking snow from our coats, something is happening. Kim has called everyone into the cafeteria. Everyone, no exceptions. Even the few people in the infirmary are wheeled in. Children, whom

I rarely see, cling to adults, some of whom I know are not their real family. Kids hang off people too old or too young to be their parents. There are heartbreaking stories here, ones I have no desire to hear. The thought of my own broken family keeps me awake at night, every night, obsessing about things I wished I'd said and done.

Seeing the whole population of our refuge together for the first time, I'm struck by the futility of our existence. I've seen the food stores. This bunker was never properly supplied. The food will run out before the winter does, even on reduced rations.

There are about two hundred and fifty of us. If we could make it through the winter, we could plant in the spring, maybe venture out into the abandoned farmland and see what animals have survived the snow. Hunt. Gather. Fracture, let the bones regrow, bent and weak. Shelter in place, just like those government safety videos advised. Wait until someone, somewhere, somehow, wins this war for us.

I envy those in the base who live by that hope. The more time passes, the more I find I don't have the strength to hang on to the idea of rescue, or a human victory. It feels hopeless. *I* feel hopeless. But maybe that's just the helplessness of having to wait for someone else to act. All the more reason to go back to Calgary, see who we can rescue and who we can kill and whether there is a way out of here, a way to the coast.

The coast is nearly a thousand miles away over a mountain range that could be swarming with Nahx.

When everyone is seated, Kim climbs onto an empty table in front of the video screen. She looks terrible, haunted. Her hair is limp and streaked with gray. Nearby, Liam stands, stoop shouldered, his arms tightly wrapped in front of him, like he's holding his own chest cavity closed.

"Any idea what's going on?" Topher says, sliding onto the bench beside me. I shake my head as Kim begins to speak.

"The Nahx killed my husband and daughter right in front of my eyes," she says.

Well, that explains some things.

"It came down to what side of a fence we were on. They were running, actually ahead of me and Liam. They ran right into a pair of Nahx, who shot them dead without a second of thought. Liam pulled me to the ground and we rolled under a car. He clamped his hand over my mouth to keep me from screaming. The Nahx came around the fence and walked right by us. My son. My hero."

Liam, who I expect to be reveling in the glory, is actually hanging his head. One of his friends pats him on the back.

"This side of a fence or the other side," Kim continues, her voice breaking. "It could have easily gone the other way." The vise that holds her together is coming apart. I can see it happening. And I think we're about to find out what pulled it open.

Without saying another word, she steps down from the table. Someone flicks a switch and the video screen clicks on.

There is no sound. The image is a map of the world. The countries, the familiar patchwork of politics and borders, are gone. The seas are blue; the continents are gray. It is like a simple puzzle for children, the shapes crude and expressionistic. Over the speakers, a woman's voice starts. Once the volume is adjusted so we can all hear it, it's easy to tell she's no one important. She doesn't have the oratory skill that even Kim has. She's reading something that someone else has written. She's the message bearer, not its creator.

" . . . that in the last forty-eight hours, the International Cooperative Defense Force have attempted to negotiate with . . . with the invading forces, now known as the Nahx."

Topher twitches next to me. The woman continues reading, tonelessly, tightly, liked a drugged widow reading a eulogy at her husband's funeral.

"To date, the human losses have been unacceptably heavy, and the ICDF has determined that losses would not only continue but increase unless hostilities cease. The Nahx's advanced technology and . . . ruthlessness make them an impossible foe."

The map starts to change. Red patches start to appear, like blood from bullet wounds. A slash from Alaska to Nevada, a patch farther east. Central western Europe, north India, parts of Africa all soaked in red.

"Those are mountain ranges," I say to Topher. His eyes are fixed on the screen. The woman's voice continues. Her pitch increases slightly, making her sound younger.

"The Nahx occupation patterns have indicated a preference for territory above twenty-five hundred feet in elevation. For this, uh, reason, the ICDF, in agreement with the nations that make up the forces, has . . ." Her voice breaks here, and there are several seconds of silence. We watch the map as the red zones spread over the land we currently live and breathe on, the Rocky Mountains and the high plains to the east. " . . . has taken the drastic and regrettable step of surrendering all territory above two thousand feet to the Nahx."

There are gasps as the map stops changing. The red stains become fixed, grotesque blotches, like third-degree burns. My vague understanding of our location puts us well inside the red zone, at least a hundred miles from any border. Somewhere in the cafeteria, someone, possibly a child, starts to cry.

"The perimeters of these territories are now heavily fortified and patrolled. The ICDF and the United Nations tried to arrange the evacuation of the surrendered territory, but the Nahx command would not communicate beyond . . . compass points and maps." The woman is crying now; I can hear it in her voice. "If you are hearing this message from within one of these regions . . . we had no choice. . . . You are now subject to Nahx rule." There is a long pause before she finishes. "God

161

bless you." Static surges over the speakers, and the map of the world fades. Someone clicks the screen off.

Topher has laid his head on the table. I lay mine down beside his. Our eyes fix on each other.

"God *bless* us?" he says. "God has completely and utterly fucked us."

The cafeteria erupts. The civilians react with all the ferocity that we militarized types keep contained. There is screaming and accusation in at least five different languages. There are a lot of tears. I expect Kim to stay, to try to restore order, but she and Liam walk out together, leaving us leaderless and broken.

It's not long before Sawyer finds us, along with Xander and Mandy. Emily slips in beside them a minute or two later. I have to force myself to make eye contact with her.

"You think anyone here knows what this means?" Mandy asks.

"Probably not," I answer. "Do you?"

She looks much calmer than I might expect, watching the civilians gathering back at tables, their voices lowered now to sepulchral tones.

"There is very little medicine left," Mandy says. "Things like high blood pressure and heart disease we can try to control with diet, I guess, but we'll lose a few to that. There's a child here with leukemia. It was just diagnosed. Funny, right?"

Xander starts to bang his forehead on the table as she continues.

"At least we can probably avoid the worst of the seasonal viruses, since we're isolated. Everybody has been cleared for HIV and hep C, and that's good because, I've got to say, we're getting through the condoms pretty quickly."

"Jesus," Xander says to the tabletop.

"People were counting on a rescue," Mandy says. "That's why everybody has been so calm, I guess. Lulled into a false sense of security by those bullshit videos. *The fight continues. We will defeat them. Shelter in place.* Ha! We'll be lucky if we come out the other side of winter."

"But will the Nahx come here?" Emily says.

Sawyer speaks at last, with some of the authority that he showed before Felix died. "This quarry is pretty low, even though we're surrounded by mountains. And we're underground. We might be trapped, but maybe we're safe here."

I sigh impatiently. "That's what you said about the camp."

"Right, and don't you think now that you should have listened to me?"

"So we could starve? And that was even higher up than here!"

"We could have made a go of it! They might never have found us!"

"Or maybe they would have!"

163

Topher's head shoots up. "Stop it! Stop it, you two!" He turns to me. "It's possible that the Nahx will ignore us since we're hidden, but I wouldn't count on it. It's immaterial though because Calgary is in the red zone, and we've made that our new objective. Right?"

"We have?" Sawyer says. Topher turns to me expectantly.

"There are survivors in Calgary. There's also a ton of supplies, medicine, food. Condoms," I add, and can't resist directing my gaze at Emily. "We can get there if we take the Humvees."

Sawyer speaks with a lower voice. "I don't think Kim will go for it."

Topher replies with his twin's intensity, scanning our little group. "But it's a good idea, right?"

I turn to look at Emily and Mandy, at Xander, whose lost expressions pretty much sum up my whole attitude too. The plan to launch a rescue mission back to Calgary now seems even more fanciful than it did an hour ago when we first conceived it. It would be like last-ditch chemotherapy on a terminal patient. Maybe give us a few more months until starvation, disease, or the Nahx get us. At least if we stay here, we will die warm. That would not have been the case at the camp. On the other hand, if we want to survive longer term, leaving is our only option. We need to start sourcing food and medicine.

It seems hopeless. But now it's our only hope. My head hurts.

Topher turns to Sawyer. Even though things have changed since we arrived at the bunker, he's still our leader. "Are you in?"

"Like I'd let a bunch of seventeen-year-olds go off on their own."

"I'm sixteen," I say. Xander grins along with me.

Sawyer reaches into his jacket and pulls out a hip flask, passing it to me.

"This is contributing to the delinquency of a minor," I point out as I uncap it. "You should be ashamed."

"There is no age of majority after an apocalypse. Can we agree on that?"

The sip of vodka stings on the way down, but the instant sensation it gives me makes me crave another.

"How do we convince Kim?" Topher asks, taking the bottle from me.

"Why do we have to?" Sawyer says. "Since when do we do things by the book?"

As we pass the bottle around our table, I realize the cafeteria has fallen silent except for the continued sobbing of a toddler. I look around in time to see another older child, a dark-skinned girl with a long braid, rise and touch the crying child's head affectionately. I expect her to say *There, there* or something, but instead she starts singing "Baby Beluga."

When the toddler's mother starts to sing along, the child

settles. But the little girl keeps going as others around her join in, one by one. Adults sing. Children sing. I'm pretty sure at least a couple of people are singing in French, and Xander seems to be singing in Chinese. Soon the whole room is singing. "Baby Beluga" is the funniest, most incongruous song to sing deep underground a thousand miles from the sea, but we bellow it out, laughing through tears, our voices ringing off the concrete, stone, and metal walls of our snow-covered tomb.

I sing too, because we need it. We are terrified. Betrayed and uncertain. Angry and heartbroken.

But united, for now. And *human*, above all. We are human. We are human.

I'm just not sure that will be enough.

I suppose I should be grateful that it is a human who finds me and not one of us, a human with a gun more suited to killing squirrels than penetrating armor. But the man scares me anyway. He screams hateful and violent things at me and empties his sad little gun, from point-blank range. The bullets *ping* off my armor, but sting enough to knock me over.

Think now. Think. My instinct is to kill him. I could snap him in half. I could certainly get a dart into him, drag him back out into the street, and drop him into a snowdrift. That's my mission. Those are my directives. Their relentless rhythm in my mind is much stronger now that I'm with others. Much harder to disobey.

Disobedient. Defective.

Spiderwebs. Snowflakes. The golden-haired human girl. I stand with my rifle raised.

The man shakes so much as I stand that he can't reload his gun. "No, please . . . ," he says. I take a step toward him. The mission is . . . the mission . . .

Run, I sign to him. He doesn't seem to understand. Some

part of me longs to pull the trigger. He's standing right there. I could crush his skull with one hand.

Run, please.

He doesn't move. I search my memory for some alternative to killing him. Can I just walk away? He might manage to shoot me in the back, but that won't injure me.

I focus on the image of the girl, her hair the warm color of new pinecones. I lower my rifle.

Where are your friends?

The man takes a step back, then another.

Your friends. Are you alone?

As he turns and runs. I hear a noise from the street above. Heavy footfalls. Not human.

No! Wait. I'll help you!

I can't stop him. He runs back out of the storeroom, knocking over boxes and shelves as he goes. I hear the outer door bang open, the whining of the dart rifle, and the *thump* of the man's body falling onto the icy sidewalk.

I tell myself there is nothing I could have done and creep back into my hiding place until the heavy footsteps fade away.

Nights in the base are quiet now. Kim seems to have disappeared. She and her cronies, the other officers, her son and his close friends, sometimes issue orders from the command level. They change snow clearing or kitchen shifts. Occasionally, sleeping arrangements are reorganized. It all smacks of a command team with nothing to command. If they're still planning an attack on the Nahx, wherever they are, they haven't shared it with the likes of me. Topher, Xander, and I train some of the other civilians in hand-to-hand combat, more as a way to pass time than for any realistic purpose.

I know how hard Nahx armor is, how it burns to touch. How fast they are. Our disarming tactics, our disabling and neutralizing techniques, are more likely to be useful on one another as our sense of community starts to fray.

Almost no one turns up for the increasingly meager dinners in the cafeteria. There is certainly no music or dancing afterward. Liam and some of his friends run NKVs sometimes on the big screen, gasping and hooting their approval. One evening Emily finds me there, facing away from the screen, working on a list of things we'll need if we're to make the mission to Calgary. She leans over, perusing the list before sitting.

"So. You know, huh?" she says, toying with her small plate of food. I stare at the space between us. "I didn't realize how serious you and Tucker were until . . ."

"It was too late?" I ask. But I find I can't muster up much emotion. I should hate her, but what would be the point of that? "It's not your fault. You weren't the first." Saying it out loud makes it true.

Emily loads her spoon with a pea, pulls it back, and flicks it precisely, across half the room, right into the back of Liam's head. I can't help but smile as Liam turns and glares back.

"Xander told me Topher says your name in his sleep," Emily says, now loading her spoon with a carefully coiled noodle.

"He's just confused. It doesn't mean anything." I wonder whether she plans to flick the noodle at me. "You're welcome to him, if that's what you're thinking."

She shrugs.

"Aren't you and Liam a thing?"

"Apparently not anymore."

Her tone is casual, but I can see it's more than that. And I actually feel sorry for her. I suppose when Tucker died she was grieving too, but she couldn't tell anyone. And now she's been dumped by a douche bag in the winter palace of the damned. I shake my head as I watch her aim her spoon. My capacity for empathy and forgiveness surprises even myself sometimes. Tucker used to call it my superpower.

Emily flicks the coiled noodle so expertly that it lands in the hood of Liam's sweatshirt. He doesn't even notice. Emily smirks at me.

"What are we doing?" I ask her.

"Making peace," she says, standing. I notice she hasn't actually eaten any of the food she's been flicking around. "No sense in dying with bitterness in your heart. Your soul should go back to the universe as clean and naked as when you arrived here." She doesn't take her plate with her as I watch her leave. She's just a girl like me, I think. She has a family too, all the way in Australia, which might as well be on another planet now. God.

I look back to see Liam approaching, a fierce expression on his face. Turning to a fresh page in my notebook, I pretend to start a drawing.

"What do you want?" he snaps as he reaches me. His friends turn and trail toward us, drawn by his tone. Disturbingly, I see Topher and Xander among them.

"Nothing," I say.

"Why are you throwing food at me?"

"I wasn't."

"Who was, then?"

I could pin it on Emily, but since she just tried to reconcile with me, that seems a bit cold. So I get up to leave. Something tells me it's time to exit this situation. I'm irritated with Topher and Xander for being part of Liam's testosterone party. And I need to think. Maybe I'll find Sawyer and we can do some proper planning.

"It was just a noodle." I tuck my notebook under my arm. "Don't be so sensitive."

Liam, astonishingly, simply steps forward and shoves me hard on the shoulders. I step back, keeping my balance easily and feel my body go into a defensive stance, legs apart, knees slightly bent, arms hanging loose but engaged at my sides, like I'm about to start a seriously competitive spar.

Behind Liam, Xander chuckles. "Wow, dude, you really don't want to get into it with her."

"I'm not scared of you," Liam says. He's drunk, I can tell. I could drop him and gut him like a fish, but I want to find Sawyer. So I turn to leave, and he charges. I see Topher dive forward in my defense at the same time as my instinct kicks in. Both my arms shoot back and take Liam by the neck. I curve one leg back around his knees. With a quick twist, he crashes down on the floor.

"Bitch!" Liam yells. "Fucking half-breed!" My fist shoots forward and cracks into his mouth. He doesn't have the protective reflexes that Topher does. Blood spurts from his lip.

This would be the moment to step back. I've won this bout,

but I'm on fire now. I have him pinned down on the floor, bloodied and dazed. My arm is drawn back to hit him again. I could beat him unconscious and barely raise a sweat, and I *want* to. Badly. I haven't heard that word he called me in years, not since I smacked a kid who slung it at my little stepcousin. It's like a curse from an ancient fairy tale that awakens a monster. I could kill Liam.

Someone grabs me from behind, pulling me off him, pinning my arms to my sides as I struggle to get free.

"Enough, Raven." Topher's voice vibrates in my ear. "Enough. Stop."

I exhale, going limp in his arms.

We're now surrounded by Liam's friends, as well as a few spectators. It is one of those scenes that make me look really cool and Liam look really dumb. I feel a twang of regret, not for his pain—I couldn't care less about that—but that I let him get to me. I have a feeling I'm going to have to pay for this one day.

Liam's friends drag him off to the bathroom to clean up. Xander trails after them, chuckling. The rest of the crowd drifts away—the entertainment over.

As I tug at Topher's arms, he releases me, and I catch my balance on the back of a chair.

"You okay?"

I flex the fingers of my right hand. They're a bit tender, but I've felt worse. "Fine."

"I didn't mean your hand." He lets a few seconds tick past. "No one else thinks of you like that."

I just shake my head. Like a "half-breed," he means, as though that's such a terrible thing. The word is pretty offensive—that much I know about my stepdad's history—but what's so wrong with being half this and half that anyway? Topher means most people think of me as white. I don't think that's true, but that doesn't matter either. What matters is that he thinks it's a compliment. I don't look white. Is he saying I *act* white?

You'd think at the end of the world I could get away from this crap, but I guess not. As for Liam, he doesn't know the first thing about me. And I don't care either, if he thinks I'm Métis, or Native, or Black. He can kiss my round, brown ass.

"I'm going to bed," I say. Topher lets me go without another word.

Mandy is not in her bunk when I get to our quarters, which means she's probably in the infirmary—maybe holding an ice pack on Liam's nose.

Looking over at the small desk, I realize I don't have my notebook. I must have dropped it when Liam jumped me. Now I'll have to go back for it, and I was so looking forward to maybe getting some sleep.

When I get back to the cafeteria, it's deserted. I search under the tables for my notebook, but it's not there. Maybe

Topher grabbed it. I can't really be bothered looking for him now. I'll ask him in the morning.

Standing in the dim empty hall, I can hear the humming of the air circulators and the faint creaking of the walls and floors in response to the lower night temperatures. A shiver passes over me, from cold, and possibility. There are large sentry parties assigned to patrol the base entrances and perimeter fences, but internal security is limited to one or two civilians doing a turn of the corridors once an hour. If I'm careful, I could wander the base all night. Maybe I was longing for sleep less than I thought. I'm wide awake suddenly.

I figure if Liam and his gang can skulk around at night when we're supposed to be in our own quarters or the communal areas, then so can I. There are parts of the base that seem to be off-limits, and if there's one thing I remember from my old life, it's that sometimes the nighttime concept of "off-limits" is as indistinct as the shadows. At least, that's what I count on as I tiptoe through the door marked RESTRICTED AREA.

The weapons store would be the obvious place to start—we're going to need weapons for our mission back to Calgary—but it's the command level that beckons me. I know only certain things are shared widely among the inhabitants of our refuge. Topher has speculated that this is about morale, but I think it's about control. We see what Kim needs us to see—the NKVs, the announcement of the surrender. But surely there are other things Kim and her inner circle have discovered from the transmissions. Maybe I can learn something about conditions on the coast or in Calgary. Maybe there's some database of survivors. I could look for my parents' names.

Above all, what we need to find out is where exactly we are. We can't navigate over unmarked roads in high mountains without that. I suppose if we follow the sunrise due east we'd eventually find the foothills, then the plains, and could make our way to Calgary from there. But we could wander in the mountains for days trying to find a way out. And that would use up all our fuel.

The location is classified, Liam told us when we arrived. I should have realized at the time that this would keep us all in, as well as keeping any invaders out. There were maps on the table when Topher and I first spoke to Kim in the command center. Maybe one of them had our location marked. That's a thin hope, but all hopes are these days.

I'm halfway up the long climb to the command level when I hear footsteps behind me. Cursing silently, I stop, pressing myself into the corner of the landing between stairways. There are emergency exits every five levels, but they're alarmed. If I tried ducking out of one, the whole base would know about it. And anyway, they go outside onto rocky plateaus. There's a spindly ladder down to the main entrance level, and up to command, but I don't fancy being chased up it in the dark and freezing night. Probably easier to face whoever this creeper is.

I step forward, calling down the stairs.

"Who's there?"

I hear a low chuckle. "I thought it would be you."

I should have known. Liam.

He appears on the landing below me, looking swollen and vaguely menacing. I could outrun him maybe. He's pretty tall compared to me, but he has recently had his face punched in. Maybe that will slow him down. But where would I run? Out into the snow?

"What do you want?"

"Nothing," he says calmly. "I was going up to find my m— Kim. I have something to show her." He lifts his hand, and I see he's holding my notebook. "Maybe you should come with me. You can discuss why you're in a restricted area after hours."

"Or . . . I could finish beating the shit out of you."

He smiles and with his free hand nudges back his hoodie, revealing a pistol in a holster.

"Jesus, Liam," I say, taking a step backward. "Chill."

"Walk."

I turn and head up the stairs as he follows. We trudge in silence as I get used to having someone with a gun behind me. Apart from the time the police briefly chased us across the park, it's never happened to me before. I can't say that I'm enjoying it.

When we reach the command level, Liam points me to a chair by one of the wide windows.

"Watch her," he says to a couple of uniformed lookouts. Liam disappears into central command, closing the door behind him.

"You're in the shit now, Rave," one of the guards says. I recognize him as one of Liam's friends. It's then I remember something else I jotted down in my notebook: a list of everyone who has committed to going to Calgary. Before I even complete this thought, Emily, Mandy, and Topher emerge from the stairway, huffing with the effort of their climb. Sawyer and Xander trail in behind them.

"Anyone know the way to Mordor?" Xander says, grinning at all of us.

Sawyer is less amused. He glares at me. "Why did I know one day you would be the cause of me being hauled out of bed in the middle of the night?"

I shrug. What can they do to us? We haven't done anything but make a tentative plan to get out of this rattrap.

Kim doesn't waste time when she calls us into the command center. I note that the long table has been cleared of maps.

"A rescue mission to Calgary?" she asks, a cool tone to her voice. Liam smirks in the corner like the stinking snitch that he is. Kim opens my notebook and reads. "A Humvee, half our weapons, and a weeks' rations? A Humvee!" Kim shouts. "And enough fuel to get you there and back, I suppose, too. Or were you going to push it?"

"We will find fuel on the way," I say. "We can recon a lot of ground that you haven't set foot in for months. There are towns and farms along the way. We might find survivors. We'll certainly find supplies."

Kim falls silent for a moment, so I forge ahead. Nothing to lose, I remind myself. "You know as well as I do that we will likely run out of medical supplies before the winter is out. There are drugstores in each town. We can raid medicine cabinets. We can give you a complete rundown on where to look when we come back."

Topher glances at me. I know that he knows what I know. We're not all that likely to make it back.

"And if you don't make it back?" Kim says. "The Nahx are still out there."

"We haven't sighted them in weeks," Sawyer points out. "Not even transports. I've seen the lookout logs."

"A million other things could go wrong."

Surprisingly, Liam pipes in. "We could take a few of the drones with us. They don't take up much space. We could send them back with data before we get to Calgary. At least that way . . . well, we would make it worth it."

I blink and shake my head. Did he just say "we"?

Kim considers her son thoughtfully. "Do you want to go with them?" she says. There is something in her voice, a tinge of pride? It turns my blood cold. She must know it's a death march too.

"I want more than to go," Liam says. "I want to command the mission."

Sawyer hangs his head and sighs.

The transport leaves me at the compound. Out on the flat land, outside the city, I linger in the yard, looking at the western sky, the foothills, and the mountains beyond. Someone shoves me so hard I fall forward onto my knees.

Inside, they sign.

I hide inside all day. They lock us inside all night. I hate being inside. I ache to climb back up into the mountains, as though I may have left something there, something important to me.

Important.

We are locked in the dark, unable to sleep, with no light to see one another by, so we can't even speak. In the morning when the light streams in, I see someone else has had their neck broken in the night.

Tenth, a girl signs as she steps over the body, like that makes it acceptable.

One night, after two days and nights locked inside, I curl up, squatting with my arms wrapped around my knees, facing into a corner. Normally, I might face out, not that it makes much difference since it is too dark to see most of the time. But it's safer to face out, easier to crawl away from any trouble that approaches in the dark. Lately, the nightmarish silence is frequently marred with the sounds of violence and the threatening or desperate growls and hisses that accompany it.

I've crawled away from an attack more than once. Someone broke the smallest finger on my left hand, for no good reason that I could discern. They simply snatched my hand and snapped my finger back. I hissed at them and shoved with my other hand. Then I heard them scuttle away. The pain wore off by morning, but I was left hurting anyway. Hurt feelings. So stupid. I don't know what I did to get my finger broken.

I keep thinking that maybe Sixth will find me here. My Sixth, I mean. There are other Sixths here, but they are not very friendly. Neither was my Sixth, of course, but . . .

Ah, but she's dead. I saw her die. She died and flew away on wings of blood.

Dead. Dead. The shape of that word doesn't seem right anymore. It's similar to our sign for "stop."

Dead. Stop. Stopped.

I press my forehead into the corner and try to focus my mind on something else. I wish I could sleep. I might dream. I might dream of . . . someone, a girl, not Sixth. . . . My brain is turning to mush. It takes all the mental strength I have to hang on to one thing.

Eighth. Will. NOT. Obey.

Defective. I make the shapes in the dark. *Disobedient.*

Dandelion.

A human girl. I know that when I lose hold of that thought, I might as well stop crawling away from danger in the night. Sometimes there is no noise at all, yet still when the light returns there is a dead one beside me. Do they just die, or do they not resist when someone comes to kill them? Perhaps they have forgotten the one thing that makes them a separate being.

The wall is cold. I can feel that through the sensory inputs in my armor. I stand and press my hands onto it, on either side of my head. Maybe I drift too far into a thought, or an attempt at a thought anyway, because I don't notice anyone beside me until I feel another hand press down on mine. I try to jerk it away, but the fingers intertwine with mine and grip tightly. I'm about to get another broken bone, I think.

But my finger isn't broken. The one beside me grips my hand tightly, but not painfully. It's so dark I can't tell if it's a boy or a girl. I don't even care. I squeeze back. It feels nice to hold hands. Sixth let me hold her hand sometimes, begrudgingly, when she grew tired of teasing me.

I feel a head drop down and rest on my shoulder, hear a little sigh of rattling breath. It's a boy, I now realize. His head is level with mine, and none of the girls are as tall as me. He rests his head there on my shoulder, clinging to my hand, breathing. In between breaths it's so quiet I can hear his heart. After a few minutes he moves but doesn't let go of my hand. I could easily yank it away, maybe even shove him so hard that he falls down, but I don't. As he walks away, I let him lead me.

We slink across the room, pressed against the wall, careful not to step on anyone or trip over their legs and feet. We both have lights, but don't dare use them. On the first night in this holding cell those who turned on lights were quickly targeted for beatings, or worse. I'm not sure I understand the logic of this. It's possible there is some directive that I haven't received. Some others seem to know what is going on more than I do.

The other one, the boy, pulls me through a doorway and down a passage. We are not supposed to leave the holding cell, but there doesn't seem to be anyone there to stop us. We reach a corner where a small light bathes us in a dim red glow.

Rank? I ask, able to see him at last.

He tilts his head to the side and lifts his free hand, palm up. It's a question hand, but I know he means something like *Do you need to ask?*

Eighth? I sign, and he nods, pulling me forward. Eighth, like me. Maybe all Eighths think for themselves, feel lonely, and like holding hands. Maybe this is something he knows and I don't.

We reach the end of the dark passageway. The other Eighth lets go of my hand, turning to the wall and sliding his fingers up and down, looking for something. I could turn and run back to the holding cell. If we are caught here, they will kill us both. I don't know where this Eighth is taking me or what he wants. There is something troubling, a slip of an idea that concerns me. I think of the human girl, and a dream that woke me drowning in shame. I can't really remember what I felt so ashamed about.

The other Eighth finds a latch. I hear a tiny *click* and feel a rush of cold air. A door slides open just enough for us to slip through, and suddenly we are outside, on a kind of walkway. He hops over the guardrail and disappears. I hesitate until I see, beyond the rail, that the ground is covered in soft, fresh snow. I swing my legs over the rail and let myself fall, landing fifteen feet below, in snow up to my ankles.

I'm overcome with such a feeling of pleasure and relief that I fall to my knees, pressing my hands into the snow. The smell of it is indescribable. I grab handfuls and hold them up to my nose, sniffing deeply. After a few seconds I feel Eighth's hand on my head. He stands above me, making a question hand.

I feel very happy, I sign. He nods and does the sign for "repeat," pointing to his own chest.

Me too.

Gesturing for me to follow, he trudges off. I follow, placing my feet in the footprints he leaves in the deep snow. The dark of night is so profound that I can barely see him ahead of me, much less where we are going. But after a few minutes we reach a high fence. It looks like something that humans

185

built, flimsy and poorly designed. Each post is crowned with a watery blue light. The other Eighth waits for me to join him, then places his index finger dramatically on the fence. It crackles with electricity. He flicks his head back a couple of times. I've seen only Sixth laugh before. On this one it's not as mean. He's laughing at the fence, not at me. Electricity is not something that deters us. The fence must be left over from whatever this place was before we arrived. Why it is still electrified, I don't know. Maybe someone thought it would prevent escapes. It's then I realize what his intention is, the other Eighth; he means to escape. He pinches a wire of the fence and pulls it easily away from the steel post. A couple of sparks hiss into the snow. He pulls another and another, until there is a gap wide enough to crawl through.

He stands back, turns to me, and holds one hand down, fingers apart, like he's grasping something large and round. Then he turns his hand upward. I've never seen this sign before, but like all of them, I somehow know what it means. It wouldn't be one that was needed very often in our lives.

Free.

I repeat it, making it a question. *Free?*

The other Eighth nods and ushers me forward. I step over the bent wire, glancing back at him as he follows me through the gap.

Turn, he signs when he reaches me. I obey without thinking, turning my back to him. I see from our shadows in the snow that he has one of our knives in his hand—a knife he should have turned in when they locked us inside. He could hurt me with that knife, but more than any fear of that I'm intrigued by his disobedience. He's defective, like me.

I feel him press the knife into the back of my neck. Maybe he is going to kill me. Part of me longs for it; part of me would rather be dead than . . . whatever this is.

There's a loud *click* and then silence.

Silence. The perpetual humming of the degraded mission directives has stopped. My thoughts empty of it so quickly, I feel faint and sway where I stand. The other Eighth takes my arm to steady me as I turn back to him. He holds out a small bundle of metal and wires, no bigger than a beetle.

Muddy death, he's beyond defective; he's crazy. Disconnecting a transponder will get us both killed.

Run, he signs.

I do as I'm told, expecting him to follow me. I run fast, taking long strides through the white drifts. After a few seconds I find myself on a raised road. The wind has kept it clear of snow. My brain works well enough to realize this means I could go either way and they couldn't track me. I'm not sure which way to go, so I turn toward the city. The mountains are past the city, and I still feel the tug of the air and trees and mist I know I'll find there.

The other Eighth appears at the edge of the road behind me. Behind him, I can barely make out that he has stepped into my footprints.

Together?

He shakes his head. I think I must have made a mistake, or maybe he intends to go the other way on the road. It's a reasonable plan, less chance of being caught.

Run, he says again.

I start to run toward the city. A hundred meters on I find a human's car, stop beside it, and look back. I don't understand what's happening. In the unfamiliar silence of my thoughts I'm confused, and the syrupy sludge isn't helping. It surges through me, trying to focus me, but without the buzz of my mission directives, it has nowhere to go, nothing to work with. The other Eighth is still standing where I left him on the road. I'm about to wave at him, or maybe go back when . . .

A shot rings out. The other Eighth clutches at his throat and tumbles forward. I dive behind the car, poking my head out just enough to see what happens next.

Three high ranks come to the side of the road. One of them throws something down on Eighth where he fell, and he explodes into flames.

I shrink back behind the car, my fists pressed in front of my mouth.

As if I could scream.

We leave a week later, all of us who signed up except Emily, who has fallen ill with some kind of stomach bug.

"I bet she's pregnant," Xander whispers conspiratorially as we run through a final supply check.

Liam overhears. "Not by me, she's not." His tone is cool. Seeing these two boys banter about a girl's fate, even a girl I don't particularly like, gives me a chill. Was there a time when people were more considerate? Maybe ages ago. There are fistfights over food now and hushed rumors that someone got raped on perimeter watch. Sometimes when I can't sleep, I fantasize that someone tries something with me, and I kill him. Is that just me being a badass, or is this place getting to me, changing me? I'm actually happy to leave the so-called safety of our refuge, happy to leave all these desperate rats in a cage.

Before the invasion it always seemed like nature was out to get us—with cold or rain or plagues of grasshoppers. Now I see we were always our own worst enemy.

Liam brings five other volunteers with him. A girl called

Britney, who I think might be Liam's new . . . whatever, a guy called Dinesh, and three white boys whose names all sound the same. I'm sure that older people volunteered, but Liam made the final selections and somehow managed to choose other teenagers. Not sure what that says about him. He's not happy that Sawyer is older than he is, that's clear.

We're heavily armed. Kim has trained me on a small but she says very powerful pistol with which my aim is slightly better. It seems powerful, but what would I have to compare it to? I know it nearly threw my arm out of the shoulder socket the first time I used it. We're low on ammo though. I have three clips for it. When those run out, I'm left with my knife. If I lose that, I'm dead.

Apart from weapons, our packs are light. We wear all our clothes, and if we don't find food in Calgary, we'll be very hungry on the way back. Mandy rejects a box of bottled water in favor of more first aid supplies.

"The ground is covered in snow, Liam," she says when he complains. "Everyone has a canteen, right?"

Liam makes a big show of confirming this with all of us and going through other items in our personal kits so pedantically I'm ready to throttle him.

We finally depart, eleven of us, in two Humvees. After all her bluster about preserving fuel, Kim clearly wants her son to travel in style and comfort. He and two of his friends are outfitted with the best in military accessories the base can come up with: Kevlar body armor, helmet-mounted cameras to record the mission, and weapons, of course.

Topher, in an improvised uniform, rides in silence, his crossbow on his lap, a rifle tucked beside him. My weapons are holstered as I've been instructed, even though it's uncomfortable to sit like this. "Too many inexperienced soldiers fumble their weapons from surprise," Liam tells me, like he's been in a battle before. "I doubt the Nahx would give you a chance to pick them up. And I don't think your whole Jackie Chan thing will help you either." He's goading me, but I don't take the bait. I need to focus on staying alive.

See a Nahx, draw my weapon, fire. Neck, shoulder, or hip joints. Chest, back, and head are bulletproof, unless you have armor-piercing bullets, which we don't. The videos taught us this. Shoot first, yell second, think later, Topher says, like that's an easy choice to make. "Code Black" is the warning call we've agreed on. The likely scenario is that if you have to use it, they will be your last two words.

The journey is slow, through remote roads piled with snow and abandoned cars, but surprisingly uneventful. We encounter no Nahx, but see enough evidence of their handiwork to fuel nightmares for a hundred people. Death is everywhere. Every rest stop, every town is littered with bodies, most in a perfect state of preservation. There is some decay, a few babies in strollers, for example, and dogs on leashes, frozen and starved. Some adults and older children too, who died in other ways. We see broken necks, smashed skulls, and some bodies that are so decayed the cause of death is unknown.

Rather than pitch our winter tents the first night, we all curl up in the Humvees, trembling, and not just from the cold.

We arrive at the city limits around midnight on the second day. Lookouts spotted Nahx transports hovering and landing at dusk, taking off an hour later. So we linger out of sight and approach from the opposite direction, setting up a rough camp inside an abandoned barn. We eat, and draw straws on who gets to take watch. Whoever it is won't get any sleep at all, since Liam wants to move out at dawn. My luck is bad and good. I draw one short straw, but Sawyer draws the other.

Liam won't let us use the cameras.

The frigid night air washes over me as the others bed down. I shiver, zipping up my jacket and pulling on a knitted hat, gathering my gun and knife in their holsters. I buckle them into place, then slip on my gloves. Sawyer and I begin our watch, heading in opposite directions around the barn.

We pace, passing each other every few minutes. Sawyer nods a greeting each time. When this gets boring, he begins telling long meandering jokes, one line at a time. I have to stifle a laugh each time he gets to the punch line, even though I can hardly remember the beginning of the joke. Eventually, he runs out of jokes, and we continue the watch in silence.

My mind drifts here and there as I trudge through snow. I think of my parents again. They might have survived. I have no way of contacting them unless we get to some kind of proper communication. Not for the first time, I try to imagine what they are going through. It's something a therapist once told me I should do. *Imagine how your parents feel when you do these things*, she said about the fighting and the drugs and the staying out all night with questionable boys. *Imagine how worried they are.*

As I walk, I have a quiet moment to think about that. There never really was that much fighting outside the dojo. And the drugs were only ever a bit of weed. And how questionable were the handsome twin sons of a nice doctor? It's possible all the other things the court-mandated therapist said to me were bullshit too. *ADHD. Attachment disorder. Anger issues*—labels every therapist loves to slap on someone who looks like me.

Argumentative I'll concede was pretty accurate. As for the rest, maybe no one ever really knew me, not even my parents. I did try to imagine their worry, but all I ever saw was disappointment that I would never be like them—a beloved English teacher and a respected Métis activist. But maybe I imagined the disappointment, too.

It's hard to imagine people when you are not sure they're alive. In a way, it's easier to imagine those who are certainly dead. I think of Tucker in his grave, and Felix and Lochie lying dead in the churchyard. I pass Sawyer, who pretends to be a zombie. I think of Topher in his sleeping bag, with Xander snuffling beside him. I'm so cold and tired I'm tempted to crawl between them and fall asleep. The next time I pass Sawyer, I'm laughing to myself about how pitiful I am. He yawns and walks on.

The yawn is catching. Suddenly, my eyes feel heavy, sticky, like they are adhered to my eyeballs with Krazy Glue. I take a deep breath of the cold night air and try to wake up. The air smells of hay, and a little horsey from the barn. There's also a faint burnt smell, like charcoal, perhaps coming from the burned-out house.

Smell is a powerful memory, I've heard. The most powerful. With that little whiff of charcoal, the Nahx in the trailer floats into my head again. My wrists ache, and my heart aches, and my mind churns like a storm. I feel like there is something important about what happened, but I can't quite grasp it. I stop, listening. I can hear Sawyer's trudging footsteps around the other side of the barn. Closing my eyes, I remember the plodding gait of the Nahx rocking as he carried me. I don't remember being picked up or set down, but I have a slip of a memory of being carried, of looking up at his shadowed shape, with the stars behind it. He was tall, straight backed, and *warm*. I remember the warmth.

When I open my eyes, he's there.

A barely visible shadow lingers in the dark by the burned-out house, looking right at me, a night-armored Nahx invader standing twenty feet away.

I'm paralyzed. *Code Black*, my mind shrieks, but nothing comes out of my mouth. I reach for my weapons, my lungs trying to take in enough breath to scream. When my gun sticks in the holster, I glance down to free it, and when I look back up, the Nahx is gone.

"Rave?" I spin around, both weapons raised. It's Sawyer, standing there, a horse blanket slung over his shoulders. "Whoa, it's me. Sawyer."

Finally I gasp, as my breath catches up to my galloping heart. I must look wild, because Sawyer raises his hands and steps slowly forward. "It's okay. It's me."

"There was a N-Nahx," I stammer, pointing back with my pistol. "Right there. Standing right there."

Sawyer frowns and looks over my shoulder, taking another step toward me. "Holster your weapons, please," he says in a firm tone, and I do so, dazed. Sawyer reaches out and touches my shoulder. His firm grip brings me back to my senses.

"There's nothing there," Sawyer says, letting go of my shoulder. "If there had been a Nahx there, you would be dead. So would I."

"I saw it," I say.

Sawyer steps back and looks at me. Then he turns me around and checks my back. "What are you looking for?"

"The videos said the darts are sometimes duds. Did you feel anything?" He searches the ground around me.

"He didn't have a weapon," I say.

"He?"

"The Nahx." I try to remember the shape of the shadow in the dark.

Sawyer frowns at me for a moment. I think he's about to tell me I imagined it, but then he shrugs off his blanket, draws his gun, and clicks the safety off. "Show me where it was standing," he says.

I take him to the spot by the house. With his free hand he pulls a small squeeze-charged flashlight from his thigh pocket and cranks it, shining the dim light on the ground.

"There's nothing here." He shines his flashlight away from the snow on to the clear ground. "I wish that tosser had given you a camera. You're *sure* you saw something?"

I don't know what to say. I had just been thinking about the Nahx when he appeared before me. I'm exhausted and paranoid, half starved and weak with cold. "Maybe . . . ," I start. Maybe what? Maybe the Nahx who captured me, who delivered me to the edge of the mountain a hundred miles away, who spared my life, followed me here? It's utterly ridiculous. I don't even finish my sentence.

Sawyer clicks his safety back on and holsters his pistol, also pocketing his flashlight. He walks back and collects his blanket from the ground, carefully laying it around my shoulders. It smells of hay and horse, but not of charcoal. "You were sleepwalking, I think, Rave," he says to me, like I am a child, but I don't know how to argue.

"Maybe you're right," I say.

In the morning we fan out from the barn and cover our tracks as best we can. We take what we need for the day, leaving the Humvees and most of the supplies. As the sky lightens we set off. I see Topher and Sawyer walking together, talking in low tones. After a few minutes Sawyer jogs up to the front of the line, and Topher drifts back until he is next to me, matching my pace in a heavy silence.

"Sawyer told you," I say finally.

"Lots of us see things," he says. "Xander sees his old dog."

"I'm not seeing things," I say. "I think it was the Nahx from the trailer. The one who left me by the fire."

"How could it find you?"

"I don't know. Maybe he's been following us."

Topher takes off his knitted hat and scratches his head under his tiny ponytail, tucking the hat into his weapon belt. "Let's say, for the sake of argument, that what you think happened is true," he says.

"Okay."

"It can only be bad. If this Nahx developed some kind of interest in you for whatever reason, its motives can only be hostile."

"Why?"

"Because it's a Nahx," Topher says, exasperated. "What kind of creature would try to annihilate an entire species, destroy a civilization, then take benevolent interest in one ordinary girl?"

Rather than protest that he called me "ordinary," I let it hang there between us for a moment.

"I should take you back to the barn, or back to the base," Topher says.

"What? What for?"

He steps closer to me and leans over to speak in my ear. "If there is a Nahx following you, even if it means you no harm, what do you imagine its plan is for the rest of us?" This gives me pause. I hadn't thought of this. "I think we should talk to Liam about it," Topher says.

"Liam? Are you joking? He's a half-wit."

"He's still our commander on this mission."

"Ugh, Toph. We're not the army. He's not really a commander. It's all just cosplay."

"With live ammo and a real alien enemy. There has to be some kind of order, don't you think?"

He has a point. But Liam knowing about the Nahx can only be bad. He will send me back, or accuse me of colluding, or worse. Either way, he's not likely to let me continue on the mission. And I'm not going to leave Topher.

"Look, forget it," I say.

"Raven . . ."

"No, I mean it. Forget it. There's no way I'm going back to the base. We have a plan. Look for survivors. Look for supplies. That is the only thing keeping me from completely cracking up." I glance over and see Topher frowning at me. "Don't tell Liam, please?"

"Fine, but stay close to me."

I give him a friendly shove. "Why? You scared?"

It sounds like a joke, but I know it's true. We're both scared. I steel myself for what we will find today. And Topher doesn't reply to my joke as we walk on in a silence so persistent it starts to feel brooding.

"Tucker would want me to protect you," he finally says.

God. That doesn't really help.

The first thing we see is the sign welcoming us to Calgary. POPULATION 1.1 MILLION AND GROWING! it proudly proclaims.

Liam poses in front of the sign, a stupid grin on his face. Several of the other soldiers laugh as they record it with Liam's camera. I don't find it very funny, especially as we pick through the rubble of bombed houses and streets.

Leaving the surface streets, we march down onto a wide freeway, which cuts into the city like a canyon. High stone walls rise on either side of us, giving us a small amount of cover, but I still feel horribly exposed. The sky is bright and blue, and though there is no wind, it is bitterly cold. The quick march is all that keeps me from freezing where I stand. After a few minutes we come upon some cars strewn untidily over the road, like children's toys.

There are remains in each car, each precisely punctuated with a dart to the forehead, each perfectly preserved. Liam pops open the hatchback of one of the cars. It is piled with boxes of food, bottles of water, clothes, and blankets— provisions for an escape that was never made. "Jason!" he says to one of his recruits. "When we're done, come back this way and clean this all out into the car with the most fuel. Then . . . borrow it."

"Check," says Jason without adding what I'm sure we're all thinking: *If we get out of this alive.*

We reach a wide tunnel, where the highway travels under the city streets, and march into it, clicking on flashlights. The tunnel is dark and cold, unlike our underground home, but it is flat, and surprisingly empty. We plod along in the dark, silent but for the sloshing of our boots.

"Anyone remember where this goes?" Liam says. "I don't think this was built last time I was here."

Mandy answers. "It comes up near the Stampede grounds, I think."

"What else is around there? Is there a mall?"

"No," she says. "But Shoppers is there." She closes her eyes and points around in the lost world she is imagining. "To the west of the grounds, down from the overpass."

After a few minutes the light changes, and soon we reach a curve that leads to the tunnel exit. Another tunnel snakes off in one direction, and a ramp climbs up to the ground level. Liam turns and walks backward.

"We need to check out the store," he says, pointing up the ramp.

Sawyer stops him. We all fall in behind him. "What?" Sawyer says. "We're starting on the other side of the river. Their neighborhood." He thumbs toward me and Topher. "We take the other tunnel. It goes under downtown."

Liam sneers at us. "The mission is to look for survivors and to scope out food and supplies, not to visit their friends. The most likely places are here in the downtown core. It had the highest density. It's the farthest from the firebombed areas. And there are a lot of places to hide. We can scope the suburbs next."

He's infuriatingly right. The downtown area is riddled with deep, spiraling underground parking garages and shopping malls. They're prone to filling with water during storms but perfect places to hide during a bomb attack. As close as we had to public bomb shelters in more peaceful times. And to

hide from a species that has admitted they prefer high elevations, what better place than underground? I look at my camp
mates. None of them seems to be able to form an argument.

Liam looks smug. "Volunteers to scout?" he says.

My hand shoots into the air.

I watched the other Eighth burn and those who shot and burned him march smartly back to the compound like nothing happened. I lay on the road behind the car, watching the flame that burned hot and blue. Eighth didn't move. I don't know whether the shot in the neck killed him or the fire, but I knew he wouldn't get up. In theory our armor is fireproof, but this was something else, something more than fire. They were done with him. They weren't going to bring him back. I wonder why he didn't run. He must have known that they'd come for him, they'd kill him. It was almost as if . . .

I twitched then, under the car, and a sliver of light appeared in my mind, as though I glimpsed something behind a door. I carried that sliver with me along the dark road back to the city. There were humans. I saw humans. I saw something so beautiful it doesn't have a name. But I wandered away. It's hard to focus without the buzzing directives. My mind leaps above the sludge with insights that seem to come from nowhere. There is more than one way to be free, I think, as the image of the other Eighth burning with blue fire plays back behind my eyes. I don't have to do this. I can walk away.

I'm free, I sign to myself. *I'm defective.*

Dead. Stopped.

It is quiet now. I think the mission is finished. The humans are finished. I've been pressed into a dark corner, between a brick wall and a large metal box for I don't know how long. I'm too scared to move.

I put my hands over my eye mask to shut out the day and try to see the sliver of light I saw by the car. I try to peel it open and look past it, but I can't. After a few hours it presses closed and is gone.

In the end five of us go. Liam feels a tight-knit team works better together. Or maybe he wants to get rid of us. Either way, myself, Topher, Xander, Sawyer, and Mandy are to scout the downtown core for forty minutes and return with our report. The rest will wait in the tunnel for our return. If we don't return after an hour, two scouts come after us. If *they* don't return, the mission is a bust, I guess.

When we leave the tunnel, cautiously emerging into the daylight, Sawyer sighs theatrically.

"Ahhhhh, feel that? Hear it?" he says. "That's the sound of the world's biggest plonker receding in the distance." He leans over and speaks directly into the camera Liam reluctantly permitted Mandy to strap to her helmet. "Did you hear that, Commander?"

The five of us giggle all the way up to the surface roads. We emerge, as expected, due south of the stadium. Snowdrifts pile up against the glass doors. We move forward to investigate, snow up to our thighs. Behind the glass doors is a scene I should be used to by now. Undecayed and decayed remains dot the wide entranceways and stairs.

"They tried to hide here, I guess," Xander says.

We continue, hugging the west side of the high stadium walls. Hundreds of cars are parked in a seemingly endless parking lot. Most of them, for a change, are empty. Sawyer opens the gas tank on a few of them and checks the contents.

"There's a lot of fuel here," he says. "We need to think of how we can get it back to the base. We should have come here weeks ago."

"We were waiting to be rescued," I say. "Shelter in place. Remember?" It almost sounds funny now.

On the other side of the parking lot, down a narrow street from the pedestrian overpass, as promised, is Shoppers, one of the ones that claims to have a large "food essentials" section. Its front windows are intact, but the door is locked, and no bodies are visible through the glass. Outside the glass are two bodies, and unbelievably, two rifles and two pistols, still loaded.

There's something unspeakably sad, I think, about two men spending their last minutes on Earth guarding food that no one will ever eat, medicines and drugs that no one will ever use. Then I remember this store could hold the goods vital for the survival of the base and silently thank the two dead guards, while Sawyer and Xander help themselves to their guns.

"Let's check this out and then poke around a bit farther into town," Sawyer says. He jangles the locked door. "Stand back."

The next second, one of the windows comes crashing down with a deafening cascade of glass. We step through.

"Right, pair up. Topher with Xander, Rave with me. Mandy, you stand watch; you're the best shot. Scope out the entire store. Exits, entrances, hidey-holes, the back room, bathrooms, everything. If the whole crew comes back here, we will need at least an hour uninterrupted. I want to know this place inside out."

Sawyer and I head left to the end of the store, while Topher and Xander head right. Mandy stands with two guns raised at the front of the store.

Sawyer leads us down the first aisle, casually perusing the shelves. He begins to pocket things. I look at him, eyebrows raised. "Matches," he says.

"We should look for medications, too," I say, thinking of the list Mandy has given us all. "Insulin, penicillin, sedatives, and, uh . . . and hearing aid batteries and—"

Sawyer raises his hand to stop me. "Right. But trust me about the matches."

I quickly stuff as many into my thigh pockets as I can. Then we move on.

We reach the end of the store. There are two double doors to our left. I poke my head through, noting a storeroom lined with packed shelves, and a large rolling door to the back.

"Exit there, closed," I say, letting the doors swing shut with a rusty squeak.

We turn and head down the next aisle. It seems to be picnic type food in all colors and textures and sizes of glass jars and plastic bags.

"Condiments," Sawyer says, turning down the aisle. "God, I've missed Tabasco." He slips a bottle into his pocket.

As we head down the aisle, there's a noise behind us. I turn to look, but Sawyer doesn't notice.

"Olives!" he says. When I turn back to him, he's opening a jar and popping small black olives into his mouth.

I hear the noise again. This time I recognize it as the rusty creak of the swinging doors.

"Wait here," I whisper, and tiptoe back to the end of the aisle. Poking my head around, I see the swinging door. Still. Nothing there.

I turn back to Sawyer. He's grinning and shoveling olives into his mouth as I jog back to him.

"Anything?" he says with his mouth full.

"When we come back, we'll need to post guards on that door."

We reach the end of the aisle and are back in the front of the store. I look over to where we left Mandy. She's not there.

My throat gets tight, and I grab Sawyer by the wrist and pull him back into the aisle.

"Where's Mandy?" I whisper.

Sawyer puts the half-eaten jar of olives back on the shelf among some jars of baby food. He draws both his guns, and quietly, muffling the sound inside his jacket, clicks the safeties off.

I draw my own pistol and do the same.

"Under the chin," I whisper, through teeth clenched with the effort of not chattering. Sawyer pokes his head around the end of the aisle and takes a look. He curses under his breath as he ducks back. We stand there, straining to hear. I hear footsteps crunching through the broken glass.

"Did we see any hidey-holes?" Sawyer whispers with a wry look. I shake my head.

"Can we get into the back room?"

Just then we hear heavy footsteps in the aisle next to us. I desperately want to call out Topher's name, but I know better. Sawyer puts a finger to his lip and points down to the bottom of the shelves. I carefully slip down to the floor and turn to look under the small gap between the shelf and the floor.

There are four sets of Nahx boots there. I turn up to Sawyer, and the look he gives back to me is more apologetic than anything else. He points to me, then to the back of the store where the storeroom is. I shake my head, *NO*. He points to his shoulder angrily. He's not properly uniformed, but if he were, that is where his lieutenant's insignia would be. He points at me again, forcefully, then to the back of the store. I look at him and I suppose my eyes must show some acquiescence. *Good-bye*, he mouths. He holds up four fingers, three fingers, two, one.

I leap up and run in one direction while he runs in the other, yelling profanities at the top of his lungs. I slam through the swinging doors as I hear four gunshots and then the whine and *thunk* of three dart guns.

Then silence. *Sawyer is dead*, I think. I squeeze my eyes shut. Tears will blur my vision. I need my vision.

I press my back against the dirty wall. Looking to my left I see a small open door, behind which is a toilet. I'm not hiding in the toilet again. An exit is what I need. I poke my head around a tall shelf to the rolling door at the back.

It is now open, and a Nahx transport is parked in the loading bay.

My heart is pounding. *How did they know we're here? How did we not hear them?* I don't want to consider that it was the Nahx from the trailer. Maybe he has been following us all this time, leading us into a trap. I can't think that.

I crawl back over to the swinging door and poke my head up to look through the grimy glass windows. There are no Nahx in my field of vision. None of my friends, either. Where are Topher and Xander? Did they find a hidey-hole on the other side of the store? Or another exit?

Run, I think. This is not the time to hide. I need to run back to the others. Find Topher first and get the hell out of there. This mission is a bust. Sawyer is almost certainly dead and so is Mandy, if she didn't give the signal. The Nahx must have seen us coming. They must have been watching all this time.

Silently, I slip through the swinging doors, easing them closed so that they don't squeak. Now I'm back in the main store. I poke my head into the aisle where I left Sawyer. It's empty. I stand still, straining to hear anything. Down the end of the aisle I can see two more transports silently hovering outside the broken glass door. How can they be silent? I've heard their engines wailing before. This must be some kind of muffler or noise-canceling thing.

My eyes sting. Now I know I'm dead too; we all are. I edge my way along the back of the store until I can poke my head down the next aisle.

Sawyer's body lies there, down the end, two darts in his chest and a pile of tumbled, broken jars around him. The smell of vinegar makes me nauseous.

At least he got to eat a few olives before he died is the stupid thing that pops into my head. The next thing I think of is Topher, and how losing him will feel. He's not perfect, but he doesn't deserve this. He should be searching for his parents, or back at the base shagging some willing girl. Or on his vengeance quest, at least, in Tucker's name.

I tiptoe down the aisle to Sawyer's body. He lies on his back, eyes open, staring at nothing, a pistol still clutched in one hand. My mind fills with dead friends: Felix, and Tucker, and Lochie, and Mandy. I'm never going to see any of them again. I'm probably never going to see anyone again. I pull one of the darts out of Sawyer's chest, break the sharp tip off, and pocket it. This seems to make sense. I ease the safety back on his pistol and tuck it into my jacket.

Edging back, out of sight of the transports in the front windows, I walk the length of the aisle. It takes forever, since I have to move like a ghost to prevent the matches from rattling in my pockets. Every muscle is clenched with the effort of remaining silent. When I reach the top of the aisle, I hear the heavy footfalls of at least three Nahx. They are feet away from seeing me. Quickly, I lie down on the floor, facedown. At the last minute I pull the dart out of my pocket and wedge it under my neck. I close my eyes and hold my breath. Hopefully, there is more than one team in here. Hopefully, they don't have some way to communicate who they have and haven't killed. Hopefully, they won't shoot me again for good measure, the way they did with Felix.

Now I know the meaning of hope. It's what tethers you to the land of the living. Lose that and you die.

The heavy footsteps turn down the aisle. They approach slowly and stop above me. One of them nudges my thigh. I tense my neck muscles to keep the dart wedged. Everything inside me is screaming, praying they won't notice that there are no black veins on my neck. I count to myself to keep from exploding. It feels like I've been holding my breath forever. Finally, the footsteps move away. I follow the sound of them to the far end of the aisle and exhale gently when they disappear. I lie there for a long time. It feels like an hour. Finally, I dare to open my eyes and move. I crawl down the aisle again, past Sawyer's body, and peek out to the front window.

The transports are gone.

I stand and move into the front of the store, walking in turning circles, two guns cocked and drawn in front of me. Behind a bench near the window we came through, I find Mandy. She has a dart protruding from one eye. Her face is a maze of dark lines. Oily silver blood drips from her nose. Her helmet camera is smashed on the floor.

Topher, I think. *Please don't be dead.* I'm not ready. I'm not ready to lose him, too.

I move along to the other side of the store, where Topher and Xander started their search. There are large open bins full of rotting and dried-out fruits and vegetables. Stacks of boxes and piles of empty buckets provide some cover. I edge behind a stack of croutons.

Silence. Looking around I take note of the details of this side of the store. The windows are out of sight. The swing doors to the back are at the other end. If Topher and Xander were here when the Nahx arrived, they might not have been seen. I slide along the floor, low and stooped, checking behind each bin and stack of boxes. I don't dare call out. There might still be Nahx somewhere. I reach the back of the section, where large high refrigerators line the walls. They are full of milk cartons. One section of the cupboard is empty. I glance at it and move on, but something stops me. I take another look. There is a clear but grimy plastic curtain at the back of the fridge. *A hidey-hole.*

I carefully open the fridge. When I've gotten it open, I crouch down and strain to see through the plastic curtain. Behind it seems to be a small room, stacked high with boxes and boxes of milk. Or what used to be milk, I think. Probably yogurt by now.

I take one last look behind me, checking for Nahx. The last thing I want to do is lead them into Topher and Xander's hiding place, if they're in here. When I'm satisfied that no one is watching, I tuck away my guns and crawl into the cupboard and through the plastic curtain, easing the door closed behind me.

The room is very dark. I take a moment for my eyes to adjust. I can't see any movement, but there are half a dozen places to hide. *Would a Nahx hide in here?* I wonder. I doubt it.

"Topher?" I finally whisper.

"Raven?" It's the most beautiful sound I've ever heard.

I find them behind a stack of whipping cream.

Xander is curled up in a corner, a pistol propped on each knee. Topher is wedged in beside him, with his crossbow loaded.

"Hide or run, huh?" he says.

I've never wanted to hug two boys more. Impulsively, I grab Topher and kiss him on the top of the head. Xander leans his head over obligingly, and I plant one on him, too.

"Did you have a gun?" I say, eyeing Topher's crossbow. He shakes his head. I dig Sawyer's pistol out and hand it to him.

"Mandy and Sawyer?" Topher says, tucking the pistol into his waistband.

"Dead," I say. Topher hangs his head between his legs and sighs heavily. Xander just looks stunned. He turns and looks at the wall.

"Are the transports gone?" Topher says, looking up.

"The ones out the front are, but there was one in the back, too, and a bunch of Nahx guarding the back door."

I look at the two boys, taking in the terror and hopelessness in their faces. What are we doing here? This scouting foray was all Liam's idea. By rights he should be dead under a counter with a dart in his eye. He should be lying in a pile of broken pickle jars.

"I'm going to murder Liam when we get back," Xander says.

"Yes, me too." I say, and don't bother reminding him Topher and I were the ones who cooked up the suicidal plan to come back to Calgary. "Where's the other door to this room?"

Topher points over to a wall, where in the dark I can just make out the outline of a door. It has a small window, too.

"Have you checked?"

"Not recently," Topher says. "Last time there were still four Nahx wandering around in there."

As quietly as I can, I get up and move to the door. The round window is so high that I have to overturn a plastic crate and stand on top to see out. I poke my eyes above for a micro-second, but don't see any movement in the storeroom on the other side.

"It's clear," I say.

"Are you sure?" Topher says.

I'm not sure. And I indicate this with a casual shrug that seems out of keeping with the deadly game we're playing.

"How long can we stay in here, do you think?" Xander asks.

"Until they find the door," Topher says.

I step down from the crate and rejoin the boys on the floor behind the whipping cream.

"You can get out the front," I say.

"What if they hear or see? They're only about a hundred feet away."

"They're going to be distracted."

Topher grabs my wrist. "No! No way! We can wait them out."

"I don't think so." I pull my wrist away. "They are searching the area. They are settling in. I'm sure they know very well that we are a recon group. They're waiting for the rest to arrive." Topher starts to protest, but I stop him. "Which they will," I continue, "if we don't get back with word. That was the arrangement, remember? The others come through after an hour. We've been here for forty minutes already. You have to get back to the tunnel before more people walk into a trap."

Topher's face hardens. "Raven, no. You can get back to the tunnel. Get past them somehow."

He's grasping for some more acceptable outcome than the one Sawyer gave to me. An extra twenty minutes of my life seems like a lot to die for. But I guess if that left me to help Xander and Topher get away, it was worth it.

"I'm not letting you go," Topher says.

"I'll go," Xander says.

"No!" Topher and I say in unison.

"No, it's okay," Xander says. "I don't have to go back out through the storeroom. If I go back out into the store through the milk and get to the front exit, I can make enough racket to draw them forward from the back room. I can outrun them if I get out into the parking lot and stay low. They won't get me. You can get out the back. Meet up at the tunnel. Then we all bug out of here."

Topher and I are silent for a moment.

"That's a *terrible* plan," Topher says.

"It's better than *her* plan."

"We haven't checked the door," I point out. "Maybe this door doesn't open from the inside."

Topher looks daggers. He gets up and steps over to the door, trying the handle. It turns and clicks, surprisingly loud. We all cringe at the noise. Topher looks through the round window and sighs.

"Nothing," he says. "They might not even still be at the back. How do we know the last transport hasn't taken off?"

"We don't," I say. "Listen, out this door and down the other end of the storeroom is a door to the main store. We can slip out of here without being heard. There's a chance we can all make it to that door, out into the store, and through the front window without them knowing about it. We just need to be quiet. They probably don't even know we're here. We can all leave together."

"I prefer that, I have to admit," Xander says.

Topher thinks for a moment. "Okay, better plan. We stick together. Everyone ready?"

"No," Xander and I say in unison. But we stand up anyway, drawing our weapons, and Topher slowly, silently, opens the door.

We emerge into the storeroom. Topher eases the door closed behind us and leads us down one wall, behind a shelf piled with brightly colored boxes of cookies. Xander grabs one and shoves it under his jacket.

We slowly make our way along the wall. I can still hear the buzzing of the transport outside the loading bay, but so far we have seen no sign of Nahx. They might have already boarded, ready to leave. Or, they might be waiting for us outside the swinging doors.

We turn, and Topher holds his hand up to stop us. He pokes his head past the shelf and ducks back, making a face. He holds up three fingers.

Three Nahx, I think. Three dart guns. If we run, we're moving targets, and much harder to hit. Maybe one of us will get back to the others to warn them. Then again, maybe the Nahx have already found them in the tunnel and inserted a dart neatly into each and every forehead.

Topher edges forward again. The swinging door is a few feet away, but to reach it we have to move from behind one shelf to another, then cross to the door, risking being seen. In fact, it's not a risk. It's almost certain; we *will* be seen.

Topher turns to us. One look at his face and I know what he's thinking. I've seen that look before, on Sawyer's face.

No, I mouth. *No, no, no*, I think. There has to be some other way out of this. All three of us need to have some chance at getting out of here. I've already forgotten what Xander's plan was and what my plan was. All I want to do is grab Topher and Xander by the wrist and drag them to safety. These are the people I have left in my life. Left in the world, maybe. This is it.

I have a feeling like I'm going to start laughing, and pinch my lips together to suppress it. Topher peeks out from behind the shelf again, and before I can stop him, he dives across the opening and behind the other shelf. He holds there for a good minute, but nothing happens. It starts to become real to me that the Nahx by the loading dock don't know that we're here. If they did, they'd be looking for us. We might have a chance to get out of this alive.

Topher stands behind the shelf and beckons to us both. I shove Xander forward. He pokes his head out from behind the shelf, takes a breath, and dives across to the other shelf.

Topher pulls him back, and they both cower there for a moment. There still isn't any reaction from the Nahx in the dock. Topher beckons to me silently. I look at him. He is white-faced and wild-eyed. Behind him Xander is trembling, scared as a child in the dark. Topher beckons me again. I shake my head.

Topher gives me a look, telling me silently, with his eyes, that he knows my plan and he doesn't approve.

Go, I mouth. His face crumples. He shakes his head. *Sorry*, I mouth. Then with a heave, I push my shelf over.

Boxes and cans come crashing down. I give Topher and Xander a final look that says, *If you don't run, this has all been for nothing*. Xander grabs Topher's arm and they run. I watch them smash through the swinging doors just as the Nahx appear inside the loading bay. I turn and bolt back into the refrigerator, slamming the door behind me. My hope is that the Nahx don't know about the plastic curtain, and I can make my escape that way. It's my only hope, slim as it is.

I push over as many stacks of whipping cream and milk as I can. Sour smells so terrible that I nearly vomit waft up, but I manage to keep myself together until I can dive back through the plastic curtain. Soon I'm wedged into the small milk cupboard once more, dripping sour-smelling goo. I reach up and try to push the glass door open. It doesn't move. Behind me I see the large door pushing against the piles of milk and cream and the muzzle of a dart gun. I pull my pistol from my jacket, cock it, and fire directly through the glass. It shatters around me.

Ears ringing, I roll forward through the broken glass and jump to my feet among the ruined food.

Run or hide? Run or hide? I could find somewhere to hide among the fruit and vegetable displays. Maybe bury myself in rotten bananas. Or I could run for my life, back outside and through the parking lot, past the stadium and down the ramp into the tunnel. I have half a second to decide. In that second I hear the roar of the transport engines firing up to full power outside. They have stopped hiding. And so have I.

I choose run.

EIGHTH

Eventually, I think I will die. Seeing the other Eighth burn made me think it's possible, at least. That thought is something of a comfort, because I can't think of any other way for this to end. I could wait or try to figure out how to hasten it. Or I could go back up to the mountains, back to the pine needles where the air is thin enough for me to take my armor off. I could think more clearly then, make a decision, one way or another. In the meantime, I stand swaying on my feet a bit and reach out to rest my left hand on the wall.

I can hear transports nearby. They fly silently sometimes, but without the sound dampeners, the noise is distinctive, aggressive, like a slice through the quiet sky. They fly like that only if they've been seen, if they are in pursuit of humans who know they are being chased.

The transport howls overhead. I could join the chase, catch the human maybe. That's what I have been instructed to do, right? But the silence in my head confuses me. I have no directives. I have no weapon. We store our weapons before being locked up. And I escaped. I'm free. Or defective. My brain doesn't seem to be working very well.

I wonder if I can string five thoughts together.

One, I turn in the direction of the noise. There is a slight buzzing in my mind, like something not quite strapped down properly, or a door blowing open in the wind. It's more like a memory of buzzing, something recorded from my missing transponder. *Dart the humans*, it tells me. But I don't want to.

Two, my rank is Eighth. It's a low rank, but I still tried to do as I was told. I creep out of the alley and onto the empty street.

Three, I should have someone with me, an Offside. She flew away. Died. Stopped. The thought of her makes my jawbone ache. I follow the sounds of the transports. They are not far away. Maybe that's a better choice than being alone.

Four, spiderwebs and sunsets. What does that have to do with anything? I need a weapon. I need to find a weapon. A large, round building rises ahead of me. I see the transports hovering above it.

Five, my mission is . . . something about a human girl. I catch a glimpse of her.

Running.

RAVEN

I dive through the broken front window, get completely airborne, and crash down on the pavement about ten feet outside the store. I don't slow down to look behind me. The parking lot and the cover of the cars is right across the street. My mind is working nearly as fast as my legs. The rest of the mission is in the tunnel, underground. If these Nahx are anything like I hope they are, they won't follow us underground. *If I can just make it back to the tunnel.*

I hear a loud noise behind me but don't look back. A shadow darkens the sky—a transport. It swoops over me. I dive down and roll under a car and keep rolling until I'm three cars away. The first car explodes in a cloud of flame and smoke. I lie there for a second, taking account of all my limbs and bones. Nothing appears to be broken, yet. I can still make it. The shadow of the transport skims over the pavement next to me, then moves away. I take a deep breath, roll out from under the car, and leap to my feet, running before I'm even fully standing.

A wild wind rises up, blowing snow and debris everywhere. I'm thankful for it, even though it turns my exposed skin to ice. The cloud of snow might do much to conceal me from the transports or even the Nahx on the ground. I risk a glance behind me. It doesn't look like any of them followed me on foot. That transport was probably the one from the loading dock.

As I run, I scan the sky. The stadium looms up ahead of me. If I can reach that I'm almost safe. Staying close to the wall will protect me somewhat from the transport. Where are Topher and Xander? Did they come this way? I don't see any sign of them. The image of Sawyer and Mandy, poisoned by darts, flares in my mind, and I can't separate it from Topher's and Xander's faces, the last time I saw them, before I pushed the shelf over. It was only a few minutes ago, but it feels distant already. My mind is playing tricks with time. I feel like I've been running forever.

I reach the wall of the stadium and stop for a moment, my breaths coming fast, each one freezing my lungs a little more. I take in my surroundings. The parking lot is clear, apart from the smoke still rising out from the exploded car. The wind has died down a bit. I can't see the Nahx transport.

I turn and begin to run down along the side of the stadium, keeping as close to the wall as possible. It curves around and away from the tunnel entrance slightly, but I follow it regardless. I need to get right to where I can sprint down into the tunnel in a straight line without having to dodge parked cars. That means I need to get past the parking lot.

I jump over a dark shape by one of the doors, realizing

afterward that it is a corpse in a tattered snowsuit. I move into a doorway for a second, taking another look around. Clear to the tunnel, I think, all clear. I can see the tunnel entrance beckoning me. It's dark and deep and safe-looking. I coil up my energy to make the fastest sprint of my life. I check to the left, to the right, above me.

When I look down, there are two Nahx emerging from the tunnel entrance.

No, no, no, I think. *I'm seeing things.* I blink a few times. When I look again, I see it's not Nahx after all; it's Topher and Xander. They see me and wave. I wave them away. Then they look up. A transport looms overhead.

"Go!" I scream. Xander grabs Topher's arm and tugs him back into the tunnel. I count on the fact that Nahx can't hear outside their transports. I have no way of knowing if this is in fact the case—I just hope. So much hope, I don't know where it all came from.

I edge back to where I don't think the transport hovering above can see me and try to think. It's not far to the entrance of the tunnel. I know I could weave back and forth, and this might prevent them from hitting me with a dart, but whatever they hit that car with was no dart; and I don't imagine one would have to get all that close to kill me.

I pull out my pistol. Of course I know that a bullet can't penetrate the transport, but it makes me feel better nonetheless. I take a quick glance upward and see the transport still hovering.

"Damn it." Up until that moment I had been pretty confident I would make it back to the tunnel. Well, except for the car exploding; that was a bit of a low point. Curling back into the doorway, I try to think. As I lean back on the glass door, it moves. I turn and push it. It's unlocked.

Without a millisecond's thought I push the door open and jump inside. There are human remains strewn throughout the large concrete entranceway and up the stairs. It's hard to believe, but I've never been in this stadium before. I always felt that watching sports was pointless, especially football and hockey. They always seemed like bloodfest fights to the death, like the gladiators or something. I suppose martial arts are too, now that I think of it. I wonder if this was why the Nahx kill us. I get that they wanted our planet. They've made that pretty clear. But why kill all of us? What kind of threat are we? Maybe it's a game for them.

I move quickly along the curved hallways around the stadium. If this is anything like I think it should be, it will have exits evenly spaced along the whole curve. I quickly formulate a plan to circumnavigate to the other side of the stadium. If the Nahx think I am trying to get into that tunnel, they will never stop watching it. So I will have to stop trying to get into the tunnel, at least that way.

If I exit the stadium exactly opposite from the entrance

that faces the tunnel, I should come out right by the river. I can climb the fence and walk over the ice back to where the tunnel comes off the freeway. It is a pretty good plan. Well, it might get me killed, but it's all I've got.

As I walk I keep a close eye on the glass doors to my left. I can't see any evidence of the Nahx or their transports. That is a good sign. Maybe there are only those three transports around. It still doesn't explain what they are doing here, but at least it gives me a feeling that I might have a chance, however remote, of getting out of this alive.

I pass three doorways, four, five. Suddenly, I realize I have no real way of knowing when I am exactly opposite from the tunnel exit, since the stadium is basically round. I curse loudly, then nearly apologize to the dead that surround me. I am trying not to look at them. There are many children among the remains, and babies, deader than dead in their dead parents' arms.

Two doors later I find what I have been hoping for: a map of the stadium and the surrounding streets. The map shows that the tunnel entrance is due south of the stadium, and that the stadium entrance I came in by was called E. I am now at Entrance J. I need to go out Entrance A. That will take me directly across from where I came in.

The streets west of the stadium are laid out in a neat grid of straight lines. Each of them is labeled with a name or number.

I try to commit some of the names to memory. I've walked these streets before, but it feels like another life. If there are signs on the streets, that might help me find my way if I have to run that way instead of taking the river. *North, then east, then south*, I say to myself. *Stay close to the buildings. Keep low.* Backup plan. I can make it.

I leave the map and continue going around the stadium, keeping the exterior wall to my left. Entrance A appears in front of me. I am seconds away from pushing through the door when something blocks out the gray daylight. I stand there, paralyzed for a second. How did they know? The bottom of a transport begins to descend into the forecourt outside the entrance. I don't take another instant to think. I turn and run up the stairs.

Tripping over bodies and other debris, I launch myself upward three steps at a time, legs burning with effort. At the top of the stairs I push through another door and am greeted by a wall of darkness. Behind me I hear an explosion. The transport has just blown out the entrance doors. This is clearly not about stealth for them anymore.

I let the door close behind me, and the last of the light disappears. I take a tentative step forward, then another. After five steps I reach a step down, then another. I tuck the pistol under my arm and dig out one of the boxes of matches from my thigh pocket. In my state of mind I can barely fish a match out of the box, much less feel my way to lighting it. Finally, by touch, I feel the hard end of the match and rough striking surface. I try and fail to light five matches before finally one bursts to life.

The tiny flame envelops me in a small circle of light. I can't see beyond about five feet in front of my face. There are remains in rows of seats to either side of me. I lean down to look more closely at one. They all have the telltale black spiderweb of veins, but there is no sign of a dart, and I wonder how these people were killed. Perhaps it was some kind of gas. There seem to be a lot of them.

The match burns down, singeing my fingers. I drop it. Behind me I hear footsteps coming up the stairs. Without really thinking, I slither along the row past a body and sit down in the first vacant seat I feel. Then I pull up the hood of my jacket and slump forward in the seat. Feeling the remains in the seat next to me, I pull them down on top of me, so the clothed corpse hangs over me like a protective blanket.

Above me, the doors burst open. Through cracked eyes I see the stadium fill with light from a spotlight. Four Nahx begin walking down the stairs. I hold my breath again. I can see the light arcing around the stadium. I can't believe how large it is, and the hundreds, no thousands, of dead in here. *How did they do this?*

The heavy Nahx footsteps pound down the concrete stairs,

past me and down. From where I rest my head, motionless, I can just see them at the bottom of the long stairway, above the slushy hockey rink. I turn my head to check behind me, slowly and carefully, trying not to let the unfortunate person on top of me slip and clatter to the floor.

There's a Nahx, standing at the end of the row, looking right at me. I freeze. He doesn't move, but continues to stare in my direction. His colleagues below are making some bang-ing noises, and from the corner of my eye I can see their light swinging around in the stadium. I hold my breath, willing the Nahx at the end of the row to move on. But he doesn't.

For a wild, optimistic moment I think that maybe this is the one who spared me in the trailer. Maybe he'll spare me again. I hold on to this delusion until he simultaneously raises a flashlight, bathing me in bright light, and his rifle beside it.

I crash to the floor as two darts *thunk* into the corpse above me. The whine of the rifle recharging is all I can hear as I scramble along the row, slithering like a snake. A dart slams into the back of a seat inches from my head. I pull another dead bundle over me and lunge for the stairs, rolling down them and slamming into the barrier at the bottom. I don't even look where I'm going. As another dart whistles past my ear, I leap over the barrier into the darkness below.

I land badly on my side, my face cracking into the icy con-crete floor. Muscles and bones lanced with pain, I yank my pistol from my jacket and fire indiscriminately into the light above me. After four shots I hear a loud *ding*, and a dart rifle sails down out of the light to land a few feet away. I swing my leg up and kick it, and it goes spiraling into the dark passageway. Then the light itself falls toward me, with the Nahx holding it. He lands above me and effortlessly swipes the gun from my hand. It goes clanking into the darkness.

I scramble for my knife, but the Nahx moves quickly, lunging down and wrenching my arm out. I feel a blaze of pain in my shoulder. With my free hand I grab at his throat, feeling for the weak area under his chin. His grip loosens for a second, and that's all I need. I swing my legs up and wrap them around his neck, contorting and clenching my abdominal muscles until I manage to flip him off me. His head slams down onto the concrete with a satisfying *crack*.

Momentarily free, I use my good arm to drag myself away, down into the deep darkness of the passageway. I have no idea what is at the other end, but if I stay at *this* end, all I will find is death. The pain in my shoulder is strangely empowering, like a hook under my collarbone tugging me away. I look back into the dimly lit stadium and see the Nahx moving again. He turns toward me and without even standing up lunges at least ten feet along the floor to jam a knife into my ankle.

Screaming, I kick out with my other leg, connecting my boot with his armored face. It sends a jarring pain up my leg, but barely seems to touch him. As he yanks the knife out, I kick with that leg and the knife goes sailing away too. He grabs my calf and pulls me along the concrete. Shoulder clenching, I try to raise my own knife, but his fist cracks my forearm away. Beyond all chance I manage to hold on to the knife, but now my arm is numb and useless.

Suddenly, the lights of the other Nahx in the stadium are focused on me, bathing me and my attacker in light. He has one of my arms clenched in his fist. My other arm lies uselessly at my side. I can feel blood pooling around my feet. With his knees the Nahx pins my body and legs to the floor. I shout obscenities at him and writhe like a trapped cat, but it makes no difference. As he looms above me, I can hear the buzzing of his breath, or whatever it is. Behind him, in the light, I see the other Nahx approaching, sloshing through puddles of dirty water, their rifles raised. Now I really am dead. It's over.

Then, somewhere in the stadium, there is the distinctive sound of a gunshot. A human gun. One of ours. I hear a voice shouting. Shouting my name.

Topher, don't do this, I think. *Run. Hide.*

The other Nahx watching us turn and run, taking their light with them. In the dimness I can see my attacker raise one armored fist above my head, knowing full well he can crush my skull with ease. It's all I can do to keep my eyes open. All I see is a blur of black. With my last molecule of strength I lurch back, and his fist connects with my rib cage instead of my face. I actually hear my ribs crack, and I scream out with the crushing of my lung. Vision blurring, I vaguely feel my knife still in my hand. My shoulder roars with pain as I try to move my arm. The Nahx above me raises his fist again.

Two things seem to happen at once. I feel my knife swish out of my hand, and at the same moment it appears in the Nahx's throat, right in the weak spot the videos taught us about. He jolts back, grabbing at his neck. There's a loud hissing noise, and then his weight sags on me, pushing down on my crushed ribs and forcing my last breath out of me. Despite my best efforts, stars float in my eyes, and I see a shadow above me before I disappear into blissful nothingness.

PART THREE
Winter

"There is something in the unselfish and self-sacrificing love of a brute, which goes directly to the heart of him who has had frequent occasion to test the paltry friendship and gossamer fidelity of mere Man."
—EDGAR ALLAN POE, *"The Black Cat"*

S he's so badly injured. I don't know what to do. One arm doesn't seem to fit her anymore, and her blood is draining out, I'm not sure from where.

Precious little human, please don't die.

I gather her up and run, run with my mind filling up with the idea of the sun on her hair and the smell of pine needles and the rushing river. But now she smells sharp and sour, of blood and fear and other things. Tears. Tears. The smell is powerful, terrifying. I stumble away with her. Halfway down the passageway, I find a dart rifle and snatch it up, slinging it over my shoulder.

Where do I go? Out into the light, out into the city. Away from the others, from my people. They didn't see me leave. They were distracted by a human with a gun.

At that moment, like my thoughts spilled out of my head and into the world, I hear the human behind me. He is yelling at me. A bullet pings off my back, another one off the top of my skull. I keep running, leaping up a flight of stairs. When I reach the top and turn to look at the human, something slices into my shoulder from front to back, between the armor plates.

The pain feels familiar, hot and harsh. I reel back and have to catch my balance. In the dim at the bottom of the stairs I see the human, with his weapon raised. He looks unnervingly familiar, too.

"GIVE HER BACK!" he screams.

He can't mean this little human. She's mine, isn't she?

Please don't die. You can't die.

I can run much faster than the human with the weapon, even with his arrow sticking out of my shoulder, even carrying the girl. I run and run and run. Up into the street, away from the human, away from my people, I run until I can no longer hear the human yelling or his footsteps behind me, until the sky grows quiet, until I find a high tower. My mind buzzes again, like there is something I've forgotten to do, or something I shouldn't have done, or something is rattling loose.

Who was that human who was chasing us? I look down at the broken human in my arms. She is the only thing that is keeping my mind tethered inside my head.

Her heart is beating fast now, but strong, too. There is blood on her face and her legs, but it's not pouring out of her anymore. I cling to her, my hand wrapped around the hole in her calf. Her blood oozes through my fingers. She is curled up in my arms as I find the stairs and start upward.

I sense movement first—upward movement. I feel myself rise, but it's not a smooth ride. It's soothing, though, like being rocked, and I drift off again. When I come back, the movement hasn't changed, but I can now see. There's a bright light rocking above me and dancing on dark gray walls. I see the number 18, then a few moments later the number 19. Then a shock of pain makes me close my eyes again.

The third time I awake, the rocking continues. This time I am able to distinguish that the numbers, which are now up to 31, are on doors. I blink and my vision clears even more. Someone is carrying me. With horror I realize it is a Nahx.

I try to move, but he clasps me tightly, my arms pinned at my sides. Struggling causes a pain like none I've ever felt before, and I feel my eyes roll back into my head as my attempt to scream for help turns into a moan of agony. The Nahx holds me even tighter, and we plod onward, upward . . . 35, 36, 37. The motion is hypnotic, and though I try to resist, I close my eyes again.

A noise wakes me, a blood-chilling, heartbreaking noise, like an animal, a dog who has been beaten half to death. It takes a full minute to realize I'm the one making the noise.

My senses return, one by one. Hearing—over my own inhuman moaning I hear someone moving nearby, clicking, the sounds of doors opening and closing, something tearing, something rattling. Smell—every negative smell imaginable assails me—the tinny metallic smell of blood, sour milk, urine? Have I pissed myself again? And charcoal, faintly, more the memory of a smell than an actual smell.

Taste—there is bile in my mouth, and blood, gurgling through my moaning. I push it out with my tongue and it dribbles down my chin.

Touch—pain, like I'm on fire. A spike in my calf, a knife in my chest, my whole right side feels like it is hanging, dangling by a strip of flesh. My face feels thick and disembodied, as though it is floating over me, throbbing with blood. The moan threatens to turn into a scream. I wrap my mouth around a familiar word, to try to capture the scream before it utterly destroys me. It comes out as a whimper.

"Topher . . . Topher . . . help . . . please. . . ."

Vision. I open my eyes, seeing only dark at first, but gradually the dark dissolves from the edges in, until I can see blurred details of a room. There are golden, glowing windows to one side, and dark shapes, low modern furniture placed far apart. *Penthouse*, I think. It's like a word in a foreign and ancient language, so far away from what my life has been for the past months that it almost makes me laugh. It's a punch line, for the longest joke in the history of humor. I'm in a freaking *luxury penthouse.* I'm dying in some spoiled bald accountant's bachelor pad.

With my good hand I feel my face gingerly. It doesn't feel like a face; my hair is matted to my forehead and my hand comes away bloody. I close one eye, then the other. They both appear to work. Searching with my tongue, I confirm that all my teeth still seem to be in place. I feel beneath me—leather. I'm lying on some kind of leather bench. I think I'm bleeding all over it.

A rivulet of blood drips back in my throat, and I cough, which sends a spasm of pain through my ribs and shoulder.

"Mama . . ." Tears mix with the blood on my face.

A shadow appears above me.

I react instinctively, launching myself somehow off the bench and onto the hard floor, landing with a bolt of pain that shoots from my skull down to my toes.

The Nahx dives over the bench after me, but I drag myself backward with my good arm, my other arm pressed into my chest.

"No . . . no . . ."

He's so large, so tall, like a hideous giant from a fairy tale. The hand that reaches out for me is metallic, segmented and big enough to crush the life out of me. Did he bring me here to kill me in private? That is somehow a million times more terrifying than being beaten to death in the stadium in front of all those corpses.

He kneels on the floor as I slide backward, leaving a trail of blood on the tiles. My shoulder is on fire and doesn't seem connected to me, like my arm is going to fall off. I stop at the wall, lean back, and clutch myself with my good arm, curling up protectively.

My vision blurs with tears so much that I can barely see him as he crawls after me. He holds his hands up, palms facing me.

"Please . . ." My voice comes out wet with snot and tears and blood. "Please don't kill me. . . ." I must imagine him shaking his head. One hand reaches forward and presses against my neck. I close my eyes, clutching at his wrist with my one good arm. At least a broken neck is fast, I think.

His hand moves over slightly, until it's pressing on my useless shoulder. I try to tear it away, but he's too strong. A nauseating pain shoots from my spine to my fingertips, making me whimper. "No . . . no . . ."

His other hand suddenly grabs my elbow and pulls. The scream of pain that empties my lungs is uncanny, like an army of banshees. It feels like he's going to tear my arm right off. Just as my eyes start rolling back in my head, I feel a jolt and hear a sickening pop as my arm bone slips back into the shoulder socket. The instant relief is almost hallucinogenic.

Streaks of light float behind my eyelids, and I find myself slipping sideways onto the floor.

When I open my eyes, he is sitting back on his heels, watching me. With the golden light from the window illuminating him, I notice something I haven't before. He has a short arrow protruding out of one shoulder. A crossbow arrow. I recognize it; it's unmistakably one of Topher's.

I try to point to it. And my movement seems to draw his attention to it for the first time. He reaches up and pulls on the fletched end. It moves a few inches and then stops. He makes a hissing noise as the arrowhead jams back into his shoulder.

I want to say something, tell him he should cut the fletch off and pull it out from the back, but I can't seem to get my mouth to work. I watch him stand and move over to the window. Gripping the curtain with one hand, he grabs the arrow with the other and pulls it. The first pull removes it only halfway. With the light coming in from the window, I can see his shape silhouetted in shadow as his shoulders rise and fall quickly. He pulls the arrow again. This time it comes out with a wet ripping noise. A brutal hiss escapes from him and he falls to his knees, pulling the curtain down from the window with him. I watch him as he kneels there, forehead on the glass, looking out into the setting sun for some minutes. *If he's a machine, how can he feel pain?* is what goes through my head. Because he looks like a machine. But he's clearly in pain. He balls up the fabric and holds it on his shoulder. When he pulls it away, I can see it's stained with something dark, like blood or oil.

Tossing the curtain and arrow away, he rotates his arm, as though testing it. Then he stares out at the setting sun some more, almost as if he's forgotten I'm here. The light begins to fade, making him harder to see. He's becoming a shadow in front of my eyes. All I can see of him is that he holds his left hand out, as though reaching for something.

I take stock of my condition. My shoulder is back as it should be, but I'm pretty sure that the forearm is broken. Blood is pooling around my ankle, and my breathing is kind of lopsided; broken ribs, I think. Also the side of my face hurts. Nothing broken there, I don't think, but I bet it's not pretty. I've had injuries before, from karate or other sports, but never this bad, and never so many all at the same time. I try to sigh, but it comes out as a whimper.

The Nahx turns and looks at me. He stands up and steps in my direction. Somehow, beyond all things plausible, I drag myself to my feet and stumble for the door, ignoring the shooting pain in my ankle and the jangling of my damaged arm. He leaps back over the bench and meets me at the door.

"Let me go, please," I say, barely above a whisper. "I won't tell anyone." I can hardly breathe. My left lung feels like it is being squeezed with a pair of pliers.

He steps out of the way as I pull the door open to a long

hallway. Without looking back, I take three steps out and stop, swaying, my head filling with sudden heat. He catches me as I fall.

"Don't hurt me," I manage as he eases me down onto the floor and sits back on his heels again. He shakes his head, holding his hands up, palms forward. I didn't imagine it this time. He really did shake his head.

"Can you understand me?"

He nods, leaning over me.

With my good hand I reach up and press on the hole in his shoulder. His thick blood seeps through my fingers. "The boy, the one who shot you with the arrow? Did you kill him?"

He shakes his head.

"Did he get away?"

He nods.

I close my eyes for a moment, feeling him pull my fingers away from his bloody shoulder. As I open my eyes, he brushes a coil of hair from my forehead. I twitch back, repulsed.

"Are you the one from the trailer? Was that you?"

He nods slowly. And maybe I'm hearing things, but I think he sighs. As he reaches for me, I flinch away again, pulling myself backward, pressing against the wall. He sits back on his heels again, his hands on his thighs.

Has he been following me all these months? My teeth chatter against one another, sending shivers of pain into the side of my head. What does he want from me? I have to get away. I have to run away as fast as I can, find Topher, and get back to the others, back to the base. Then I have to disappear somewhere this *thing* can't find me.

The hallway is almost completely dark, except for the weak twilight streaming through the open door to the penthouse. The Nahx kneels there, facing me, though for all I know his eyes could be closed. I try to get a good look at him, but it's too dark and my vision is beginning to blur again. He doesn't seem as large, kneeling and close up, but his armor and mask, if that's what it is, still seem to suck what little light there is. The armor makes a dull clicking noise as he moves, and his breathing is a low buzz, halfway between a sick wasp and the purring of a cat.

The face of his mask is vaguely humanoid, large, glassy, reflective black eye shapes, a ridge where the nose would be, and a kind of grille over the mouth. It reminds me of a gas mask from World War II. There's no sign of the movement in the segmented plates that I remember, no sign of the sharp spines on his face. Maybe that's something that happens during an attack, or when he's frightened. And why would he be frightened now? He could kill me with one finger.

Neither his helmet, mask, nor the rest of his armor looks shiny or new. Instead, it's dirty and there are marks and abrasions like healed scars all over him, including a star-shaped mark on his chest. Is it possible this is his skin? Does it heal? I consider the arrow hole in his shoulder. The bleeding seems to be slowing down. But it doesn't look like blood.

What is he? What does he want? The possibilities are too much to contemplate.

I realize I've been holding my head up. My neck spasms, and I lie back, saying the first word that comes to my mind.

"Tuck . . ." Then the tears are pouring out of my eyes. I stare up at the dark ceiling and give in to it, crying out all the horror that I haven't given full vent to since that day we buried him. The Nahx watches me for a moment, then stands, and leaving the door propped open so some faint light can trickle into the hallway, leaves me there and goes inside.

Who knows how long I lie there? Maybe I pass out from blood loss, or maybe I fall asleep from exhaustion, but when I wake up, I'm lying on a bed, my good wrist shackled to the bedpost.

EIGHTH

I watch her in the dim light from some candles I found and left burning on the little table by the bed. It feels wrong to touch her as she sleeps, but I want to try to treat her injuries. I seem to know things about treating injuries, without knowing how. I focus on her, on the details of her, her smell. Without that effort I will lose myself.

She twitches and gasps. Before I even reach her, she's wailing and tugging at the restraint.

"No . . . uhh, no . . . untie me, please. . . ."

As I kneel beside the bed, she pulls herself as far away as she can get, her shackled arm stretched out. The speed and strength of her emotions is slightly surprising to me. She's crying and furious at the same time.

"Untie me, you piece of shit! You son of a bitch!" Then she closes her eyes and turns away from me, curling up, her bleeding ankle leaving a streak of blood on the sheet. I move to the other side of the bed to face her, but she turns away again. I move back and she turns away. Finally, in desperation, I grab her face and turn it to me. She snarls something I don't quite understand, then spits on me.

I won't hurt you, I sign.

Her good leg swings up and curls around my neck. Before I know what is happening, she has flipped me down on the bed and is crushing my neck between her knees. As I pry them apart, she kicks me hard in my injured shoulder and then in the side of the head. I tumble backward on the floor, my helmet banging on the edge of a chair as I fall.

"Don't fucking touch me!" she yells. I stand, head throbbing, shoulder stinging, and take two steps back. Focus now. This is going to be harder than I thought. I didn't really think at all. I just grabbed her and ran. It seemed like a good idea at the time. Now I take a moment to reconsider my options.

I could leave her, let her die.

No, I can't do that. Not after finding her again. That has to mean something.

I could hope that her injuries aren't as bad as I think they are.

I'm pretty sure they are.

I could try to find her people.

They would kill me. Or worse, my people would kill her.

I could try to knock her out again, like I did in the trailer.

Ah no. Anything but that. Think.

I can overpower her. I'm much stronger than her, despite her fighting spirit. But the thought of it makes me feel sick. There will be screaming and crying. As it is, the scent of her fear nearly chokes me.

Please, I sign. But of course she doesn't know the signs.

Her face is soaked with blood, mucus, and tears. She lifts her injured arm to wipe it, but I think both the bones of her forearm are broken. She gasps and whimpers as her hand flops unnaturally.

There's a bath in the next room. I step in there to grab towels, and when I come back she has hauled herself up to the bedpost and is biting at the binding on her wrist. Her mouth is already bloody.

Stop. Stop, I sign. I drop the towels and try to pull her teeth away. She twists her head and bites down on my hand. Hard. There's no way she could bite through the armored glove, but I feel it well enough. I could break her jaw trying to peel her off me. Instead, I pinch down hard on her cheek. She yelps and releases me. A bright red welt blooms on her face. My fingerprints.

Sorry. Sorry. Very sorry.

"Can't you talk? I don't know what those signs mean!" she snarls through bloodied teeth.

Of course she doesn't. I could try to teach her some of them, but I don't have time. Her leg is still bleeding, her pant leg and boot now soaked with blood. Her arm must be excruciating.

Kneeling again by the side of the bed, I reach forward with one of the towels. I think perhaps she's too tired to move, because though she tenses, she lets me wipe some of the blood from her mouth.

"What do you want from me?"

I set the towels down on the bed. *I want to fix you.*

"What does that mean?"

I point to her arm. *Broken.* That's an obvious one. *Broken.*

"My arm is broken. Yes, I know."

I turn the "broken" sign upside down and do it again, back-ward.

Fix. Broken. Fix. Broken.

"You want to fix my arm?"

Ah, thank you. I nod. I point to her leg and hold up one finger.

"First my leg?"

My mind floods with giddy relief. I can do this if I can make her understand me. I rest my forehead down on the bed, nod-ding, trying to keep my thoughts from swirling into vapor. When I look up, she's staring at me, eyes wide, swollen, and red rimmed.

"Can I ask you a question?"

I nod.

She looks sick as she begins to speak, and what little color was left drains from her face. "Did you do this to me? In the stadium? Was it you who beat me up?"

RAVEN

He lurches back, like he's been punched. Holding both hands out, palms up, he shakes his head over and over, slowly at first, then faster. I guess that's a no. He lifts his hands up and lets his head fall into them, holding it there, still on his knees by the side of the bed. My mind suddenly flashes back to the video of the Nahx girl being decapitated. It's frighteningly vivid, almost like a waking dream. I must gasp, because he looks up sharply.

A rush of heat starts at my feet and shoots up my body, over my stomach and chest. My neck and face get painfully hot, and I can't help but moan. He dives forward, grabbing a candle from the bedside table, and leans down to look into my face. The candle flickers on his eye mask.

"I feel sick," I murmur. Maybe for both of us, this represents something of a truce. He quickly reaches over to the restraint on my wrist. I don't know what he does, but it clicks open. Just as he helps me sits up, I vomit all over myself. He doesn't even flinch, but pulls a towel from the pile on the bed and mops me up as much as he can. Tossing the towel aside, he places one gloved hand on my forehead.

It feels surprisingly soft, almost like flesh, but cool.

"I have a fever." He nods, laying me back on the pillows. I press my newly freed hand onto my forehead. It's as hot as a sidewalk in the sun, almost as if it could burn me.

He turns and unlaces my boot. My whole leg tingles with pain as he slips it off. The army pants I wear are loose enough that he can push the leg up to my knee, but the blood-soaked thermals underneath are too fitted. He slips a knife from somewhere in his armor. I cringe at the sight of it, then again when he cuts the cloth away, and I see the severity of the wound. It looks like the knife went right between the two bones of my shin, completely through my calf from front to back. It's swollen and kaleidoscope-colored. The blood still seeping out is red mixed with bright yellow pus.

"That looks really painful." The Nahx turns to me, and I imagine a perplexed expression in the tilt of his head. "Just trying to lighten the mood." My words are starting to slur.

I lie back and let the room swim around me. When I look up again, he has a bowl of sudsy water and another pile of towels as well as torn strips of lighter fabric, possibly a sheet. Washing the wound involves the kind of pain people probably go mad from, but I'm already pretty delirious, so I giggle through most of it, when I can keep from whimpering. Maybe the pain is bad enough for me to zone out again, because the next time I look at my leg, it's loosely bandaged in clean, torn sheets.

The next few minutes pass in a haze as he helps me sit up and slips off my layers of coat and sweaters. When he lays me back, wearing just a bra and cotton undershirt, the cool sheets soothe my scorched skin. He reaches forward, uncertainly, delicately, and lifts the side of my undershirt. My ribs are eggplant-colored and puffed up like a cake that's ready to come out of the oven. He runs his fingers over the bruising, and though his touch is achingly gentle, bolts of pain shoot through me.

By this time I think the fever must have risen dangerously. The daylight is completely gone, the scene lit only by candlelight. When I turn my head from side to side, the candles streak in my vision, like shooting stars. My mouth is as dry as the ashes of the burnt forest where . . .

"Was that you too?" I ask, then remembering that he's not privy to my thoughts, add: "By the river. You let us float away?"

He nods, pulling my undershirt back down. That's all the torture in that area for now. As he prods my bruised cheek, I find my words getting thick as uncooked sausages. My lips feel like they are inflated.

"Have you been following me?"

A second passes before he shrugs. There's a small part of me that is outraged by this answer; how can he not know? Either he has followed me or he hasn't. But the fevered part of me understands completely. Sometimes a path is something you float along, not something you make. The path followed me; he just followed the path. That makes a kind of delirious sense.

I try to look at him in the near dark, but he looks more like the absence of himself than anything solid. He's like a negation of a person, the blank space left when a person is lost. How many people did he . . . ? But I can't finish this thought because my eyes fill with tears.

"*Tuck . . .* ," I whisper. "*Tucker. . . .*"

And Lochie, and Felix, and Sawyer, and Mandy. And God knows who else. My parents, Tucker's parents. Xander's family. Millions, billions. All our shared history, good and bad. Gone. It's hard to reconcile this gentle one with that level of destruction.

"Just following orders . . . ," I hear myself mumble. He wriggles his fingers in front of his mouth, and I must be high as a kite, because I understand this sign immediately.

What did you say? What are you talking about? Explain.

"Just following orders, right?" I say, in a wave of lucidity. "I could tell you stories from our history about that. Is that why you do what you do? Walk around with a rifle creating human mannequins? How many of us have you dispatched, anyway?"

He turns away from me, staring out at the dark window. I hear him take a deep, rattling breath in and out. His hands find my broken forearm. The shot of pain makes a red flash in my eyes. He produces a little light from somewhere and shines it down on my arm. I can see a raised, swollen bump there, but no bone sticking out—that's something.

"It's going to really hurt, isn't it? If you set it?"

He doesn't look at me as he nods. He stands, and I see he has the shackle in his other hand.

"Don't. Please. I won't go anywhere. I promise. I can barely sit up."

He hesitates, but tucks the shackle away and looks down at me, his head cocked to the side.

"So," I say. My voice is like two sheets of sandpaper rustling together. "Should we do the arm with screaming or without?"

He makes a circle with his thumb and forefinger. *Zero*. I guess that means no screaming.

"Maybe if I had something to bite down on?" He flicks his head back twice, like a reverse nod, and holds out the hand that I bit earlier.

Really? He's making jokes? I guess I'd laugh if I could, or smile, if my face weren't so mangled. The fever is starting make everything look like it's been decorated in gaudy streamers and glitter, like I'm at a New Year's Eve party.

Wait, he signs. Another unmistakable one. He disappears for a few moments and comes back with several kitchen utensils, some for biting and some splint shaped. He also has, mercifully, a bottle of bourbon.

I don't really like bourbon. I'm not averse to a little under-age drinking, but purloined wine and beer are my usual poisons. Broken prisoners of hostile aliens cannot be choosers, I guess. I uncap the bottle and take a swig. It burns on the way down. I imagine it will probably feel as bad if not worse on the way back up.

While I drink, he wets a cloth and presses into onto my steaming forehead. I wonder if he knows what the fever means. How much can he know about human medical care?

"My leg is getting infected, I think," I say. "Do you know what that means?"

He nods slowly.

"I need antibiotics. Can you look for some? After you do the arm?"

He wriggles his fingers in front of his mouth. *Explain.*

"Antibiotics. Medicine." I blearily recite the words Mandy made us all memorize. "Erythromycin, penicillin, amoxicillin . . . cipro . . . floox . . . flox . . . flux . . . little pills in a little jar."

He leaps up and disappears into the bathroom, returning seconds later with handfuls of pill bottles, which he pours onto the bed. He holds each one under the flashlight and shows me. I try to remember the names I learned from Mandy and the ones I've heard at home. Mom's pills. Jack's pills. The mountain of daily pills Jack's dad would bring with him when he visited. Then I have to blink away that memory, because it's too distracting from my own life-or-death situation. I focus on the tiny typing on the labels instead.

"Antidepressants, I think," I say, studying one. "Antianxiety, anti–blood pressure, anti-cholesterol. Wow. This guy had it all." I push the pills aside. "None of these are any good. Sorry." The Nahx shoves them onto the floor and they rattle away. He taps his eye mask.

Look. Me. Look.

Then he points to the pills.

"You can look after the screaming, yes." I take another gulp of bourbon, trying not to cough. Mostly failing though. I clutch my ruined ribs and moan.

On top of the fever, the bourbon is working its magic. I expect I'll still feel every bit of the pain, but maybe I won't care as much. I tuck the bottle into the crook of my good arm and recap it.

"I think I'm ready now."

I wish there were some way I could turn off my hearing. Her screams will be . . . Hearing her scream in the stadium nearly finished me. I could barely think. I can still barely think, though seeing her again has sharpened my mind a little bit. I remember, at least, that I'm a rebel and a deserter; that's helpful. And I remember pretty much everything about her. I'm not very clear on what has been going on since the last time I saw her though, or how I found her again. Maybe that will come back when I calm down a bit.

Then there's the human who chased us. *Give her back,* he shouted. Does she belong to him? For a moment when I picked her up, I thought she belonged to me, but that doesn't seem right anymore, not like I belonged to Sixth, anyway. But that other human could be looking for her. And I don't know whether she was running away from him. Maybe he treated her as Sixth treated me.

She said his name. Topher. Or Tucker. I'm not sure what I heard. I have no way to ask her.

I need to think, to focus. There is too much sludge churning through me. It's making me confused.

"Are we doing this?" she asks. I kneel down by the bed again.

I've set a bone before, one of my own, I think. That seems like something from behind the door in my mind. I understand the principle of it though. I feel the break a bit first. It's only displaced one of the bones. I check the other one; it seems to be sound. That's good. But I'll have to be careful. I doubt her bones are as strong as mine.

I found a wooden spoon in the kitchen. I give it to her and she clenches it in her mouth, but then pulls it out again. "Wait."

She uncaps the bottle and takes several large gulps, gasping. Then she returns the spoon to her mouth and nods. I have to turn my eyes away from the fear in her face.

Little human, I don't want to hurt you.

I should have taken her when . . . the first time, from the river or the second time I saw her, in that village. I could have taken her up into the mountains with me. None of this would have happened.

I grip her arm. She clenches her teeth and growls. And I do it. I fix it. I pull her arm apart and put it back together over the sound of her screaming.

When it's done, she closes her eyes and shivers and lets me wipe the tears from her cheeks.

Slow sweet muddy death. I need to sit down.

Time seems to pass, or I dream of time passing, at least. The problem is the same time repeats. Over and over the Nahx in the stadium flies down toward me. Sometimes I wake screaming, pain shooting through my rib cage, only to sink back into feverish sleep. Sometimes the dream progresses beyond what actually happened. He kills me in some. In others I become a Nahx like him and turn on Topher as he tries to rescue me, crushing him with my armored fists. In one dream Topher kills the Nahx, then takes me in his arms, pulling me down onto the ground, kissing the blood from my mouth. In another Topher *is* the Nahx, and it is Tucker who rescues and embraces me. Eventually, my dreams degrade into the fat, ill-fitting, and misshapen dreams of fever, with no more fighting or kissing.

Sometimes *my* Nahx is there when I open my eyes and sometimes not. Once I wake to find him spooning something hot and salty into my mouth. I swallow, painfully, and feel the warmth sinking down into me. But the next time I wake, I'm vomiting it all up again. My Nahx appears with a cloth and wipes my face and neck.

"What are you?" I ask, more than once, it seems. He makes signs, but I don't understand them. Sometimes he just shrugs. If he ever gives me a coherent answer, I'm not conscious enough to process it. In the delirium I give him my own designations: monster, demon, killer, alien, machine.

And I blearily remind myself of my own designation: Rage, the fighter, the soldier who won't surrender. Not to this Nahx, not to anyone. And not to death.

I dream of fire. My skin is on fire. I feel the heat rising off me in waves. He lays wet cloths on my head and chest. The pain in my leg takes over my thoughts for a while, until I can't fit a single idea in with it. I lie in ignorant silence, not hearing, not seeing, floating on a bed of knives and hot coals and fire.

How many days this goes on, I don't know. I see sunlight and darkness in approximately equal measures. And I see the Nahx, at my side sometimes and sometimes in the shadows in the corner of the room. If I cry out in pain, it's not long before he appears, and once as he looks at me and checks my wound, I see him shake his head. Does he think I'm going to die? I wonder. Is he preparing himself? And why does he care?

Once I wake in the night, at least I feel that I'm awake, and see Tucker standing by the window, looking out at the dark sky. I will him to turn, to look at me, but he continues to stare out silently. This is what the dead become, I think, grim sentinels who see and hear nothing, who watch the stars. Maybe if I die, I'll see Tucker again.

Another night, after a few days of floating in this fevered world, I lose myself. It takes only a moment. One minute I'm aware, a brief twinkling of lucidity, that my fever has reached some place beyond life and recovery. It's a kind of psychic dressing room where I strip off everything that makes me myself so I can enter into a world where only naked spirits can go. I let go of anger. Anger at my parents, anger at Tuck and Emily, anger at myself. Anger at the Nahx. I let go of them too, my parents, Tuck, Emily, all of them. Even Topher, though he is hard to release. His fingers lock on to mine, but in the end the gravity of what awaits is too strong. He slips away. I let go of rage, and then everything slips away. I slip away from everything. I have no shape, no size, no memory, no name. All I have is what is immediate, what I feel and see. I feel hot. I see fire. I see a shadow move in the fire.

Then nothing.

EIGHTH

S he wakes up screaming. My first instinct is to hold my
hands over my ears.

The pills aren't working. She's going to die. All I can
do now is watch.

Not quite right. I could leave her. Go back to my people.
No one would know.

I should leave her.

I should.

Leave.

Her.

But I can't. I kneel at her bedside, finding her scorching
hand. She clutches at me, but weakly. As her scream subsides,
her trembling spreads up my fingers and arm, into my mind.

Beautiful human. Don't leave me.

I choke. My throat spasms around the tube. The thick fluid
pulses through me. Suddenly, I'm angry, so angry at the heat
in her, the fire that is killing her. I could crush it, break it
down, kill it, kill . . .

Human. Brave girl, get better. Please. You must. Obey me.

Think. Try to think.

If she dies, I'll jump from the terrace. We're forty floors up. The fall would kill me, wouldn't it? I couldn't just walk away from her if she doesn't get up. I can't go back to the mission. I close my eyes and think of that other Eighth burning on the road and wish I could trade places with him. Or that I had stayed with him. I don't want to be alone. And no one would miss me.

Missing. Important.

Sixth? What do I do? Tell me what to do. I have to do something.

Ah, my mind is dripping, slipping away. She is as transparent as a cloud. Her hair lies in wet tendrils around her head. Her face is still black-and-blue and swollen. She smells of death, tears, waste, soap, and pine needles. She's more beautiful than a spiderweb or a dandelion. Or a snowflake.

A snowflake.

The terrace.

Snow.

The terrace door has been open for hours, to let the cold night air in. I carry her outside. A thick layer of snow spreads around us.

There's a little twist in my thoughts. I could leap over the railing with her in my arms. But she would never choose that. She chose life before. She has chosen life over and over. She wants to live.

I was supposed to put a dart in her.

You don't have to do this, she said to me.

Yes, I remember.

You can just walk away.

But I can't, pretty Dandelion. I can't walk away from you.

Please don't kill me, she said. I shook my head. I told her no. I made a kind of promise.

I could never kill her. I could never dart her. Anything but that.

She sags in my arms. Over the wind blowing around my ear sensors, I can no longer hear her heartbeat.

Please don't kill me, human girl.

As I lay her down, her arms flop up by her head. I move them, making wings for her in the thick snow.

Angel.

The word creeps out from behind the door, mocks me with possibility, then slams the door behind itself.

Sixth was an empty green angel in the grass, with blood-black wings. This one is a shimmering ice angel, with snowflakes in her hair.

I never even learned her name.

When the dream starts, it is cold and dark. But as light seeps in, I see I am floating in the lake, with snowflakes drifting down around me. I turn my head to the dock and see Tucker standing there. Or Topher. I can't tell them apart anymore. I try to move, to swim to shore, but the water is frigid. I'm numb, paralyzed. And scared. So terrified. Because there is something under the water coming for me. I can see the ripples getting closer, closer.

On the dock, Tucker yells, but his voice is wrong. He's too sad, too dark, too tense. That's how I know it's Topher yelling. He jumps into the water and swims toward me, as the unknown ripple approaches from the other direction. I float, naked, unable to move or scream. Something emerges from the ripples in the water. A Nahx, *the* Nahx. He reaches me as Topher flails in the cold. The Nahx gathers me and holds me. He says things to me.

I will take you anywhere.

I'm not sure how he has a voice. He has no lips. I want to go to the shore, to the dock, to Topher. But Topher is drowning. I try to tell the Nahx. I try to entreat him to save Topher, but my own lips are numb and swollen. My hands can't move to make the signs.

Please, please.

Topher sinks in the dark water, leaving bubbles on the surface.

I relax my body as the Nahx releases me and sink down, searching for Topher in the murk. The cold permeates my skull and my brain.

Tucker, I will never get you back. You're gone. Like the world, the one I never really appreciated. It was imperfect but all we had.

Topher, loving me would only ever hurt you. All we can be is partners in grief and revenge.

Mom? Can you ever forgive me?

Jack? Can I start calling you Dad?

An armored hand closes around my wrist and pulls me to the surface. "Who are you?" I say. He slips his arms around me again, grasps me tightly, and together we sink to the bottom of the dark lake.

I wake up, lake water choking me, drowning me, though when I cough, it is cold air that comes out. I open my eyes. I'm lying outside, half naked in the cold, in a puddle of water, melted snow, and tears. It is daylight, the sun beats down on me, and I feel almost normal. Numb and cold, really cold, but normal.

Through the glare I see the Nahx kneeling a few feet away, his head resting in his hands on the floor in front of him.

"H-hey."

His head shoots up.

"I'm kind of cold."

He lunges forward and scoops me up.

The sickroom stinks of vomit and other worse things. He steps right through it and along the hallway, setting me down on the wide leather bench in the living room.

Wait, he signs. Like I could go anywhere in my condition. I can barely focus my eyes.

He returns with piles of clean towels and blankets. Wrapping me in a blanket, he dries my head, hands, and feet, holding my fingers and toes for a few extra seconds. His hands are unnaturally warm.

There is still pain in my side, but no longer the acute ache throughout my whole body. My leg feels slightly numb but not too sore. My broken arm is splinted and bandaged, but feels almost normal. But I am parched and dizzy, and also something . . .

"I need to pee," I croak out. "I need . . ."

He tilts his head to the side.

"Please," I say, "I need to pee. Pee?" Helpless, I move one hand over the thick blanket and grab my crotch. The Nahx nods and, sliding his hand behind my back, helps me stand, the blanket wrapped around me.

I sway for a moment and he moves to lift me, but I wave him off. "Help me walk," I say. He walks me, limping excruciatingly slowly down the narrow hallway, and opens the door to a small room. There is a flash of light, and a second later a candle in an ornate candleholder illuminates a toilet and a sink. There is a bucket of water on the floor next to the toilet.

Shrugging off the blanket, I look down at my body and realize I am wearing nothing but the bloody rags of my undershirt and some soaked men's boxers. Suddenly, I'm horribly embarrassed. The Nahx simply points to the toilet and the bucket, and then he stands there, looking at me.

"Can I have some privacy?" I ask.

He turns around.

"I mean actual privacy?"

He glances back at me, then walks off, disappearing down the hall. After I use the toilet and rinse it out, I sit on the closed lid and use the rest of the water in the bucket to wash my body as well as I can with one hand.

I emerge, hopping on my good leg, wearing nothing but the blanket wrapped around me. I left my reeking underclothes in the sink. The Nahx stands in the middle of the living room, watching me carefully. The effort of hopping soon catches up to me and I stumble. He grabs me and eases me into a chair. I look up at him.

"Are there any clean clothes?" I ask. He disappears into

a room, returning with a pair of men's pajamas. He turns politely, while I struggle to put them on. My muscles are variously stiff and floppy as noodles, my whole body lopsided.

"How long have I been here?" I ask while I dress. He reaches back without turning around, holding all five fingers out. Then he closes his fist and opens it again, this time with three fingers.

"Eight days?" I can't quite believe that. It seems impossible. But what would be his motive for lying?

"You can't speak?" I ask. I can't remember if we discussed this before. Probably should have, but I was busy dying. "Like, with a voice?"

He shakes his head.

"You can turn around." He turns and helps me sit on the low sofa, kneeling on one knee in front of me.

"Can't you take your armor off? We're not in a battle now."

He shakes his head and, laying both hands on his chest, closes his fists tightly.

Crush.

"Oh. Our atmosphere is wrong or something?"

He nods. And then we have an awkward silence as he stares at me and I stare at his weird segmented boots.

"Do you have a name?" I ask when it finally becomes too awkward, even for me.

He looks at me for a moment, and I see daylight shining

in from the window and reflecting in the black lenses of his mask. I wonder if there are eyes behind the mask or if the mask is all he is. Have we talked about this, too?

He points to the second finger on his left hand.

"Finger?" I say. "Your name is Finger?"

He flicks his head back a couple of times, and there is a little grumble in his breathing. Is he laughing?

He reaches over to the bookshelf and taps his finger theatrically on the books. One, two, three . . . all the way up to ten. Then he taps again on the eighth book.

"Eight?"

He shakes his head, tapping the book.

"Eighth?"

He nods.

"Your name is Eighth? That's a weird name. Eighth what?"

He points to the sky and draws a circle with his finger.

"Sun? Moon! Eighth Moon?" I'm playing charades with an alien who has knocked me unconscious and seen me pee my pants at least twice. I'm not very good at it, clearly. He's unsatisfied with "Eighth Moon." He draws a circle in the sky, then moves his hand and draws a half circle, then moves his hand again and draws a thin crescent.

"Moon cycle? Like month?" He nods enthusiastically. "Like the eighth month. August?"

He gazes at me for a moment, not moving, then nods.

"August," I say, trying it out. Though I have a feeling it's not quite what he was trying to tell me, it does seem to suit him somehow. He's very imposing. And imperial. Like the emperor that watched Rome burn. But that was another guy, I think. I almost laugh at the thought of social studies classes. Ancient history? *We* are the ancient history now. We are the dead civilization. This thing saw to that.

"I'm terribly hungry," I say, to cover my disgust. He starts to get up, but I stop him. "Wait."

He kneels back down, his hands resting on one raised knee.

I examine him properly for the first time with a clear head, free of pain. He is extraordinarily tall; even kneeling, he is looking down on me where I sit. His shoulders are broad, and in the daylight I can see a small mark in the segmented armor where he pulled Topher's arrow out. It seems, somehow, healed, like a scar, although how there can be a scar on armor I don't know. There is a similar, larger but possibly older scar on his chest. I wonder, again, if this is his skin.

Skin or armor, it seems to suck the surrounding light away, making him difficult to focus on. The hard plates cover his whole body, moving and rippling as he moves. His chest rises and falls. It *looks* like he's breathing, but the buzzing sound this makes is more machinelike than alive.

My heart is pounding, I suddenly realize, and I'm frightened, so horribly frightened of him. I see the Nahx in the stadium falling on me, I see this Nahx, August, wrenching me out of the toilet in the trailer and hanging me by my wrists until they almost broke. I think of him with his rifle pointed at my head, the tiny sharp spikes quivering on his face. Can this gentle August be the same Nahx, changed somehow? Reformed? Or is this some perverse new game? How many of my people did he kill with that rifle before he took pity on me? Was he the one that killed Sawyer and Mandy? I'm so sickened I want to look away. I want to run away. I turn my head to the door, the window, trying to find a way to get out. Perhaps I could get up and leave, walk down those endless flights of stairs and through the city, somehow find the tunnel again, and then go back to the barn, find the others. But that was days ago. I've been missing for over a week. They have returned to the base by now and told everyone I'm dead. If I am to survive, much less get back to the base, it depends on him. Whatever his plans for me, I'm at his mercy. This makes my stomach turn. I want nothing more at that moment than to hide from him.

I'm hanging my head, unable to look at him anymore, when he makes a noise, like a purr.

"What?" I say, looking up. He points to his own chest, then to mine. When I don't react, he repeats it, raising one hand, palm up, like a question.

"Oh! Raven," I say. He nods and points to the sky, making

a waving motion with his hand. "Yes, it's a bird. A black bird."

Nodding, he reaches out, very slowly with one hand, and gently fingers my damp golden ringlets, shaking his head. I must flinch, because he quickly draws his hand away.

"I'd rather you didn't touch me," I say. He nods slowly and turns his head toward the wall.

For some reason, as he stands up and walks into the other room, I blush with shame. Perhaps I should have said, *It's nothing personal.* But of course it is.

While he's in the other room, I stand, experimentally putting weight on my injured leg. Pain shoots up to my hip, not quite bearable but nearly. In a few days, maybe a week, I could walk out of here. I'll need clothes. Men's pajamas will not do, and although it's hazy, I'm pretty sure he cut my clothes to pieces when he was treating my injuries or . . .

My skin prickles as I remember the men's boxers I woke up in. I wasn't wearing them when I got attacked, which means he undressed me at some point.

The beginnings of a scream take root inside me. I catch it, pressing my lips together before it comes out and alerts him to my distress. I don't need to see him now, and I don't want him to see how the thought of being unconscious, half naked, with him hanging over me threatens to undo me. I need to focus.

Focus. I need warm clothes. I'll snoop through the drawers and closets.

Find some kind of a bag, pack some food. Maybe try to purloin a weapon. Then I'll leave.

I sit back on the sofa, leaning on the pillows. My eyes sting with frustrated tears.

It's a ridiculous plan. I'll freeze or starve, and where would I go? The base is hundreds of miles from here. I guess I could try to find human survivors, the ones we hoped were hidden in the labyrinthine parking garages under the city. I don't remember seeing any evidence of them.

Maybe I could hide on my own. Maybe somewhere near that store where everything went so horribly wrong. There's enough food in there to keep one person alive until spring. If I leave in spring I could hike over the mountains and head for the coast.

Nearly a thousand miles away.

I wipe my face. This is not how I expected it to turn out. I expected Topher and I would get away, kill some Nahx, and escape together, head west like Lewis and Clark. Or something. That was stupid. I know that now. Topher is probably dead. Just because this Nahx didn't kill him doesn't mean one of the other billion didn't.

This thought makes me sob and sob until my ribs hurt. Topher can't be dead. How could I have been so stupid to become so attached to him? Or to anyone in this world? We're all going to die. Through the blur of tears, I see the Nahx,

August, returning with a steaming bowl. He sets it down on the coffee table and kneels next to me again, putting his hand on my splinted arm.

"Please don't touch me."

He sits back, picks up the bowl and holds it out to me. Believe it or not, it's actually chicken soup. What are the odds?

"I'll eat it later. Can you leave me alone?"

He sets the soup down, hesitating, but finally walks down the hallway to the bedroom and closes the door.

Even in the state I'm in, I take note that he hasn't tried to restrain me. Maybe he knows how hopeless it is too.

It feels like another life now, when I had so much hope. But if I take a second to tally it up, maybe it wasn't that much after all. It was only ever faint glimmers, like satellites exploding against a dark sky. I hoped I might make it up to Mom and Jack, that I might find them again. I hoped we might escape from the Nahx, that Topher might help me forget Tucker, or become him even, just take his place the way he seemed destined to. What evidence did I have that any of that was even possible? All I ever had was hope. So many tiny pinpoints of hope.

Now I don't even have that. This Nahx took it all away.

I can barely look at him. His touch makes my skin crawl. The thought that he sat and watched me lying there in nothing but underwear for more than a week horrifies me. I was so delirious he could have done anything, looked at me, touched me.

Maybe he thinks I should be grateful to him for saving my life, but I'm not grateful. I hate him.

Yes.

I hate him. I don't care if he saved me. I'm a soldier. I'll watch him, learn about him and his kind. Then I'll kill him.

Maybe if I were more sure of this, I would feel less humiliated.

Augustis my name now. I'm still a rebel and a deserter. I'm still a sentimental idiot. Weak-minded and stupid.

Defective. Disobedient.

The moment the human has the strength, she will do her best to kill me. Not that I don't deserve it for the things I've done. But I doubt she'll be able to. It's the trying that scares me. It's the things I could do to her in my own defense.

The room where she didn't die smells of twenty different things, most of them not very nice. I tear the sheets from the bed, then another cover, but discover the mattress is soaked with everything too. I haul the whole mess out onto the terrace and throw it over the railing, watching it sail down and land with a satisfying crash. My mind relaxes enough, for an instant, to think how much fun it would be to throw things over the railing for the rest of the day. Or to set them on fire and throw them out all night. Who among my people thinks like I do? That's ridiculous.

I'm very good at breaking things—that's still the case. *August* can break things, like doors and locks. I have terrible aim with my rifle, but I don't need it. She's right there, helpless. I could snap her neck like a dandelion stem. Crush her like a fragile baby bird and throw the pieces over the railing too.

The thought of it makes me gag. I reach out with my left hand and find the cold brick wall of the terrace. Even walking away right now would be killing her. She's too weak to survive alone.

I step back into the room and gather the piles of towels from the floor. Balling them up, I pitch them out the patio door, where they flap open and flutter on the wind, like giant snowflakes. Less pretty though. Snowflakes are so pretty. The thought of them skims a thin slice of misery away, and I feel light as air for an instant. But snowflakes make me think of the human girl. And why not? She's in the next room, plotting ways of ridding herself of me.

Maybe I should tell her she can just walk away. Maybe she would believe that. Maybe if I concentrated really hard, I could let her go. I could go back to my people. I could beg them to fix me. They could close her behind the door in my mind with the angels and the other almost memories.

August. She gave me a name. It's not what I meant to say to her. The names of the human months mean nothing to us, but we used their moon as part of our process. I'm from the eighth moon cycle. Eighth. Like all the others. It's not really a name. It's a rank. The ranks mean so much to us, but I guess they mean nothing to her.

August. Eighth Cycle of the Moon.

She told me I don't have to be who I am. She gave me more than Sixth ever did. All Sixth ever gave me were orders. And mysteries. Questions she wouldn't answer.

How much time has passed? I've been standing in the middle of the bedroom with a damp towel in my hand for what seems like hours. The sun will set soon. I could watch it from the other room. But she hates me so much, it hurts to be in the same room with her. I should be used to it by now. Stupid defective Eighth, I thought that if I saved her life, she might not be so repelled. She might be grateful. If Eighth had saved Sixth . . .

Not Eighth. August. August is even stupider. August has feelings like a human. Stupid feelings that make me pathetic. Disgusting, perverse feelings that make me not want to leave her when I know I should.

I should leave her.

Once I thought of leaving Sixth. I thought of turning away from her while we walked in a heavy rainstorm. I let my hand fall from her shoulder experimentally, and she snapped her head back. *Stay together*, she signed. That was about as close to affection as she ever got. That was also the moment I realized to get away from her I would have to kill her. And that I couldn't kill her because I loved her so much.

Love is not really permitted. We are supposed to feel protective toward the girls, and the girls are supposed to lead us, and mentor us, because they are more experienced. I knew this. There are other things that Sixth knew that I didn't. I'm not sure if she was supposed to explain them to me, if she was waiting for the right time, or if she neglected to, or refused to, because she hated me. I was supposed to feel attached to her, and dependent on her. And I did. That's how the pairs are supposed to work.

But love? It should not have mattered to me, the names she called me. And the violence is just part of how we are. I should have probably fought back, crushed her fingers as she slept, or thrown hot coals at her. But I couldn't hurt her, and that made her think I was weak, and stupid. Which made her angry, and more inclined to violence, or plain meanness. Calling me names, letting me eat things that made me sick. Laughing at me when the humans with their guns startled me. She would have laughed if she'd seen me lingering by her lifeless body, pacing, my throat convulsing around the tube. She would have laughed if she'd seen how I trembled when I disconnected, high in the mountain after she didn't get up. How I lay down beside the fire and cried about her until my head ached like it was split open again. She would have been disgusted with me.

And now, how appalled would she be, that I have captured a little human pet, nursed her back to health, and now can't let her go like I should. She mocked the humans with their cats and dogs, that they would waste time going back for them as they tried to flee. She tore a dog apart once, in front of the screaming family, before darting them all into silence. She would tear this one apart too, to spite me, then laugh as I grieved. Blood-winged angel Sixth, she was quite something, now that I think of it. If she were still alive I think I would be able to snap her neck to protect the little dandelion in the next room.

I suppose that means I don't love Sixth anymore.

When I dare to poke my head into the other room, she has fallen asleep on the bench, piled with blankets. The bowl is empty. As quietly as I can, I gather it and carry it out onto the west-facing terrace. I drop it over the rail and wait for the dull thump it makes as it hits the deep snow forty stories below us. I could have washed it, but that's something a human would do. There are a lot of bowls and plates in the kitchen. I'm not washing them. When I run out of bowls, maybe I'll leave her. Maybe I'll tear the tube from my throat and wait for the heaviness of the air to press the life from my lungs. We don't get up from that, I hear. If she still hates me when the bowls run out, I'll do it.

The sky turns pink and orange. The colors in this world are heartbreaking. Heartbreak is something I should not understand. Why should I feel the pain of losing a planet that was never mine? I should be happy, proud of what we've achieved. I'm supposed to hate these vulgar humans. I have been told how they are. Wasteful. Cruel. Disorganized and petty. Weak and stupid. They don't deserve such an enchanting world. I'm supposed to look on them as vermin.

But I love the human girl so much it makes my chest hurt.

The next morning greets me with a headache—a ball-shrinking headache, Xander would have called it—in addition to the pains in my body. There's a bowl of dry cereal on the table next to me, and a glass of water. Lined up neatly next to that are several bottles of prescription pills. Reading the labels, I have some insight into why the only memories I have of my illness feel like hallucinogenic dreams.

Oxycodone. Percocet. A couple of different antibiotics. The Nahx must have been force-feeding this to me the whole time. No wonder I have a headache. I'm coming down from opiates. Perfect. I sweep the collection into a small garbage can I find under the side table. I don't need a drug problem now on top of everything else.

The penthouse is quiet. "Hello?" I call out. There's no answer.

My head throbs as I stand and test my weight on my leg. If anything, it feels worse than yesterday, but that's probably because the sledgehammer drug cocktail has worn off. What I need is some aspirin or ibuprofen, but the search will make the pain worse. In seconds my mind is hurling silent curses at the Nahx again. It's hard to think of anything else with my head pounding like this, but the significance of being alone is not lost on me. I could leave now, run away. Well, hobble away, limp away. I almost laugh at the thought as I take two tentative steps, pain shooting from my foot to my hip.

An agonizing eternity later, I'm in the hall bathroom, but the medicine cabinet is empty, and my swollen and bruised face scowls back at me from the beveled mirror. Under the bruises, my color looks dreadful—a dull khaki rather than my normal golden brown, my freckles like sad bugs crawling on my cheeks. And my Afro looks pretty much like you'd expect for someone who has been in bed for more than a week—frizzy, squashed, and lopsided—but I don't have the energy or the tools to fix it.

Focusing on my reflection only worsens my headache. Rather than endure the long journey down to the other bedroom to search for painkillers, I cross into the kitchen. It's a fascinating mess. All the dishes have been pulled out and strewn across the counter. Another pile of pill bottles litters the draining board. None of them are painkillers. Towels and sheets are piled up, some of them torn into strips. And there are boxes and cans of food everywhere, not just in cupboards but on the breakfast bar, the top of the stove. I'm not game to open the fridge though. Not sure I want to know what pestilence lurks in there after . . . What has it been since a human lived here? Six months?

A human apart from me, I mean.

The Nahx has been creating a little hoard, it seems. Is he planning to keep me here forever? My eyes fall on the knife block. The paring knife looks pretty sharp. If I had some kind of a holster, I could keep it on me. As it is, weapons are hard to conceal in men's pajamas. Socks, maybe. I could keep one in my sock.

There's a faint noise behind me, and I spin without thinking, knife raised in my good hand, in as close to a defensive posture as I can get.

It's only him, the Nahx, August. I recognize him by the scrappy state of his armor plates, the dirt, the scuffs, the star-shaped scar on his shoulder. He doesn't seem to react to my knife apart from tilting his head slowly to the side. He slips his rifle from his shoulder and sets it on the breakfast bar.

"Don't sneak up on me," I say. "Unless you'd like to be filleted."

Before I can blink, he has plucked the knife out of my grip, as easily as if I handed it to him as a gift. I step back as he lays his palm on the butcher block. Raising the knife above his head, he slams it down into the back of his hand.

"No!" I slap my hand over my mouth.

There's a loud *ping* as the blade snaps in two. He shows it to me before tossing it away.

Edging back, I watch him reach out. He points to the joint

in his armor over his wrist, bending his hand up and down to show me the plates opening and closing. He points to his elbow and the scar on his shoulder. Weak spots.

Now I'm cornered against the counter as he steps forward. I reach for the knife block again, but he gets there before me, shoving it hard onto the floor, where it crashes and slides away. One long, sharp knife remains in his hand. He flips it over, holding the handle end out to me. I don't move, but he nods encouragingly, extending the knife, inviting me to take it.

I snatch it from his hand and hold it out, aimed at his throat. He flicks his head back a couple of times and steps forward.

"Don't come any closer," I say.

He takes another small step, until his neck is pressed against the tip of the blade. I feel it click between the plates. If I gave a hard push, it would go right through his throat. I want to. After everything I've seen these monsters do, I really want to. And I think he's daring me.

I pull the knife back, clutching it to my chest. "There's only one killer here."

He hisses abruptly and strides out of the kitchen, across the living room, and out the door into the hallway. After his footsteps recede I notice he's left his rifle.

Awkwardly tying a dish towel around my waist, I fashion a kind of holster for the knife, which I tuck into place. I can't know when he'll come back for his rifle, but in the meantime I can get a close look at it. Like him, it's a dull gray metallic color. It even smells a bit like he does, vaguely chemical and smoky, like charcoal. It's much heavier than any rifle I've ever held, so heavy it would be unwieldy for all but the strongest human soldier to carry. But the Nahx are very strong. We know that.

For months I've wanted to get a close look at a live dart. The only ones I've ever seen are spent—and they are completely empty, without a trace of the toxin left to study, according to one video I saw. Awkwardly, because of my bandaged arm, I prop the rifle on the breakfast bar and try a few switches and levers. As I flick something, a loud whine begins and a second later a dart *thunks* into a cupboard door.

I limp forward to inspect it, but hear him pounding back up the hallway. He mustn't have been very far away. Turning back to the front door, I'm so surprised by his speed across the living room that I accidentally fire the rifle at him. He snatches the dart right out of the air and hurls it across the room. His hands slash through the air as he lunges at me.

Break BREAK.

I recognize that one. And he points at me as I stumble backward, sliding his thumb across his throat.

Kill you. Break you.

"Don't!" I fling the rifle across the floor, sliding down to crouch in the corner, my good arm curled up protectively.

He stops moving, becoming still, apart from his breathing. After a moment where I stare at him from under my elbow, burning with the rage of being so scared of him that I can barely move, he raises his hands, palms forward, shaking his head. He bends down slowly, retrieving the rifle and slinging it over his back.

Dropping to one knee, he makes some signs. *Break* I see again, and he points at me, raising one hand like a half shrug.

Break you?

"No, I'm not hurt." I'm trembling though, and fighting not to. It's withdrawal, I tell myself. Cold, tremors, nausea. Maybe it's the lingering infection. I don't think I was this scared yesterday. But I was drugged then.

The Nahx pats his rifle. *Hurt you*, he signs firmly, a warning, not a threat.

"I won't touch it again. I just wanted to know how the darts work."

He tilts his head to the side again, retrieving the rifle. With a *click*, one of the darts pops out. He holds it out.

I've never actually seen a veterinarian tranquilizer dart in real life, but this one looks a bit like the ones I've seen in nature documentaries. Like a futuristic version of one, and maybe it's blood rushing in my ears, but it seems to hum.

Touch. No. Hurt you. Kill you.

"Okay. I won't." I'm surprised how many of his signs I seem

to know already. They're intuitive, and I vaguely remember him talking to me while I was half conscious. I guess I absorbed some of it.

He slaps his palm on his chest and stands, holding his hand down for me.

"I don't need help."

He steps back as I struggle to stand. Then we face each other, him towering over me, me small, helpless, addled by drugs, bent with pain. I don't think it would be much of a fight if it came to that. I have the little knife—that's something. And I have my hate, my fear, my rage.

"Are you still using that rifle? Is that where you go in the day? Off to find survivors and kill them?"

He shakes his head. I want him to go away now, so I can suffer in peace. My head is on fire, throbbing so hard that I'm seeing stars. But I try to think like a soldier, or a survivor, try to ignore the pain and ignore how scared I am. I have to . . . make him care about me? Isn't that how it goes in the movies? But that's not really my style. And it probably wouldn't do any good anyway.

"Why do you carry the rifle around if you're not using it?"

He huffs a little breath, like he's thinking about it. *Look good.*

I snort back a laugh, choking on the thought of how very human that is. So like a man to want to be armed for fashion reasons. But as he moves to leave me, my mind trips on another thought. I don't think he said his rifle "looks good"; I think he said it "looks *right*," as though to the outside world he needs to still look like the rest of them.

"August?"

He turns in the doorway.

"Are there . . . others . . . like you? Outside?"

He nods. *You stay. Hurt you.*

A warning. Not a threat.

We pause there, while I absorb that reality. So, there is some secrecy to whatever is happening here, to what he's doing with me. Maybe I should be comforted by his protection from others of his kind, but there's something horrifying, too, about being the secret consort of a monster. I'd probably cry if I didn't think it would take my headache from merely ball-shrinking to heart-stopping.

"I can't take those pills you found for me anymore," I say, turning away to look out the window, at the fridge, anywhere but him. "They'll make me sick. I need ones that come in bigger white bottles, not the little yellow ones. Can you look for me?"

He takes one step forward and opens the narrow cupboard by the sink. It's full of various medicines, Band-Aids, sunscreen. Plenty of everyday ibuprofen. Whoever lived here was well supplied.

August trusts me to dose myself with these pills, I guess. He turns back to the doorway and strides off, disappearing into the hall.

Humans have photographs. I have no sign for that, but the sound of the word plays clearly in my head. *Photograph.* I draw the shape of it in the air, a rectangle or square. There's odd familiarity to this peculiar human habit, as though this is something from the hidden parts of my mind. But there's also something wrong about the photographs I find. The shape of them is off, or the color. And they are treated so carelessly for such precious objects, tossed into drawers, stuck behind magnets on doors, pinned to walls. If I had a photograph of the human girl, I would keep it somewhere safe, I think. Maybe the ones the humans left behind aren't their precious ones. Maybe they took those with them when they ran.

For humans, memories can be held inside the mind as thoughts, or outside as objects. I have few memories to keep as thoughts, and no objects to keep at all. I wish I had taken something from Sixth after she . . . died. Or whatever happened. But what? I could have taken her rifle, I suppose, or her knife. At least that would help me remember how violent she was. Sometimes when I think of her I still miss her steady shoulder. I have to keep reminding myself that's wrong. It's like the memory of the mission directives humming in my mind. I still hear their echo sometimes, still think I should dart a human if I see one.

But I see no humans, not alive, at least. The city is quiet. I find evidence of my kind once in a while and occasionally hear the grumble of a distant transport, but so far I don't encounter any. I don't know what I will do if it happens. They would want me to go with them, but I can't leave the human, Raven. She would die without me. Or the others would find her and dart her. Or she would be left alone in a dead city.

The empty human streets spread out like a maze around the high tower where I took her. My search of them has become a compulsion. I know it's another echo of the directives— search, search for humans, flush them out of hiding places, and dart them, all of them. Leave none standing. But if I found one, I think I could resist. That's my plan—find another human, capture it, and bring it to her. Make it understand that she needs help. Then I could leave her, as she wants. I should have given her to the human who shot me with the arrow. It was a mistake not to; I see that now. The sludge inside me makes every emotion urgent and catastrophic. It is so hard to think in moments like that and without the focus of the directives, without Sixth to guide me. . . .

I make mistakes. I've made many mistakes.

I've searched for days and haven't found a single living human.

She is sleeping when I come back to our refuge in the sky. I have other bottles of the pills she wants—I hope they are the right kind. And I have thick blankets I took from beds two flights down. There are darted humans still lying in some of the beds. I leave their blankets in place; it feels wrong to disturb them, and anyway, the directives were to leave them where they fall. I take blankets only from empty beds, secure in the knowledge that the darted humans mean this building has already been processed. There is no reason for any of my kind to come back through here.

I suppose if her people are all gone, and my people are all gone, then the two of us could stay here indefinitely. There is plenty of food for her, and though the elevation is low, I could recharge if I needed to, if I was quick about it. I could protect her and take care of her until spring. Or summer? And then what?

Something comes next, and though I don't know what it is, I'm sure it's not good, for me, for her, for dandelions or snowflakes or spiderwebs. How can any of this be good?

RAVEN

The hallway outside the door is approximately one hundred feet long. I know this because I pace it out several times a day. There are four penthouse apartments on this floor. August has broken the locks and propped the doors open on all of them, and as my leg improves, I wander in and out as I please, sometimes stopping to practice a karate kata with my shadow on the walls. The door to the stairwell has been torn off its hinges too. I usually hobble down a few flights of stairs and back up once a day too, trying to build the strength back in my leg and lungs. I want to keep going, every single day, want to complete the journey down to the street below, back to the stadium and the tunnel, toward my human friends. Away from him.

But I know to leave now would be suicide. Still, some days even suicide seems preferable to . . . whatever this is.

Counting the eight days I floated in a fever, I have been here for just under three weeks. I rarely see the Nahx, August, now. He leaves food out for me, usually cold, although sometimes if I happen to be awake when he brings it, he will slip back into the kitchen and return a few minutes later with a steaming bowl. I'm not sure how he heats it. Oddly, when I finish eating, he throws the bowls off the balcony. Once I hobbled out there with my bowl, ate, then called out to him when I finished. When he appeared, I handed him the empty bowl expectantly. He held it over the railing and dropped it, with what I'm almost sure was a sigh.

Broken, he signed. This was the first sign he had made in days.

He doesn't communicate much. He doesn't touch me or come near me except to check my injuries. But I learn a few signs.

One, where he waves two fingers in front of his chest, is a useful one. It seems to mean "repeat."

Repeat. Speak, he'll sign if he hasn't heard something I've said. But he also uses it for "more" or "very."

Repeat cold, he signed one night as he arrived with a pile of new blankets. It is cold. With the power off, the apartment isn't heated. The sun blazing in the many windows keeps it warm enough during the day, but at night the temperature drops to close to freezing. I pile the blankets over me and shiver myself to sleep. Sometimes I wake in the night and find him kneeling or standing nearby, never looking at me, but his body radiates heat. He doesn't seem to sleep. I think he's trying to keep me warm in the night. It's kind of skeevy to have him so close to me as I sleep, but I'm so tired and cold that I tolerate it.

This is how I learn his sign for "sad." One night a dream of Tucker drags me out of sleep with a sob, tears streaming down my face. August leans down to check on me.

Feel broken? he signs. The sign means "pain," I've learned. He worries about the lingering pain in my ribs and leg.

"Just sad," I say. He draws a finger down his face, like a tear. *Sad.*

"Yes, sad. I had a sad dream."

He draws a swirl on his forehead, and a few cells in the region of my heart flicker at the idea that he has shared his word for "dream." He says it again.

Sad dream.

Something about the way he nods to himself as he leaves me makes my breath catch in my throat. Does he dream? Are his dreams sad? I have a horrible feeling that he knows a kind of sadness I can only aspire to. I have people to get back to, after all. What does he have? He knows I hate him. I know he hates himself. He turned all the mirrors and every reflective art piece to the wall, like a vampire or something. He doesn't even like his shadow. Once he stood in the doorway to the hall as I made my daily laps. The sunlight streaming in behind him outlined his shape on the wall. I watched him look at it for an instant and then step quickly out of the light.

He made a sign once, after I changed into some flowered thermal pajamas he found for me. I think he might have done it subconsciously; it wasn't really directed at me. He glanced at me and looked away, making a shape with his hand. "Pretty," I took it to mean, because he did it again, one night looking at the sunset, adding the repeat sign.

Repeat pretty.

When he saw his shadow, he made this sign backward with a shake of his head, negating it. He thinks he is ugly. I might have agreed with him once, but now I think maybe that's a little unfair. He is what he is, no different from a toad or a hyena, or one of nature's other less attractive offerings. Still not something you want to get close to, but I'm used to him now anyway. I don't jump out of my skin every time I see him anymore, though I still don't like it when he touches me or comes near me. I try to be civil. If I'm civil, I can earn his trust, and maybe get him to reveal things he shouldn't. If I'm civil, he's less likely to turn on me. So I do it because my life depends on it. But with all this rage embedded in me like a stubborn, bloated tick, even civility is a challenge.

Daily, I fantasize about leaving. I imagine marching through the mountains, alone, determined, a crust of ice forming on my face, my eyelashes freezing together. Sometimes the daydreams end with Topher finding me, with us running into each other's arms in slow motion. Sometimes they end with me dead in the snow. It's hard to decide which daydream I enjoy more.

August has other signs, most having to do with my care. "Hungry" and "tired," he uses daily. "Scared," which involves a closed fist in front of the mouth, he used a lot early on, when he approached me to check my leg or ribs. *Scared*, he would sign, shaking his head, subverting it. *Don't be scared*. He doesn't need to use it anymore. I turn away when he tends to my wounds. I'm not scared of him. And there's nothing else to be scared of up here in the clouds.

I reach the end of the hallway, my good leg aching with the extra weight I still put on it. A musty breeze blows up the stairwell. I'm about to begin the difficult trip down two or three flights when I hear footsteps coming up. I freeze and edge backward. It's probably him, but if it isn't . . . I listen, straining. It sounds like one set of footsteps. It must be him.

Peering over the banister, I look into the deep, narrow abyss down the center of the railings. I can see his left hand, well, *someone's* left hand, trailing on the metal bar. For some reason, I wait, neither descending nor retreating as he reaches the landing below me. He stops as he sees me.

"Hello," I say. The dark stairwell makes him hard to see, shadowy. His armor clicks as he nods a reply. He's carrying a large cardboard box. "What have you got?"

He carries the box up to my level and sets it down on the floor. Reaching in, he fishes around a bit and then pulls out a small pink teddy bear. It's wearing floral pajamas very much like mine. He hands it to me.

At first I don't know what to say. I feel a mix of amusement and revulsion as I look into the bear's little pink face. It has a wide smile and bright blue button eyes, as well as a little red felt nose. Stitched on the front of the pajama top is a name: *Lucy.* I don't know if that is the bear's name or the name of the child who loved it. Suddenly, I feel a surge of nauseating anger rising up in me.

"This belonged to a child, you know," I say. I can tell August hears the accusing tone in my voice. He takes a small step backward. "The child is dead, right?"

A second passes before he shrugs.

"What do you mean, you don't know? All the children are dead. Everyone is dead. You killed them all." He shakes his head.

Not me.

"You're one of them though. One of those that killed everyone here. Aren't you?"

His nod is barely there, tiny. I shake the teddy bear in his face.

"This is pirate plunder, Viking plunder. Don't pillage on my behalf anymore. I don't want things you've stolen from dead children."

I reach forward and drop the bear into the abyss, watching

as it sails down and disappears into the dark. When I turn, August is looking at me, still except for the rising and falling of his shoulders. I glance down and see the box is full of sweaters, thick socks, and mittens. Things I desperately need. Struggling to conceal the desire in my eyes, I turn back and stare defiantly at him.

He moves so quickly sometimes, it takes my breath away. In a flash he picks up the box and disappears into the hallway. I hobble after him, as fast as I can, seeing him stepping into the penthouse we have been living in. By the time I get there, he is out on the balcony, emptying the contents of the box over the railing.

"Don't!" I say, but he throws the empty box, leaning over to watch it fall. "You're being stupid. Stop it!"

He pushes past me, gathering up the blankets that make my bed, the extra clothes I've amassed, slippers, socks, even a cheesy romance novel he gave me, which I've been secretly reading, and takes the whole pile out to the terrace.

"August, don't, please!" But he heaves the pile over the railing. The wind catches some of it, blowing it up and away, before it wafts downward and out of sight.

He makes a sign that looks like "sad" but backward, adding a question hand.

Happy?

"No, I'm not happy. Why did you do that? I'll freeze."

He crosses his arms, leaning back on the railing. I feel frustrated tears prickling the back of my eyes. It's the kind of thing bullies used to do to me in school—throw my mittens out of the bus window or drop my hat in a puddle of slush. They did these things because they liked me, people used to say. The idea is horrifying. Better to remember that they did these things until the first time I knocked one of them flat with an uppercut, though I have no chance of knocking August over in this way. Even to wipe his legs out from under him, I would have to take him by surprise. Not likely, since he's staring back at me now, sulking. My mind ticks over. I didn't know I could upset him like that, enough for him to become so stubborn. It's so unlike his usual emotionless attention to my every need.

The wind blows through my pajamas. My bare feet ache from the cold concrete terrace floor. I wrap my arms around myself and look over the railing. Far below, the clothes and blankets are strewn over cars and snowbanks. Now is as good a time as any to test my power over him, I guess.

"Go down and get that. Right now."

He shakes his head.

Despite desperately wanting not to, I start to shiver. "You have to! I'll freeze tonight."

He turns his head away, arms still crossed, still defiant.

You go. He flicks the sign at me with one dismissive hand.

"I can't! I can't walk all that way down and back up. Go down and get it!"

He doesn't react at all. Apparently, he's better at this game than I thought he would be.

"I can die from freezing, you know. Is that what you want?" I turn and stomp dramatically back into the relative warmth of the penthouse, wincing as the pain in my leg flares up. All my bedding is gone, sheets, blankets, quilts, everything. All the extra clothes I bundle into each night are gone too, and all the ones I've been setting aside for my journey away from here. This part is not a game so much. Maybe he doesn't even know how much this will hurt me. It could kill me tonight if it gets cold enough. I'm already shivering, and the sun isn't even touching the horizon yet. Worse, all the provisions I've gathered for my escape are gone.

Behind me, I hear the terrace door slide closed. I slump into the sofa and hug my knees, hanging my head, hiding my face, until I know that he's kneeling in front of me.

"Do you know how bad it feels to be so dependent on you?" I say into my knees. "My life is in your hands. I have to pretend to like you, because if you change your mind, or get bored of me and leave, I'm dead. That's repulsive." I hear him sigh and fidget, his armor clicking. A little farther, I think. What does it matter about his feelings anyway? He's a killer.

"And what if that's not enough? I don't know what you are,

or what you think you want. Whatever it is, I have to give it, if I want to live. Right?" I look up at him. He's shaking his head, both palms raised at his sides.

"Just go away," I say, but before he can get up, I stop him. "No, wait. I have a better idea." He sits back on his heels, expectant. I open the high collar of my pajama top, exposing my neck. "If you want me dead, do it now." I lean forward, pressing my bare neck toward him. "Go on. Get it over with."

He exhales roughly, almost like a growl, and recoils. As we stare at each other, I realize that I've conjured up some tears from somewhere, and I'm not even sure if they're real. Wiping them away elicits a sob, and seconds later I'm crying for real, curled up on the sofa, shivering with cold and crying in front of this monstrous alien who holds my life in his blood-ied hands. I cover my face again because I think I've probably cried enough to make my point, but I'm not sure that I can stop. After a few seconds I feel his warm hands on my feet.

And unlike I normally would, I don't flinch away.

AUGUST

Her skin is cool and smooth. Cold, in fact. Without all her blankets and clothes she could freeze tonight. I know this isn't really what she wants. It's not what I want either, and yet I feel something tugging me away, urging me to turn and run, down the stairs three at a time and out into the streets, away from her, because part of me wants this torment to be over.

It's exhausting being the object of her hate, her disdain and disgust. I'm so tired. Between her and Sixth, the effort of being the only creature on this planet who even marginally cares whether I live or die has worn me out. I'll leave her. It's something I should have done weeks ago. I feel the oily sludge bubbling up, erasing my own thoughts, thinking for me.

It would be easier if she would look at me, so I could say something to her at least, maybe good-bye.

Open your eyes, Dandelion, please.

I feel the pain in my chest before I realize I'm hitting myself there.

Please, please, please.

Her feet are so delicate, so slender and pretty. Sometimes

when I look at her I think of unspeakable things, things that make me want . . . to be anyone but who I am.

I make a noise, with my breathing, like a hiss, and pull my fingers away from her cold skin. She looks up at me.

Sorry. Sorry. Very sorry forever.

She slides down to the end of the sofa, away from me.

Don't be scared.

"I'm not."

She's lying. I can smell the adrenaline flowing through her.

Sorry forever.

"Right, I get it," she says, mockingly imitating my last sign, shooting her hand upward, to the stars. "Big sorry. Forever sorry." She wipes the tears from her face. "Go get my clothes and blankets now. It's cold in here."

Of course. Of course I will. My body is on fire with shame. I try to lower my temperature to something more comfortable, but fail. Even though it is close to freezing, I'm burning. I have to fight to keep from gagging on the tube in my throat as I stagger to the door.

"August."

I turn to the sound of her voice.

"Don't ever touch me again, okay? I mean it. My leg is healed. My ribs are fine. I can take the splint off my arm. So just . . . don't touch me. Don't come near me. Don't even look at me. Unless you really are going to kill me, keep your creepy hands to yourself."

Before I can stop myself, I make a set of signs to her, a terrible curse I learned from Sixth.

Die in mud and pain, defective low rank.

I regret it immediately and hope that she didn't understand.

"Yeah, fuck you, too," she says, adding her own sign, and two of mine. "Fuck you, pervert, *repeat forever.*"

Outside the door, out of her sight, I rest my left hand on the wall and stand there, trying to get my thoughts to flow properly again. The numbing fluid is churning in me. I badly want to break something, but I've already broken almost all the locks and kicked in almost all the doors in this building. Instead, I rest my head on my hand, breathing in and out, while the spasms in my throat subside. Inside the apartment, I can hear her crying.

It's about the worst thing I've ever heard.

The blankets return, and all the clothes. Even the book comes back, damp but undamaged. He also brings two bowls that miraculously survived the fall, and a pile of bowls I assume he found in another apartment. He doesn't look in my direction as he delivers these things.

Later, after I've eaten the food he gives me and he's disappeared, I find the teddy bear in the bathroom. It's in two pieces, its head torn right off. I'm not sure if this is some kind of warning to me, or an admission of guilt or an oversight on his part. I wet the head in the bucket of water and use it to wash my face and under my arms before throwing it in the bath.

He doesn't reappear that night, and despite the piles of blankets the cold is a punishment I did not anticipate. I shiver and toss and turn, tucking and retucking the blankets around me. I dream, when I finally sleep, of crawling into his warm lap, having him wrap his arms around me. He breathes in my ear and whispers vivid, violent, and terrifying things. I wake in the dark, paralyzed with fear and cold. And missing him. Missing his warmth, his protective shadow.

Missing *August*. The one who perpetually seems inches away from killing me, simply out of habit. I wish I didn't know his name or the details of him that I've gathered over the weeks. How he loves sunsets and falling snow. How he checks my breathing when I sleep. Sometimes I pretend to be sleeping and hold my breath, just to bug him. If he knows I'm doing this he doesn't let on. He doesn't eat, or sleep. He never sits; he rarely even kneels. Sometimes, especially after I've said something unforgivable, he leans against the wall or doorframe, always with his left hand.

I say unforgivable things to him a lot, call him a creep if I catch him watching me at night, accuse him of murder when my mind won't stop replaying Felix's death behind my eyes. I let the venom out of me as words, sometimes barely knowing whether it's under my control at all. My parents were smart putting me in martial arts all those years ago, and my teachers were right—anger needs to be controlled. It's as though with my body weak and wounded, my words are the only outlet I have.

But when I can manage it, I still fake civility, and it's tragic how no amount of venom seems to change his attitude toward me. I can see he's sad, and frustrated, but his manner is always kind, indulgent even. So I try to get him to answer questions.

"What is the poison in the darts?" I say one day when I find him in the hallway, leaning on the wall. He shrugs.

"What are your plans for my planet?"

I have no plans.

His word for "plans" is like three lines drawn over his right ear.

"Your people," I say. "What plans do your people have for my planet?"

He just shakes his head and walks away. He does that for about 50 percent of the questions I ask him. At first this made me angry, but now I think maybe he's tired of telling me he doesn't know. I'm reminded of school, of lessons I hadn't done the reading for, and how teachers seemed to relish putting me and the other slackers in our place by asking us questions we couldn't possibly answer. Say *I don't know* enough times and it starts to sounds like *I'm a fucking idiot.*

I let August get close to me only so I can study his armor, and I no longer care if he decides to off me as I sleep, or abandon me. I know, even with his help, it's nearly impossible that I will ever see the others again. Topher thinks I'm dead. He saw it, I think. I have a vague memory of knowing he was nearby in the stadium. From his point of view, that Nahx killed me, beat me to death. That Nahx that wasn't August. That August says wasn't him. I have no way of being sure he's not lying. I don't remember it very well. In my mind the attacker and the rescuer blend together as one, blend and spin together in pain and terror until I'm nauseous just thinking about it.

He knows how angry I am at him, at his kind, at the whole world. And he does try. As if the decapitated teddy bear wasn't enough, there begins now a parade of gifts and offerings, each more unexpected or inappropriate than the last. There are over a hundred apartments in this building, and he is pilfering through each, one by one, in search of some trinket that might appease me. It's a rather sad and poignant quest actually, the kind of thing some sick person might write a poem about one day, but it has little effect on me. Though the day he finds an unopened box of Belgian chocolates is a good day. The day he turns up with someone's diamond bracelet is a bad day. A very bad day. But he stands stoically for twenty minutes while I tell him a made-up story of the man who splurged on the bracelet for the woman he loved, maybe for her birthday, their anniversary, or Valentine's Day, only to watch her be murdered by the Nahx, then succumb himself, a poison dart in his heart.

"Were their bodies still there?" I ask accusingly. "Did you take this right off her wrist?"

He simply snatches the bracelet back and sends it sailing over the balcony. I don't see him for a day and night after that. Another cold night, shivering, wondering if he'll ever come back, struggling to not regret the things I said. I only need him, I remind myself; I don't care about him. Once I get back to the mountains, back to the base, I could cut his throat without a second thought. My fingers slip around the knife concealed in the lining under the sofa.

He can still surprise me though. One day, as I doze on the sofa, afternoon sunlight streaming in through the sliding doors, he tosses something onto the blankets. I open my eyes, closing my fingers around a small hardcover book. My breath catches as I see what it is. It's an illustrated book of the Edgar Allan Poe poem "The Raven." He stands there, silent, as I stare at it for a few moments.

"Can you read?" I ask. He nods slowly. I'm quite surprised. "You can? Did you read this?" He nods again.

Sad. Repeat sad.

"It is sad, yes. Very sad." I open it and flip through a page or two. As I read, I'm dimly aware of him taking a step forward, then another. He kneels in front of me.

Zero repeat forever.

"Repeat?" I say, imitating his sign.

He taps the book in my lap. This is as close as he's come to me since the blankets came back. *Zero repeat forever.*

My mind translates it this time to "nothing again forever."

"Oh! Nevermore?"

He nods firmly, satisfied. *Sad,* he signs before standing and disappearing into the kitchen.

The cold stone inside me breaks for him then, a little bit. What he must think of this terrible story of a man haunted by the memory of his lost love, Lenore. Of all of human literature, that he should read this one, this depressing, fatalistic dish of melancholy. It can't have been good for him. The fact that he seemed to understand it so well tells me something about him too. I see him then, as that miserable wretch, cowering in his lonely chamber, unable to let go of who he is, what he's done, and all that he's lost. I swallow a sob, crushing the blankets over my mouth so he won't hear.

All this time I thought I was the saddest person in the world, when really, it's probably him. It takes an hour of intense concentration for me to finally convince myself that he deserves all the sadness he feels. That the things I think about him and his sorrow must be imagined. That I know nothing about his life before he rescued me in the stadium. That I don't care. That I only need him until I find Topher again. That Topher will put an arrow into his neck this time, and that will be the end of it, the end of August, the Nahx.

Then I will think of him nevermore.

The day comes when I am able walk down to the ground floor and back up, forty flights. I sweat and pant, but there is no discernible strain to my convalescing lungs or leg. I took the splint off in the previous week, and my arm feels strong too, as I jab and block at my shadow in the hallway. I feel strong. Strong enough to leave, maybe, but probably not strong enough to fight him off if he tries to stop me.

We have been here for five weeks. August still brings me things nearly every day. Food mainly, though I prepare my own meals now, and clothes. I have shown him that warm clothes make me happy, so he piles them up all over the apartment. So far they are all indoor clothes. I haven't figured out a way to express a desire for outdoor clothes without revealing my intention to leave him. After all this time, I'm still not sure he would let me.

I remember an outdoor equipment supplier on the outskirts of town. Tucker and I bought our sleeping bags for camp there. It's a half-hour walk, an hour, tops. If I bundle up with enough sweaters and the day is fine, I'll make it with no trouble. My plan is to leave soon, but I don't set a date or a deadline. I want to wait for the right moment, then slip away. I don't want him to sense my anticipation. Feeling less dependent on him softens my hatred somewhat. I don't want him to know I'm leaving and try to stop me, because I would have to kill him. There are still sharp knives in the kitchen. I know exactly where they all are, as well as the one under the sofa where I sleep, and others wrapped among the pile of clothes I've amassed. I have studied his neck, where the armor is weaker, when he's not looking. I know I could do it, if I caught him by surprise, but I don't want to as much as I once did. He saved my life, though I never asked him to. He deserves at least that much consideration in return.

Though my mood improves with my recovery, his does not. I often find him in the long hallway, leaning on the wall, holding his head in his left hand. Occasionally I find him the other way, leaning on the right, with his left hand extended, like he is reaching for something. Once, unable to help myself, I ask him what's wrong.

Tired, he signs, letting his left hand fall. I don't think he means from lack of sleep. I think he's growing tired of me and my venom. Who could blame him?

One day, to my astonishment, he brings me a working laptop computer. There are two computers in the penthouse and several in the other apartments, but none of them are working. There is no power—that's part of the problem—but the laptops at least should have had some battery time left, but they don't. This is why I'm so surprised when this one boots up, like nothing happened. Seeing the home screen with the owner's files, the full battery icon, and boxes popping up fills me with nostalgia for a world that feels centuries past, not just months.

I spot the wireless icon flashing, one weak signal bar. Somehow, it has connected with a network. This could be . . . I slam the laptop shut.

"Thanks," I say evenly. "I'll play with it later, maybe. I don't want to waste the battery."

He nods lightly and leaves me, unaware, I hope, of what he has given me.

Later that day, after I watch him trail his left hand down the wall of the long hallway and disappear into the stairwell, I take the computer around the apartment, searching for a better signal. Not surprisingly, out on the west-facing terrace is best. There are several high buildings in my sight line, and even, in the distance, what looks like a cell phone tower. According to Kim, lots of these are fitted with solar-powered transmitters and connected to the emergency broadcast system.

"Damn . . . ," I whisper. It's amazing what you don't know in this world until everything goes to hell.

I look at my watch—oddly enough, after everything, it still keeps good time—it's three in the afternoon. I close the computer then, knowing my chances of receiving anything are best at noon. Maybe my chances of sending anything are best then too. What would I send? Mayday? SOS? Would anyone come?

It's a while before I can get the laptop out onto the terrace at noon. For some reason August lurks around until after midday for three days, after kneeling by me through the night. Perhaps because it has been particularly cold, or perhaps he has his own reasons. I struggle not to show my frustration. Finally, on the third day, in the morning, I try to entice him out of the penthouse with a promise of my fleeting happiness.

"I'd love to have some more of that chocolate," I say. It's embarrassing how quickly he reacts. In seconds he has fled, practically running as I listen to his heavy metallic footsteps echoing down the stairs. Why is he so quick to try to provide the things I want when surely he must know what I want most is to leave him? I start to wonder if he's really what's keeping me here. Or was it my injuries? Maybe I'm too scared to set off on my own.

I grab the laptop and take it back out onto the terrace. The sun is approaching its apex in the sky, still low on the southern horizon, but it's a bright day, and warm enough that I don't even bother putting socks or slippers on.

If there is any signal at all, it should be easy to find it. I'll ration the battery time. Ten minutes to search for signals, send messages, or download information. Twenty minutes to view files or anything else I've found. Half an hour per day. That way, if this is a good battery, it should last for a week or two. Maybe I won't be here for that long, but I have to always plan for the worst.

I give a little shudder then. That's the kind of thing Topher would say. *Plan for the worst.* This *is* the worst, Topher. I'm hundreds of miles away from you, a prisoner. Did you have a plan for this?

Setting the computer down on a glass and metal table, I find the signal easily. It's an unsecured network called NKV82. Though I know what I'm going to find, I connect anyway. I'm immediately taken to a directory of video files. Nahx kill videos all. They are sorted by popularity. The most popular one has over twenty million hits. *Twenty million?* There must be a lot of survivors, then. What Kim hoped about the coastal areas might be true after all. It's strange to think how isolated we've become, how our human connections depend so much on technology that without it we are like lost ships floating in a sunless, windless sea.

I stop then, for a moment, and consider backtracking. Maybe there is another signal, one not dedicated to these alien snuff movies. Maybe there is some kind of search and rescue network I can log on to. I remember the one time I watched videos like this, how sick they made me feel. But I'm curious to see if I will still feel the same way. I can't afford to waste time thinking about it. At the very least, if these videos have comments, I should comment on the most popular one. Tell people where I am. Maybe someone can send help. I click on the top file. As the video uploads surprisingly fast and starts to play, I recognize it immediately. It's the one where the female Nahx is decapitated. My first instinct is revulsion, but then I find I can't look away. The way the girl Nahx looks up before losing her head mesmerizes me. I pause the video and watch that moment over and over. There is something very familiar about her posture, about the subtle changes with the position of her head and shoulders. Something I recognize. Resignation. I find I'm blinking away tears.

The video ends and returns me to the directory page. I forgot to check if there were comments. I click again to get back, and the video begins again. Again, I find I can't stop watching. My bare feet start to ache from cold. Over and over the Nahx girl is taunted, pushed over, and kicked. Over and over she growls until I feel I can understand exactly what she's saying. It's not a threat. It's a plea. *Please don't kill me.*

Maybe, if she could have spoken, she would have said, *Just walk away.*

Over and over the machete falls and her head rolls away in a gush of blood. *Please don't kill me.* Resignation. *Please don't . . .*

A shadow falls across the laptop. The machete falls. I feel August clutch a handful of my hair just as the Nahx girl's head comes off.

I yelp as he yanks me off the chair by my hair. He releases me as soon as I tumble to the tiles.

"Don't sneak up on me, and you won't see things you don't like!" I snarl, cornered by the table and his dark shape. My scalp aches from where he grabbed me.

His shoulders rise and fall, his breath growling as he grabs the laptop and flings it over the railing. Seconds later I hear it clang mournfully against the roof of a car. Hating myself for not managing to send any call for help, I try to slither past him, but he steps to the side, blocking me. His hands are clenched and raised in front of his chest.

"You don't scare me." I kick out feebly with one leg. "You wouldn't dare hit me."

His fists come crashing down on the table. It explodes into a million shards of glass. I throw my arms over my face. While he is occupied with hurling the tangled metal remains of the table over the railing, I try to crawl away. There is broken glass everywhere. He reaches down and picks me up like a toy, carrying me back into the apartment.

"Don't touch me! Put me down!" I kick and scratch at him as he shoves me into the sofa. My hands fly back and wrap around a vase on the sofa table. I swing it out and smash it across his head, shattering it, and showering myself in more glass. "See? Two can play that game!" Before I can dive off the sofa, he grabs me up again, pinning my arms at my sides. Glass tinkles to the floor as I writhe in his arms.

As he carries me away, I kick out and connect my foot to one of the pictures he had turned to the wall. It smashes to the floor in another shower of glass. He moves into the hallway, which is lined with art. I drag my legs along the wall, sending each piece crashing down, all the while hurling abuse at him, spitting and biting like a trapped viper.

When I manage to get an arm free, I grab one of the ornate mirrors he had turned, waving it in his face. "Is this what you're scared of? Monsters? Mutants?" He smacks it away and it shatters against the wall. I slide down, but he scoops me up before I reach the floor.

"Stop it! Stop it! You're hurting me!" Then my words dissolve into unformed wordless screaming as he carries me flailing down to the bedroom, my feet still scraping framed art from the walls. He kicks the door open, and I see the room where I lingered between life and death for the first time since I came out of my fever-induced haze. The bed is minus its mattress, and most evidence of my sickness is gone. I tear another mirror from the wall, and it splinters on the floor. August presses me down on the box spring, clutching my twisting wrists in one of his hands. In his other hand I see the shackles appear from somewhere in his armor.

"No! August, you can't! Don't, please, don't!" I twist and squirm, but he manages to attach one of my wrists to the metal bedpost. I swing my other fist at his head, cracking my knuckles painfully against the hard armor. "Let me go!" I scream, and worse things, until tears are streaming down my cheeks. Somehow he has managed to restrain my good leg too. The shame and betrayal that boil up inside me turn into a terrible rage. I could kill him right now. I could kill him for this. I kick my injured leg around until he grabs me by the ankle, trying to hold my foot in front of his face.

"Is that it?" I snarl. "You have a foot fetish? Fuck you, you pervert! You deviant!" I wrench my foot from his grip and kick out. He steps back, crunching broken glass under his boots, holding his hands palms out, as though he might dive forward and grab me, all his . . . whatever . . . everything he's held inside all this time about to spill out. Like he's going to kill me after all, or something worse. Or he's trying to placate me, maybe. It's hard to tell. It's hard to see through the tears pouring out of my eyes. "You're disgusting. I hate you!" I wail between sobbing, pulling, and clawing at the restraints. He takes another step backward. I grab things from the bedside table and hurl them at him—candles, a clock radio, the lamp. He steps back again and puts both hands on top of his head.

"You feel bad now? You should feel bad, asshole! I hate you! I hate you *repeat forever*! I wish you were dead!"

We fall silent for a moment, staring at each other. He makes a tiny movement, as though he might step toward me, and I suck saliva into my mouth and spit at him. He jerks back as my spit sprays his chest, retreating until his back is pressed against the wall by the door. Before I can plead with him to stop, he turns and runs down the hallway.

"Come back! Don't leave me like this! August, please, don't leave me! Come back!"

Over my sobbing screams I hear the front door open and close.

AUGUST

What.

Just.

Happened?

I fall to my knees at the top of the stairs, tearing at my throat. I can't breathe. I can't breathe.

The door to the roof is propped open. I crawl out into the sunlight, gagging, gasping. I need to disconnect. Now. Something is malfunctioning. I can't breathe. My mind is fragmenting, shattering like glass. Glass. Glass. There was so much glass on the floor. Her feet were bare. Her feet.

Something bubbles inside me, and I feel like I might vomit, though I know I can't. But the breathing tube constricts and contracts all the way back up into my mouth. I cough violently and the tube unwinds and snakes back downward, back into my lungs and insides, filling me with thick sludge, wiping my mind clean for a second, until I can catch my breath.

I rest there, on my hands and knees, trying to hang on to my slippery thoughts. The syrup wants to push them away, turn them into anger, turn me against the vermin, the humans, the girl. . . .

What happened? She was watching something, a video, a girl. A girl being killed. One of us.

Like Sixth. My girl. I wish she were here. She would know what to do. But she's dead. Wings of blood pooled around her neck.

The edge of the roof is only a few feet away. I struggle to my feet and stumble forward, hanging my head over the side. Below me is the terrace off the bedroom. Over the wind I can hear her screaming and crying. Maybe I imagine it. I could hop down; it's only fifteen feet. I could hop down and be with her in seconds, unbinding her and begging her to forgive me. I don't have a sign for "forgive," but I'll make one up.

I don't even know what half those words mean, those things she called me.

There's another edge behind me, at the other side of the roof, with no terrace below it. Forty-one stories straight down. The fall will probably kill me. Probably. What do I believe more? That she'll ever forgive me, or that the fall will kill me? What do I want more? Forgiveness? Or death?

Or sunsets. Or spiderwebs. Pine needles.

Snowflakes.

Dandelions.

Slippery thoughts slither away. I lean my head over the edge until I imagine I can hear her again. Screaming my name. I can't leave her there. Hold on to that thought. I can't forget that she's down there, tied up, alone. If I die, she dies. Starves, freezes. Tied to a bed like . . .

What have I done?

How long have I been up here? Time seems to have passed. The sun is kissing the mountaintops, the light changing from golden to indigo. I stand and measure the distance to each edge, moving my feet slightly until it is exactly even.

The orange orb of the sun dipping behind the snowcapped mountains catches my mind for a second, enough for me to think more clearly than I have in days.

I can string five thoughts together, I think. Try anyway. It's important.

One, she doesn't love me. She never will. *Zero repeat forever.* Nevermore. I doesn't matter what I bring her or how I care for her. I can never make her love me. It's embarrassing to think how hard I've tried.

Two, I love her so completely I can barely think of anything else. That feels like something I won't be able to forget, no matter what.

Three, she'll die if I leave her. Hang on to that. It's important.

Four, it hasn't snowed in six days. That's not really relevant, I get that, but it's true. The fact that I can even remember the last time it snowed is something to celebrate at this point.

Five, I can be by her side in seconds. And she hates me,

thinks I'm a monster, which I am. But I don't care. I'll do whatever she wants, whatever it takes, let her hate me, abuse me, even kill me. I don't care. That makes me a sentimental fool, as well as a pervert and a deviant. Defective, stupid, weak . . .

My head clears. Absolute clarity. I step toward the roof edge, barely aware of which direction I have chosen.

RAVEN

Here's the thing about being handcuffed: It's a lot worse when you don't know when or how it's going to end.

I scream his name and beg him to come back, beg and scream and cry until all my self-respect is gone. Then I cry for Topher, even for Xander and Emily. My parents. I cry for anyone who would never do this to me. And I cry for the dead, Sawyer and Felix and Tucker and the little child whose teddy bear lies decapitated in the bath. And after I cry about the laptop computer smashed below us, I relive the exploding glass table and the Nahx girl losing her head, drifting into exhaustion and jerking awake again and again.

When my arm and leg are both numb and aching, and the fingers on my free hand bleeding from tearing at the shackles, I relive the vase smashing over August's head, and the mirrors and the pictures on the wall. The sun sinks low on the horizon. Golden light streams in through the terrace windows. I turn my head away and look down the hallway, where the debris of the broken picture frames makes long shadows, and the broken glass glitters golden on the floor like distant stars.

Oh my God, the glass on the floor.

Broken glass all over the floor. And I have bare feet. Something inside me cracks and spiderwebs, like a windshield, and all the little shards tinkle down to join the destruction. This is certainly not the first time I've fallen apart, but it's the first time when I'm not sure I want to pick up all the pieces and put myself back together. Because somewhere among the shards is the piece of me that hated August so much that I dreamed of killing him. That I got pleasure from mocking him. That hurled insults and curses even though I know they burned him like acid. What kind of person would be so cruel and distrustful to someone who saved their life? He's never done anything but try to help me and make me happy.

"August . . . ," I whimper. "Come back, please. . . ."

Tugging at the restraints, I lift my free foot back, turning it awkwardly. There is a small cut on one side, nothing serious. I wriggle my other foot. It feels sound.

Time passes. The sun touches the snowy mountaintops and sinks. The twinkling stars in the hallway blink out. I'm so ashamed of myself, I actually long for darkness. If he ever does come back, I don't want him to see me like this. If he ever does come back, the girl they would have called Rage, the fighter, the angry, lost soldier, is gone. Someone else has taken her place, someone nobody would recognize.

Above the mountains the first star appears. It's probably

Venus, but I don't care; I press my eyes shut and make a wish anyway, whispering, "Please let him come back. . . ."

Outside on the terrace I hear something *thump* onto the concrete floor. The sliding door opens.

With the fading sunset behind him all I see is his silhouette. He steps forward and kneels by the bed.

Sorry. Repeat sorry. Forever.

"Me too," I manage, though my heart is lodged in my throat.

He reaches up and clicks something on my wrist restraint, releasing it, then does the same with my ankle. I slide backward, away from him, and tumble onto the floor. When he comes around the bed, I'm pressed into the corner of the room, rubbing the feeling back into my wrist and ankle.

Four. Give.

It's the first time I've seen him use that phrase. Probably not the last. I can forgive—I do forgive—but my mouth won't work.

He hangs his head and slowly kneels in front of me, then falls forward until his forehead is on the floor, both his hands on the top of his helmet. It's an impressive display of remorse, I have to admit. Even Tucker's impassioned apologies were never this all-encompassing, this visceral. But Tucker's anger was never so explosive, either. I mean at least he never smashed a table in front of me.

"It was because of the broken glass, right? You didn't want me to cut my feet?"

He moves his head slightly, nodding into the floor.

"Why did you get so angry? Did you know that girl? The one in the video?"

He taps the thumb on his left hand. I'm not sure what this means. When I don't respond, he makes two other familiar signs.

Feel broken.

"I'm okay. You didn't really hurt me."

I—I—I— feel broken.

He sits up, leaning back on his heels. Hanging his head, not looking at me, he signs slowly with one hand. I translate it effortlessly in my head.

You make me very, very sad.

This feels like an attack more than an admission. I reach forward and lift his chin up so he can see me, making his signs as I speak, slicing my thumb across my throat. "You make me feel like killing myself."

He pulls his chin away and turns his head slightly, just enough that I know he's not looking at me anymore.

Repeat me.

Repeat.

Forever.

I couldn't hate him now if I found him torturing puppies. All I want is to put my arms around him and tell him that everything will be all right. But of course I realize that's the last thing he needs. Because it would be a lie. And no one needs that.

"You went up onto the roof, didn't you? When you left me?"

He nods, still looking away.

"Were you going to jump?"

He falls slowly forward again, this time cradling his head on the floor in the crook of his right elbow. His left hand inches forward until his gloved fingertips barely touch my foot. I don't move it away. I feel a strange connection to him, knowing that suicide has been on his mind too. I'm not sure I realized how much it's been on *my* mind until a few seconds ago.

"I don't think we should be around each other anymore."

He shakes his head.

"I have to get back to my people, back to my friends somehow."

He nods slowly.

Squeezing my eyes shut doesn't make it any harder to see the reality of my situation, of our situation. As much as we need to be rid of each other, it's not to be. Not for a while anyway.

"I don't think I can find my way back alone. It's too far."

A long time passes before he nods again, his head still cradled in his arm.

It's the hardest thing I've ever had to ask of anyone. Harder than asking Xander to help us put Tucker's body in the ground.

"Will you come with me?"

He nods right away this time and sighs a long, growling sigh.

"It's a long way. More than two hundred miles."

He keeps nodding, but clenches the fingers away from my foot.

We sit there until I start to tremble from the cold. The sun has dipped well below the horizon by this time, and the room is dark but for the lingering twilight.

"August . . ."

He stands quickly, perfunctorily, and glancing across the room and through the door, leans down and lifts me easily into his arms. Since I don't struggle, he's able to hold me, like a groom holds a bride, and carry me down the long, dark hallway. Glass crunches under his feet as he walks.

He tucks me into the sofa, folding blankets around me, always his face turned away. He doesn't want to see me. As he finishes, I take hold of one of his hands, whispering, like I'm sharing a secret.

"There's a place, a time maybe, or a universe, where we can be friends, right?"

He makes his sign for "pretty" then. I'm not sure why. And nods.

Later, in the dark, I hear him sweeping up the broken glass.

AUGUST

riends.

Not in this world though. Not in this universe, somewhere else. But that's enough, I suppose. It's more than I deserve after frightening her so much.

When the sun rises, I have a surprise for her. It wasn't that hard to manage, and I finally figured out how to give her something that I'm sure she'll love, without having to steal it from a dead human. I nudge her sleeping form. As she stirs, I move back. I know she doesn't like me touching her.

"Hello," she says, opening her eyes. She sits up a little and looks around, out the window. "Nice day for a hike, huh?"

I nod, the happy feeling in my mind making it easy to focus. I make her name sign.

Raven.

"Yes?" she says with a smile. Ah, she's beautiful.

I gesture, standing up and stepping backward.

Follow, I sign. She seems to understand. With the blanket still wrapped around her, she follows me down the hallway to the bathroom. I hold the door open for her. Scented steam wafts out.

"Is that . . . *hot* water? A hot bath?"

I nod. I'm starting to feel a little dizzy.

"Wow. August. I don't know what to say. How did you do this? It's amazing. . . ."

She's smiling so brightly now that it almost hurts to look at her. This is the happiness I have been trying for all along. Sweet Dandelion with a smile on her face. It's too much to bear. I turn away, reaching for the wall with my left hand.

"Are you okay?"

Good. Happy. You?

"Very happy, thank you. I'm going to have my bath now."

I have forgotten how to move, I think. The smile fades from her face.

"You weren't hoping to watch, were you?"

No. No. No. No. Sorry. No.

I step out and close the door behind me. Stupid August. That was really stupid.

By the time she emerges wrapped in her blanket, her hair in a towel, I have piled up new clothes on the sofa, things I searched all night for. I stand there and watch her reaction as she sees the offerings. Thermal underwear, a warm coat, insulated snow pants, waterproof mittens . . .

"Boots," she says, and then, for some reason, she looks sad. She covers her mouth.

I'm not really sure what to do or say. I'm trying not to

look at her bare thigh, which pokes out from the blanket. She smells phenomenal, exquisite, like a mixture of wildflowers and bees and *her* smell, but clean and new. So human, so much a part of her beautiful planet. I reach for her without even thinking. She takes a step back.

Sorry.

"No, it's okay." She sniffs. "Really, I'm fine. I'll get dressed now. Can you . . . ?"

I step out the front door and close it behind me.

In the hallway I struggle not to imagine the blanket slipping off, her pulling the towel from her head, the golden dandelion wisps of her hair springing back and falling on her shoulders. The Dandelion in my thoughts is even more beautiful, if that's possible.

My mind opens up and I see things, mysterious but familiar, that I know come from behind the door. The overpowering feeling of seeing her happy has cracked it open again, and I see others like me, hundreds of others lined up, something almost remembered about seeing myself in a mirror, a row of mirrors. My heart jumps in my chest as the door slides closed, the sliver of light disappearing.

I'm kneeling, my whole body leaning on the wall when she finds me.

"Are you all right?"

She is completely outfitted in the clothes I gathered for her, all black and dark gray because we will need to keep to the shadows—a tight black hat that pulls down and ties under her chin, a black scarf over her mouth and nose, a fitted waterproof jacket, mittens, the snow pants tied into the boots. She's very small, compared to me, but if another glanced at her from far away, she would look like one of us. That's the idea. If we are seen, and not looked at too closely, the others might ignore us. Seeing her makes me feel better about going out into the world.

I shake off the unease of the vision, and stand.

Good forever. You?

"Great. How do I look?"

You look like you're getting ready to leave me, Dandelion. But she doesn't know all the signs for that so I just sign *good*.

He suggests, instructs rather, that I nap in the afternoon.

Sleep now, please.

"I'm not that tired."

Then he makes a long series of signs, most of which I've never seen before. But somehow the meaning is clear anyway.

Sleep now or you'll be so tired I'll have to carry you all night.

He laughs along with me, tipping his head back as I curl up on the sofa. When I wake, it's dark and quiet in the apartment. Moonlight trickles in from the terrace as I sit up and pull on my boots, taking a last look around.

If this were another world and I were another person, this place would be a dream come true—a million-dollar penthouse in the clouds. In the dark it looks almost as though it could still be that, though I know by daylight it's a bit of a mess. Clothes piled everywhere, food packets discarded on every surface. Neither one of us is very good at housework. He's been throwing the dirty dishes over the railing, after all. We've basically trashed the place, like a couple of drug-addicted squatters. I feel a twinge of guilt then. What if the owner, the bald, single accountant, survived somehow, in a refugee camp or something? What if, when all this is over, he comes back and finds this mess? Maybe I should leave him a note. I wonder how I could explain what happened here.

"August?" I say then, suddenly uncomfortable in the dark. There is no answer. He'll be back soon, I tell myself. He always comes back, no matter what.

I feel my way down to the bathroom, light a candle, and use the toilet one last time. Digging through the drawers, I collect a few toothbrushes and some toothpaste. I grab some moist disinfecting wipe things and some sunscreen.

I can't help but smile at the assortment of skin care, hair oil, and shampoo gifts August gathered over the weeks. I picture him scouring store shelves, taking any bottle or box with a model that looks vaguely like me. I have enough African hair products to last two apocalypses. I wish I could carry it all, but one jar of shea butter will have to do. For now I take some time to properly comb my hair, styling it into flat twists that will be comfortable under my hat. I figure I've earned a little pampering.

When I'm done, I slip everything into a small case and carry it back into the living room, tucking it into my backpack, which beyond all reason, I still have. It's been through everything with me, barely the worse for wear. I shake my head, looking through the window at the stars.

"August?" I say to my reflection. It seems I'm still alone. I fuss with the zipper of my backpack—it's always been a bit stubborn. When I look back up at my reflection, there is a large shadow behind me, just inside the door.

"Jesus! Don't sneak up on me."

A second later I know it's not him.

I dive down to the floor, sliding my hand under the sofa, searching for the knife that I sliced into the upholstery. My hand feels around as the shadow moves toward me. I have only enough brain cells left over to realize this is a probably a girl Nahx before my hand closes over the knife. She gives the coffee table a shove with her foot, and it goes sliding across the room.

"AUGUST!" I scream, swinging my leg around. Her feet go out from under her, and she crashes down onto the floor in front of me. I have to make a split-second decision. I could jump her and try to lodge the knife into her neck, or I could run.

Ah, run or fight. Either way my chances are basically nil.

"AUGUST!"

The girl grabs my ankle, like the one in the stadium did. I pull my other leg back and kick her hard in the head. Maybe this one is not quite as robust, because this seems to stun her. Gripping the knife, I leap to my feet and vault over her, heading for the door.

Throwing the door open, I launch myself into the hallway. I catch a glimpse of the girl Nahx clambering to her feet before the door swings closed. It's almost completely dark in the hall, and I don't have a light. In fact, I have nothing but the knife in my hand. I don't even have that fantastic coat on. All I'm wearing is the snow pants, boots, and a couple of sweaters. Damn it, where is August?!

I race down the hallway, dragging my hand along the wall to find my way. When I reach the stairwell, I glance back to see the Nahx emerging from the penthouse. *Oh God, I'm dead*, I think, and even have the logic to remember that Nahx don't usually travel alone. Whoever this Nahx is, her partner, a boy, likely much larger and stronger than her, is somewhere nearby.

I leap down the first flight of stairs, my ankles jolting painfully as I land. Then I slide down the banister to the next level and fly out into the hallway. Thankfully, August has kicked open all the doors on this level too. I've never been more grateful for this particular one of his peculiarities. I run halfway down the hallway and, pulling the scarf from around my neck, toss it into an apartment. Then I double back and duck quickly behind the door of the first apartment. I'm not sure that the Nahx work by smell, but I've long suspected it. Maybe this will be how I find out once and for all.

The apartment I find myself in is similar to the penthouse,

but smaller. I run to the kitchen first and take a second to arm myself with another sharp knife. Then I bolt down to the bedroom, into the en suite bathroom, and lock the door. I crawl into the bath and pull the sliding glass across.

And wait.

It's not long before I hear the front door bang open. The irony is not lost on me. I'm cowering in a bathroom again, a knife in each hand. Shoot, maybe I can make this one fall in love with me too.

Fall in love? Did I just think that? Do I really think August is in love with me?

I hear metallic footsteps approaching down the hardwood floor in the hallway.

Of course August is in love with me. Of course he is. What the hell have I been thinking?

"Oh God, oh God, oh God," I whisper, not sure whether I'm panicking about the girl Nahx who is coming down the hall to kill me, or the boy Nahx who is out there in the city somewhere, in love with me. How did I let either of these things happen?

The bedroom door opens. I make a rash and stupid decision. This girl will be expecting me to cower in hiding, like I did when August found me. But I'm going down slashing. As quietly as I can, I slide the glass door open and step out of the bath. A shaft of moonlight through a frosted window is all the illumination I have to work with, but it's enough to guide me back to the bathroom door. I doubt I can slowly ease the lock back without making noise, so I decide to go for fast and loud. *Click, bang!* I throw the door open.

The Nahx is bent over, looking under the bed, her rifle lying on the coverlet. She barely has time to turn her head before I leap on her back, bounce down onto the bed, hooking one foot through the strap of her rifle, and then plow into the sliding door, my arms crossed in front of my face. The glass shatters around me, and I land on my knees, my face smacking into the railing. That will hurt tomorrow, I think, spinning back to see the Nahx climbing over the bed toward me.

She moves slowly at first. I'm sure she knows that the only way out for me is down, but I'm counting on her aggression taking over at the last minute. My other encounters with Nahx have all been about a slow stalk culminating in a high-speed hand-to-hand assault. I've lost track of where her rifle went. She doesn't have it and I don't have it—that's all I know. She steps down off the bed. I crouch, gripping my knives. With a swish, she produces her own knife. The polished blade glints in the moonlight.

"Oh shit," I say. I don't really care if she knows how scared I am. Bravado is going to get me nowhere at this stage. I have one chance to end this in my favor. I try to frame my plan into words in my head. They should be very familiar words to me, martial arts prodigy that I am, but I can't quite think. Glass crunches under the Nahx's boots.

"AUGUST!?" I yell into the night.

Something about using my enemy's momentum to do something. I have no earthly idea. She steps onto the terrace and, with lightning speed, lunges at me. Dropping the knives, I dive down and grab her ankles. She smacks into the railing as I roll onto my back, still holding her ankles, and get my feet under me. Then, knees trembling with effort, I press up. She gives a nasty growl as I flip her over the railing. One of her hands shoots out and grabs the metal as she falls. She swings down, hanging by one hand.

Damn it. This is like one of those movie scenes where the good guy stupidly helps the bad guy not fall to their death. The second it takes for me to think this is enough for us to both realize where the dart rifle is—right under the railing, right in front of her. She flings her knife away before her fingers close on the rifle. This time I don't even think. I swing around and kick, neatly swiping her hand right off the rail. She lets out a wild hiss as she falls.

I look over the railing as she disappears below me, and something zips past my ear.

Bitch actually fired that dart rifle as she fell thirty-nine stories straight down.

I fall to my knees on the terrace, the snow pants cushioning the impact somewhat. Something trickles down my face. I reach up and find blood dripping from a cut on my eyebrow. I'm cold now too. Now that the adrenaline is wearing off, I realize how bitingly cold it is out here. I have no hat or gloves or coat, either, and I've just smashed the window. I struggle to my feet. Leaning over the railing, I can see the Nahx girl splayed out, a dark speck on the road far below. I stumble back into the apartment and sit on the bed.

Now I have to decide what to do. Do I go and look for August, risking running into this girl's partner, or do I hide for a while and hope August can find me? Hide or fight? Hide or run? Hide or search?

And then there is the whole thing of August being in love with me. I'm not as sure of this as I was a few minutes ago, when death was so close. Now I think maybe that was just my brain twitching in the heat of the moment. He cares about me, cares about my survival, but love? I think it's possible he loves me about as much as Topher does, which is to say not really at all. He feels an obligation to me, a perverse attraction, and a good deal of the old-fashioned hormonal confusion brought by grief and fear and being a boy. Yes, that makes more sense. Grief and fear turn us all into morons.

I wish Topher were here, so I could tell him that killing a Nahx doesn't feel as good as we thought it would. In fact I feel sick to my stomach. She was wild and determined to dart me, for whatever reasons the Nahx have, but some part of her must have been like August, a thinking being. He can't be the only one who thinks like he does. Did she like sunsets too? Snowflakes? Was she afraid of her own reflection? He was driven like her once too. He stormed into that trailer planning to kill whatever he found there, but changed his mind for some reason. If he could change his mind, then can't they all? The strength of this revelation makes me dizzy. I lie back on the bed and stare at the dark ceiling. If I made August change his mind, then why can't I . . . do something . . . you know? Save the world or something?

Why does my life have to be so complicated?

I encounter the boy on the fourth floor. He turns at the sounds of my footsteps on the stairs behind him. We can't show emotion. We aren't supposed to feel any emotion, but I can tell he's surprised to see me.

Rank? he signs.

Sixth, I lie.

My mind spits up a piece of procedure. Something Sixth may or may not have told me. *Split up. I start at the top, you at the bottom. We meet in the middle.* Though I never searched a high-rise with her, I know what this means. There is a girl on the top floor; this one's Offside is up where Dandelion was. Right now. And I can't move from dreading she'll dart Dandelion and this will all be over.

Too late I remember I should have asked for the boy's rank too. He's a high rank. A Third maybe. His armor is shiny clean.

What are you doing? he asks me, impatiently, because I've been standing there staring at him like a dull-witted Twelfth.

Preparing, I sign. *I have searched this building.*

Where is your Offside?

Dead. I think of the shape she left in the crushed grass,

the wings of blood. *Dead* doesn't seem like the right answer anymore.

Upstairs, I say, in a rare moment of inspiration. *What is your rank?*

Third, he snaps. *Come with me.*

I have no time to think or plan. I step up behind him as he turns, grab his head, and kick his feet out from under him. That's been done to me enough times that I am something of an expert. His knife flashes in the dark as he falls. I hold my hands on his head and twist until I hear a crack, then push his body down the stairs. The knife *clinks* onto the concrete. Stepping down, I pick it up and stare at it for a moment.

It is easier than I thought it would be, to kill one of my own kind, in cold blood. I killed the one who was attacking Dandelion in the stadium, but that was different, a moment of rage and terror, fueled by the sludge churning inside me. This broken-necked boy on the stairs was a rational choice. I wonder now why I didn't kill Sixth that day in the rain.

Kill. Dead. Stop. Stopped.

I should just walk away. This Third cared nothing for me, and even less for humans. But I can't shake my sense of allegiance to him. I flip his lifeless body over. With the knife I dig the transponder out of the back of his neck, dropping it and crushing it under my boot on the concrete floor. At least now if he ever wakes up, maybe he'll be free like me.

Dandelion is sitting in the dark when I find her, in our apartment, wrapped in a blanket, a sharp knife in each hand, the smell of fear wafting around her. Fear and bees and wildflowers. Her hair is tightly twisted to her head, with feathery puffs escaping the edges. Not a dandelion now so much as a bird. A scared bird. A bold, defiant bird.

Raven.

"I killed a . . . one of you," she says. There's a line of blood down one side of her face.

Me too.

"What will they do to you if they find out?"

I draw my thumb across my throat, then hand her coat to her.

I give her the knife I took from the boy and point to the spot under my chin. I'd like to explain that the blades are specially designed to cut through my armor. *Why* has never been explained to me.

"I know," she says, sliding the knife into a holster she has strapped to her thigh.

Don't be scared, I sign. I don't want to tell her there's a chance one or both of them will get up eventually.

"I'm not."

I reach forward and unzip one of the coat pockets. Then I slip in a small pistol I found, dropping two ammunition clips into the other pocket. I tap my chin again.

As we leave the tower that has been our home for so long, we pass the bodies of my two colleagues, one limp on the stairs, one twisted and broken out in the snow.

The beginning of our journey is not as happy as I had hoped. But at least we're together.

I'm not sure why I didn't get angry at August for leaving me alone to be attacked by a Nahx in the dark. Maybe I've finally realized that none of this is his fault. None of it is my fault either, I now know too. Nothing either of us could have done would have made a difference. I couldn't have known, and he has no power or influence. I'm not even sure how I know this now—I just do. It's clear that he is an underling, a foot soldier. He's AWOL, a deserter, too, which I'm sure is not good, for either of us.

Both of us are on the run now, but only one of us has somewhere to go. As we creep along the dark streets, I wonder what will become of him when we part. I wonder, and I wonder, and I begin to worry and obsess, chiding myself, reminding myself that he's not my problem. He walks slightly behind me, rifle raised in one hand, the other hand resting on my shoulder. I shove it off periodically, but it always finds its way back there. Eventually, I ignore it. He's used to walking like that, or he wants us to look like a normal pair of Nahx, whatever. It's irritating, but at least he doesn't chatter the whole time the way Xander did.

Even at night I can see that we are walking through a nightmare. I focus my eyes on my feet, so as not to have to bear witness to the devastation around me. After an hour of walking I begin to realize a small voice in the back of my head has been counting, despite my efforts, noticing each of the dead humans we pass. I become aware of it at around five hundred. Many of them are so covered in snow they look like indistinct shapes of white fluff. But I know what they are.

The darkness is still profound when we reach the stadium. It rises above us like looming cliffs against the starry sky. I feel a perverse desire to go inside, to examine the place where I fought with the Nahx, where August rescued me. I'm not sure what I expect to find. My bloodstains, maybe. The body of that Nahx. Did August kill him? I've never asked. Or have I? The attacker and rescuer swirl together again. August grabs my arm as I stumble in the snow.

Feel broken?

"Fine. I slipped."

I tell myself that what happened in the stadium doesn't matter. And it doesn't. All I need is an escort back to the base, back to safety, and then August will not matter to me anymore, nor what he did or didn't do, nor why.

We skirt around the stadium, staying close to the wall. We haven't talked about where those two Nahx came from earlier. August doesn't seem very worried about it, and there doesn't seem to be any sign of more Nahx behind them. Maybe they were a routine patrol or something. I count on August knowing if more are likely to follow. I count on him to be able to spot the transports, which can fly silently. I count on him for everything. If I ran off, would he follow? Would he let me do something so stupid?

I count on the answer being no.

August hands me a small flashlight when we reach the entrance to the tunnel. He hesitates as I head down the ramp, but follows me as I descend, his hand on my shoulder.

The tunnel is dark and cold and smells of fuel and damp, something I didn't notice last time I was here. My flashlight, and one August clips to his rifle, provide a small pool of light to guide us. I walk ahead, with August trailing, and I feel his tentative pace, almost as though he doesn't want to be down here with me.

"Is this too low for you? You prefer the high ground, right?" I shine my flashlight at him as he nods. "Will you be all right?" He rolls his finger in a circle, which I interpret as "Let's get on with it." It's strange how familiar many of these signs are to me now.

If he's some sort of machine, I think as I walk, then why would they make him so he can't talk? Surely that's a limitation his makers should have thought of. Perhaps I could ask him about it later. Now is probably not the best time. I think of the weeks we spent in the comfortable penthouse when I could have been learning to communicate with him better, when I could have been asking him every possible question. But instead I seethed with anger, avoided him out of fear and disgust, or wasted time trying to make him feel bad. All those years of effort I put into trying to contain and channel my rage through martial arts and philosophy came to nothing, I guess, when it mattered. Thinking of it makes me want to kick something.

We slosh through a fetid puddle and soon we are up to our ankles in suspiciously oily water. I take back what I said about the chatter. It's creepy down here with nothing to listen to but my thoughts. To fill the silence I start to chatter myself and hope that August doesn't mind.

"I used to be afraid of the dark, you know." Stupid thing to say, but the echo of my voice off the weeping walls provides a bit of atmosphere. "I guess in a world without electricity that's a pretty crippling phobia. Darkness is a natural thing, after all. Like death." His feet slosh behind mine. "Why is the electricity off anyway? Do you guys bomb the power stations? Wait, was it like one of those, what are they called, EMPs? An electromagnetic pulse? Those antiterrorist nuts used to talk about that. You guys showed them, huh? Way to incite terror. Kill everyone. That's pretty terrifying."

We walk in silence for several minutes during which

my face burns. I don't even know if it's anger or shame at this point. God, if we have to walk back to the base, it will take weeks. I'm going to lose my mind, being stretched out between resenting him and needing him and feeling sorry for him and wishing he were dead. And wishing I were dead. When finally I can't help but release a shaky sigh, he gives my shoulder a squeeze. Even through my coat and sweaters I can feel his hand is hot. Unnaturally hot, like an iron or a kettle. If it weren't for the thick layers of clothes, it feels like it might burn me.

Stopping, I turn and shine my flashlight at him. In the near dark his armored plates disappear into shadows somehow so I can barely see him. He drops his hand from my shoulder and lowers the rifle he carries, tilting his head to the side.

"Are you a machine?" I've asked this before, but this is one of the questions he walked away from. "Answer me this time."

He makes a sign with his hand, moving his fingers like he is pressing buttons or levers.

"Machine, right. Well? Are you a machine?"

He sighs and, after a moment, shrugs.

"What do you mean? How can you not know?"

Reaching forward, he taps me on the shoulder.

You. Machine?

"No, I'm not. I'm a human being, of course."

He simply raises his hand to form a question without any

words attached to it. I somehow know he's asking me *Are you sure?* I walk on, unable to find the right answer to that. A moment later, his hand appears on my shoulder again. Is it so odd that he doesn't know what he is? If someone had asked me a year ago what my purpose was and why I was here, I wouldn't have had a clue. I would have shrugged like the surly teenager I am, neglected my homework, and slumped into a chair to waste more time blasting space zombies, all the while slowly becoming one. Outside the dojo, was I any less a mindless machine than August? And inside the dojo all I ever wanted was a win for myself. August was part of a mission at least, part of an encroaching army that had a shared goal, a plan, and a pattern of operations.

Space zombies. That's funny.

I shove his hand from my shoulder, but a minute later it reappears. I wonder how we would look from far away, if we look like two Nahx strolling about their business of ridding the Earth of human scum. I imagine myself joining this mission, firing darts, and laying waste to a civilization. I know it took thousands of years to build, but maybe it wasn't all that great anyway. Maybe we deserved what we got. And I might like being a Nahx. I've always preferred wearing dark colors anyway.

As though he knows what I'm thinking, he squeezes my shoulder again.

With nothing but the circle of light in front of us to look at, it's easy for my mind to conjure other images. I picture August reaching out to the left with his hand, leaning on the wall, on furniture, reaching for something that is not there. Something, or someone. Someone. I think of the way the Nahx walked in those fuzzy videos, one with their hand on the other's shoulder. The one where the head disintegrated. And that girl who lost her head had someone leaning on her, too, once, I imagine.

I really hate this tunnel. It's dark and wet and making me maudlin and stupid.

"Who was it?" I say to August eventually, when I can no longer resist. "The one you reach for? When you are upset or in pain, you reach to the left. Who are you reaching for? Someone you used to walk with, like this?"

He grips my shoulder hard and pulls me to a stop.

"Never mind," I say quickly. "Forget it. It's not my business."

Turning my flashlight to him, I can see he is looking away from me, though his hand is still on my shoulder. I don't know why I keep talking. It's as though there is some bridge that needs crossing that I need to draw us over if we're to get where we're going.

"Was it a girl? The girl you traveled with?"

He nods, still looking away. My flashlight illuminates his profile, which in its lack of detail, still looks disarmingly human. A strong chin, the sweep of a nose, even a slight brow ridge in a permanent frown. He sighs then, a long growling sigh, which resonates down the tunnel.

"Did you love her?" I don't know what the hell is happening to my mouth. It seems to be proceeding without any reference to my brain or what might be sensible things to ask him. It's several long seconds before he nods again, slowly.

I barely take the time to process that this creature, who may or may not be a machine, has admitted to loving someone. "Where is she?"

He takes his hand from my shoulder and draws it across his throat.

Dead.

He puts his hand back on my shoulder and squeezes, letting his head drop and hang down. Then he gives me a little shove. I turn my flashlight forward and walk on, blinking, blinking, and thinking of Edgar Allan Poe.

Zero repeat forever.

Nothing again forever.

Nevermore.

"My boyfriend died too," I say a few minutes later, for no other reason than I think he should know. He pulls me to a stop, tapping his shoulder where Topher shot him with the arrow, and shakes his head.

"No, that wasn't my boyfriend. That was Topher. He's just a friend. His brother, Tucker, was the one I loved. But he died.

He was killed by . . . one of you. A Nahx. A while ago."

See Topher? he signs, tapping his eye and his shoulder. It's nice the way he's given him a sign name, just like that.

"We're looking for him, yes."

See Topher repeat.

"I hope so," I say. "I hope I see him again. He's a good friend." I say this with conviction, though I'm not sure I know what friendship is anymore. Maybe I only call Topher a friend because he's the same species as me.

August stares at me for a moment, then nods and, gripping my shoulder, nudges me forward once more.

Ahead of us in the tunnel I see a dark shape. I shine my flashlight forward and there, parked neatly, across two lanes in the middle of the road facing away from us, is a bright red old-style pickup truck, something I'm sure wasn't here the last time I came this way. I tug away from August's hand and run. With his clanking footsteps falling in behind me, I reach the back of the truck and jump up to look at the flatbed.

It is lined with fuel canisters. Full canisters, I discover on shaking one. Enough gasoline to drive hundreds of miles.

"Yes!" Yes!" I leap down and throw the driver's door open. Miraculously, the light comes on. On the seat is a plain white envelope. I tug my mittens off and tear it open with trembling fingers, climbing into the driver's seat. August appears in the open door, but I ignore him.

There is a map. A hand-drawn map on a white sheet of paper. *Start at the camp*, it says. I know the way to the camp from town. The map shows the way from there to the base. The secret base. No one who doesn't know what camp we were at could ever use this map. It's brilliant.

There is also a letter. From Topher.

Dear Raven,

I've been searching for you for three days, and Liam says we can't wait anymore. I can't believe you're dead. I won't believe that. I chased that Nahx for miles, but he was too fast and I lost him. Please forgive me for letting him take you. Please forgive me for not searching for you forever.

I'm out of my mind not knowing what happened to you, and I'm an idiot for hoping you're still alive. But I hope you are and that you come back here and find this truck, this map, and this letter. Xander made the map. The route is mostly lower ground and back roads so it should be safer. We found the truck deep in a parking garage. Just touch the wires together and it will start. Since it's so old, the ignition is simple. It should start. I pray it starts.

I hope we find each other again. I miss you, Raven, and I promise I will never forget you.

Please come back to me.

—Toph

I read it again, then again, to make sure that I didn't imagine the more fanciful parts. The part where he says he'll never forget me. The part where he says "come back to me." August stands stoically, staring forward in the tunnel while I read the note one last time before folding it into my pocket with the pistol. Then I set my forehead down on the steering wheel and resist the urge to scream.

Come back to me? To ME? There is a sense of inevitability to it, that Topher would take his twin's place as easily, in the end, as putting on his boots. I wonder if it will be that easy for me.

My heart is pounding in my chest so hard that my ribs ache. I tug at the scarf around my neck, loosening it, and take deep breaths.

After a few minutes I feel August's hand on my shoulder.

Feel broken?

For once I don't have tears in my eyes. I think I'm in too much shock to cry. "I'm fine," I say, the millionth lie I've told him. "It's just exciting. It means I can drive. At least part of the way. I'll get there in a day or two, instead of weeks."

August nods. His hand turns up to form a question, but I don't know what about.

"I'm sorry I . . ."

He taps himself in the chest, with his other hand still making a question.

Me?

"What about you?"

August reaches past me and points to the passenger seat.

Me?

He wants to know if I still want him to come along. Like I would leave him here alone in the tunnel. Like I'm that kind of person.

Like that isn't exactly what I should do.

"Of course, August. I mean, if you want to. It's still pretty dangerous out there, right?"

He nods and looks ahead into the tunnel again. Then he gently closes the driver's door and walks around the truck. I lean over and open the passenger door for him.

"Hop in."

He hesitates at the door. I realize I have never seen him sitting down. He has kneeled and sat back on his heels, but I've never seen him sit, either on the floor or on a chair. Also, he's very tall. I'm not sure he'll fit. He leans his head in, and I hear him take a deep breath. I breathe in too and notice that the cab smells like cigarettes and beer. Not my favorite smell, but I'll take it rather than leave it.

But August, who lived with the smell of me dying for a week, apparently prefers not to. He closes the door, steps back, and deftly hops into the bed of the truck, squatting among the gas canisters.

I roll my window down and lean out to look at him.

"Are you sure?" He nods and clicks off his flashlight as I start the engine, swiping the two wires against each other. It purrs beautifully, and the headlights glow in front of us, lighting up the wet tunnel, the way out, and the thoughts in my head that swirl like a blizzard.

I'm almost there. I'm going back to Topher, to other humans, to somewhere safe, somewhere August will leave me behind and we'll never see each other again. I focus on the road, pressing my lips together so that last thought won't tear me apart.

S he drives until her head begins to nod down, when the dark of the next day is already approaching. Now that we are away from the city, I think it's safe to travel by day. Safer even, because I could see the transports in the sky even if they were flying silent. So far we have been unmolested, but I can't count on that continuing.

We park the vehicle under the cover of some trees as the light fades. She is quiet, subdued. The time she spent under the tree where we broke our journey earlier today is weighing heavily on her, though I'm not sure I understand why. She kneeled there in the snow and cried a little. I stood off to the side, not wanting to intrude. I think it's possible that her boy is buried under the ground there. The humans bury their dead sometimes, like seeds that they expect to grow into something else, a flower or a tree. As though burying them will change their destiny. It's sad and kind of funny to me. I left Sixth where she fell because . . . well, because I couldn't stand to look at her anymore.

Dandelion sits in the truck until I have built a fire. It is dangerously cold, and I think it's worth the risk that the smoke will be seen. This kind of cold can kill humans, I know. I've seen it. I could keep her warm, just by being close to her, but she doesn't care for closeness, not with me anyway. She sits opposite me, the heat of the fire distorting her pretty face. I dig out a can of some kind of food from my pack. She eats without comment, then curls up and goes to sleep.

I wish she would talk to me again, like in the tunnel when she asked me about my life and shared things from hers. It bothered me, the things she asked and the things she said, but it was better than this silence. When she sleeps, I feel alone and bound at the same time. I'm both with and without. With and without her, with and without my own people. With and without Sixth. With and without a reason to keep living.

But her questions unnerve me too. The things she wanted to know about our darts, our plans, that I couldn't quite answer. And she spoke of me loving Sixth as though that was a normal thing for someone like me. She wants to know who and what I am, wants me to tell her, but I think she knows more about that than I do.

Tomorrow we will reach our destination and all this will be over. I'll be on my own again. There is no going back this time.

My mind drifts in and out of focus. I think of noting the location of her refuge and reporting it back to the high ranks. I know that's wrong, but it seems to fit. It's the right thing to think, even though I would never, I could never betray

Dandelion like that. I think of tearing my breathing tube out. I think of following her back to her people and hoping they . . . what? Like me? Accept me? Tolerate me as she does? I think of darting her as she sleeps and then wandering off into the snow until I find something to jump off or somewhere to sit and think. The dread of my last moment with her has so infused me in sludge right now, I can barely string two thoughts together. But at least they're *my* thoughts. The hum of directives is a faint memory. If they changed, if there were new directives, I would never know. I have given myself new directives anyway. Save the life of *this* human. That's what matters.

I tuck the cans of food she rejected back into the pack. As I reorganize things, I find a slim book and discover, remember rather, that I can read. "The Raven," this book is called.

Ah, right, that's her name. Raven. It does not suit her. Dandelion suits her much better. It's not just her prettiness, or her cloud of sunny hair. She reminds me of the bright little flowers that grew everywhere during the summer, unbowed by the destruction my people wrought. It was as though they refused to be conquered. But I suppose ravens are like that too. And humans. *This* human in particular.

I read the raven book, then read it again. Why do humans read things like this? Are they masochists in love with pain? I have to resist the urge to throw it into the fire, so miserable it makes me. I wonder if there is a written thing on this planet that is sadder.

Slipping my hand into her pocket as she sleeps, I unfold the letter that inflamed her so much her body wafted with endorphins. It is not mine to read—I know this somehow, this rule of privacy that the humans treasure so much. It is not part of my culture—we don't have secrets—but I understand it anyway. This doesn't stop me from reading the letter from the boy who shot me, Topher. The boy who loves Dandelion. The one she loves back, though I'm not sure she knows it.

My head starts to hurt as I read. We are low, for me. The altimeter on my sleeve reads 2,000 feet, about 500 feet lower than is healthy. Soon my muscles and bones will ache too. Eventually, probably, I will die, gasping for breath, blood drowning my lungs. I think that's what happens. Maybe Sixth explained this to me once.

The letter transfixes me. I can't stop reading it, and I find it *is* sadder than the raven book. I don't think after reading it countless times that he loves her as much as I do, but to her, I suppose that doesn't matter. I would never have stopped searching though, if I were him. I would never have left her side. That other one in the stadium would have to have killed me first before he touched her. This Topher is stupid and weak like all human men. I could crush him like a snail on a rock and eat his remains.

We've been told not to eat human remains, although some ignore that advice. Personally, I keep away from humans dead or alive. Except Dandelion. I can't keep away from her.

When I turn to her, she is looking at me, her face a mask of horror. I still have the letter in my hand.

"Give that back!" she says, sitting up. The fire blazes in her eyes. "That's mine!"

I don't know why I do it. I'm so hurt and angry at that moment, for no good reason either. She doesn't belong to me. We are not bound together as Sixth and I were. She owes me nothing. She has promised me nothing. Nothing is what I deserve.

I throw the letter into the fire.

"No!" she cries. I grab her wrists before she can dive after it. The fire consumes the paper quickly, in a flash of flame and smoke. She flicks her wrists back and away.

There follows a silence so deep and long that I'm genuinely afraid she will kill me with the knife I gave her. I burn, I burn so hot that I plunge my hands into the deep snow beside me. Finally, she speaks, her voice low and cracked and swollen with fury.

"You . . . despicable . . . horrible . . . . MONSTER!"

I nod. *Yes. Yes.* She's right. She's absolutely right.

"How could you do that?"

I've made her cry again. I hate myself so much right now, if throwing myself into the fire would help, I would do it.

"I might never see him again," she sobs. I turn away and shield my eyes with my hands. "Look at me! Look at me!"

Sorry. Sorry. Forever sorry.

"Stop saying that! You can't do horrible things and expect to be forgiven because you say you're sorry. You have to stop doing horrible things. Stop ruining things. Stop hurting me."

I hit myself in the chest.

Please, please, please. Sorry, sorry, sorry.

"Shut up!" she screams, although I have not made any noise. I stand and walk into the trees, away from her. The smell of pine needles gives me a few blissful seconds and I forget why she's angry, but then she yells after me.

"I might never see him again! He could be dead!"

I keep walking, winding in and out of the trunks and branches, until the glow of the fire is just a speck in the distance. She doesn't follow or call after me. I could keep going. She'll be safe enough, out here, in the middle of nowhere. At any rate, if my people took her in an hour or a day, or if she froze or starved or was eaten by a wolf, I would never know. I could pretend forever that she was still alive. That we might be together again. I could dream like that boy Topher does. Like she does. She dreams of being with him again. She says his name as she sleeps.

I burned his letter to her. Why did I do it?

I'm a monster. How could I do that? I want her to be happy. That can never be while I'm around. I wish I could make a hot bath for her again, or find her some of that sweet food she liked so much. But I can give her only one thing that will make her happy. I can bring her safely back to the human boy. I can do this. I will do this. My head is now pounding so hard I can barely focus my eyes as I turn and trudge back to her, back to the fire. She sits, her arms wrapped around her legs, staring into the flames.

Say something.

"What do you want me to say?"

I kneel down on one knee across from her and tuck another log into the fire. She looks away. I reach over the fire and lift her chin, so she's looking at me.

I promise you will see Topher again.

She repeats the sign for "promise," like an arrow over the mouth. "I don't know what that means."

How can I explain a promise? In our signs it means something more like "I will obey" or "I will succeed," but I know to the humans it means something different. It is less formal, more personal, coming from a warmer place; and it implies something about a shared future. How I know this is a mystery.

Good words. Forever.

"Good speak? Like truth? Promise? Why would I believe

a promise from you?" Shaking her head, she lies down by the fire again, pulling the blanket over herself. "If we do ever find Topher, there's a very good chance he'll kill you. That's my promise."

Topher can try, I think. Maybe I'll let him.

I promise to try to not fight back, when he comes after me.

RAVEN

There are two types of silences with August. There is the silence inherent in the fact that he doesn't talk. The everyday silence that almost achieves companionability at times. The silence that has never scared or unnerved me, never felt like punishment or perversion, that feels natural. It feels like he is offering as much as he can, hiding nothing, and it is almost enough.

Then there is this kind of silence—the silence that hangs over me like a sentence of solitary confinement. When looking at him feels like spying. When despite his size he seems to shrink down to near invisibility, when he turns his head away from me, away from the rising sun, away from his shadow in the snow. This kind of silence would make a grave seem lively.

His remorse is impressive, as always. And for a moment on waking, when I see that he has roused me by poking my foot with a long stick, I wonder what it's for. Then I remember the letter and the flames. At least he didn't burn the map, I tell myself. Topher will write other notes.

He kicks snow on the smoking embers of the fire and slings the packs into the cab of the truck. As I unravel myself from the blanket, stretching and struggling to my feet, he stares down the dirt road back the way we came, then off into the trees in the other direction.

I go now, he signs as I approach.

I look into the trees and visualize him walking slowly through the snow, headed nowhere, forever, or until the land runs out, or he runs out. Maybe he could reach the Arctic Ocean or the Gulf of Mexico, the Atlantic, the Pacific. I wonder if he can swim.

"Don't go," I say. I feel the words "We have more time" forming in my throat. Why would I say that though? I stare back at the remains of the fire, Topher's letter now dust among the charred wood and ashes. I know why August burned it. He thinks he loves me. He's jealous. I should be angry, furious, but instead I'm just sad. "Come with me, August," I say. "It's okay."

Yes?

God. What I am going to do with him?

He crouches in the back as I drive and drive, his rifle in one hand, the other hand gripping the edge of the flatbed. The going is infuriatingly slow over icy roads piled with snow-drifts. We stop to refuel with our last canister when, by the map, which I've been carefully marking with a red pencil I found in the truck, I estimate we are still more than a hundred miles away.

"We might run out of gas," I say.

Walk, he says, shrugging.

"It could be far."

I'll carry you.

I turn away so he can't see the smile on my face. Stupid alien robot thing. It's so hard to stay mad at him.

As I feared, the fuel runs out in a wide treeless expanse of flat white nothing. The truck coughs and rattles, and I say a silent prayer, though I know it's useless. The engine sputters, and I feel tears in the corners of my eyes, not knowing how close we are or how far. After we roll to a stop, I unfold the map and stare at it in my lap until the rocking tells me August has climbed out of the back. He taps on the window. Still staring at the map, I roll it down.

Behind him, in the white, there are no landmarks, no features to indicate or even suggest where we are. The last part of the map is represented by a ten-mile winding, swirling road that I remember made me quite ill when we drove out an eternity ago. We have been driving along a straight, wide highway since dawn. No sign of winding roads. None of the turnoffs looked right. But maybe I missed it. I slam my hands into the steering wheel in frustration, over and over, harder and harder until August reaches through the window and grabs my hands, stilling them. Holding them. Gently at first but then squeezing them until they start to hurt. He releases me as soon as I pull away.

Promise, he signs.

I'd like to tell him to shove his promise up his ass, but what would that accomplish? Instead, I open the door and step out into the snow. It's much warmer than I expected, though it is overcast. My watch tells me it's midafternoon. We have a couple of hours of sunlight left at most. I'm not sure whether to camp here in the truck for the night or keep walking, in the hopes that we find some shelter or cover before dark. With no idea how far we have to go, it's hard to make a call like that, but August seems to have his own ideas. He scoops the larger pack from the cab and slings it over his shoulder, turning to look at me expectantly.

Carry?

I sniff back a laugh. "I think I'll walk, thank you."

He simply lays his left hand on my right shoulder, turning me gently and nudging me forward along the road. Then we're walking again. Minutes later he pulls me to a stop and tugs my hood, scarf, and cap up over my hair, tucking away the puffs of errant curls escaping from the twists as he does so.

"Do I look like you now?" I say, holding my arms out for inspection.

He turns his head to the side appraisingly. *Prettier*, he signs, making the "pretty" sign while lifting his hand above his head. Despite the cool wind, my face burns as I turn and walk away. After a few seconds his hand drops down on my shoulder as soft as a butterfly. We trudge down the sparkling ice road. I imagine from the sky we must look like two determined beetles or ants, vainly searching for home. I hope that from the sky we look like two Nahx, doing whatever it is Nahx do.

An hour passes, the flat white giving way to sparse trees, then thicker forest on either side of the road. He stops and makes me drink from a bottle that he has kept tucked into his armor somehow. The water is so warm it's like flavorless tea. After another hour he hands me a packet of dry Asian noodles, which he knows I love. I munch them gratefully as we walk.

Another hour later the light changes, the air changes, and it begins to snow. Fat, ripe snowflakes drift down, quieting the wind, absorbing the sounds of our footsteps until it feels like we are walking in the silent vacuum of space, with stars tumbling around us. A sudden lightness settles on me, and I walk ten paces before I realize August has taken his hand off my shoulder.

I look back to see him standing next to the pack, with his arms out wide, face turned to the sky, feather snowflakes drifting down onto him. It's almost as though he is worshipping. Though I feel like an intruder, I can't help but watch. His shoulders rise and fall with deep grumbling breaths. After long minutes he slowly lowers himself onto his knees and presses his hands into the fresh snow. Now I really am intruding. As I turn, something zips past my ear and lands in the snow ahead of me. A snowball.

Behind me Augusts kneels primly, innocently, his snow-dusted hands folded in front. He raises them as if to say, *What?*

"I see. Is that how it's going to be, then?" I crouch down and form a snowball. The temperature is warm enough for the snow to be nice and sticky, and soon I have a good, round projectile. August doesn't even flinch as I send it sailing three feet to the left of him. As I stoop to pack another snowball, he pulls one out of the snow and sends it flying precisely. I turn and it disintegrates on my back.

I launch a counterstrike. This one flies about ten feet over his head. Now August is laughing at me, tipping his head back and shaking.

"Oh yeah?" I say, gathering a handful of snow. "How about a point-blank attack?" I run at him before he has a chance to clamber to his feet and mash the snow into his head. As he tries to escape, I swing my leg, sweeping his feet out from under him. He falls backward into the snow.

"Oh! Sorry! Are you okay?"

He lies there for a second, like a fallen angel, a black silhouette on a white background.

"August?"

Shooting upward, he flings more snow at me. I leap down on him, pushing him backward, and land on top of his chest, my knees pressing his arms down.

It's hard to say how I know he's laughing as I shovel snow

onto his head. He flicks his head back and shakes and doesn't try very hard to escape. But suddenly he twitches upward, and I find myself flipped over on my back. By this time the snow is deep enough to form a cushion around me, like a supersoft feather bed. Kneeling beside me, he sprinkles snow from my head to my feet.

I'm not sure what is happening. We should be moving, getting as far as we can before dark, but time seems to have stopped. It's as though we've both been spirited out of the world with all its horror and into a dream. The falling snow hypnotizes me. I can almost feel my blood pressure lowering as he lets the snow trickle between his fingers.

"You like snow, don't you?" I say, blowing snowflakes from my lips. He nods, scooping up another handful. "Why?"

Makes me feel very happy, he signs, sprinkling my knees.

I feel very happy at that moment too. The snow is comfortable underneath me, and the air is cool and fresh. The fat, falling snowflakes tickle my face as they fall and decorate August's armor until he looks like a postapocalyptic Christmas card. All the antagonism I've felt for him melts along with the snowflakes on my eyelids. Lying back with my face to the sky, it's easy to forget the devastation that surrounds us, or that his people stole my world. It's easy to forget the weeks I spent hating him and how he once frightened me. It's easy to forget how he burned Topher's letter. Not why, though.

You make me feel very happy.

"I thought I made you very very sad," I say. Not cruelly, I hope, but his reply reassures me.

Happy. Sad. Happy. Sad. Then he draws a spiral on his forehead. Sitting back on his heels, he looks out into the distance. A large snowflake drifts down and lands on his face, around where his eyebrow might be. I sit up and brush it away.

"Can you feel that? The snowflakes falling on you?"

He nods.

"Do you ever take your armor off? I mean, I know you're not a machine inside, are you?"

He shakes his head, signing. *Breathing here hurts my chest.* Pointing up to the mountains in the distance he continues. *Up the mountains, breathing is better.*

"Oh! Where the air is thinner?" That explains the Nahx preferring the high country, such a simple explanation for something that screwed us all over so thoroughly.

August nods again, looking at the mountains. Another snowflake lands near his nose. I brush that one away too. Then I pull off one of my mittens and lay my hand on the side of his head. He turns and presses his head into my hand, the way a cat would. I run my fingers from the top of his head to his chin. His armor seems to be pulsing hot and cold—some snowflakes melt and some don't. His breath rattles deeply, like the purring of a tiger.

His left hand rises up slowly and lingers there for a moment, suspended in the air, before coming to rest on my shoulder. Seconds later he slides it onto my face.

We sit like that, snowflakes drifting down on us, for several minutes. August purrs softly, as meanwhile I have things caught in my throat. Words. Stuff I should say and stuff I want to say and a whole lot of things that are ridiculous.

August's hand slips down from my face, slowly, and stops, curved around my breast. With my coat on and all, it's possible he doesn't really know what he's doing. At least I think that until he squeezes, gently but definitely intentionally. I feel my face get hot.

"August, I . . ."

He pulls his hand away as though he's been burned, freezes there for an instant, then leaps to his feet, striding back to where he left the pack.

"It's okay. Really," I say, clambering to my feet as he passes me. "Wait."

He pauses on the road as I catch up, facing our destination, not turning to meet my eyes. I take one step in front of him, and his hand falls on my shoulder, shoving me a little roughly. We walk in silence, back into the silence that feels like punishment, though I've done nothing wrong. We walk until night falls, still not finding the winding road that heralds the hidden base. He stops me then, and I sit and have some water and food while he stares off into the dark.

"So I suppose you were just curious? Or you misunderstood . . . ?" I ask when I can stand the silence no longer. I probably should be angrier at him, but if I'm honest, I think maybe I wanted him to touch me like that. Or something.

He kneels facing me, resting back on his heels.

Sorry. Sorry. Sorry.

"I accept your apology."

Not scare you?

"No. If I thought you were going to hurt me, I would have punched you in the face."

He hangs his head, impressively remorseful, as usual.

"It's really no big deal. You're not very old, are you?"

Speak, he signs with a question hand.

"I mean, you're not a man, quite. You're young, like me. Just a boy. Right?" He's always seemed young to me, and so like the boys I know, in some ways. Why else would he throw dirty dishes off the balcony?

He shrugs and nods, evidence, if there ever was, that's he's a teenager, who doesn't know and knows at the same time.

"Well, anyway, boys do stuff like that all the time. It's not exactly accepted behavior, but it's not the end of the world either. Boys are jerks sometimes. They need to grow up." I have to suppress a smile, thinking of Tucker's first fumbling move on me, uninvited and pretty clueless but not exactly unwelcome. And the time Xander tried to pinch my ass and ended up on the floor of the dojo with my knee on his neck. And Topher, that time the night we arrived at the base. But that wasn't so funny.

I don't know whether I can laugh at August having his hand on me like that either. I don't think such a gesture is just raging hormones or showing off for him. Who would he be showing off for anyway?

The worst part about this, the part that makes me bite back my smile, turn away to the frozen horizon, my heart skipping in my throat, is that I feel like if he tried to touch me again, I might let him.

Night falls, but we walk on. I guide her gently, with a little pressure on her shoulder, letting her walk in front, but leading the way myself as she begins to meander. It grows colder and colder; she hunches over as the wind rises and walks with her eyes closed, asleep on her feet almost. Finally, she simply falls. One step lands true and straight, leaving a small, sure footprint; the next crumples beneath her. I catch her, one arm wrapped around her chest, and lift her. She mumbles something but doesn't resist as I tuck her head onto my shoulder and press her frozen hands onto my chest between us.

Her trembling reminds me of how sick she was, how she nearly died, and me along with her. She whimpers in my arms, and I realize she has fallen asleep. I make myself as warm as I can and hold her close, stepping forward, searching the dark for the high, rocky hills she has described, the entrance to the haven she seeks.

My mind is coming apart again. I want to stop now, turn off the road, and leave with her, to the high mountains, to hide away from the humans and from my people.

Step forward, still stepping forward.

The human boy is the goal. The promise.

One foot in front of the other.

The night cold dissolves the clouds, stars peek out, and the wide, icy landscape turns silver in the moonlight. I look down at her sleeping face, resting on my shoulder. Unable to resist, I lean over, breathing deeply, inhaling her drowsy warmth. She smells of . . . something . . . fragile and impermanent, like a spiderweb or a snowflake. Like a human, a forgiving human girl.

I can carry her forever and keep her from freezing indefinitely. I would do it. But her food will run out soon if we don't find something. The last town we passed was hours back. I could turn around, take her back there, but I promised her I would find the human boy. I promised.

Dizzy with having her in my arms again, I try not to stumble. I try to focus on the journey, on the road ahead of us, not on the smell of her, her frozen eyelashes, try to ignore the perplexing, tantalizing images that her closeness draws into my half-drowned brain.

I try to forget that the end of this journey is also the end of us.

I wake in the dark, bathed in warmth, curled up, my hands and face resting on something that radiates heat. So comfortable that I don't want to move. I'm warmer than I feel like I have been in weeks, months, since we left the base to go on our ill-fated mission back to Calgary. I enjoy a brief delusion that I have somehow arrived back at the base before I come to realize that I'm actually curled up in August's lap.

He's sitting, cross-legged, in a windbreak dug in the snow, his arms slung over me, my head resting on one of his thighs, my own legs drawn up with my feet tucked under his other thigh. In the moonlight I see his face above me, his head hanging. I watch for a moment as his shoulders rise and fall with his breaths. It's mesmerizing, staring at him like this. The moon behind him creates a kind of blue halo where it reflects on the few shiny parts of his armor. His breathing is rattling and slow. In between his breaths, in the silent stillness, I hear something else, a kind of low tapping noise. Shocked, I move my head slightly, careful not to disturb him, and press my ear onto his abdomen.

His heart. I can hear his heart beating.

He has a heart.

For a tiny second I'm tempted by the rhythm of it, tempted to surrender myself to the comfort of his warmth, his selfless devotion, to give up my fragile humanity in exchange for his monstrous security, for the safety of his arms. He could protect me in this terrifying new world. Maybe he's the only one who could really protect me.

"August," I whisper. He takes a breath and turns his head to look at me. "Were you asleep?"

Think, he signs. Then points off into the distance.

"Your thoughts were far away? What were you thinking about?"

He lifts his arms from me and rests them on his knees. After a moment he raises his left hand and suspends it in the air for a few seconds before letting it fall again. I slide out of his lap and face him.

"I've never seen you sitting before."

Feel broken, he signs, awkwardly pulling himself to his knees. He taps the armor over his hip.

"It hurts to sit? Because of your armor?" He nods a little, then looks away. "Thank you, then, for keeping me warm."

Happy.

But he doesn't look happy. He looks miserable and defeated, his shoulders sagging as he turns his head and looks off to the side. I follow his gaze and make out dark, craggy shadows to the north of us. They have the flat, hacked-off tops I remember. "I think those are the hills."

He nods slowly. His left hand drifts up for a second and then falls again. He's thinking of her.

"How did she die?" I ask. "The girl you loved. What happened to her?"

Topher, he signs after a second ticks by.

Somewhere under all my clothes and sweaters and coats, I feel a little prickle. "Topher? In the city, where you found me? Topher killed her?"

August shakes his head. I watch him inhale and exhale slowly.

Repeat, Topher, he signs.

He uses repeat to mean "the same" sometimes. Alike. Someone like Topher.

I imagine I hear a rumble, an avalanche gathering in the cliffs above us.

"He looked like Topher?" I whisper. I can't seem to get my vocal cords to work. My voice comes out like paper rustling in a bottom drawer. "Someone who looked like Topher killed her?"

August nods, hanging his head.

I close my eyes and calculate, but I can't think. I can't count the weeks and months since we found Tucker with a Nahx dart in his spine. It feels like forever ago and yesterday.

"S-s-summer?" I splutter. "It was summer? The end of sum-mer?"

August reaches for me. I high-block his arm, hard enough that the crack of his armor echoes across the snow, and the pain of it zings up my arm to my head, blowing the truth up like a firework.

"You killed him, right? You killed the one who killed your girlfriend?" I'm on my feet, backing away.

Stop. Stop.

I look down at the indentation between us, where we curled up together. My brain empties itself of everything except the few bits of information that I need to put together like puzzle pieces. But I can't make my thoughts obey me. I bend down and hold my head in my hands, moaning as the memory of Topher's vengeance quest fills me like poison, like a hallucino-gen. I feel like I might vomit.

"Have you been following me all this time?"

No. I don't know.

"How can you not know!?"

He hisses as I turn and take two long strides in the snow, breaking into a run. I think I'm still going in the right direc-tion, though it's dark and I don't know where we are. Going in the right direction doesn't matter anymore, only that I run away from him. Barely conscious of his footsteps crunching in the snow after me, I smash my shins into a rock or something and fall face forward, landing hard on my elbows. I manage to crawl to my feet, blinded by tears, and stumble onward. I veer into the dark, and the ground drops out from under me. Falling, I think of Tucker in his grave.

I land facedown. My chin slams into something hard and I taste blood in my mouth. When I roll over, I feel pain shooting through my ribs. As I struggle to take a breath, I look up and see something dark falling toward me. This time I'm not going to resist, I tell myself. This time I'm going to let him kill me. But when my eyes focus, I see the shackles in his hand.

"No!" I kick out, connecting with his shoulder, knocking him off balance. "Don't you dare!" I kick his hand, and the shackles fly off into the dark.

He hisses and growls as he leaps for me, and I scramble pathetically away. I can't escape. He's too fast, too strong, too determined. He lands on top of me, pinning my legs down.

I'm not even sure how it happens. All I hear is the ring of steel on leather. There is a flash of moonlight and star light on something metal, and my muscles move, coil up, and spring out, seemingly of their own volition. When stillness and silence return, we are locked together, pressing knives into each other's throats. I'm vaguely aware that I drew first, though only by a millisecond. Somehow I am pushed back against a rock or tree, or ice, pushed back and held in place by a Nahx with a knife.

"Go ahead," I say. "If that's what you want."

The plates on his face pulse, revealing a glimpse of the sharp spikes hidden beneath. He doesn't move his knife. Neither do I. But he pulls one hand away, making signs so firmly they whistle in the cold night.

Look. Listen!

"How long have you known? How long have you known who I am? Who Tucker was?" I can feel the armor plates on his neck giving under the blade of my knife.

Listen. Please.

"You killed Tucker," I say into the cloud of mist between us, though of course I know he knows. "He was running away. You could have let him get away." I don't even know how I can say this. If it had been the other way around, I would have chased Tucker's killer until one or both of us collapsed from exhaustion. But I don't need to chase him. I have him. I have my knife at his throat just like I planned the first moment I met him. If I had known then who he was, I would have done it.

He starts making signs, quickly but clearly, like he's enunciating as to be sure I understand.

If you kill me, you die. You freeze.

"Maybe it would be worth it."

I die fast. You die slow.

"I don't care."

He puts his hand on his head for a moment, then signs again, now taking his time, his fingers fluid, almost like a dance. But he growls as he signs.

You die fast. I die slow. He takes the knife from my throat and signs with both hands, incorporating the knife into the word somehow, giving it power, presenting it like a challenge as he makes the shape around my outstretched arm and the blade at his own throat. It's a new word, one I've never seen before, but the meaning is clear enough.

Choose.

I'm paralyzed, noting that he doesn't let go of his knife as his body relaxes out of its defensive stance. That's because if I choose a fast death for me, he will make it happen. A fast death for me, and a slow, lonely, heartbroken death for him. How long would it take? Would he hurry it along somehow? And if I choose the other, would he let me put the knife through his neck, even though it would mean I freeze out here? I've been assuming he would never let me be the architect of my own death, that when it came to it, he would put a stop to any stupid, reckless impulses, but maybe that's finally changed. Maybe he's had enough of me, though perhaps not enough to stop doing my bidding, whatever it is.

Please, he signs.

"Please what?"

He lowers himself to his knees, slowly enough that I can

keep the knife at his neck. Kneeling, he looks me as he tucks his own knife into a holster in his armor. In his long, mournful sigh, I almost hear another noise, like a whimper, as though he has overcome his muteness with a tiny vocalization, an expression of . . . what . . . surrender? Resignation? I half expect him to tell me I can just walk away. He holds his hands out at his sides for a moment, palms up, then signs.

Please let me give you a life for a life.

"Whose life?"

Your life. Please. Choose.

His hands fall back down to his knees and are still. His shoulders droop, his head tilts to the side. He looks tired, suddenly, exhausted.

"Why were you going to shackle me, before?"

He shrugs. *My mind is broken.*

Broken, like my arm, my ribs, like all the locks on all the doors in the apartment building. Like the world. Is there a thing left on Earth that isn't broken? We were friends, August and I, for only a few hours, it seems. Now that's broken too.

I pull my hand with the knife away from his throat and start talking, with a feeling that his words are actually coming out of my mouth. I might still find my way to the base if I killed him. But I don't want to kill him. And one day I'll have to tell Topher why I didn't do it.

Maybe if he can explain it, I can let it go. "You were walking with her, the girl?" I ask. "Patrolling or hunting, whatever you do?"

He nods, not looking at me. I need to go on. I need to know about Tucker's last minutes before I take another step of life without him.

He points to the scar on his chest. Not the one Topher made, the other, more faded one. He taps it hard and hunches over, clutching himself with one hand, reaching with the other.

"He shot you first? Then her?" Tucker could reload the crossbow as fast as Emily. He had practiced for hours. In between . . . the other stuff.

August looks up, tilting his head backward, pointing to the gaps between the armor on his neck.

"An arrow went through her neck. That killed her." Like we speculated. Just as August once showed me. There's a weakness in the neck.

He doesn't reply. Doesn't nod or acknowledge me. Lowering himself, he leans forward and buries his hands in the snow.

"And you were scared because you were lost. Lost without her. She took care of you, right? You didn't know what to do."

He hisses out a long, shaky sigh.

"Did you chase him?"

Still hanging over the snow, he chops one hand into his chest hard. *Sorry*.

I find I can't say any more. Tucker's death plays behind my

closed eyelids like the worst kind of horror movie. I wonder if he yelled as he ran, if he screamed. I wonder if he knew in those last moments that he was going to die. Did he think of me? Or Topher? Or only of himself? Minutes tick past. I see Tucker fall, face forward, the soft mulch of pine needles and willow leaves cushioning his fall. I hear the whine of the dart gun. I feel the punch of the dart at the base of my neck and the sour stinging of the Nahx poison rushing through my veins and out my eyes.

"Was it painful?" I say at last. "Did he suffer?"

August shakes his head.

"Was it painful for you?"

After a moment he answers, signing fluidly, and clearly, though one of the words is new to me.

Tucker had a square machine.

"A square machine?"

He makes the square in front of his face, pointing at his eyes. *Picture. Machine. Like the time I broke the table.*

Oh. God.

"A video? He had a video. On his phone?"

Yes.

"A video of him killing your . . . the girl? The girl you loved?"

Yes.

So.

There's the truth at last. Tucker wasn't hunting for food when he left my bunk that night. He was hunting for glory. Why would he do that? He knew already that I hated the videos. That I thought they were stupid.

But Emily liked them. I'm not sure why that changes everything, but it does. Tucker filmed his attack on August and his companion, and it was playing back when August caught him. Maybe they both watched it as Tucker died. Then poor August smashed the phone to pieces.

He lifts one hand out of the snow and lays it on his chest over the scar, over his heart, if he's anything like me inside.

I reimagine the scene, this time from August's point of view, and it breaks me. Bleeding from his chest and in terrible pain, his only companion murdered in front of him, a dead human boy under a tree, lost and scared and alone on a planet full of people who want him dead. With a video playing back the moment his life fell apart. I can't imagine his pain.

I could no more kill him now than myself, than Topher, than my own poor parents who tried so hard to keep me out of trouble, who forgave so much and lost me anyway. Tucker will never get his vengeance, not from me. I drop the knife. It rings like a bell when it hits the ice at our feet.

The world, which may or may not have ground to a halt while we resolved this catastrophe, starts moving again. I feel it lurch beneath my feet, unbalancing me, while things that have cycled between terrifying and familiar so many times they became a blur settle on familiar again. There's a kind of finality to it. I trust him now, and that won't change again. Trust is enough for us to go on.

Standing, August takes two steps before turning back to me, holding out his hand. I reach for him, his fingers close around mine, and we walk like that, holding hands like two children, back to where we left the packs, as the sky lightens around us. His hand pulses warm in mine and squeezes to the knife-edge of too tight, to the precipice of painful. The stinging and heat radiates up my arm, my shoulder, and neck. I wonder if he doesn't know his own strength or if the grip is intentional, if there is some unspoken message in it.

If he is angry with me, at last, I suppose I deserve it. Angry, fed up, exhausted, frustrated—it's not like it's a new sensation to me, to inspire such emotions. But this time I decide to give myself a little break. I have the right to grieve and be bitter and resentful. And so does he. There are no easy answers, not anymore. Probably there never were any.

Morning breaks, and a blue sky blossoms above us, making a wonderland of the craggy rocks and hills ahead. But the day passes in silence. August lets go of my hand only to give me water or food. I open my mouth only to drink or eat. Was it just a few days ago that I told him we could be friends in a different time or universe? I'm not sure I meant it then, but now I think I'd like to be his friend. It feels safe walking hand in hand with him, the first time I've felt safe in what seems like forever. I know who he is and what he did, but that was somewhere else. Maybe *this* is the universe in which we can be friends.

It is dusk when we reach the helipad at the canyon's edge; it emerges from the ice haze like a mirage. August silently considers the dormant helicopter, tucked away under camouflage tarps and a thick layer of snow. He turns and looks at me, setting the pack down between us.

I breathe deeply, exhausted from our daylong walk, and emotional, too. Emotionally exhausted, like I've been watching children die. I feel as fragile as glass, a stained glass replica of myself.

Before this all happened, I had never said a real good-bye. I close my eyes and picture Sawyer, in the grocery store, the expression on his face, the silent something we shared the second before he gave his life for mine. Tucker and I never had that chance. He snuck out of my bunk as I slept, took his crossbow into the forest, and I never saw him alive again. But that is death. In a way it is a better good-bye, because at least you don't wonder forever. My parents, if they live, must wonder about me, as I do about them. Topher wonders about me. Wonders whether I am alive or dead. What must have been going on in his head when he saw August carry me away?

That kind of good-bye is torture that never ends.

I will never see August again. Never know what happened to him, whether he lived or died. Whether he rejoined his kind and their pillage of our planet. Or if he snuck away and hid somewhere, alone in exile, until . . . what? He died? Can he even die? There are still so many unanswered questions. And no more time.

"I have to walk to the base," I say, struggling to keep my voice even. "There's a narrow path, and the entrance is kind of hidden. It's a secret base."

He nods at this last fact.

"You can't tell your people where we are."

He shakes his head. Behind him he opens the pack he's been carrying and tucks my own smaller backpack inside. Then he carefully slings the whole thing over my shoulder. It's heavy. He takes time to adjust the strap and hands me a flashlight, which I stash away.

I go now, he signs finally. He adjusts his rifle, slinging it over his back, and takes a step away from me, as though to leave, just like that.

"August."

The light is fading, and he is doing that thing where his shape gets less distinct the less light there is. It is a shadow that turns back to me expectantly.

"Where will you go?"

The shadow shrugs.

"What will you do?"

See you nevermore.

It's like being stabbed with three sharp and perfect icicles. *Zero. Repeat. Forever.* I'm not even sure that Tucker could have been so beautifully pitiful. Not even if he were angling for the best roll of his life. August has nothing to gain from me. He's just being honest.

"No, probably not. Here, I want you to keep this." I dig in the bag he's slung over my shoulder and come up with the slim book, "The Raven," and my red pencil.

To August, I write on the title page. *Take care, from Raven.*

I don't quite have the heart to write "love."

August purrs softly as he reads the inscription, before tucking the book away somewhere in his armor.

Sad. He makes the sign on his own face first, then repeats it on mine, tracing the track of the single tear I can't stop. He moves to leave again.

"Will you go back to your people?" He shakes his head. "Why not?"

He makes a new sign, like a little cage with his hand, then he flips it upside down. The meaning is clear.

I'm free.

"You are free, August. Don't forget that."

You made me free.

I almost gasp. "No, you did that for yourself."

He nods, although I get the sense that he doesn't believe me. Or maybe I misread his signs. It's possible he meant "You made me a prisoner and now I'm free."

I have so many things I want to say to him all of a sudden, things I should have said before. And questions to ask, although I'm not sure how he would answer them. I don't even really know where to start, but I have to get this all out in about thirty seconds, because if I don't, I'll never be able to leave him.

"August, just . . . please don't harm yourself. Okay? I know you think there is nothing in the world for you. I know that. And I know that you are so much better than what is expected of you from your . . . people, whatever they are. I know how you feel about . . ."

I almost say me, but what would be the point of that?

" . . . things. I know you're different from the others. You must be." I'm rambling nonsense. I'd be embarrassed if I weren't so miserable. The problem is I can't imagine a future for him that doesn't involve despair or death, most likely both.

"Find somewhere to hide, August. Just hide away from all this. That's what I'm going to do."

With Topher?

"With other humans, yes. We're going to hide here. You won't tell anyone?"

No. Forever.

"You won't . . . harm yourself, will you?"

Promise.

He's so sincere somehow, without facial expressions or a tone of voice; I believe his promise more than I have ever believed anything in my life. Letting my head fall into my mittens, I release a shaky sigh. Eventually, I feel his hand on my left shoulder again.

"I don't know why you've been so kind to me," I say, looking up at him. He draws a little swirl on his forehead, which I take to mean something like "I'm confused." He puts his other hand on my shoulder and slowly draws me forward. I step toward him as though in a dream, one step, two, three, until I am pressed up against his chest, his breastbone at my eye level. Then he wraps his arms around me and squeezes me, so tenderly that my heart seems to contract in my rib cage, and expand again like a bird discovering its wings.

"August," I whisper, because I can't think of anything else to say. He's held me before, carried me like a child, but this is different. I encircle his waist with my arms and lay my head on his chest, letting tears drip down his armor, which is as warm as a hot water bottle. He drops his head and rests it on top of mine. I feel him slip my hood down and pull back the knitted cap. His fingers curl into the unraveling twists of my hair, his rattling, buzzing breath going in and out. I can feel his sorrow almost as acutely as my own and wish there were something I could do about it. I want to tell him we might be together again one day, that everything will be all right, that he makes me very, very happy.

But only one of those things is true.

We stand like that for a while, as the daylight fades. Finally, it is he who steps back. I wipe my eyes on my mittens.

"Thank you for saving my life," I say. I can't believe I haven't said this before. When I think of some of the things I *did* say to him . . .

There are subtleties to his language that I am just beginning to understand. Things I will never fully learn now. Important differences that matter. Like the difference between me and my. The difference between happiness and pleasure.

My pleasure, he signs. After a moment he adds, *Say good-bye.*

I try but I can't. My mouth opens, but nothing comes out. August takes my shoulders again, turns me and gives me a little nudge toward the path to the base. I take one step, two, three, before I turn back to see he is walking away, disappearing into the shadows of the mountains beyond. I watch him until he puts both hands on his head. Then his image blurs too much to see.

I walk until darkness covers me, until I'm sure if I looked back, I would not be able to see her, even if she hasn't moved from where we parted. If I looked back, I would not be able to see the empty place where she stood, the deficiency of her. This is the thing I don't want to see.

I will see her nevermore.

After the battle in the city Sixth warned me about many things. That was when she still felt some responsibility for me, before I disappointed and frustrated her so much that she stopped caring what happened to me. She warned me not to disconnect below 4,000 feet, by the human measures, because I wouldn't be able to breathe. And to never disconnect where humans could see. She warned me about the Elevenths and Twelfths, that they were mostly lost, defective, and not to be trusted if I should encounter one. And she warned me about human girls. I listened obediently, watching her hands make signs I knew but barely used. Of all the things she said to me, so many of which I've forgotten, I remember this: *Human girls will interest you. You will feel things just by looking at them. You will confuse your devotion to me with feelings for them. This is a human trick. They will trick you into sympathy, into letting them go, letting them live. Higher ranks than you have been destroyed because they couldn't bring themselves to dart a human girl. Stay focused and stay away from them.*

So. There. I failed her one last time.

I hurt all over. My insides hurt. Parts of me that aren't even real hurt. Like my mind, my memories, such as they are, the part of me that resists all that is expected of me. I wonder if those parts are dying now that she's gone forever. I wonder whether I can go back to being a soldier, an assassin, go back to my people and resume my duties now that she has been excised from my life.

If she made me rebel, surely her absence might make me comply. But I would rather die a million painful muddy deaths than return to that unliving life. I don't care if it was all a trick. I am free.

In the darkness the idea that captured me once, twice, more times I am too ashamed to admit even to myself, takes me again. I pull my arm back and hurl my rifle far into the night. Faintly, I hear it *thump* in the distance. Without it I feel as light as the mist rising from the fresh snow.

My mind drifts back to that sunset on the roof when I stood there staring into nothing while she screamed at me, screamed and screamed and cried, shackled to the bed below. There is something so vulgar about that, so unspeakably vile, something I don't quite understand. How she ever forgave me, I will never know. How she forgave me for anything, for everything, not that I deserved it.

She would never know, would she, if I broke my promise? Just like I will never know whether she lives or dies, she would never know if I drew my knife and slipped it between the armor plates on my neck.

I would do it. I would. But I'm not sure I can actually die. If I can't die, maybe Sixth is not dead. Maybe she is out in the world somewhere searching for me, waiting for me, waiting to judge my failures again.

PART FOUR
Spring

"The boundaries which divide Life from Death are at best shadowy and vague. Who shall say where the one ends, and where the other begins?"
—EDGAR ALLAN POE, *"The Premature Burial"*

Time passes, snowflake by snowflake, sunrise by sunrise. I'm scared that if I disconnect and purge my body of the thick oil that keeps me alive and awake, the memory of her might go with it. Or worse, I might forget that I have promised to leave her and her friends alone. I have promised not to reveal her location to my people. What if I forget that?

So instead I wander through the trees, hiding from daylight like a . . . something . . . a vampire? That was in one of the other books I left behind in the tower. I lurk in my tree trunk chamber dreading the raven who will tell me *nevermore*.

Raven. Nevermore. Like I need reminding. I look at the book sometimes, but the words swim in my vision. I think I have forgotten how to read.

Nevermore.

It stops snowing and starts raining. I imagine the raindrops dripping down the armor over my nose are tears. I only ever remember crying once, after I lost Sixth. I wasn't sure what was happening. I thought maybe I was very sick or dying, it felt so bad. But after a while it became familiar, and the familiarity coalesced into a word, and I knew I was crying. I was ashamed at first, because I thought crying was for humans and children, but later it felt good, like the tears were sucking the malice out of me. That was when I began to resist, before I first saw Dandelion. Was that the reason I didn't shoot her in the river? Because I remembered how to cry? Was it actually the pain of losing Sixth that saved me?

Irony. A word I didn't know I knew flops out of the sludge in my brain and gasps on the shore for a few seconds, like a dying fish. Irony. What possible use could that knowledge be to anyone, least of all me? Why remember these useless things now?

So much is remembered as I roam through the dark forest. The broken parts of my brain have finally repaired themselves. But the charge of the armor is wearing out. It no longer keeps me entirely awake. Sometimes I find myself dozing on my feet, my back resting against a tree. It no longer ties my thoughts up in knots. Images wriggle out and dance behind my eyes. I remember being on the big ship with the others. I remember being smaller, and eating, and injections that made me sleep without dreams. I remember waking up so full of hate for the humans, I attacked the one who woke me and squeezed their throat until others tore me off.

I don't remember being punished for this.

A *human* woke me—this I remember distinctly. I don't

know how that can be. A human on the big ship? Maybe I'm remembering that wrong. The captured fragments of story in my head seem so implausible. We are preparing, but for what? There is a great battle coming, but with whom? Surely not the humans. They are all gone. And anyway, even with the living ones, it would not be much of a battle.

I'm soaked in oily fluid, but its power is waning too, along with my strength. Once, when I kneel to look at a fallen bird's nest, I forget momentarily how to stand up. Like a baby. I think Sixth might have warned me about this, too. If I stayed in the armor for too long, if I let the power cells run out, it would start to shut down my nonessential systems first. Speaking, walking, thinking. It is getting hard to think. I know I have an organic brain too, my own brain that can think for itself, but it has been so long contained and infiltrated by the sludge that I'm not sure it works.

For the first time, I recognize this as something stolen from me, as a terrible violation. My mind was stolen, my history. I try to claw it back but can't tell which parts are real and which are imagined.

Sometimes I do the signs to myself.

I feel very, very sad.

When I remember to do it and it feels safe, I stand in the sun, if the clouds clear. But the solar is just a backup. I should recharge properly, disconnect, and recharge. But I'm scared.

Scared.

I'm scared I'll forget her. Forget my promises. I hear the transports sometimes, and hide from them as they swoop in low, careful patterns. They are searching, but what could they be searching for? I feel like I should know.

Recharge. Eat and sleep, Sixth would say. Eat and sleep, like a human.

Eat. Sleep.

I make the human girl's names with my fingers. *Raven. Dandelion.* Again and again until my hands ache.

Time has passed. The moon has bloated and shrunk. The Firsts, Seconds, Thirds, and Fourths have all begun their second year.

If that boy . . . His name is gone, something about an arrow in the shoulder . . . If he were there waiting for Dandelion, she . . .

She . . . Dandelion . . . she has another name, doesn't she? A speck of black in the bright sky. Something about memory.

A transport hums above the mountains. Searching.

Someone should warn . . . her . . . the flower . . . and the bird.

The rain drips off my face. I turn my body away from the setting sun and meander off into the dark.

I need to disconnect, to take off this monstrous armor for a few hours. To recharge by eating and sleeping.

Like a human.

S pring arrives at the base like a funeral cortege. The first point of order is the digging of graves for those who did not survive the winter. Now that the ground has thawed out, our dead friends can be laid to rest more gracefully than simply being stacked in the snow outside the north exit. A man with diabetes died, as he predicted, and the kid with leukemia. There were two suicides. A heart attack. And an old woman who died in her sleep, her great-grandson asleep beside her. Someone overdosed on homemade liquor. Maybe an accident, maybe not. And people died on two ill-fated raiding missions to nearby towns.

Those not darted by the Nahx are buried first, because their remains will decay. I volunteer to dig since I have a strong back and a cold heart. I view these deaths not with resignation, but determination. Staying here is slow suicide; eventually the food will run out, and we'll all succumb like sharks in a too-small tank. There is only one hope now. Over the months since my return I have daily negotiated with Liam about an exodus to the coast. Now that spring is here, it becomes a real idea, not just something to argue about in dim hallways. He prefers to wait, to arm ourselves, to scheme and plot against the Nahx who are as absent now as myths. Only the gray veins in Britney's dead face stand to remind us. Her encounter with them was the last any of us have seen of them. We may wait forever for a chance at revenge.

I had my chance, of course, and let it go, like snowflakes on the wind. Now I don't want to waste everything he gave to me, everything he gave up for me, only to let myself starve in a cave. I owe him that. I owe it to everyone who never lost hope in me. Tucker, my parents, Topher even. Topher who saw me carried off by a Nahx and still never gave up.

And August. He brought me back from certain death. My life is his life.

Liam now commands the base, since Kim died two months ago on a raid for food and medicine. Liam, whose mental state is questionable at best; many of his friends died on the same mission. Kim we bury first because, for whatever reason, the Nahx who caught her chose to break her neck over darting her. Britney's corpse is as pretty and delicate as she was in life. We bury her beside Kim, and leave Liam there sitting in the mud, his face a mask.

Topher pulls me behind one of the trucks and we hold each other, breathing the sweat of digging all morning, the damp, rotting smell of spring, and pine needles, the trees stirring back to life around us. We do this sometimes. Fall into each other's arms not quite like lovers, but more than like friends. The first time was the night I arrived back at the base, when Topher ran out into the snow in bare feet and carried me back inside, where we collapsed together on the floor, sobbing. Him with relief, me with something else entirely.

Many times since then we have fallen together this way, when we can no longer stand the ruined world around us. We close ourselves in a private circle of comfort and regret. It never lasts very long. Sometimes we kiss, but mostly not.

"I love you, Raven," he lies, whispering into my ear. I press my lips onto his mouth because I don't want him to say more, like he sometimes does. Keeps saying sweet things, increasingly desperate things, waiting for something to change between us. But it doesn't. He can't know why. My heart is elsewhere, left out in the snow at the top of the hidden path, now thawing and melting into the soft earth with everything else. Or maybe marching on other hiding humans, trying not to remember me. Or dead. Maybe dead.

Probably. Hopefully dead.

I have told no one about August. Everyone in the base considers my return a miracle. The story I told was that the Nahx who Topher saw grab me collapsed from the arrow wound a few minutes later. I crawled inside a small grocery store, treated my injuries, and recuperated alone until I was strong enough to walk back to the tunnel. I found the truck. I drove until the fuel ran out. I hiked from there. It's implausible in the extreme, but no one questions it. Topher suspects, I'm sure, but maybe he doesn't want to know.

Four months have passed since my miraculous return. Four months since I've seen August, apart from nightly in my dreams.

"I say it, and it's like you don't even hear me," Topher says. But I've told him I love him back, many times. It's Topher who can't hear how complete that is. How that is all there will ever be.

None of this is real. His idea of loving me is no more real than a memory. I know that. I know the difference. Sometimes it matters and sometimes it doesn't.

"Tucker is not coming back. We can belong to each other," he says, tucking a ringlet of my hair back under my sweaty bandanna.

Sometimes I feel I'm having these conversations with a corpse. Because all that Topher says he feels for me is imaginary. He is as dead inside as his twin is in every way. Possibly, that doesn't matter either. His body pressed against mine makes my skin tingle, my heart thump against my ribs. I need this right now. And so does he. What's the harm? I kiss him again.

"Why don't you have some respect, you assholes," Liam says, appearing around the truck. "We just buried nine people." Topher is actually chastened. In theory he's Liam's second-in-command, and I'm the last person Liam wants in his inner circle, so our relationship, such as it is, is a point of contention between them.

"You're right, sorry," Topher says, stepping away from me. "Raven was upset and we . . ." I don't contradict this plausible lie. "It won't happen again."

Liam raises an eyebrow a bit too salaciously for my tastes. I consider, briefly, spitting in his face but think better of it.

"I need to see you in command, Raven," Liam says, turning. "You have five minutes."

"Me too?" Topher says.

"No. Dig another grave. There was a suicide last night."

I take my time climbing up to the command center, much more than five minutes, more like twenty. I like to make Liam wait. And it gives me time to reassure myself about the suicide; I saw everyone here that I care about at breakfast.

Liam is calm when I arrive though. He invites me to sit at one of the long tables and sits across from me. We've sat across this table many times, me advocating bugging out and following a route Xander has mapped out that will bring us out of the occupied high ground in as little as a week, Liam dismissing my argument. He recruits from the civilians every day, so that only a few elderly or very young are left unarmed. Raiding parties bring as many weapons as food and medicines back from raids on nearby cabins and farms. The raiding parties that come back, that is. Some come back in pieces, like Britney and Kim's party. Some don't come back at all. I quietly hope that they turned back into the mountains and followed Xander's map, that they are on their way to freedom. But that's probably a forlorn dream. The Nahx could dispense with a six-person raiding party in seconds, quietly, barely blowing up dust.

"Who was the suicide?" I ask as I sit. I've never made any new friends here. The ones I arrived with are down to Topher, Xander, and Emily, but whatever friendship I had with her is long gone. A coldness settled on her during my absence. There are rumors of a miscarriage, but I've never asked for details. In a way, I admire the ice in her. It is hard, impenetrable. Like armor.

As for Liam, he and I discuss strategy, argue mostly, and occasionally he sits with me at meals, trying to make small talk about the old days, books I read or music that I like. It's awkward, but I tolerate it. As much as I hate to admit it, I need Liam as an ally. But everyone else is a stranger to me.

"Jill. That girl whose boyfriend never came back from patrol. You know her?"

I shake my head, though her face swims in front of my eyes. We never spoke, but I recognized her pain well enough. I know what it's like when someone you care about disappears from your life. I don't bother asking how she did it. Some details don't really matter.

"It's time to consider retreat," I say, because I know I'm expected to. "I mean really consider it. We could reach the coast by summer. Even if there's nothing there, that would give us time to establish some sort of settlement before winter sets in."

"We're not going anywhere."

"Liam, we have a chance. A real chance. Xander's map is rock solid. The route is well below two thousand feet for nearly ninety percent of the way. One of the videos even suggested there might be human patrols as close as Prince George. That's not even two hundred miles from here. Two weeks at most and we could be rescued."

"You're not going anywhere," Liam says, and something about his tone makes me tense in my seat, as though I might need to make a quick exit. But then I think he's probably mad about me and Topher. Mad that we have something together. Mad that Topher hasn't surrendered the last vestiges of his humanity the way Liam wants us all to. I don't really have the heart for Liam's anger today. I stand up to leave.

Liam slams both hands down on the table before I've even straightened my back.

"Sit the fuck down!"

I sit. This is more than Liam's ordinary bad mood. I start searching my recent behaviors, trying to find something that might earn this kind of confrontation. But Liam's demeanor calms. He rests his hands palm down on the table for a few seconds, breathing in and out, before reaching over to a large folder at the edge of the table. Extracting a slim book, he tosses it faceup in front of me.

It's "The Raven," by Edgar Allan Poe. And I've seen this particular book before. I stare at it until my vision blurs, afraid to look back into Liam's face. Afraid to show him mine.

"Well?" he says.

"Well what?"

As Liam reaches for the book, I resist the urge to snatch it away and run. To where I don't know. Nor why. If August gave up this treasure, he's either lost any interest or memory of me, or he's dead. Or worse, I suppose. There is a third option. I find I can't stand dragging it out. But before I open my mouth, Liam has opened the book. He reads my inscription.

"'To August, Take care, from Raven.' Simple, really. Concise. Were you in a hurry when you wrote this? I don't know who August is, but I'm sorry to tell you he's probably dead. We found this on a Nahx."

"Dead?" I manage. I'm trying to piece it together in my head from Liam's point of view. Of course he wouldn't assume that August was the one I gave the book to. That August *is* the Nahx. But now I'm not sure what he's so angry about.

"Your friend August led a Nahx scout here somehow. I'm

sure he's dead out in the slush now, and he goddamn deserves it too, for being so stupid."

Right. A human boy. Who Liam thinks is August. Somehow followed by a Nahx. Who I think actually *is* August.

August. Is. Here.

"Is he . . . ? I mean is it . . . ? Did you kill the Nahx?"

Liam sits back, a little smile on his face. "Raven. That's cold. You're not worried about whoever this August is? Some hapless yokel who escorted you at least part of the way here, I imagine. Did you make it worth his while? Is that why he came after you? So he could have another serving of what Topher's enjoying so much?"

He wants me to go for him. I know this. Liam goads me whenever he gets the chance, because what he wants more than anything is a reason to beat the living shit out of me in a knock-down, drag-out brawl. I'd love to give him the satisfaction, but there are more important things right now.

"Is the Nahx dead?" I ask. "I mean, if he . . . if it got away, then we definitely need to bug out. It'll bring a legion of them. We'll be finished." If only Liam knew how untrue this is. If only he knew how my heart is pounding in my chest, hanging on the faint hope that August, the real August, my Nahx, is alive.

"We didn't kill the Nahx," Liam says with a smug grin. "We did one better. We took it prisoner."

AUGUST

I reach for my knee. But my hand is tangled in something, some chain. I try the other hand, but that is tangled too. I pull on the chain to break it. I am good at breaking things.

There's a swish of movement and something *thunks* behind me. A wall? Am I inside?

"Stop doing that," a voice says. "I don't want to keep hurting you."

"Don't waste arrows. If it does it again, put one in the other shoulder."

I don't think it's nighttime, but I'm having trouble seeing. And though I should be fully recharged after the days I spent in the rocks and snow, pulling hibernating creatures out of dens and swallowing them practically whole, I feel weak. And the pain is disorienting. Blinding. Maybe that's why I can't see.

"Take the hood off it, for God's sake. At least let it see."

A black shadow slips off my head, like a cloud in the wind. And I smell blood. *My* blood. Lots of it. The bright light blinds me, but as my vision clears I look down. I'm kneeling in it. Blood. There's an arrow in my knee, another in my shoulder, another through my wrist. Blood pools beneath me. At the sight of it the tube in my throat constricts, and I gag until it relaxes back, unwinding down into my stomach, pulsing. The fluid of my armor torrents through me. I can feel it trying to close the wounds, trying to block the pain sensors sufficiently for me to move, to escape. But in the swirling maelstrom it's hard to think. My thoughts keep getting sucked away before I can complete them.

I'm inside. In a . . . something. There are humans with me.

And injured. Badly. I need to rest, away from here. Away from these humans and their arrows.

"Is that blood, do you think?" one of the humans says. "It looks like motor oil."

"Why don't we take its armor off?"

"Tried. Can't. I'm not sure it *is* armor. And it's boiling hot."

The other human trains his weapon on me, an arrow poised to pierce into me. As he takes a step forward, I growl with as much force as I can manage. His quick recoil satisfies me. Weak and stupid human. He's still scared of me when I'm chained up and half dead.

"DON'T do that again!" the human says.

Or what, stupid human? You'll poke another hole in me?

My shoulder spasms with sharp pain. I look down to see the arrowhead sticking out. Shot in the back, I think, and this reminds me of something. A name. A tap on the shoulder over a star-shaped scar. Thick sludge gurgles in my brain. My hand makes the signs for "bird" and "black."

Ah, death, muddy death. I'm the stupidest creature who ever lived.

Pretty. Wind. Flower.

Dandelion.

I came back for her, as if she even remembers me.

Topher finds me in my quarters, curled up on the bottom bunk, fists pressed into my eyes, trying to get my breathing to be normal.

"I just heard," he says, sitting on my chair. "We're going to get together a search party tomorrow. See if we can find your friend, this August. Why didn't he come all the way to the base with you?"

I don't answer. Of course I don't answer.

"Liam says there's probably another group of refugees somewhere. Is that right? Why didn't you say anything? Do you know where they are? Liam says you stopped answering his questions."

I press my hand over my mouth because if I open it, I'm afraid of what will come out. Topher rolls the chair forward and touches me, his fingers gentle on my cheek. "He might not be dead. He might have dropped the book or . . ." But he doesn't believe this. He gets out of the chair and kneels by the bed, curling his arms around me. "We'll find him, Raven. If that's what you want."

I know what he's thinking. That this human boy, August,

is the obstacle between us and the thing neither of us really wants. And maybe that Topher's willingness to search for this imaginary boy is enough of a demonstration that I might finally begin to thaw toward the absurd idea of us. But it's so insincere it is almost nauseating. Because Topher knows as well as I do that if there ever was a human boy called August, he's dead. Their "search party" is not a rescue mission. It's a recovery. Topher expects to find him with a dart in his chest and learn a new thing about the Nahx—that they sometimes take trophies from their victims.

"Can you tell me about him?" Topher says. "Tell me what happened. Where you were all those weeks."

I turn my face to the wall.

"It's not going to hurt my feelings or anything, if you had something with him. I just want to know why he didn't come back here with you. Unless he had somewhere else to go. That's what Liam is thinking. That he was part of a group of refugees that were heading west, but that you wanted to come back here for . . ."

I know what Liam would think of this. That romantic sentimentality will get us all killed. I didn't go with August because I'm in love with Topher. August came back for me because he's in love with me. A Nahx trailed him, killed him, and maybe transmitted our location to his command. We've all been fucked over by love.

If only they knew that love might be the one thing to save us.

"Do you want to bug out?" I say to the wall. "Head west, I mean. Use Xander's map and get the hell out of here?"

Topher doesn't answer quickly enough for me. In his hesitation I see all the hours he and the other boys and men have spent training, adapting the weapons, planning assaults. It all comes down to fight or run again. I have no fight left in me. And sometimes I think Topher is nothing *but* fight.

"I want to get you out," he says finally, and I guess I have to be satisfied with that.

"What are they going to do with the Nahx they captured?"

Topher sits back in the chair, his hands on his knees. I'm struck by his appearance, taking a moment to really look at him for the first time in months. He looks much older than seventeen, and the last vestiges of the warmth that made him look like Tucker are fading. For all his lies about love, Topher is hard as the icy mountains that separate us from the rest of the human world.

"They're going to try to interrogate it, I guess."

"Interrogate? You mean, like torture?"

"I guess that depends on how much it's willing to tell us."

An urge from my past, long since forgotten, to punch Topher in his pretty face, crashes over me. "The Nahx don't speak," I say before I can stop myself.

Topher leans back, studying me. "They don't speak to us.

When have they had an opportunity before this? As far as the NKVs go, this is only the second time one has been captured. They've never even managed to bring one in dead."

"They don't . . ." But how can I explain what I know? How can I make Topher understand? His hate for them is like a living thing, as ugly and consuming as it was that day by Tucker's grave. I backtrack, trying to get us onto a safer topic. "I know a way we can get to the coast. Safely, I mean."

"Xander's map?"

"Yes. But that's not all." I press my eyes shut. "An escort. Someone who knows the way. Who knows everything about the Nahx. Knows where they are and how to evade them."

Unexpectedly, Topher slides out of his chair and kneels in front of me again. "Raven . . . he's . . . August is dead. I shouldn't have said what I did before. There's no way that Nahx would have left him alive. That's never happened. Never. I know what you think happened back in the trailer park, but that was some kind of hallucination. There's no such thing as a Nahx that leaves people alive. That Nahx they caught? It killed August."

I search his eyes. Search for the spark of joy that I once loved so much in Tucker. But there's nothing left. My own eyes fill with tears. For Tucker. For the world. For the fact that Topher is the human left that I trust the most, and I can't trust him with the truth. But I have no choice.

"Topher," I say, my hands on either side of his face. "The Nahx they caught *is* August."

A gust of wind in the quadrangle rattles my window suddenly. Topher glances at it and looks back at me, his face inscrutable. He looks like someone trying to figure out the punch line of a particularly complex joke. Then realization dawns on him like a new day. Slowly. And colorfully. But it's a new day broken by winter, like everything else around here. He stands abruptly and steps out the door.

"Call a security team!" he yells down the hallway. "Right now!" There's a muffled reply, and the sound of a door opening and closing.

"Topher," I try.

"You shut up!"

He remains in the doorway, silhouetted by the bright hallway lights. Finally, he turns back to me, and I see that truly, Tucker is gone. Topher is gone. All that remains now is a vengeful soldier. I'm neither surprised nor disappointed. Resignation is what I feel, like the Nahx girl in the video, just before she lost her head.

"Stand up," he says. "Turn around."

I turn to the window, my mind naturally traveling back to that first night on the base when Topher pressed himself into my back, his drunkenness, his heartbreak, his disdain for me so potent I wanted to kill him with my bare hands. Maybe everything that I thought had changed was an illusion. I don't even think we were ever really friends. And he was never going to be Tucker. Even Tucker wasn't who I thought he was. Neither of them was. I feel like I just keep taking their masks off but never get to the real person underneath.

"Put your hands behind your back."

"Topher, please." Like all the senior officers, he carries around cable ties, to truss up anyone who gets out of hand. It's been happening more and more, with the younger men especially. Cabin fever and homemade alcohol. I've never seen Topher restrain a girl before though. "Come on. Where am I going to go?"

"Hands. Behind. Your back."

I do it. And flinch when he pulls the cable tie much too tight.

"You brought a Nahx here." His voice is choked with fury. "You brought a Nahx to the one safe place left on Earth."

"I had no other way of getting back. I couldn't have done it without him. He saved my life."

"Are you that stupid? It was a trick. It tricked you into leading it here."

Outside, the wind turns to rain, fat drops clicking against the small window like distant gunfire. Topher yanks me back and pushes me into the chair, my hands crumpling uncomfortably behind me.

"You have about sixty seconds until security gets here. It's time to tell me everything you know."

"About what?" I ask stupidly.

"Did this Nahx have any others with him?"

"No. He killed the only other one we encountered."

That makes Topher frown. "What about communications? A radio? A transmitter?"

"None that I saw. He was lost. Like separated from his . . . whatever . . . platoon. I think he was basically AWOL."

"Or a spy."

I almost laugh at that. August seemed so confused most of the time; I can't imagine him stringing together that kind of deception.

"I *saw* the one he killed. If he was a spy, why would he kill one of his own people?"

"Did you see him actually kill it? This other one?"

"No. But I know he did. There were two of them. A male and a female. I killed the female and August killed the male."

"How do you know he killed it?"

It occurs to me that Topher has started referring to August as "he" and not "it." Perhaps I should file that away as a minor victory. "He told me. Why would he lie?"

"To gain your trust, of course. You haven't been watching the videos. Most of the time when you think one of them is dead, they get up and walk away a few hours later. So he pretended to kill it, to prove he was on your side so you would lead him right here. Jesus, Raven."

He begins to pace.

"That's not what happened. He abandoned his people. He saved my life."

"Saved your life? All I saw was a Nahx beating the crap out of you. I thought you were dead when he picked you up."

My blood turns to ice. "That wasn't him," I say. "He picked me up *after* the other one knocked me out. He killed that one too, I think." Out in the hallway, I hear the door burst open and the sound of boots on the concrete floor. "Topher, there were two Nahx there with me in the stadium, right? You saw him. You saw him save me."

"I don't remember."

"You must remember! A dead Nahx with my knife in its throat would have been right there! August killed him to save me."

"Raven, I was out of my mind. I thought you were dead. This Nahx was running off with you. I was firing arrows at him and chasing you. I didn't stop to check out the scenery."

Before I can convince him, the security team arrives. Xander and Emily.

"What's going on?" Xander says.

"Take her down to a detention cell," Topher says.

Xander, bless him, scratches his head, looking down at me. "Toph?"

"You heard me. Take her. I'm right behind you."

Xander thinks about it for a few seconds until Emily steps forward and hoists me up. I bite back a whimper of pain.

Faces turn to me as we travel through the base, toward the long stairway down to the detention cells. And we pass people I know. People I recognize. They don't seem very surprised to see me being hauled away in restraints. But I suppose nothing much surprises anyone anymore. Faces turn away from me just as quickly.

While the command deck is about two hundred feet above the residence decks, the detention cells are deep beneath, tucked among the storerooms, the generator, and water heaters that feed off an underground river and hot springs. Under many feet of rock and ice. Uncomfortably claustrophobic for me, a cell will be a nightmare for August.

"Let me speak to him," I say, twisting my neck back to look at Topher. "Let me see the Nahx. He can help us get out of the occupied territory. I know he can."

"I thought you said they can't speak," Topher says.

"They don't. Not with voices. They have signs. I learned a lot of them. And he can read. Maybe he can write."

Topher walks in silence behind us as I watch him, my neck cramping from the effort of twisting it back.

"Put her in an empty cell," he says, then turns to me. "Liam is on his way down. You need to speak to him."

I stumble as Emily shoves me into a cell, and I fall painfully to my knees. Topher stares down at me from the doorway as I roll awkwardly into a sitting position.

"Can you untie me now?"

"A black belt in karate? Would that be wise?"

"You're a black belt too."

"You know I can't take you, Raven. I've never been able to." I guess the irony of the truncheon and pistol holstered at his hip is lost on him. But then he shrugs and cuts the bindings with a pocketknife. I hear voices out in the corridor, as Topher steps back through the door, clicking it shut behind him.

The walls seem to close around me. After a few minutes I hear Liam's voice outside. He is yelling. He is not happy.

"Go back up to command!" he bellows "Make sure the sentry patrols are doubled. You take an attack team to the north entrance."

"Yes, sir," I hear Topher say. It gives me chills.

The lock on the door clicks open and Liam stands there staring down at me, with Xander and Emily behind him as guards. I twitch involuntarily, my shoulders aching. Liam steps forward. He looks as though he might say something. But then in the blink of an eye, before I can react, he pulls his fist back and punches me so hard in the face I feel my brain jangle against my skull.

"What the fuck did you do?" he says as I struggle back up onto my knees, my face throbbing. "That piece of shit in the next cell is your doing. When its army arrives and kills us all, it will be your fault."

"No army is arriving," I say. "August is on our side. He left his platoon. He saved my life. He can help us get out of here. He could help us get to the coast. He wants to help us."

"Why would he want to help us? He's part of their army!"

"Army? Do you think he volunteered for this?" I edge backward, not sure he's done inflicting violence on me. I could take him, no doubt, but what would that accomplish? I'm in a prison cell, at long last.

I feel something warm dripping down from my nose. Blood. For some reason the taste of it helps me to focus. Of all the times I have tried to convince Liam that the thing to do is to get the hell out of here, this is the most critical. This is the moment where he can choose to fight, to kill the Nahx he has in captivity already. Or to use his enemy to help us get to safety.

Of all the persuasion I've tried, all the arguments, all the begging, this is the most important. I need to appeal to Liam's sense of reason, his survival instinct, if he has one. But maybe, like Topher, he is nothing but fight.

"You need to listen to me," I say. "This is our last and only chance. August will not bring the Nahx here. But they will come eventually. I don't really understand what their project is, what their goal is. What this is all about. But I'm pretty sure that their main idea is that no humans are left alive. Not in the high lands anyway. Maybe eventually they will take every human on Earth. But for the time being we're pretty sure it's safe on the coast. If we can get there, we can live. All these people in the base. All the people that your mother swore to protect. They can live."

Liam stares at me. He does look as though he's considering what I've said. But then his lips turn into a smirk and I know I've lost him. Or that maybe I never had him. Maybe he never had the well-being of all people on the base as his priority. Maybe watching his father get killed, watching his sister die, watching his mother's body being brought back from a raid destroyed him in the same way that Tucker's death destroyed Topher.

I suppose because we grew up so safe, deceptively safe, without war, with little crime, with everything we needed to survive, we never learned what this kind of life would do to you. I wonder how many people there are left at the base who have any desire to escape, who haven't had their spirits turned to anger and revenge. I think of my stepfather's stories of the badass hunters and trappers he knew up north, and the darker stories he had. There must be people in the base who have stared down despair, hunger, and cold before too. I'll make them my allies if I ever get out of here.

But that doesn't seem likely. Liam leans over and spits on me, his saliva mixing with the blood on my lips. "Bring her into the Nahx's cell," he says. This time Xander reaches down and gently lifts me to my feet.

AUGUST

Blood. My face mask reflects back up at me from the pool of blood on the floor.

Blood. When you break a dandelion stem, it bleeds white. Like the milk the humans drink. I drank milk once. Sixth said I could. It made me sick too. Dandelion blood. Her smell is overpowering, intoxicating. My mind swims back through the thick mist of syrupy memory to those days in the sky, those days she died slowly, skin on fire, bloody and blue with bruises. She didn't die.

She didn't die.

"Wake up!"

Have I been sleeping? That's not normal.

I lift my head up and blink the past from my eyes.

Blood. Blood on her face.

The guards stumble back as I hiss and pull at the chains.

"Settle down, Nahx, unless you want another arrow in you."

It's the pale, thin one again, the one who gives the orders. The one I tried to surrender to. I tried to show him Dandelion's book. He put the first arrow through my knee.

Blood. He smells of her blood.

Rage surges through me. I'm more awake now than I've been in days. Weeks. As awake as I was the day I left her. That took all my strength, to not carry her away with me and keep her.

Blood. Blood. Her blood on him. Blood on her face.

My right shoulder pulses with pain as I pull my arm forward. There's a creak; and the humans recoil as the chain bursts from the wall. As I yank down the other chain, someone fires an arrow into the wall behind me. My own blood sprays the room as I pull the arrow from my shoulder. One fist connects with the boy's head while the other lashes out with the arrow at a girl with a crossbow. She falls in a heap.

Then Dandelion is screaming. Screaming. The other girl has an arrow in her eye—an arrow dripping with my oily, gray blood. The thin boy lies crumpled on the floor. I pull his pistol out of his hand and point it at the black-haired one.

"August! NO!"

The black-haired one drops his crossbow and raises his hands over his head.

I count time with her breaths. One, two, three, four.

Blood. Ah no. What have I done?

"Xander? Are there more guards outside the door?" she

says, not taking her eyes off me. Her eyes. "Xander?" Her voice is like the rushing river. But tight. Like the rushing river pushed through a crack in the ice. The black-haired one was in the river with her. I remember him now. I remember her bravery in pulling him down, saving him.

"No," he says. "Topher's putting together extra sentry teams and attack squads. Everyone was called up to the command level."

Dandelion takes a tentative step toward me, her hands outstretched.

"August? Can I have the pistol?"

My breathing makes a bubbly sound. There might be blood in my lungs. I'm trying to figure out what just happened. I think I killed two people. But they were . . .

"August?"

. . . hurting her.

I flip the pistol and hold it out. She steps forward and takes it, tucking it into the back of her belt.

"Xander is my friend, okay? Please don't hurt him."

I shake my head. I pull arrows out of my wrist and knee. The blaze of pain is like lightning. Blood drips off my fingers as I drop the arrows and sign her name.

Dandelion.

"I don't know what that one means, August."

Something about flying. Black flying night feathers feather never nevermore.

Raven. I thought I'd see you nevermore.

She touches my face, and I wrap my aching arms around her.

"I've missed you, too," she says, and lets me lift her up.

RAVEN

We stay like that, me lifted up, floating above the horror August wrought. His armor is almost too hot to touch, and yet I cling to him. Cradled in his arms, time stops for me; the world disappears and I don't have to face what is next. It is Xander who eventually breaks the spell.

"Rave? Liam is still breathing."

August moves. Lunging forward onto one knee, he somehow manages to tuck me protectively behind him while simultaneously shoving Liam's limp form across the cell. One hand lashes out and grabs Xander's crossbow from the floor.

"No! August, no!"

He stops and looks back at me, still coiled up like a snake preparing to pounce.

"Give me the crossbow, too, please." I make the "please" sign, pressing my fist into my breastbone. August glances in Xander's direction. "Xander's a friend. Right, Xander?"

Xander shrugs, his black eyes wide with fear. But August tosses the crossbow down. I snatch it up and note the arrow loaded into the channel. Could I shoot August? I wonder as I stand and face up to our situation. Could I aim that arrow at the weak point in his neck and let fly? Hopefully, I won't have to find out.

"Come here, August. Xander's going to check out . . . these two, okay? Everything is okay. Calm down." August steps back toward me, reaching for my face. I flinch away and he lets his hand fall.

Don't be scared.

"I *am* scared. You killed someone right in front of me!"

Sorry sorry repeat sorry forever sorry four give. Four give . . .

"Stop it!"

His hands still. Then after a second or two, he drops slowly to his knees, sitting back on his heels. I wipe my eyes and watch as Xander hangs over Emily. The eye she has left is open and staring, her skin changing to the color of cooling ash.

"She's dead," Xander says, unhelpfully. He takes Liam's pulse and checks under his eyelids. "He's still with us. Not sure if he'll ever wake up again. I'll go get a medic, I guess."

Xander stands, and as the three of us look at one another, a moment passes so full of possibility and disaster that I feel I could choke on it.

"Xander, August and I are leaving."

Xander blinks. "Okay," he says uncertainly.

"We need you to help us get out of the base. Will you do that?"

"Do I have a choice?"

August looks up at me, and I have the chilling realization that he would kill Xander where he stands if I wanted. That he would kill every human in the base if I asked him to. I'm still not sure what I did to have such power over him, or if that power is absolute. Maybe one day August will finally tire of me.

"No," I say to Xander. "You don't have a choice. Bind Liam's hands."

Xander pulls a cable tie from his pocket and fastens it tightly around Liam's wrists. Liam moans softly, but does not quite come around.

"Where are you going to go?" he asks as he finishes.

"Away from here. West. Toward the coast. August, you can get me to the coast, right? To the human territory?"

He looks up at me for a moment, then nods slowly, turning his face toward the floor. I have just asked him to deliver me out of his life again, I realize. I wonder how many times I will ask this of him. How many times he will do it. And whether we will ever truly be rid of each other. Somehow between here and the coast I'm going to have to make him understand that he doesn't belong in my world.

But August doesn't belong in his own world either. He doesn't belong anywhere.

"You're covered in his blood," Xander says, frowning thoughtfully. I've seen this look from him before, before

August captured me in Calgary. It's a mixture of panic and practicality. As though he's putting off a scream of terror while he figures out how to avoid what's inciting it. "We can get out through the thermal vents, I guess. Down to the river and out via the walkways to the northwest exits. That's my favorite sentry shift because it's so warm."

"Will there be sentries there?"

Xander bends over and closes Emily's staring eye. "Maybe. Probably. Likely sleeping though, if they're anything like me." He straightens up and shakes his head. "This is fucked up."

Sorry. Repeat sorry.

"What do those signs mean?" Xander asks.

"He just apologized. He does that a lot."

"How very Canadian. Can you ask him not to kill the sentries at the northwest exits, if they're awake?"

"Ask him yourself."

Xander takes a tentative step toward August, who rises slowly to his feet. Next to this giant alien, Xander looks slight and small, almost childlike, though I've never thought of him like that before.

"Well, August? Can you get out of here without killing anyone else?"

August studies Xander for a moment, then nods.

Promise.

"He promises," I say.

"I see. And does he usually keep his promises?"

If you only knew how much, I think.

The low-ceilinged hallways outside the detention cells mean August has to stoop, which he does with one hand resting lightly on my shoulder. Xander leads us, and I make sure he knows I have the pistol in my hand. The crossbow hangs over my back.

"Did you have a rifle, August?" I ask as Xander checks the entrance to the thermal generators. August shakes his head. "Do you need a weapon? Where's your knife?" He shakes his head and shrugs. I suppose I could give him the crossbow if we get into a fight. I don't know how good he would be with it. And I wonder how Liam and his team subdued him, if they took his weapons. I never had a chance to ask someone how it all went down. Maybe August can explain it to me when we get a moment.

August's boots clang against the metal catwalk above the humming generators, but apart from that, we walk in silence. As the minutes pass, August's limp lessens until he walks just as easily as he ever did. Whatever he is, his resilience is extraordinary. He had three arrows in him not ten minutes ago. Now he's walking along as though nothing happened.

"Are you in pain?" I ask him.

A little, he signs, holding his index finger and thumb an inch apart.

"Will you be okay?"

Don't be scared, he signs, which I translate to "Don't worry."

Sure. Nothing to worry about. Escaping a veritable fortress with an enemy killer. No big deal.

As we begin the descent to the river, he starts to wheeze a bit, but repeats his *Don't worry* when I turn back to scrutinize him. "If the Nahx do come, you should bring the civilians down here," I say to Xander. "Nahx don't like being underground, and this is getting low for them, I think. Isn't that right, August?"

He nods as Xander turns and walks backward for a few steps.

"Why do you walk like that?" Xander asks, pointing at the hand August rests on my shoulder.

Push down. Danger, August signs, wheezing. I translate.

"And it's always a male and a female, right? Like you're a bodyguard or something?"

August nods.

"Well, that's very chivalrous, I guess. Kind of old-fashioned."

August takes his hand off my shoulder then and places it on his head, rubbing, as though he has a headache. We walk in silence for a minute, until my thoughts threaten to bubble up and leak out as hopeless tears again.

"August, would it be okay if I told Xander some things about you? About the girl you traveled with?"

He takes my hand, giving it a little squeeze. I take that as a yes.

And so as we walk along the catwalk, now above the steaming river, our progress marked by the rhythmic clanging of August's footsteps, I tell Xander the tale. What I know of it, anyway. How Tucker killed this girl that August was bound to. How August killed Tucker, then wandered lost and alone until fate put him outside that bathroom door in the trailer park. Until he let me live and lost his whole world.

Xander sighs as he walks in front of us, and I think I see him wipe his eyes. We both know what it is to lose a whole world.

"Does Topher know?" Xander asks. "That he's the one who . . . ?"

"No. And I don't think you should tell him. It will only make it worse."

August's response is a low grumble.

We arrive at the northwest exit, which is remarkable only in its lack of pretension, a small metal door with a pitifully small lock. While Xander slips outside to locate the sentries, August taps me on the shoulder.

You are my world, he signs. Then, because I'm sure he sees something in my eyes, *I'm sorry.*

"You don't need to apologize. I owe you my life."

No. Nothing give please.

Ah, I don't owe him anything? If only that were true. I let go of his hand and try to run my fingers through my sweaty, tangled hair. Xander returns toting an assault rifle and a pistol. He hands them calmly to August as he gives us the update.

"The sentries are heading out to the perimeter gate to join the patrol. I told them I'd take this post." He presses his eyes closed. "You should be able to hoof it up the mountain just west of here. It's steep, but I've done it before. The path from the helipad will be crawling with patrols, and the helipad, too now, so you can't go that way. No one will take the helicopter without Liam's say-so, but someone will think of it. Then they'll look for him. Then you're fucked." He takes a breath and sighs it out. "But failing that, you need to get to the service road south of the Yellowhead Highway and then into the rail tunnels. You still have a copy of the map?"

I do, in my pocket. Half the people on the base do. Xander has been obsessively making copies of them and handing them out. We stare at each other.

"What are you going to do?" I say. He pushes the door wide open and gazes up at the frost-covered mountains.

"I could create a diversion, I guess. Or make sure I'm on whatever patrol manages to follow you. Someone will figure it out. I . . ." He looks hopeless suddenly, another expression I've rarely seen on Xander. He's the eternal optimist. The one who believes all things can be overcome. "This is suicide, Rave. If

Liam's crew catch up to you, they will kill you both."

"They won't catch up to us." I turn to August, who is listening, still wheezing slightly, the rifle slung over his shoulder. "Will they?"

Carry you.

"Right. August can move scarily fast if he wants to. Even carrying me."

"You have no supplies. Barely any weapons. And the Nahx could still be out there."

"We'll manage."

Xander shakes his head, looking forlorn again. "I never wanted to be a soldier," he says finally, simply. This is how Xander has felt all along. As much as he enjoyed a spar in the dojo, he was never up for this war.

"So why don't you come with us?" I say. "To the coast?"

August takes my hand and squeezes, a little impatiently, tugging me out the door. I take one step away from Xander, two steps, until I'm on the landing of a small set of stairs leading down to the muddy ground below.

"I don't think he could carry both of us," Xander says. "You'll send people back, right? A rescue mission? If you can?"

"Of course!" I dive back inside and throw my arms around him, ignoring the little growl August emits. "Take care of Topher, okay?"

"I'll do my best." He lets me go and leans out the door as I join August on the stairs. "Hey, August? Look after her."

Promise, August signs, then takes my hand again. As I take the last two steps out of the base, I'm overcome with the realization that I might be their last hope. I hope that August and I can get away without being killed. I hope that he can get me to the human cities on the coast. I hope those left at the base can somehow continue to survive, that Liam won't regain consciousness all the more determined to lead them to a massacre in the snow. I hope they will wait to be rescued.

So much hope hinging on me and August, disappearing in the fading afternoon light. We are the future of something unfinished and unformed, something powerful and important. I'm so scared and yet so certain that I'm doing the right thing. August squeezes my fingers and pulls me forward, away from the base, from my people, from Xander, from Topher, from Tucker's memory, from everything I ever knew.

He pulls me away from the human race, and I follow.

Xander didn't lie. The climb is steep and our progress slow. As August's wheezing subsides, mine increases with every yard of elevation we gain. The cold isn't helping; I'm not dressed for it, wearing my regular indoor uniform of cargo pants and a man's hoodie over a long-sleeved T-shirt. And we have no water and no food. As far as escapes go, this one is poorly planned. Maybe because neither of us thinks we'll actually get away. Maybe this is all some kind of last act of defiance. A final fuck-you to the species that failed to hold on to this planet.

When we have to scale rocky outcrops, August calmly invites me to climb on his back, where I cling like a chimpanzee baby until we reach more manageable terrain. I'm not a bad climber, actually. It's another adrenaline sport I pursued when my life lacked any real excitement. But I don't have the right shoes or any gear. That's only part of my excuse. Maybe I'm just tired. Or maybe I like being so close to him.

Pausing on a plateau, I look back down at the base, now tiny and unthreatening in the distance. It doesn't look like anything unusual is happening. We've been climbing, I estimate, for about two hours. If Liam has woken up, he's not speaking. If Xander has run into Topher, he hasn't betrayed us. Maybe they'll let us just walk away. What would anyone gain by a pursuit? Maybe logic will prevail.

After another hour of climbing, it begins to grow dark. For me each breath grows more and more difficult, while August seems to buzz with renewed energy. I'm beginning to see why the Nahx prefer the high ground. Although he's always seemed strong and fast to me, up here he's extraordinary, leaping up cliff faces with me clinging to him, or casually hoisting me over smaller obstacles with one hand. As night falls, we reach the snow line, and though the cold will be harsh, August seems to want to stop. He leads me under an overhang, which turns out to be a small cave. When August turns on his light, I see the remains of a fire.

"Have you been here before?"

He nods, pointing at the blackened rocks and ash and making a sign, along with the question hand.

Want a fire?

"Won't it be smoky?"

He shrugs. *You cold?*

"I think I'll be okay if we sit close."

He flicks his head back a few times like that's funny. Which I guess it is. Then he puts his hand on his head and taps his helmet nervously, before sitting next to me, easing himself down with a low hiss.

"I'm sorry. I forgot that's uncomfortable for you." He merely shakes his head. "Do you know where we're going?"

Your human friends. Long walk.

"Do you think we can make it?"

He thinks for a moment before signing. *Find clothes. Find food. Hide from my people. Yes.*

The more I speak to him, the more the nuances of his language translate easily in my head. *I will make sure you are safe. I'll get you there, back to your people. I promise.*

"I hope so."

He taps his head and makes a sign that looks like my name, but not quite.

"I'm sorry I don't . . . fly think? Fly dream? What does that mean?"

You said it just before.

"I . . . I hope so? Hope? That's how you say hope? Flying dream?"

He nods.

"That's a very pretty way of saying it. Hope is my middle name."

He tilts his head, raising a question hand.

"I know. It's kind of ironic. I've been called 'hopeless' enough times. A hopeless case."

Raven. Hope, he signs, but I see it as "Flying Black Dream."

I've never felt my name suited me less. It sounds like some kind of advanced stealth aircraft.

"My mom thought Hope was a lucky name, I guess. She pictured a black-haired, clever, and hopeful daughter. And she got me." I turn from him and blink away the thought of her panicked face, the thought of the silent car ride home from the police station, Mom and Jack in the front seat, me in the back, burning with shame. I'd tell August about it if I thought I could without losing my mind.

"I really miss my parents," I say instead. It seems like this is the first time I've ever admitted this, but that can't be right. It feels good to say it anyway; the words keep me connected to them. And I'm starting to think Mom was right all along.

It's all inside me. The hope has kept me sane all this time. The raven has kept me alive. If only I had something that would let me keep . . . August.

After a few seconds I feel his hand on my shoulder.

Why hopeless? he signs when I look back at him.

"Oh, you know, I was a brat." Understatement, but whatever. "I broke rules," I add when he seems to not understand.

I broke hard promises too.

"Hard promises?" He flicks his head back a couple of times. "Your language is interesting."

You are interesting.

We sit in silence for a moment while my face gets hot. "On the road again," I say finally. A weak attempt at humor.

Happy, he says.

"You are?"

He nods. *Happy to be outside. Happy to be moving. Happy to be with you.* He changes position slightly, his armor creaking. *I don't like being alone. I don't like my own people. I don't like your people. But I like you.*

This is about the longest speech he's ever made. Maybe the saddest, too.

"You know when we get to the coast, you'll have to leave me, right?" I say, putting my hand on his knee. His armor is almost too hot to touch. "We won't be able to stay together."

He places his armored glove over my hand and squeezes

gently. *Maybe the world will end*, he signs. *Maybe the sky will fall.* Then he signs another sentence I don't quite catch.

"Maybe something and something will be friends? What were those two signs?"

With his finger he draws two childish pictures in the dirt. A bear and a bee.

"Maybe bears and bees will be friends?" I don't know whether to laugh or cry as he nods.

Maybe snowflakes will rise and time will stop moving.

The way he says maybe is "almost hope." Almost a flying dream. With every word I know him better. I had no idea he was such a philosopher. So many things I don't know about him. So much to learn and such a limited time in which to learn it. But then again, as he says, maybe time will stop moving, and I will come to know him better than I know myself.

I want to get out of here, back to my parents, to safety. I want to save Topher and Xander and everyone else I can. I want the human race to survive. I want us to have a chance to redeem ourselves.

But I almost hope time stops moving too.

She sleeps, eventually, her little head tumbling onto my aching knee as I rest my hand in her hair and stare out at the dark beyond the cave entrance. I don't think the other humans would be foolish enough to come after us at night. But I have miscalculated their foolishness before.

As for my own foolishness, that knows no bounds. I will take her to the ends of the earth, descending to elevations that will make my nose bleed inside my mask. I will see spots and my joints will seize up, if Sixth's words are anything to go by. Maybe those were all lies. Maybe I could slip my armor off and stroll into the human refugee camps without anyone noticing. I don't look that different from them. Taller, my skin made dull by the sludge in my veins. Mainly, I think my behavior would give me away. I'd probably kill someone in a jealous rage within the first day.

Anyway, Sixth was probably telling the truth.

I check the altimeter on my sleeve. 3,900 feet. I could disconnect for a few minutes and . . . what? I don't even know. Watch her sleep without my mask between us? Breathe the same air as her? Wake her and ask her to put her hand on my face again? The possibilities are too numerous to consider. But it's a noisy, messy thing disconnecting from armor so recently recharged. She would be terrified and maybe run away and fall, tumble off a cliff in the dark, her last thoughts of the monster that woke her.

Tomorrow we head south, to a small town I've visited before. I can find her the clothes and food she will need for the journey. Then, unless my addled brain betrays me, we turn north and look for a series of low tunnels through the rock. Early on, long before I met Dandelion, some humans tried to escape that way. Tried. We watched it from a distant cliff, but the noise of the explosion was enough to rattle my eardrums. Sixth celebrated by embracing me tightly, then was so angry with herself she pulled out her knife and chased me down the mountain until I hid in a human car. She drove her fist through the windshield and dragged me out, but by that time her anger had abated. At least her desire to stab me had. That was the time she let me drink the fizzy brown drink that nearly killed me.

But the tunnels, long quiet now that most of the humans are processed, are the safest road west. They will be dark, and many miles long in places. And under tons of rock, and low most of the way. If Sixth is right, it could finish me.

Dandelion murmurs in her sleep, and I gently let her head slide off my knee and onto the ground, tugging the hood of her jacket up to protect her from the dust and ash. I pull myself to standing and stretch out my aching limbs. At the cave opening I see a wisp of movement and have weapons in each hand before even taking a breath. But when I step forward to investigate, I see that the movement was only a fat snowflake drifting onto the ledge outside the cave. Another follows it, then another, until the air is full of snowflakes, each one like a . . . a tiny human with wings. A magical creature . . .

Fairy. I capture the word and hold it a moment in the dungeon of my ruined mind. Something about this small rescued memory along with the glinting snowflakes fills me with a sense of peace and resolve. My objective is clearer than it has ever been. Dandelion must reach the human territory.

If, for me, that's a path to death, so be it.

I wake to shouts. It takes a moment for me to interpret the noise as bad news. A moment to remember that I'm with August, and he neither shouts nor speaks. That shouting means trouble. Leaping up, I look around to see I'm alone. I tuck my pistol into the back of my belt and poke my head out the cave opening. My throat clenches back a yell as I duck backward and process what I caught a glimpse of.

On the plateau below us, twenty feet away, is August, hands above his head, a crossbow pressed into his neck.

A crossbow that Topher is holding.

"Where is she?" I hear him shout again. August, of course, is silent.

"They don't talk," another voice says. Xander. Thank God. A voice of reason.

"He's darted her and left her somewhere. WHERE IS SHE?!"

I hear the crack of metal on metal, then the unmistakable clatter of August tumbling over on the rocky ground. "Get up!" I risk another look.

Topher and Xander have August hemmed in, facing him,

weapons raised and a steep cliff face behind him. I know August could scale that cliff effortlessly, but beyond climbing slowly back to his feet, he doesn't move or make any attempt to escape. Because of me. He could run, get away easily. If one of them managed to get an arrow into him, he would pull it out and be good as new in a day. But he won't leave me. And Topher looks like he would kill him.

I step out of the cave. "Hey!"

"There she is," Xander says. "I told you."

All three of them seem to relax a bit. As I step out of the cave, I catch a flash of movement from the other direction. And the still morning air precisely frames the unmistakable sound of a bowstring being pulled back. In one movement I turn my head, shouting at the shape in the shadows of the rocks and leaping recklessly down to the plateau.

Gravity bends, slows down, and I feel that I hover in the air for far too long, my head still turned toward the movement in the rocks. Liam, an arrow nocked, bowstring drawn. He looks at me as I yell, his face lighting up with recognition.

Time stops then, and I start to think maybe August was right. I'm stuck in the second I jumped out of the cave, in the moment I'm suspended above the plateau. The moment I meet Liam's eyes and see his surprise that I would attempt such a leap. The surprise that makes him jerk backward, lose his aim on August, twitch his bow and arrow slightly upward in my direction. The arrow sails toward me in slow motion as I turn in the air. When it hits, I expect a noise, but it slices through me like a warm knife in butter. Silent.

I land hard, my knees giving way under me. I just manage to stop myself falling on my face with my hands. And I have this tiny thought in the moment before everything falls apart.

August, I'm so sorry.

I would do the "sorry" hand sign, but the arrowhead is poking out of my chest in the exact spot where the side of my hand would go. Instead, I look up at him as he turns. As Topher turns. As Xander takes a tentative, stunned step forward.

August hisses, a loud, harsh hiss, and in the microsecond that Topher loses his concentration, August lashes out, grabs the crossbow, and smacks Topher hard in the face with it. Then he dives for me. Dives and catches me as I slide downward.

As he lays me on my side, the noises he makes are terrible. Growling, woeful hisses. Vaguely, behind him I see Xander helping Topher to his feet. I feel August snatch the pistol out of the back of my pants.

"*No,*" I croak, but August ignores them, pointing the gun instead at an approaching shadow, hissing, his free hand cradling my head.

"It was an accident. I didn't mean to hit her. I swear I was aiming for him." I'm not sure Liam is talking to August. He seems to be directing his words to Topher and Xander, who step toward us cautiously. August pulls back the safety on the pistol, snarling, making Liam take a step back. "I didn't mean to hit her," he says, raising his hands up. "She surprised me. I lost grip on the arrow. I swear."

I turn my head as much as I can to look at him, standing there five feet away in the thin snow, looking as insipid as ever. His face is bruised, one eye circled in black. Concussed, pale with shock and fear. Cold, scared. I almost feel sorry for him. He lost all the things I hope to find again one day.

Hoped.

I have a second, which stretches out like a slingshot, in which to see that Liam is wearing one of the helmet cameras. And I half complete the thought that one day maybe he'll let go of his lust for blood and glory before the question becomes irrelevant.

August hisses once, I feel his fingers twitch in my hair, and he pulls the trigger.

The world disappears. For that second the sound of the gunshot erases everything—the mountains, the snow, the sun, the sky. The past, present, and future shrink down to the size of a mote of dust and then nothing. Nothing but the red spray of Liam's life exploding out of the back of his skull, and the slow, almost graceful fall of his body.

"Oh, August . . . ," I say. I watch him breathe as the world slowly returns. I turn back toward the boys. Topher unarmed, blood dripping down his face from a cut near his hairline, and Xander, behind him, his own weapon dropped carelessly to the ground.

I blink, but it seems to take a long time. While my eyes are closed, I hear a soft *snip* and feel the swish of the arrow being pulled out from between my ribs. I assume that the person who screamed in pain was me.

When I open my eyes, August has pulled me up into his lap, hanging over me with the hand holding the pistol pressed to his head. Above him Xander tosses the remains of the arrow away.

"Can I take a look?" he says. August nods. He's shaking, his armor pulsing scorching hot and freezing cold. Xander crouches down and lifts up my hoodie and shirt. They're both soaked with blood. I try to curl my head up to see, but that effort seems to push more blood from the wound. I feel it dribble down my side.

"Oh fuck," Xander says. "Try not to move. Uh . . ."

Topher appears, stepping into my field of view. This seems to snap August out of whatever trance he's been in. His hand whisks out, pointing the pistol in Topher's face.

"No!" I cry, pushing another bubble of blood out. "No more. August, give Xander the gun, okay?"

He obeys without hesitation, flipping the pistol and handing it over. Xander tucks it away as Topher approaches, pulling his jacket off. Xander bunches it up and presses it over my wound. Pulling his own jacket off, he tucks it behind me, over the hole where the arrow entered.

"Pressure, here and here," he says to August, who wraps his hands around the front and back of my ribs, the gentle pressure making pain begin to register properly for the first time since it happened. Since Liam accidentally shot me with an arrow.

I could almost laugh.

If I weren't so sure I was dying, that is, I could probably laugh.

"I'll go back for a medic. Or we could take her back to the base," Topher says. But his voice has the tone he used when he talked about us loving each other, belonging to each other. He doesn't believe it.

"It's three hours at least," Xander says. "She doesn't . . ."

August starts to rock. He lets the blood-soaked jackets fall away and pulls me closer, hugging me to his chest.

"I'm sorry, August," I say.

No. No.

"Please, can you take my friends through the pass? To the human territory?"

No. No. No. Leave you nevermore.

I lift my hand up and touch the side of his face, the metal still pulsing hot and cold. He hisses mournfully.

"I told you we would be friends one day."

He makes a series of signs then. Some I know, and some I've seen before but never quite understood. Some new ones. But now, in this hazy space before death, they make perfect sense.

You walk in my dreams, Pretty Wind Flower.

"You too, August," I say, registering the nickname he's given me properly for the first time. He's said it a million times, but I never understood what it meant until now.

Pretty Wind Flower.

Dandelion. Yes. I think there's a dandelion inside me too, somewhere, with the raven and the hope. I'm apparently not as invincible as I thought.

When I blink next it's hard to get my eyes back open. Only the sound of Topher crying gives me the strength.

"I'll go back to the base," he says through his tears. "I'll bring back a medic."

Xander, who is sitting by my feet, calls after him. "Topher! Wait! It's not . . ." Then he glances at me, his face not hiding the hard truth he was about to yell out. "It's dangerous!" he finally says, but there's no spirit in him, either.

I turn my head to look at Topher, standing by the path down from the plateau. He looks at me, but I don't have the strength to interpret his expression. And he, I think, lacks the will to speak. He just turns and walks away.

He walks away. Didn't he tell me once he would never leave me? Or was that someone else?

August pulls me closer again and moves one thumb to wipe a tear from my face.

"Try to hang on, Rave," Xander says.

I try. But I can feel myself unraveling, and the puddle of blood I'm lying in is getting larger.

Feel broken?

How many times has August asked me this and how many times have I lied and said no?

"Yes," I say.

Repeat me.

We stare at each other until my reflection in the glass of his eye mask starts to blur and darken.

Breathe, he signs. I needed the reminder. But the next breath I take has bubbles of blood in it, which drip down my chin. As August wipes it away, I see his hand is shaking. He's trembling. He pulls me into his lap, sliding down to sit cross-legged beneath me, cradling me as he did that night before I learned the truth about what happened to Tucker. About who August was.

Despite the warmth he surrounds me with, I'm shivering too as my mind travels backward, back through the months I didn't know whether August was alive or dead. The months I tried to love Topher, tried to ignore the coldness growing inside him. Through the days August and I walked through the snow to return me to a life of hiding and scheming, through the weeks in the penthouse, hating him, fearing him, longing for him when he was gone. And the rocking climb up the stairs half conscious in his arms, and the glimpse of him outside the barn when Sawyer thought I was dreaming, and him carrying me, carrying me, with snowflakes drifting down around us, with the stars falling. And staring at that latch on the bathroom in the trailer, staring and wishing I had locked that door. Though with his propensity for breaking locks, he probably would have just torn the door from its hinges. Maybe that act of violence would have been enough to incite anger toward me. Maybe he would have darted me and walked away.

Either way, that unlatched door is the reason we're both here now, my life leaking away, his heart breaking. Either way, when he opened the door he saw something that made him hesitate, and that was all it took.

He remembered the girl who floated away in the river and didn't want to let her float away again.

I wonder if there is such a thing as love at first sight. I thought once that Tucker loved me. I see now that I was wrong. This is what love feels like: August's trembling hands trying to hold my blood inside me. In my memory, as he carried me away from the trailer park, he trembled too. Was he scared of me? Or scared of losing me? Maybe both.

I blink again. When I open my eyes, my hand is resting on August's face, his own warm hand pressed over it.

"Can you take this off?" I ask. "Your helmet? Your armor? Can you take it off?"

No. Yes. Die.

"You die if you take it off? Even for a minute?"

He adjusts the hand sign slightly—I'm not even sure how—but it changes the tense to passive.

Not die. Be killed.

"Who would kill you? Other Nahx? It's forbidden to take it off? No one will know, August."

He looks up to Xander, who I had forgotten was even here. Xander sniffs wetly before answering.

"I'm not going to tell anyone."

August turns his face back down to me, and with the morning sun shining on him, I can almost imagine I see his eyes behind the mask. "Would you take it off? Please? I'd like to see what you look like."

He stares down at me, running his trembling fingers over my hair. Finally, he reaches out with one arm and touches Xander on the shoulder.

Take, he signs. *Take her.*

Xander moves to sit closer as August gently slides me into his lap. The movement causes a fresh burst of blood to bubble out, and Xander clumsily presses his bare hand over it.

"God," he says quietly. And then "Okay . . ." I wish I could have spared him this. I wish I could have spared everyone everything.

August rises up to rest on one knee. He looks around the plateau and then back to me, with his head turned to the side. I bite back a whimper as a sudden spasm of pain lances through me.

"Please," I say, and I don't add *there's not much time.*

August reaches up to his helmet and pulls on something. There's a loud crack, almost like a gunshot, and when black fluid drips down his shoulder, I panic for a moment that he has been shot, but he just reaches over and snaps something on the other side of his helmet. Another loud bang. Xander twitches under me.

August slowly leans forward to rest on both knees, with one hand on the ground. Reaching, he grabs the back of his helmet and pulls. There's another noise, a wet squooshing sound, and the helmet splits in two, front and back, and falls to the ground. His head emerges, wet, covered in the same fluid that leaked out. It looks like what I've always thought of as his blood.

He holds there, his head hanging down, and I can see that the helmet is still connected to him via a dripping tube, which splits into three as it seems to originate in his mouth and nostrils.

"What the . . . ," Xander says.

August starts to cough and choke. With a shaking hand he grabs the slimy tube and pulls about a foot of it out, then another few inches until finally the whole thing slithers out, along with a stream of sludge. He hangs there for a moment as I watch him cough and gag. Then he ejects a torrent of black vomit onto the snow. A few seconds pass. Finally, he takes a wet, wheezing breath.

"August?"

He sits back on his knees and does something to his wrists. With two more cracking noises and more sludge his gloves come away. He gathers a handful of the fresh snow and rubs away the fluid from his hands, revealing pale, almost gray skin beneath. Clambering over the puddle of vomit, he returns to my side and looks down on me.

"Oh my God," Xander says as August takes me, sliding me back to cradle in his lap. August wipes his face and scrapes some of the fluid from his eyes. He bows his head, looking down at me from inches away.

"You're . . . you're . . ." For a moment I've forgotten the word. When it pops back into my head I almost laugh. "You're human?"

Repeat human, he signs.

"Can't you speak? Now that you've taken the mask off? You can't speak?"

No. Cut voice. He tilts his head back to show me a mass of scars and some metallic implants that form part of his neck.

"But you're human? I mean apart from . . ." I reach up to touch

471

the implants on his neck and jaw. "You look just like a human."

Repeat human.

At first I think he's agreeing with me, because repeat means "alike." But then I realize it can also mean something else.

"Copy human? You mean, like a clone?"

He nods then, and moves one hand up to touch my hair, my brow. A little sigh escapes him. And he smiles.

Human. But not. There are things about him that don't look quite right. His teeth look sharp. His irises are pure black, and larger than they should be. And his skin, where I can see it as he wipes more of the black gunk away, is actually gray. When I run my fingers over his lips and teeth, and he opens his mouth, I see that his tongue is black too. His face is smooth and hairless and what hair he has on his head looks messily shorn and mashed and matted with the oily fluid.

But somehow, despite all this, he is unspeakably beautiful. If I had to guess, I would say at least one of his parents or grandparents was Chinese. He has a delicate nose and angled eyes along with a strong jaw and prominent cheekbones—one of them marred with a bright white scar from his temple to his bow-shaped upper lip.

I use the sleeve of my hoodie to wipe more slime from his pretty face. He looks so harmless for how frightened I've been of him, for the things he's done, the people he's killed. He looks innocent.

"How old are you?" I ask.

August shrugs, never taking his black eyes from mine. I become aware that his breathing is a bit forced. "Are you okay? Can you breathe like this?"

Don't worry about me.

And saying this seems to release something in him. His eyes fill with silvery tears.

I'm sorry sorry sorry.

It's getting hard to think through the throbbing burning from the broken flesh inside me and the ache in my heart, but dimly, I'm aware that Xander is crying too. Strange that I don't think I've ever felt as loved as I do this moment. Two beautiful boys crying over my imminent death. I couldn't have dreamed up a better scene. I feel like Juliet.

"Xan-Xander? Will you tell . . . my parents what happened to me, if you find them?"

He nods, sobbing.

Dandelion. I promise I will take that black-haired boy to the humans.

I laugh, but it turns into a moan of pain.

August gulps air and clings to me, pulling me close.

"Put your mask back on if you can't breathe."

He shakes his head, and gasps.

"Dude, come on. . . ." Xander reaches for him, but August shoves him back.

No!

"August, please. You just promised to take Xander home. You promised."

He shakes his head, his beautiful face now streaked with gray tears.

Live. Live. Live?

"I'm sorry. I don't think I will." My vision is starting to turn dark at the edges.

Live forever?

"No. No one lives forever."

August takes a raspy gulp of air, leaning down to me, clutching my chin in his warm fingers. With his other hand he points to his eyes and ears.

Look! Listen! he signs with a low hiss.

"I'm listening," I say, trying to maintain focus on his face. Trying to fix all his expressions of sorrow and frustration in my mind. After so many months never seeing him like this, of having to guess his emotions, it's precious.

He signs slowly, adding punctuation with firm hand movements.

Do. You. Want. To. Live. Forever?

"Everyone does. But that's . . ."

He presses his hand over my mouth. *Yes or no?*

In my fading vision I see a small spark of light, like a firefly. I try to reach for it, but my arms are too heavy.

Yes or no!?

"Yes," I say, more to the firefly than to anything else. It's buzzing closer now. If I could just lift my hand . . .

August hoists me up roughly and reaches to his thigh under my back. When he lowers me down, I see what he has in his hand.

A Nahx dart.

His face is a mask of regret and sadness, eyebrows drawn together, his sharp white teeth digging into his top lip, his eyes streaming with tears. He bites something off the end of the dart, revealing the needle tip.

Yes? Say yes.

"Yes," I say. To him, to the firefly, to Xander, who is nothing but a muttering ghost at the edges of the light. To Topher, who walked away. To someone . . .

August jams the dart into my neck. The firefly explodes, sucking away the light like a collapsing star.

"What . . . ," I say, but fire is coursing through me. My body spasms, spine curling backward as I try to escape the inferno inside. I open my mouth to scream, but nothing comes out, the light of my voice sucked away with everything else.

"What was that? WHAT DID YOU DO?" I hear Xander screaming.

I begin to shake, and as August holds me up, I see that the blood leaking from my stomach is changing color. Everything is changing color. The black at the edges of my vision becomes hard and thick. I look up and meet August's eyes. He shakes his head and presses the side of his hand into his chest.

Sorry. Sorry. Sorry.

Then he lifts my hands and puts them on either side of his face. Looking into his eyes, locking on to him as my mind drowns in darkness, something of the mystery of August begins to unfurl and sail above the waves, something of the mystery of the Nahx, of their darts, their strange blood. What they are doing to our planet. It makes sense at last, and with that comes such relief that I think I smile. August smiles back at me through his tears. I tug his face down until our lips touch. His kiss tastes like fresh snow and the smoke of a campfire. He pulls back and touches his lips with his fingers.

I feel my heart stop, like it has stepped into quicksand and sunk without a struggle. Things start to move slowly. August blinks, and it seems to take an hour, a day. The poison of the dart infuses all parts of me now, and I know. This is time stopping, just as August said. I know what the darts are for. I feel the beginnings of disdain for my own weak, imperfect species. This is how we become perfect. This is how we live forever.

My brain focuses on his face, which is frozen, inches from mine, his eyes wide and frightened, snowflakes suspended in the air around him, like stars.

There is darkness underneath me, like that murky lake of

my dream. There is something under the water, pulling at me, something I've forgotten, something vital. If the Nahx darts are human perfection, if they are immortality, then what have I forgotten? Something too terrible to remember. Something under the earth, under the snow, something under the shadows of a leafless tree.

It comes back to me as August's face dissolves into nothing. With the last impulse of my human body, I form the word and whisper it through half-frozen lips.

"Tucker . . ."

Then the darkness sucks me down.

AUGUST

Her eyes are open, but I know what she sees. Nothing. I can remember the nothing.

"You should close her eyes," the black-haired boy says. He wipes snot from his nose with his sleeve. "What did you inject her with? Was it medicine or something?"

I can't move. I don't want to close her eyes or stop looking at her. I know when she opens them again, if she opens them again, she won't be my Dandelion anymore. Even now there are streaks of black in her golden hair, veins of spiderwebs on her skin, no longer warm sunlight brown, but gray as a storm cloud. Gray as mine.

"I guess it didn't work. Unless . . . well, she was going to die anyway. I think the arrow went through her spine." He wipes his dark eyes. His tears are as clear as ice, unlike mine. They smell of salt, and sorrow. "She was in a lot of pain."

I gulp for air, and it feels like swallowing claws and teeth.

"You need to put your mask back on," the boy says, reaching for it. When his fingers are a few inches away, the tentacles of the breathing tube spring to life and wind around his hand.

"Ugh! Get it off!" he says. But the mask rejects him, the

tentacles curling back and falling slack. "What the fuck is that?"

I gulp another breath. But before I put the mask on, I bend down and kiss Dandelion's cold lips again. And close her eyes.

The boy looks away as I reconnect to the mask, the tubes finding their way into my nose and mouth, making me gag and cough. When I fix the helmet into place and latch it closed, I'm rewarded, or punished maybe, with a burst of slug syrup. The relief of pain lasts only a moment, because I cling to Dandelion and remind myself she's gone. And I'm not sure how to bring her back.

I lift her into my arms and hold her tight. My mind struggles with the thought-numbing fluid, tries to hang on to the feeling of losing her. I think if I lose that, I lose everything. If I stop caring, I'll kill the black-haired boy and dump Dandelion somewhere for the others to gather. They know how to bring her back, but then she really will be lost to me forever. They'll cut parts of her away, her mind, her heart, the part of her that begged for life, the part that told me I have a choice. I hang on to the pain and wish that I had said more things to her, that I had a voice to tell her how much I love her. I'll hang on until I'm sure the pain has carved a permanent mark in my syrupy brain.

"The ground is too hard up here to bury her," the black-haired one says. "But we could make a cairn. There are enough rocks." He grimaces as he glances at the dead body slumped in a puddle of blood. "For Liam, too. We should cover them."

I ignore him, pulling Dandelion closer, pressing my face into her hair. After a moment I feel the boy's hand on my shoulder.

"She was pretty special, wasn't she?"

Before I can stop myself, I hiss at him. He stumbles backward.

"Not that . . . There was never anything between us. . . . We were just friends, right? She explained that to you? Right?"

I put my face back into her hair.

"Really though. We should, you know, bury them or whatever."

Stupid human. I'm back where I started. He doesn't know my words or understand what has happened. And he's terrified of me. I hate him. I could break him in two and toss him down the mountain.

No. Think. He and I are so alike. Looking at him I wonder now how I could have ever believed that I was so different from the humans.

Think.

Dandelion's eyelids streaked with black veins. The smell of her hair. Not pine needles now. Charcoal. Like me. Dead but not dead.

Stopped.

I might have been someone else once too. We all might have been.

I try to breathe out the hate for the black-haired boy. I promised Dandelion I would save him. And I will, but first . . .

She wanted something else in her last second.

Tucker.

"I'm sorry. I don't know what that means."

I close my eyes behind the mask and try to remember the shapes, the letters. I know I can read. I can make letters, too. Remember.

I trace letters in the snow between us.

T U K R

"Oh. I'm sure she just said that because, you know, your life flashes in front of your eyes apparently, when you die. But he's been dead for a long time."

Tucker's not dead. It's odd how I'm not sure when exactly I realized this.

"I'm sorry, I don't . . ."

I growl with frustration, and the black-haired one recoils.

Tucker and Dandelion are not dead.

He shrugs. It's unfair how humans can put an apology on their face so easily. Or any feeling. It's hard to stay mad at them.

Xander. He needs a sign name.

I draw a *Z* in the snow and point to him.

"Yeah. Actually it's *X*, but . . ." I growl again. I will have a daily struggle not to kill this one. "No, *Z* is fine. *Z* it is," he says, his hands up.

I make the *Z* in the air and point to him. Then I make my own sign name.

Eighth Cycle of the Moon.

I haven't used this since Dandelion renamed me.

"August, right? I'm Xander. Xander Liu." He holds out his hand expectantly. It takes me a moment, but some splinter of memory eventually surfaces, and I reach forward. We shake hands like friends. He smiles back at me, though there are still tears in his eyes. His teeth are large and white.

Maybe it won't be so hard not to throw him from a cliff.

I stand with Dandelion in my arms. Then I indicate with my head and hands that Xander should collect and carry the weapons. We will find more on the way. He needs clothes and food, too.

Follow me, I sign, and he seems to understand. I turn and begin walking along the plateau. In the town where I will find clothes and food for him, I hope we can find a vehicle.

Xander watches me walk for a moment, and part of me hopes he will not follow. Maybe he'll go back to the base and continue scheming battles he can never win.

"Shouldn't we bury her?" he says at last, hurrying after me. "I mean, you're not going to just carry her around? That's so weird."

I ignore him. We reach the edge of the plateau, and I jump

down the five meters to the path below. Xander scrambles down after me, but I don't wait for him.

"You can't carry a dead human around. It's disrespectful. I mean, we can leave Liam, I guess, but we need to bury Raven."

I walk away. I can hear his footsteps behind me.

"She IS dead, isn't she? ISN'T SHE?"

I keep walking, driven to one goal. Though my eyes are wide open, it is all I can see.

"ISN'T SHE?!" Xander yells.

I could turn back maybe, and explain it to him. It might make things easier.

I should explain it, what I think has happened. Is happening. Will happen. I could try to explain it.

But I don't think I know the words.

Acknowledgments

Writing is lonely work and often by the time a book is done I feel like I'm the only person on earth, struggling alone and unloved in an inconsiderate void.

Then I get over myself.

If you're reading this, there are a whole slew of people who helped me get this book through your eyeballs, ears, or fingers and into your brain: the bookseller, librarian, parent, teacher, or friend who put it in your hands, for example, and the bloggers and reviewers who alerted the world to its existence. They all get my heartfelt thanks. If not for them, we'd be piling books up in warehouses wondering why we don't have money to eat.

Then there are the people who made it so you read a published *book* and not just four hundred pages of insensible rambling scribbled onto the backs of chain restaurant menus. The inventor of the laptop computer is one example, and Bill Gates (bless him) for creating Microsoft Word.

But seriously and more importantly, the team at Simon & Schuster Books for Young Readers shepherded and shaped this book until it met their exacting standards. Zareen Jaffery and Mekisha Telfer deserve particular thanks—working with you guys has been a dream. Sarah and Nita from Simon &

Schuster Canada and Jane from S&S UK, everyone at Oceano and Intrinseca, as well as Heather Baror-Shapiro, who has worked on all the international deals. And Lizzy Bromley for designing a ridiculously cool cover.

Speaking of deals, Barbara Poelle deserves an entire paragraph of thanks. The first time we spoke on the phone, I mentioned "shooting for the moon" and she got right onboard and piloted me and my book out past the orbit of Pluto! You're the agent of my dreams, Barbara. Here's to many *many* more of my books for you to send into space. Thanks also to Brita Lundberg and everyone else at the Irene Goodman Agency for all your tireless work on contracts and payments and general awesomeness. I LOVE YOU GUYS!

And then there are the readers—no, not you, though you're great too—the early readers who took the time to look over this manuscript at various stages to help me make sure I had something good and not something horrifying. Hannah Gómez and Jenna Beacom, who beta read with a critical eye toward the depiction of identity and language, and Calais LaFontaine for her answers about Métis culture. Angie Fleming at Pinkindle for her rigorous beta reading, Deb McIntyre and Becka McIntosh for their copious edit notes, and AJ Downey for insisting that yes this was in fact a good book and deserving of a good publishing deal. Thank you all!

Thanks to the NaNoWriMo organization for providing the

boost I needed to write the first draft of this book one cold November in 2011.

My family are, as always, slightly mystified but still supportive. My husband, Len, and daughter, Lucy, both inspire and endure me. My lovely sisters and mother are my biggest fans.

Thank you all so much.